AGE OF DECEPTION

The Firebird Chronicles

By T.A. White

To my grandmothers.
I miss you both.

TABLE OF CONTENTS

ONE 1

TWO 15

THREE 24

FOUR 37

FIVE 52

SIX 70

SEVEN 84

EIGHT 96

NINE 116

TEN 134

ELEVEN 149

TWELVE 164

THIRTEEN 182

FOURTEEN 196

FIFTEEN 207

SIXTEEN 221

SEVENTEEN 237

EIGHTEEN 252

NINETEEN 265

TWENTY 281

TWENTY-ONE 295

TWENTY-TWO 311

TWENTY-THREE 329

TWENTY-FOUR 342

TWENTY-FIVE 357

TWENTY-SIX 375

TWENTY-SEVEN 386

TUANN TERMS 395

TUANN HOUSES 396

DISCOVER MORE BY T.A. WHITE 397

CONNECT WITH ME 397
ABOUT THE AUTHOR 398

ONE

BEING STRUCK SPEECHLESS was a new experience for Kira, but then the man sitting across from her had a disturbing way of surprising her.

Graydon rested his chin on his hand and raised his eyebrows at her in silent invitation.

He couldn't have said what she thought she'd heard.

"Would you like to repeat that?" Because it had sounded an awful lot like he'd said he was keeping her—which was absurd.

A fact he had to know.

Graydon smirked, a cocky twist of the lips that made her want to reach across the table and punch him. "Is your hearing bad?"

The man known as the Emperor's Face was built like a mountain. Authority was stamped on every feature; arrogance along with it. The synth armor he wore seemed to eat the light, appearing a black so deep she was surprised she couldn't see her reflection in it. He was tall and broad-shouldered, with clearly delineated muscles even his armor couldn't hide.

His features warned of the stubborn personality inside even as they invited you to sit and stare a while. He was handsome, almost brutally so. He knew it, too. Dark hair framed intense, stormy gray eyes and a face chiseled from granite. Thin lips that looked indescribably soft.

Yes, handsome if not for the fact smug superiority oozed from his pores.

Kira's eyes narrowed.

Was this revenge? Some type of retaliation for hurt pride?

He'd asked her to stay, and she'd refused for reasons she couldn't reveal to him. Her mission was dangerous, requiring focus and sacrifice. Graydon was a temptation she couldn't afford.

She wouldn't have thought it of him. He was too self-assured for such petty things.

No, this was something else.

"Not at all," Kira said icily. "I just wanted to see if you're really as stupid as you're acting."

Graydon's smile flashed again, an amused lion impressed by his prey's struggles.

She ignored him in favor of examining the rest of those taking part in this farce. Liara, the Overlord of House Luatha, sat to the right of Graydon, her eyes bruised and her features exhausted. The battle for the planet had taken its toll on Kira's cousin.

Liara seemed resigned to events, her careful mask providing no hint to what she thought of the current situation.

Kira dismissed Liara almost in the same instant. Her cousin might hold a measure of familial loyalty to Kira, but she wouldn't risk the safety of her people for one she'd known for a handful of days.

She also dismissed Shandry, the healer who'd tended to Kira during her brief stay in Shandry's healing room. The healer lacked any true power to influence current events.

Her attention shifted to the true threats. Silas and Quillon. Until now, they were unknowns. Maybe a little too interested in Kira, but ultimately unimportant. Except they'd proven they were capable of much more than she'd assumed.

She'd played right into House Roake's hands. Hadn't seen the ambush until she was already caught in it.

Kira sucked in a deep breath. Patience. Control. She needed to keep it.

"Jin?"

The drone who was Kira's best friend hovered over her shoulder, his round spherical body no bigger than her head.

"They have a case," he said after a drawn-out moment where he considered.

Kira fought the urge to curse. Of course, they did. She had no doubt she would be here if they hadn't thought out every possible outcome from this conversation.

She was in the midst of a battle she'd had no idea was even taking place. They were three steps ahead while she was still struggling to see the game board.

The two men regarded her patiently. The color of their synth armor was a blue so deep and dark it reminded Kira of midnight. Its design was simpler than that of Liara's bodyguards, more in line with Graydon's people. It was serviceable, meant for battle rather than to impress.

House Roake. Her father's people. A man she had never met and hadn't given much thought to while struggling to survive the hell of her childhood.

Until recently, Kira had thought she was the product of experiments to create a super-soldier. Someone whose DNA had been tinkered with before birth to create a killing weapon, meant to be aimed at the enemy and fired.

Turned out she was wrong. Instead, she was apparently a member of an alien race called the Tuann. Technologically advanced with social customs more suited to the feudal societies of old Earth, they had odd notions of how long-lost members of their race should be treated. Few of their people strayed from the accepted molds, which made Kira something of an anomaly.

"Let's all stay calm," Jace cautioned. The words might have been said to the room, but they were meant for Kira. Her former commander knew about her temper. "I'm sure there's an easy solution to this."

"Yeah, Kira is once again humanity's bargaining chip for their continued survival," Jin said.

Jace slid him a quelling look. "It's not going to come to that."

But it would. Humanity was between a rock and a hard place with their old enemy the Tsavitee back on the galactic stage. They'd barely come out the winner during their last war with the alien race known as the scourge. There was no guarantee they'd triumph again—especially with Kira not quite up to her old standards.

The price for losing would be annihilation.

Neither humanity nor the Consortium would risk that, not with the Tuann offering ships and people to operate those ships.

The walls threatened to close in on Kira. Not a good feeling for someone who'd just transformed back from a monstrous creature that had ripped dozens of Tsavitee apart.

"Calm," Jace said, meeting Kira's gaze, his expression saying trust me.

Kira consciously relaxed, forcing panic and helplessness away. For someone used to controlling every aspect of her life—for soldiers, losing control usually resulted in death—it wasn't easy having that independence threatened. Jace had earned her trust. She'd give him a shot at this.

When he faced the Tuann again, Jace was poised, his bearing that of the rear admiral he'd become. "This news is unexpected. I'm sure you understand if we need a little time to process."

Silas's smile was conciliatory. "Of course. We want to make this transition as easy for the child of our House as possible."

"You could always let her go," Jin muttered.

"Jin," Jace warned.

Jin grumbled but didn't say anything else.

Silas acknowledged Jin before turning to Kira. "I'm afraid that is the one thing we cannot do. Your father was a special person for our people. His daughter will be welcomed with open arms. Please let us get to know you as you get to know us. That's all we're asking."

Kira stared at him with narrowed eyes.

He seemed earnest. Caring even.

"Why do you care?" Kira asked.

Silas's smile was peaceful and tranquil. "Because you're one of us and shouldn't face this world alone."

Raider snorted. "Good luck with that."

Kira had a long history of going it alone—as evidenced by her heading off to live in a ship by herself rather than face the remnants of her old team.

"We are aware accommodations need to be made for your circumstances," Silas continued. "We're willing to arrange what you need to be comfortable with this."

Mighty big of him when he had driven a space cruiser through Kira's plans.

"This is a highly unusual ask," Jace said, carefully not looking at Kira. "We will need to contact our superiors. They need to be present for this conversation."

Raider crossed his arms and leaned back in his chair, a neutral expression on his face.

Silas inclined his head. "We understand. The Emperor's Face anticipated this request and has a deep space connection standing by."

Jace's smile didn't reach his eyes. "How very thoughtful."

Graydon's lips tilted up the barest bit, warning Kira he found this entirely too amusing for her comfort. He must be doing cartwheels inside at having so thoroughly thwarted her. She'd be impressed if she wasn't so infuriated.

One of Graydon's oshota—elite warriors who were some of the deadliest fighters Kira had ever seen—stepped forward carrying what looked like a small rock. Amila's nod was respectful as she set the silvery amethyst stone in front of Jace.

They all looked at the rock. It sat there, doing what rocks do.

Jace's expression was befuddled while Raider raised an eyebrow.

The rock didn't move. No tricks were performed as it lay there—inert.

Jace cleared his throat uncomfortably. "I'm not familiar with this technology."

"Place your hand on it and think of who you want to contact. The anchor will do the rest," Amila said.

Jin made a fascinated sound as he drifted closer, pointing the lens on his front that acted as his eye, at the rock. It was an unnecessary affectation, an inside joke taken from old movies and TV shows from Earth. He had hundreds of mini-cameras built into his case, allowing him a 360-degree view of his surroundings at all times.

"It's mental-based, isn't it? Like the Nexus?" Jin asked.

No one answered for a long moment.

"Yes," Amila said when the silence deepened further.

Jace placed his hand on the rock, his forehead furrowing.

"This is the *CSS Valiant*. You're using an unauthorized channel," a disembodied voice barked.

"This is Rear Admiral Jace Skarsdale. Confirm voice ID print, code alpha, romeo, delta, sierra, one, niner, two."

"Stand by." The voice sounded slightly startled. Seconds later, the person said, "Code confirmed. What can I do for you, sir?"

"I want a link to Admiral Akira Himoto, top priority, highly classified," Jace said.

"Roger that."

There was a click, and then a man appeared at the end of the table, his hands folded in front of him, his expression contemplative.

Admiral Himoto had been part of Kira's life almost since the moment she'd freed herself from her childhood captors. He was a father figure and mentor all rolled into one. He was the reason she'd joined the Space Force and the person who had forced her to see her unique traits as tools to be used and embraced rather than fought and feared.

He'd told her that her abilities might have arisen from the evil acts of greedy men, but she could choose what to do with her talents. She'd never forgotten that lesson.

Forces outside her control might shape her, but she was in charge of what she became. No one else.

For that reason, she would always love him, even if she no longer trusted him.

He had the weight of an entire race on his shoulders. One lost lamb didn't outweigh the duties he wore like a mantle.

No longer the young man of her childhood, Himoto had aged in the years she'd been away. He was of Japanese descent, and his hair had more gray and white now than black, with faint lines riddling his face. Despite that, the impact of his gaze showcased that same forceful personality she remembered from their first meeting. Eyes that were calm, yet held a wisdom as deep as the ocean.

He didn't seem surprised by his abrupt summons, regarding them calmly. "Lord Graydon, to what do I owe this pleasure? I trust Kira hasn't been too difficult."

Graydon's teeth flashed. "You're a canny human. You knew exactly what we faced. A warning would have been nice."

Himoto allowed himself the briefest of smiles. "I did try. It's not my fault you refused to listen."

Graydon's chuckle was deep, but it didn't fool Kira. Despite the slight teasing, Graydon was a tiger with a man's shape, waiting for his enemy to show weakness. Only then would he pounce.

Himoto's thoughtful gaze moved over them. To Jace, he said, "I assume since you are calling me in this manner, things have not gone as planned."

"We've encountered a slight problem," Jace confirmed.

Himoto let out a weary sigh. "That is always the way."

Next to Himoto, a second man appeared. Younger than Himoto, his hair was buzzed close to his skull, creating the faintest shadow. A permanently dissatisfied frown had taken up residence on his face.

Himoto gestured to the second. "I've taken the liberty of inviting Admiral John Kent to take part in this conversation."

Jace looked like he'd bitten into a lemon.

It didn't take long for Kira to guess why when the man's deep brown eyes swung her way and his lip curled. "What did you do?"

Kira lifted an eyebrow, studying him for several long seconds. It was obvious this man disliked her despite never having met her. Why? An innate dislike for aliens? Or something else?

"That's some greeting you have there. Did you skip diplomacy school while becoming an admiral?" Kira drawled.

"Your reputation precedes you, Captain Forrest."

"Heh, and that makes you an expert," Kira guessed.

Raider's snicker was low, a smile playing over his lips before he looked down, hiding it. "He does have a point."

Jin chortled beside her.

Kira gritted her teeth. "Why are you here again?"

"To make sure you don't do anything stupid, remember?" Raider taunted.

"Good luck with that," Jin muttered.

Kira ignored both of them, studying Himoto instead. His lips tightened faintly. He wasn't thrilled with the other admiral's presence. That more than anything else told her something was going on at Centcom.

Politics. Great. As if she wasn't getting her fill of them already.

Graydon caught her glance.

"This isn't going to work," she mouthed at him.

"We'll see," he mouthed back. "It'll be fun watching you struggle."

Her eyes narrowed. Definitely a little bit of revenge in this ambush.

She caught sight of Finn's carefully blank face from his position against the wall. The oshota had shadowed Kira almost since her arrival on Luatha. She'd accepted him as her shield, which made them responsible for each other in some way Kira still didn't quite understand.

Finn's eyes met hers. He'd tried to warn her during her last encounter with Graydon that things weren't over. Kira should have paid more attention.

She tuned back in as Jace was explaining the situation. "The Tuann have graciously decided to keep their word; however, there is a problem."

"What sort of problem?" Kent demanded.

"We're happy to give you the ships," Silas spoke up. "But you will find yourself unable to leave the planet with them."

Himoto's expression remained calm as Kent's eyes narrowed. "What good are ships if you won't let them out of your system?"

"I don't think we're explaining correctly," Silas said, his forehead furrowing slightly.

"It's not that they won't let us fly them home; it's that we can't," Jace said.

Kent's severe expression didn't thaw. If anything, he seemed more frustrated than before. Himoto shifted in his chair, steepling his fingertips in front of him as a thoughtful frown settled on his face.

Kent was the opposite, aiming a look at Jace that said he thought the rear admiral was an imbecile. "Have the Tuann give you a crash course in flying one of their boats and then bring it home."

Kira fought the urge to roll her eyes. As if flying a complicated piece of technology like a Tuann ship was as easy as flicking a switch. It seemed Kent's rise in the military hadn't come with a set of brains.

"Our ships are keyed to our specific attributes," Silas said. "I'm afraid unless you are Tuann and are able to harness *ki* you will not be able to operate them."

"And who are you?" Kent demanded, squinting at the Tuann.

Silas smiled and inclined his head. "My name is Silas. My companion and I represent House Roake."

"House what?" Kent asked.

The skin around Himoto's eyes tightened the tiniest bit.

"Real stellar leadership you have there," Kira murmured in Japanese.

"He has many other admirable attributes," Himoto told her, again in Japanese.

Kira resisted the urge to blow a raspberry, tempted to call bullshit. What kind of leader engaged with a hostile ally without learning the cultural mores upon which their society was founded? Not a good one—especially in light of the often fractious relationship the Consortium enjoyed with the Tuann. They'd misjudged the Tuann during first contact, and nothing since had eased the stigma their past actions had generated.

Kent's attention came to her, and he frowned again. "What will it take for your people to teach us what we need to know to make these work?"

Silas cocked his head as Graydon lifted an eyebrow.

"He's being deliberately obtuse," Jin murmured.

Raider and Jace didn't say anything. The look on their faces told her they agreed, but their ranks in the military meant they couldn't publicly chide Kent no matter how much they wanted to.

"I think I agree with you, Jin," Kira muttered back.

She tapped her fingertips against the table as she considered. The question was if Kent was doing it deliberately.

It would make a deceptively useful tactic. More so when it was used like it was now, as a bludgeon to try to force the outcome he wanted.

It might have worked had these people been human. Not so much with Tuann, who could do quietly-stubborn better than even Kira. She could already see the mood in the room shifting. Any gains Jace and the Curs, an elite squad who had accompanied her to Ta Da'an, had won during their actions against the Tsavitee invasion were rapidly disappearing.

The Tuann appreciated the fine art of subtlety. They were the sleek snake in the grass, not the boar driving its head mindlessly against the nearest obstacle.

Kira briefly considered interfering and saving Kent from himself, but why do that when he was being the perfect distraction.

"What are our options?" Kira stuck to Japanese as she lowered her voice so only Jin would hear.

Raider shifted beside her, leaning closer.

She'd prefer to have this conversation in private, but she doubted she would be afforded that privilege.

"Not many," Jin admitted. "They have you over a barrel. There is precedent. It's rare, but it's there."

Kira refocused. When they'd arrived on this planet—ostensibly to meet her mother's people, House Luatha—Jin had gone through the Tuann laws—those he could get his hands on. An informed Kira was a smart Kira. They'd thought getting Liara to give up her family claim to Kira would be the end of things. Turned out that assumption was wrong because Kira was uncommon in the Tuann community.

Her parents weren't from one House but two, a marriage meant to cement an alliance between two foes. It left Kira in the rare position of being dual House. Since she'd been kidnapped before her parents could designate her as one House or the other, it meant both Houses had a claim. And lucky Kira, she'd convinced Liara to rescind her claim, clearing the field nicely for Roake.

Kira rubbed her forehead. What a clusterfuck.

It wasn't Jin's fault he'd missed this. Neither one of them was familiar enough with Tuann culture to understand all of its nuances. It placed them in the unenviable position of having to feel their way through half-blind.

"We could run, but—" Jin trailed off.

Yes, but.

The Tsavitee were back. Humans would need all their allies.

She might have pulled away from humanity, needing the distance to heal while putting her long-term plans in motion, but she had no desire to see the Consortium fall. She cared for too many of them.

Kira stared at the table, hating she'd been pushed to this point. Options were limited. There was no easy path forward; whichever way she turned, something would be lost.

Since she'd never formalized her retirement, it left her open to the military's will. A will Himoto had already exercised once by ordering her to Ta Da'an, House Luatha's planet.

As soon as Kent figured out what the Tuann really wanted, it'd happen again.

The only thing she was surprised about was that Himoto hadn't already acted. She lifted her eyes to meet his impenetrable stare. He'd never been easy to read with that stoic face. Age hadn't changed that much.

"I don't think you have a choice," Jin said, knowing where her mind had gone.

"I think you're right." She hated that it had come to this. Hated that she was going to have to shut a door she'd kept deliberately cracked.

"What are you about to do?" Raider asked, the lazy amusement on his face disappearing.

He'd known her long enough to know she wasn't going to let herself be caged. Not unless it was her will.

"Nothing I don't have to," Kira assured him.

Raider appeared less than reassured. But then, he knew her better than any of those present, except for Jin. Their history was long. Even if it was fraught with tension and soured with dislike toward the end, there had been a time where they'd been as close as siblings.

"I don't care if you have to tow the damn things," Kent was saying, his eyes snapping fire as he glared at Jace. "Just find a way to get them here."

"Admiral, we are happy to provide the people required to fly our ships to a human station of your choosing," Silas offered.

Silence reigned. Kent's gaze flicked from Silas to Jace to Kira and back again. "What are we talking about then?"

"There's a price for their cooperation," Kira said, finally stirring.

Kent stared at her. "Don't leave us in suspense."

"In exchange for our cooperation, we would like the Lady Kira to accompany us to our home," Silas said, inclining his head showing respect to Kira.

Kent was quiet for several seconds, his forehead furrowed as if he was trying to decipher whether there was a hidden message in there. "Let me see if I have this straight. You'll give us the ships, people to operate the ships, and all you want is her?"

"We would like the opportunity for her to get to know us. This seems to be the only way to make it happen." Silas's smile was genial.

"More like keep her indefinitely," Jin muttered.

"Is that a drone?" Kent asked, squinting at her friend. "What is a drone doing giving its opinion in a situation like this? Is that even possible?"

Kira's hands tightened into fists, no longer finding the brash admiral quite so amusing.

Kent didn't wait for an answer, flicking his hand dismissively. "It doesn't matter. This problem is easily solved. Take her. Rear Admiral Skarsdale, please accompany those ships home."

"No." Kira's words ripped through the air, forestalling the admiral from flicking off his screen.

He frowned at her. "What do you mean no?"

Kira ignored him, focusing on Himoto. "You asked for ships. I got you ships. You asked me to free myself. I did. My debt is paid."

Himoto didn't speak as he regarded her thoughtfully.

"You don't get to say no," Kent said disdainfully. "You're a member of the Space Force. You serve at our needs, just like every other soldier."

"Jin."

"Already done," Jin said.

"What are you doing?" Jace asked, his attention swinging to Kira.

"What I have to," Kira said, not second-guessing herself. She focused on Kent again. "Regulation 5.63—any service member who has served their first two tours can put in a packet to end their service

11

if they have not been called to a combat rotation for the preceding three years."

Raider made a choked sound.

Kira took a deep breath. Was she really doing this? Yes. Yes, she was. She wouldn't bow to the dictates of someone like Kent.

This move was drastic, but it would give her room to maneuver. More importantly, it meant none of her actions beyond this point could be used against the Consortium.

"I won't be trapped again. I've defended humanity above and beyond what most ever hope to commit. I've sacrificed again and again. This was the last time."

"This won't work. That packet has to be hand-delivered," Kent warned.

"Nothing in those regulations says it has to be done by the person submitting the packet."

Kira and Kent were locked in a staring match. Each daring the other to blink. Only this time, Kira didn't plan for it to be her.

"You're bluffing," he said finally.

"Tell me again how you order me to give up my freedom for a few ships that won't even protect you when the Tsavitee come," Kira dared.

Fury and stubbornness lit Kent's eyes. He was going to do it. He was going to force her hand.

"Kira, think. You can't take this back," Raider said urgently.

"It should have been done a long time ago," she said softly. "There's no going back. Only forward."

It hurt to break Kent's gaze and look at her longtime friend, sometimes enemy.

Jace was silent, frozen disbelief on his face.

"You wouldn't dare," Kent said. He didn't realize she was a wolf whose leg was caught in a trap, willing to chew it off.

A knock sounded from out of sight.

Himoto met her gaze, his lips twitching. "This is unexpected. Quite the element of surprise."

"I learned from the best."

His head dipped in a nod. "Come in."

Kira thought she saw momentary surprise flash across his face before he composed his expression.

Graydon shifted, the tension rolling off him drawing Kira's

attention like a bee to honey. His eyes were fierce, his shoulders tense.

That's right. Breathe it in. She'd outmaneuvered him.

"I win," she mouthed.

His eyebrows snapped together.

"That doesn't mean anything," Kent tried.

"For someone of your position, you're not particularly smart," Jin said. "The Tuann are sitting right here. What kind of people do you want them to think you are? The kind who would sacrifice your own people? The kind who lies for your own self-interests? You're not really presenting humans in a sympathetic light here."

"J1N, shut down," Kent snapped. "That's an order."

A chuckle rolled from Jin. "I don't take orders from you, meat sack."

Kira ignored the exchange.

Himoto looked considering before he speared her with a gaze. "Well done, dear, but I still have one move left. You really shouldn't have wasted time gloating."

Kira's lips parted.

Himoto didn't wait, reaching forward and tapping a button out of sight. There was a brief tone as Himoto's hologram snapped out of existence, leaving them staring at empty air.

Kira shook her head and blinked. She stood slowly.

He couldn't have.

A smile broadened on Kent's face. "Remember—last order given."

Then Kent's feed snapped off too.

Kira shook her head again. No. This wasn't happening.

"I'll be damned. That old fox outsmarted you," Jin said with awe.

Kira's teeth clenched; her gaze still focused on the spot where Himoto had been.

"The regulation you cited only works if you can confirm receipt of your resignation," Raider said thoughtfully. "Until you do, you're still considered active."

"Which means you have to obey the last order given," Jace finished.

And that was to accompany the Roake home.

Graydon's smirk caught her eye. He mouthed, "I guess it's still my win, *coli.*"

Kira inhaled deeply. Strangling the Emperor's Face wouldn't help her situation—even if it would make her feel better.

Kira slapped her hands on the table and shoved her seat back. "No,

I'll find him and cram that resignation down his throat."

Himoto wasn't winning like this.

"That would be considered leaving your post without orders. You'd be considered AWOL," Raider said, studying his fingernails. "They still court-martial for that."

"I don't care," Kira hissed, too far gone to care about the ramifications of her actions any longer.

"Oh, boy," Jin said. "She's snapped. Someone needs to do something before she does something drastic."

"You're dying," Shandry said, her words cutting through the drama.

TWO

KIRA FROZE, HER chest tight as her gaze locked on where Luatha's healer had been sitting quietly until now.

Raider stiffened as soft realization stole into his expression.

Jin snorted. "No, she's not. Right, Kira?"

Raider held her gaze, reading the truth there before she could even think of denying it. Her silence was answer enough.

"But then, I think you know that," Shandry continued.

That drew the barest flinch from Kira.

Jin made a broken sound of denial.

"How long have you known?" Shandry inquired.

Kira placed her hands flat on the table as she urged herself to stay calm. She breathed in then out slowly, doing it again and again.

"Since Rothchild." Jin's voice held grim realization as he put the pieces together.

"Is this why you cornered me?" Kira asked, her voice deadly calm as she glanced at Graydon.

Graydon's expression was hard to read, but she caught a thread of irritation in the look he threw the healer. So—he hadn't planned to use this information against her.

That had been all Shandry's doing. Good to know.

Kira lifted her head and faced her oldest friend, reading the emotional turbulence in him as clearly as if he'd been human.

"Before," Kira admitted softly.

There was a choked sound from Jace as he sat hard. Raider's expression closed down, a stoic mask descending.

"Why didn't you tell us?" Jace asked. "We could have helped."

"How?" Her voice sounded dead. She'd never wanted anyone to know this. It had been her burden to bear.

15

"I don't know. Someone else could have taken your place."

Kira scoffed. "It was war, Jace. Every one of us faced death each time we suited up. Mine was simply a little more inescapable."

"You didn't always have to be on the front lines," he argued. "There would have been options if you'd simply told somebody."

"Who would you have had me send in my place?" she challenged. "Who should I have chosen? Elise? Raider? You? I knew the risks. Everyone did. That didn't change because there was something inside tearing me apart."

He shook his head. He folded his arms across his chest, his jaw clenching as if he were biting back more words.

"No doubt whatever you were doing to help the humans made things worse," Shandry said crisply.

Kira fixed a look on her, that monstrous creature inside that took over when times were dark fixated on Shandry. It longed to break the healer's neck. It would be so easy.

The healer looked soft. Zero combat ability.

Two seconds and Kira could be across the table. A second after that and crack, no more annoying healer.

Finn shifted, correctly interpreting Kira's precarious mood. Her control right now was gossamer thin.

"The Tuann pay a price for our power," Silas said into the silence. "Left unchecked the effects of unbalanced *ki* kill."

Jace's gaze sharpened. "What are you saying?"

"We can heal you," Silas promised, his eyes never leaving Kira's.

"And all you want in exchange is everything I am," she said bitterly.

"You would be alive."

Her smile was brief and didn't reach her eyes. "There are things worse than death."

Shandry slapped the table. "You're making this more difficult than it has to be. We're offering you a way to survive. Don't you want to live?"

Of course, she did. Almost more than anything else in the world.

But that was the sticking point—almost. There were important things she needed to do. Things that no one else could.

Kira touched a spot on the inside of her elbow. One such thing suddenly felt unbearably heavy.

She was at a crossroads. Go with Roake and let them fix her. But then, who knew how long it would take her to get the data she'd downloaded from the Nexus to Odin.

Or don't go with them and seal her fate.

What a choice to make.

"How long does she have?" Jace asked.

Shandry shrugged. "It's difficult to say. Five to ten years maybe. Less if she keeps abusing her *ki* the way she is."

Raider made a derisive sound. "Your notion of immediacy needs work."

He wasn't wrong. The Tuann life span hadn't been definitively confirmed but she knew they lived for hundreds of years, perhaps longer. To them, ten years would feel like a blink of an eye.

Kira lifted her chin. "I've been beating impossible odds my whole life. Nothing says I can't do it again."

Shandry made a scornful sound. "Your ignorance is going to see you dead."

Kira bared her teeth at the healer and leaned forward. Satisfaction filled her as the other woman flinched. "It's my life to risk."

"You're going to do this," Jin said calmly.

Kira sent a hard glance at him. "You don't speak for me. I don't care what our history is."

No one had that right.

"You're going to give them a chance," he continued as if she hadn't spoken.

"You overstep." There was a threat in Kira's voice.

Jin swung around to face her, pointing his eye at her. "They're giving you a chance the rest of the forty-three didn't have."

Graydon shifted, interest in his expression.

"And you're going to throw it away because you're afraid they'll make you care again," Jin accused.

"This isn't the time for this conversation." Never would be Kira's preference.

"You lied. You said there wasn't anything to worry about." Grief and rage boiled in his voice, enough so the Tuann across from them looked at him with interest.

Most saw Jin as a machine; he wasn't. He had been a person once. A boy like her who, after being mortally wounded, had somehow attached his soul to a military-grade combat drone.

Kira's mouth clicked shut as she stared at her friend, guilt a boulder in her chest. Her gaze dropped, and she rubbed her forehead. Her

17

reasons had been sound, but that didn't change the fact she'd lied. Something she'd said she'd never do with him.

"You're going to do this for me. You're going to give them a chance," he said in a calm voice that belied the upheaval she could sense through their bond.

Kira started to protest. She'd do a lot for him, die if necessary, but this was asking a bit much.

"Elise isn't the only one you made promises to," he hissed.

Kira flinched. Her mouth snapped closed on what she'd been about to say. The resulting silence had a weight, awkward and horrible, as she forced herself to keep her eyes up and her attention on her friend.

Next to her, Raider had stilled as he watched the two of them with barely veiled interest.

"You promised me things too," Jin told her, his voice grave. "You don't get to leave because you're afraid. I know you better than you know yourself. You're going with them, and you're going to let them help you."

"And if I don't?" she forced herself to ask. She had to know.

"We're done, and I never want to see you again."

Kira inhaled deeply, not letting herself outwardly react. Of any threat he could have made, he knew this one would hit home. Worse, she could tell he meant it. This wasn't one of those times where he'd get angry and then forgive her a few hours later. If she walked away now, she was doing it alone.

She folded her arms across her chest, resisting the urge to hunch in on herself. She'd never been separated from Jin for any length of time. The prospect of losing him—it was too terrible to contemplate.

Sometimes you didn't know what you had until you lost it. Sometimes you knew, but you managed to fuck it up anyway.

He had a point. She had made him promises. Herself too.

Like it or not, they were both defined by what had happened to them as children. It was a weight they dragged behind them no matter where they went or what they did to escape it. They had forced themselves to rise above it but still carried the scars.

Kira's were too many to enumerate; Jin's fewer but more complicated.

He feared abandonment, of facing this world alone, a monster no one could ever truly understand.

Those first few years had been difficult, and Kira thought she'd lose him again. She'd vowed to find him a way back to a body—barring that, she would never leave his side.

"If I may, there might be an easy solution," Silas said when the silence lengthened.

Kira cut an angry glance at him.

"Come to Ta Sa'Riel. See who we are. Learn about us," Silas offered.

"And once I'm there, I'll likely never leave," Kira pointed out.

"We're not interested in caging you," Silas said. "All we want is to see you thrive. If you truly cannot find a place there, you will be free to go. We only ask that you wait until your *ki* has been healed, and we've been assured you can protect yourself. Passing the sequence of trials leading to the adva ka would go a long way to doing that. Until then, you will be a treasured guest of our House."

Kira studied him. He seemed sincere, but she also didn't know him well enough to know if he was faking.

"We hope, of course, you will come to find your place among us and won't wish to leave," he said with a gentle smile.

Not likely. Kira had a place once. It was gone. She didn't plan to chance the pain of having a home ripped from her again.

Graydon's sober expression caught her attention. "Silas is honorable. If he says you can walk away at any time, he means it."

For all that they were on opposing sides, Kira found herself trusting Graydon. He hadn't given her a reason to do otherwise.

"All right, I'll do it. I'll come with you," Kira said.

There was a slight whirring noise as Jin started for the door.

"Where are you going?" Kira asked.

"Away. I don't want to see your face right now."

The door shut behind him, leaving Kira staring at the place where he'd disappeared.

"Ouch. I didn't know Tin Man could get that angry with you," Raider murmured.

Kira didn't answer. She couldn't. He'd left her. Even after she'd given in. This was a nightmare from which there was no escape.

"Is now really the time for this?" Jace asked.

Raider smiled. "There's no better time."

Her nostrils flared as she inhaled deeply, trying to compose herself, all too aware the Tuann were still watching.

Concentration was difficult with the incredible pressure in her chest. It was filling her up, making it hard to think or breathe.

He was gone. Jin had left her. She was alone, her secrets exposed. Vulnerable. Weak.

Kira's eyes locked on Shandry, idly noting the other woman's casual posture, the slightly smug look on her face as if she'd won a point on an invisible scoreboard.

Shandry noticed her looking at her and her smile widened. Gloating as she basked in her victory.

She'd done this. Upended Kira's life, exposed one of her most closely guarded secrets, and driven a wedge between Kira and her oldest friend.

Now Shandry was happy.

Kira's body moved without conscious thought. She was out of the chair, halfway across the table before anyone could blink.

The room erupted, oshota springing forward. To Kira, their shouts sounded like nothing more than angry buzzing as she lost herself to the red haze in her head.

She'd lost control, she realized distantly. Even knowing what could happen from such a breach, she couldn't bring herself to care, intent on destroying the person who had hurt her.

Hard arms wrapped around her lower body, slamming her into the table. A second set pinned her upper half to the table. Raider and Jace hauled her toward them, shoving her into her seat.

Raider's arm ended up wrapped around her neck, nearly cutting off her oxygen. Jace was at her front, forcing her to stay in her chair.

Kira lurched forward before she gathered herself, letting them keep her there as she panted. Rage, the likes of which she'd lost herself to only a few times in her life, coursed through her.

Staying seated was hard. All she wanted to do was eliminate the threat, the thing that had already hurt her.

Instincts warred with control. She wasn't proud to admit control was losing.

"It's been a while since she's done this," Raider grunted, not daring to move even when she remained still.

"Let's keep it that way, shall we?" Jace didn't let up as she quivered from the urge to attack, somehow retaining enough of herself not to hurt her friends. "I'd forgotten how damn terrifying she is."

"No shit," Raider snapped.

Finn appeared next to them. Not touching, his physical presence was threat enough.

Kira forced herself not to move, not to struggle. As much as she hated what Shandry had done, what she had revealed without Kira's permission, it wasn't the healer's fault Jin had left. It was Kira's. She'd been the one who'd chosen to hide the extent of the damage her power caused her. She'd been the one to decide against upsetting him with the inevitable.

She had no one to blame for his current abandonment but herself.

After one final breath, Kira reached up and tapped Raider on the forearm. "You can let me go. I won't attack her."

Raider's grip didn't loosen. "Are you sure? I don't think they'll give us ships or people to fly them if you kill one of their people."

"Let me go, asshole."

Raider chuckled, his arm loosening as he stepped back. "Just like old times, Phoenix."

Kira mumbled to herself as she fiddled with her sleeves, straightening them before twitching them into place. Only when she had finished did she look up, her face expressionless.

Everyone in the room stared at her with varying expressions of disbelief.

She stared blandly back. Hadn't they ever seen a grown woman lose her shit before?

Liara was shocked, her oshota reflecting their Overlord's dismay. Graydon and his warriors were poised to interfere if the humans couldn't keep her contained.

Silas seemed thoughtful as he watched her regain her composure.

"You'll have to forgive Kira," Jace said smoothly into the silence. "In our culture, a doctor revealing such personal information as yours just did to such a public forum is considered a grave breach of privacy and trust. For someone with her issues, it acted like a trigger."

"It is similar for us as well," Graydon said, shooting Shandry a hard look. "Such things are not to be done lightly and should have been handled with caution and respect. Something Luatha's healer seems to have forgotten."

Shandry flushed slightly at the rebuke, her gaze shifting.

The exchange allowed Kira to regain the last of her composure. She settled in her chair and fixed Graydon and Silas with a cool stare. "Can you really fix what's wrong with me?"

For so long, Kira had lived with the knowledge that using her powers was slowly killing her. She was afraid to let herself hope.

21

What she'd told Jace had been true. The life of a Cur was dangerous. You risked death anytime you left for battle on a hoverboard.

In that situation, it had been easy to ignore how her body was slowly killing her. She'd done what she needed to do like any good soldier, never really expecting to survive the war.

When she lived, and so many others didn't, she'd had to find a new way forward. It had lengthened her life expectancy, but she knew it was only a matter of time. She could feel the broken bits bleeding her out slowly.

"We can," Graydon promised.

Kira closed her eyes. It was harder than she thought to let them try. Death had been a familiar stalker since she could remember.

So why was she hesitant to take their help now?

"Take the hand they're offering you, Kira," Jace urged.

There was no choice, she realized. Even if Jin hadn't thrown his ultimatum, she would have had to take this road. She was stubborn, not stupid. No matter how much she wanted to knock Graydon and the rest of the arrogant Tuann down a peg or two, she wouldn't kill herself to do it.

"How are you going to fix me?" she asked.

Silas and Quillon exchanged a look. This time Quillon was the one to answer her. "Our species rarely spend extended time away from our planets. The Mea'Ave provides something vital so we can live. Those who have not had contact with it weaken. If enough time goes by, they eventually die."

"With enough time, the planet will heal me," Kira guessed.

"That is an oversimplification. A healer will need to guide the process, but yes. We are familiar with this ailment. It is something we can fix," Quillon said.

Easily, it sounded like.

"Looks like this round goes to you," Kira told Graydon. "Don't think you'll always get your way."

Graydon watched her for several seconds. Kira could see the thoughts moving behind his eyes, the plots, the schemes. Graydon wasn't the sort to let life happen around him. He prodded and guided until he got the outcome he wanted.

She didn't know why he'd fixated on her, but she had no doubt he would try to figure out a way to make her stay. She looked forward to the battle.

"Good enough. There will be time later to change your mind," he promised.

She snorted. "Not likely, but you're welcome to try."

His smile was wicked as it curved his lips. "I look forward to it."

Shandry sat forward. "I have a healing regimen that should help things along."

Kira's glance was cutting. "You're not touching me."

Shandry's mouth dropped open, shocked disbelief on her face. "You can't mean that."

"I do exactly mean that. I don't trust you. It'll be a cold day in hell before I let you close to me." The tone of Kira's voice made the depth of her resolve unmistakable.

Quillon's nod was sharp, his expression understanding. "This is acceptable. House Roake has many skilled healers, including myself."

The tight ball in Kira's stomach loosened. Her history with doctors and the like was a complicated one. They were a necessary evil in her mind. She needed them; her life had been too dangerous not to. But they reminded her of a childhood spent being poked and prodded, experimented on like a common lab rat.

"Fine," Kira finally said, sweeping her gaze over the room. This wasn't what she would have chosen, but it was a path forward. Sometimes that was all you could ask for.

Adapting was one of the first tenets of warfare. She'd gotten good at that. The Tuann were about to learn how good.

THREE

A DAY LATER Kira stood in front of an archway that stretched three stories high, symbols and runes carved along its sides. Different metals were etched into the design, creating a complex pattern that wove between the symbols. Like most of the Citadel of Light, the structure was breathtaking. Awe-inspiring even. Impossibly delicate while at the same time speaking of strength and an endurance that would outlast even the fall of empires.

Humanity had many marvels in its history. All those achievements paled in the face of this.

A gate, designed to take you from world to world without ever setting off into space. An impossible dream that turned out to be all too real.

The physics of it was mind-boggling in the extreme. Kira didn't pretend to understand, but she didn't need to. All she needed to do was walk through when the time came. That, and pray she survived the experience.

Graydon and Silas had decided it was their best option for reaching Ta Sa'Riel. Traveling by ship was too dangerous after the incursion by the Tsavitee. Both Graydon and Silas's vessels were diplomatic ships, not equipped for war. They had their fangs, sure, but they wouldn't last long against anything over elite class.

"We have to travel through that?" Raider didn't bother to hide his skepticism as he set his duffel bag next to Kira's and peered up at the giant structure. He shifted a second bag to his other hand.

"Doesn't really inspire confidence, does it?" he told her.

She frowned at him. "What are you doing here?"

Blue darted forward before he could answer, a small sound of wonder escaping her. "These runes aren't like any of the others I've

24

seen in the Citadel. How does it work?"

Blue was short and wiry, her coloring pointing to an Asian descent. She'd been an orphan when Kira had found her and was now a Cur along with Raider. Her real name was Yuki, but everyone knew her as Blue.

The tips of her hair were the color of her namesake; a color Blue had used in one way or another since the day they'd met. Her bone structure made her appear delicate, and more than one person had mistaken her as weak.

Blue was always quick to teach them the error of their assumptions. She was a scrapper, and she didn't always fight fair. Actually, she almost never fought fair. That was one of the perks of being scary smart.

An ever-present curiosity lit her expression. Kira could practically see the gears turning as she schemed how to take the gate apart to pry its secrets from the scattered pieces.

Blue drifted toward the gate, almost as if she couldn't help herself.

"No touching, Blue. You know the rules," Jace ordered. "We can't afford to upset our hosts."

The look Blue shot him said she wasn't dumb. Kira hid her grin, knowing that was exactly what she'd been considering. Blue was nothing if not predictable in this. She had a bad habit of disassembling the things that interested her so she could find out how they worked. It had often led her into trouble in the past.

"The pathway to other worlds is one of the most heavily guarded secrets of the Tuann. You should count yourselves lucky to experience it," Liara said.

Kira could see why. Something like this would offer its owner a strategic advantage.

Liara moved toward them, dressed much the same as she'd been the first time Kira had seen her. The synth armor polished to a deep green that reminded Kira of the forest, a cape trailing behind her. It was far too long to be considered anything but a liability during a fight.

Liara's eyes were fierce and guarded as she studied the four of them. She was still pale but no longer looked as if she could be knocked over with a gentle push.

Kira frowned at Raider and Jace again, not having forgotten her question.

Raider jerked his head at Jace. "He managed to convince them of the necessity of joint training operations."

Kira considered Jace. Now, how had he managed that? The Tuann didn't exactly consider humans trustworthy—or even overly useful.

Jace lifted a shoulder. "It wasn't hard. The attack proved the Tsavitee aren't interested in only humans. They've made themselves everyone's problem. It'll be a lot easier to deal with them if we work together. Familiarizing ourselves with the Tuann's society and military capabilities can only help both of us in the long run."

Maybe so, but Kira doubted the Tuann would have accepted that argument so easily. They were nothing if not reclusive, and they didn't like others playing in their sandbox.

"And they're sending you?" Kira didn't bother hiding her skepticism. Raider had never been known for his diplomacy. From what she had seen, time hadn't changed that much.

"They have a version of our waveboards," Raider said. "I'm the best pilot we have, so it made sense."

"Second best," Kira corrected.

"Seven years is a long time. I've improved a lot since the old days." Raider's grin was sly. "And we both know you're not up to your old standards."

Kira glared. "On my worst day, I could still kick your ass on a board."

"Promises, promises."

Jace was well accustomed to their arguing and waited with only the slightest hint of impatience for them to stop before continuing. "Blue and Raider will accompany you to Ta Sa'Riel and participate in joint training. I expect all of you to represent the human race with dignity and poise." He leveled a no-nonsense stare on them, waiting for their grudging agreement before relenting. "Maverick, Tank, and I will escort the ships back to a station of Centcom's choosing."

Kira whistled. "I don't know which of us has the worst task."

Cooped up on a ship with Tuann who didn't like you and saw you as a burden. The end destination a nest of vipers and bureaucracy. She didn't envy him his mission.

"Him, definitely," Raider said.

Jace's expression was pained.

"One of the many perks of not being a rear admiral," Kira teased.

"You'll be among the first humans to ever travel this path," Liara told Raider.

"Lucky me," Raider muttered.

Jace sent him a quelling look. Raider's mouth pulled down on one side even as he straightened and made a half-assed effort to mask his dour expression. Kira should have felt sympathy for him, but found herself amused instead. He never did do well when strange things happened. Raider liked order and the universe obeying the laws he knew.

It made her wonder why he had chosen to accompany her. Jace could easily have sent either Tank or Maverick. Probably should have given the history between Raider and her.

That Raider was here meant he wanted to be here. And *that* she didn't understand.

"What can you tell me about House Roake?" Kira asked Liara.

If this was really to be her future, it paid to know all she could. Kira was nothing if not a realist. Her goals relied on her being fighting fit. She'd never intended her mission to be a one-way ticket, but she'd accepted that might be the cost. With Roake's help, she could hedge her bets.

She was a person of action. Patience had never come easy. Ever since Rothchild she'd had to take a masterclass in the attribute. Roake's demands were another bump on the way. A delay in a long line of them. A detour—but a necessary one.

Liara hesitated, her gaze going to Silas and Quillon. Warriors, unless Kira's instincts were wrong.

Silas's manner was gentle, quiet, almost unassuming, but she sensed a thread of steel running through him. He wasn't a pushover even if his eyes were kind.

There was a hint of gray in Silas's hair, the finest of lines on his face, but that wasn't what made him seem ancient. It was the years she could feel pressing in his gaze when he looked at her.

Quillon was the same. She knew he was a healer, but the way he moved, like a predator anticipating an attack, made it clear he was a warrior too. And not in charge. That duty lay fully on Silas's shoulders.

It behooved her to learn all she could about them. Their strengths. Their weaknesses. They were the first of House Roake that she'd had contact with. She needed to know what she'd be up against.

"They're a small House. Much smaller than mine, yet they are unchallenged," Liara said in a pensive tone.

"You sound afraid of them," Kira observed.

Raider was attentive beside her. He seemed brash and bold,

27

hotheaded even. He was all those things, but he was also observant and smart when he wasn't letting emotions rule him.

Once, he'd been a good man to have at her back.

Liara shrugged. "It's hard not to respect a *lu-ong's* ability to swallow you whole even if you know they have no interest in you."

"You said before my mother married my father to create an alliance. Are your Houses enemies?"

Liara's expression was pensive as she considered Kira's question. "Perhaps once; before the Sorrowing. Everything changed after that."

Kira suspected it had. Losing so many of your people and loved ones to an attack tended to do that. Add in having your children stolen, and Kira thought the Tuann might have reason to be as reclusive as they were.

"Luatha no longer dares be so free with the word enemy. We lost too much during that time, and we aren't as strong as we once were," Liara said.

"The Luatha Overlord plays well with the meaning of words." Graydon strode toward them, his expression arrogant and amused as he regarded them.

Unlike Liara, he'd left off the cape, his footsteps echoing in the large space. He moved with purpose and efficiency. He looked like a knight striding out of humanity's past. Powerful. Brutal. Dangerous.

"The relationship between Luatha and Roake has been—" there was a brief hesitation as Graydon considered the right phrasing. "Fraught with tension since the Sorrowing."

Liara didn't speak, her chin lifting in challenge.

Kira didn't have to ask whether Graydon's assessment was correct or not. She could read the answer in Liara's suddenly smooth expression; all emotion wiped away.

Yup, there was definitely something there.

"If you want to know about House Roake, you should ask the Emperor's Face. After all, he was one of them once," Liara said, her tone cutting.

Graydon's expression remained amused.

Liara flicked a glance at Kira. "Did you ever wonder how they learned about you? That information isn't floating around. Someone would have had to tell them—and it wasn't us."

This wasn't about Kira. This was a power play. Liara was upset with Graydon and still hurting from the attack on her House.

"Sowing dissent, cousin?" Kira asked.

It was to Liara's credit that she flushed at the question.

Kira's smile was soft. "I'm not a tool to be used against others."

It was best Liara learned that now, before she made a mistake she couldn't come back from.

Movement from the doorway attracted Kira's attention as Ziva and Joule appeared. Kira had rescued the two children back on O'Riley Station when the air gondola they'd been riding in had been sabotaged and was in the process of crashing. That one act had set this entire situation in motion, but she found she couldn't regret it.

The two had somehow found a way past her defenses. They were persistent. Joule intent on protecting those he had no business trying to protect. He looked to be in his early teens. Thirteen or fourteen at most.

His face still held the slightest trace of baby fat, but his facial bones were defined. One day he was going to break hearts.

Ziva was an adorable mini-replica, modeling her behavior off the older boy. Several years younger than Joule, she had white-blond hair and eyes of the deepest blue. Her cuteness belied the fighter within. Right now she was small, but Kira knew with the right training and time to grow she'd be fierce. Already she didn't let her young age or small size stop her from throwing herself into the midst of danger.

What were they doing here?

They approached with hesitant steps. Joule's gaze came up to meet hers, his expression filling with guilt and something else. Stubbornness. That's what it was.

Well, well, it looked like he'd finally gotten over his hero worship.

Joule's attention slid to where Silas regarded him steadily.

Joule took a deep breath, steeling himself. "We've come to petition to join House Roake. If accepted, we would train there until we pass our *adva ka*."

Kira started to object.

Liara stopped her with a touch on her wrist. "Don't interfere. This is his choice."

"Who is your sponsor?" Silas asked.

"I am," Graydon rumbled from beside Kira.

Kira fixed Graydon with a hard look. That hadn't been the agreement.

"To gain entrance into Roake, he needs a sponsor. Same with the *adva ka.* Do you really want him trained by her warriors?" Graydon asked. "I thought you liked the boy. He'll have a far better shot at becoming an Overlord if trained by Roake."

Liara pressed her lips together tight but didn't argue. Kira took that to mean Graydon was right.

"You said they were welcome in your House," Kira told her.

"And they are, but we're stretched thin. We cannot provide the type of training he wants. It is customary for children to apprentice and learn at the feet of other Houses. It's how we keep our skills relevant."

New blood would bring innovation. Humans had had a similar custom in their distant past. Where the sons of knights and lords would foster with another household to learn their skills before going on their way. It was an important apprenticeship and only practiced sparingly now.

Silas's gaze was appraising as he regarded the two young ones still bent in their respectful bows. He glanced at Kira.

She worked to keep her face expressionless, unsure which way she wanted him to decide. The events during the attack had made it clear she had an attachment to the two children. A wise man might seek to use that against her. Himoto certainly would have.

Silas crouched so he was at eye level. "Why do you wish to join the warriors?"

Joule straightened, his gaze steady despite the slight shaking she could see in his legs. He was terrified—whether of Silas or rejection was hard to say.

"House Maxiim was attacked by Tuann pirates, roamers who banded together to bring us down so we couldn't interfere with them anymore. Most were killed. I am the only one who has a chance of becoming Overlord, but I cannot pass the *adva ka* as I am."

"And you, young one?" Silas's gaze shifted to Ziva.

She drew herself up, lifting her chin. "I am going to be his first. I'm not going to let anyone hurt us ever again."

Silas made a thoughtful sound. "Put your hand in mine and let me test your resolve."

"Silas can determine a person's affinity and strength with a touch," Graydon told Kira quietly. "Right now, he's determining if they have what it takes to make it through the rigorous training."

"Hmm." Kira couldn't help the skeptical sound. More than a touch was needed to determine something like that.

Graydon's hand was warm on her back. "You forget he was there in the Nexus. He watched them try to defend their companions against the Tsavitee. Many warriors wouldn't have demonstrated the bravery they did. They'll pass his test, but whether he accepts them is still unknown."

"Why?"

Graydon thought a moment. "We're dangerous. The oshota and Overlords particularly so. To develop their talents is a responsibility House Roake takes seriously. Those who pass become weapons. They must make sure those weapons can never threaten them or the Tuann as a whole."

The look he aimed at Raider was significant. "This is the training you and the other humans agreed to undertake."

Now she saw why Graydon was explaining this. It wasn't just a kindness but a warning as well.

She had a feeling that those whose minds cracked or exhibited weakness never left House Roake again.

"Understood," Raider said, his expression slightly grim.

Both of them had seen enough soldiers whose minds or temperament were unsuited to a soldier's lifestyle. Some got off on the power. Some stopped seeing the white and black, only seeing shades of gray. Those were the ones you had to watch out for because they could justify anything. They'd commit unspeakable crimes and never blink an eye.

Power in any form should be carefully guarded because there were always those who would abuse it to prey on the weak.

It made Kira like House Roake just a little bit more to know they were careful about who they let loose in the galaxy.

"Both of you have amazing potential. With the right tools, conquering the *adva ka* should be no problem." Silas's hands dropped to his side, and he straightened as the children's faces lit up.

Silas's gaze was somber. "The boy can come, but the girl wouldn't be a good fit at this time."

Joule's expression froze, the hope of seconds before fading. Devastation settled on Ziva's face, her gaze going blank.

Silas rested a hand on Ziva's shoulder. "Your goals do you credit and someone as passionate and brave as you would fit in well with Roake. However, I'd be doing your future a disservice by allowing you to attend right now. You're too young, and there are still things you can only learn here."

Ziva's face threatened to crumple. She scrubbed one hand over her eyes, wiping away any tears that might have escaped her iron control. "When I'm older, then? Can I try again?"

Silas's gaze was wise and kind. "It would be my honor."

Ziva's nod was short and abrupt, resolve filling her delicate features.

Silas directed his attention to Liara. "If this is acceptable to you, Overlord."

Liara's smile was faint. "Of course. We're pleased Joule will get this chance. The remnants of their House and I will expect regular reports and visits to ensure their continued wellbeing."

Kira's attention jerked to her cousin. Now she saw why Liara had been willing to let Joule and Ziva make this attempt. It wasn't because she thought they'd be better off—although Kira had no doubt that was part of it. Instead, Liara had neatly managed to come up with a way to keep tabs on Kira.

Respect crept into Silas's gaze, and he inclined his head in a formal bow.

"Well played," Graydon murmured.

There was the slightest quirk to Liara's lips that said she heard and appreciated the compliment.

It left an uneasy feeling in Kira's gut. She didn't like the thought of Joule and Ziva being pawns in a larger game. She'd been in that position too many times to be comfortable sentencing someone else to that fate.

"Ziva," Joule said, sounding lost and shocked. This turn of events had been nowhere in his calculations, Kira was sure. It was a harsh, but necessary, lesson that things wouldn't always go his way.

"You need to go," Ziva said in a strong voice. She had a cocky smile on her face even as Kira caught the faintest tremble in her hands. "I'll catch up soon enough."

Joule shook his head, the sting of betrayal in his eyes. Kira could see his resolve wavering. She didn't blame him. Both children had lost more than any should have to bear. They'd probably clung to each other harder as a result. Now, their goals threatened to separate them for an unknown length of time.

Kira exhaled heavily and moved toward them. She set a hand on Joule's head, before flicking him in the forehead.

Joule touched the spot and glared, anger replacing the lost look he'd had. Good. The other expression hadn't suited him at all. "What was that for?"

She leveled a censorious glance on him. "Are you thinking clearly again?"

His gaze fell, his shoulders rounding before he nodded.

"Good, it looks like we're about to move. Why don't you say goodbye to Liara?" Kira told him.

His lips flattened mulishly before his gaze went to Ziva. His eyes softened, and he jerked his chin down slowly, a wealth of promise there. "I won't let us down."

Ziva's small body shook next to Kira, but she still managed an enthusiastic cry of approval. Joule spun, striding toward Luatha's Overlord.

There was a sniffle next to Kira, Ziva's composure cracking. Kira saw the girl glaring at the gate even as tears trailed down her cheek.

The girl had done well to put up a front for this long.

Kira dropped to a knee, getting to Ziva's level and blocking her from the rest of those in the room. By now silent sobs wracked Ziva's small body, the girl's hands clenched into fists as determination blazed from her eyes. Kira smiled. That was her girl.

She pulled Ziva into a hug, pressing the child's face against her shoulder and ignoring the tears soaking her shirt. "Well done."

"I don't want to be left behind," Ziva gasped.

Kira nodded. She understood that feeling. She'd been left behind more times than she liked to think about. She'd done the leaving a time or two. It never got any easier. "I don't think anyone does."

Kira ran a hand over Ziva's silky hair. She saw too much of herself in Ziva. The girl was a survivor. Incredibly brave and foolish at the same time with a chip on her shoulder. Joule too. They both made Kira remember the lost little girl she'd once been. She couldn't walk away, not without making sure Ziva would be all right. "This is going to hurt. You're going to feel lonely. That's okay. Use those feelings to make yourself stronger."

Kira drew back, her gaze finding Ziva's as she shared the things she wished someone would have told her. "You're going to be tempted to close yourself off from others. Don't let yourself fall into that trap. You will both experience many things from now on. It will change you. Your worlds will slowly shift, and you will grow. Make those friends, Ziva. They will help during darker times."

Both Joule and Ziva were so young. It was entirely possible that by the time they found their way back to each other, they would be different than the other remembered, neither fitting so easily into the other's world.

Kira hoped that didn't happen, but that was the way of life. You grew. You evolved. Sometimes toward one another; other times away. Only the two of them could decide which direction they'd take.

Ziva's tears had faded, and she had a focused look on her face that said she was internalizing Kira's words. Kira squeezed her shoulder and stood. She hoped they were helpful, that they'd provide comfort in the lonely days ahead.

"I will make our dream a reality," Ziva promised in a fervent voice.

Kira couldn't help a small smile at that statement. The arrogance of youth. She could do with a little of that herself.

Ziva's shoulders were straight and square as she moved toward the door, her stride full of purpose. Already, she was shaking off the blow of Silas's rejection.

"If only some of us were capable of taking our own advice," Raider mused, joining Kira.

"I'm simply discerning in the people I choose as friends." Kira faced the gate as the Tuann arranged themselves in preparation for travel.

Silas stood in front of it, waiting. "Are we finally ready?"

Kira shot another look over her shoulder at the door. Still no Jin.

She fought to hide her disappointment. No matter how angry he had been, she hadn't thought he'd let her leave without him.

Seeing her hesitation, Silas offered. "We can wait a little longer for you to say your goodbyes."

Raider nudged her. "Tin Man will forgive you. He always does. Give him a little time to come around."

Kira jerked up a shoulder. She knew he would. That didn't make the intervening time any easier.

She didn't like leaving him behind. This felt wrong—down to the very core of her soul wrong.

Kira took a deep breath. Sometimes to do right, you had to do things that felt wrong. This was one of those times.

"Right now, he's angry with you and them. They may have made it clear he wasn't welcome," Raider said in a quiet voice.

Kira shot him a sharp look. Raider lifted a shoulder in answer.

That still didn't explain why he hadn't come to say goodbye.

After several more minutes where it became increasingly clear Jin wasn't coming, Kira forced herself to face the gate. "We can go."

Waiting would prolong the inevitable.

Jin would cool off—eventually. Until he did, the only thing she could do was take the first steps to repair the breach between them.

"Let's do this." She met Silas's gaze, resolve in hers. He gave her a tiny nod of respect.

In Tuann, he barked several words, of which she only caught a few.

Without Jin here to translate via the comms patch inserted into her ear, she was left reliant on her own language skills. She knew some Tuann but she was far from fluent. It was a weakness she'd have to address.

There was a thrum as the runes along the edges pulsed. Blue made an interested sound, her eyes as wide as a child seeing a magic show for the first time. She drifted closer, her gaze wondering. Resigned, Kira grabbed her by her shirt and hauled her several steps back.

Blue was smart, but sometimes her curiosity got the better of her.

"Let's keep our distance until we get the all clear," Kira warned her.

Blue barely acknowledged Kira's words; her attention still fixed on the gate. "Whatever you say, Nixxy."

Raider glanced at Blue before shaking his head in resignation. "You're fighting a losing battle. She's going to latch onto it eventually."

"But perhaps not until after it does its thing," Kira shot back.

Raider shrugged. "Whatever you say. You're the boss."

Kira kept her grumble to herself. If only that were true.

A pulse went up from the gate; one Kira felt through her bones. It set them vibrating, not exactly unpleasant but not comfortable either.

Light coalesced in the center of the arches until the air rippled.

"The path has stabilized," a Luathan tech called.

Finn appeared at her shoulder, looking at the arches with a complicated expression on his face.

"We will leave after Silas steps through," he said.

"You're coming with us?" That surprised her. With the level of barely concealed tension between Liara and those from Roake, she hadn't thought they'd let any of Liara's people into their House.

His eyes lowered to meet hers. "I'm originally from House Roake. Where you go; I will follow."

Her eyes widened. She twisted to find Graydon and glared. He met her gaze calmly.

Tricky bastard. He'd planned this from the beginning. He'd appointed Finn as her oshota specifically so he would stay with her even when House Roake claimed her.

Would any of this have been possible if she hadn't negotiated her freedom from Liara? Did he anticipate that too?

His eyes smiled at her before he stepped through the doorway after Silas.

Raider paused beside her. "I think you might have a problem with that one. He's nearly as tricky as you."

Kira slid a sidelong look at him. Raider's snicker was quiet as she marched toward the gate. "I definitely would have preferred any of the other three over you," she muttered.

FOUR

KIRA BRACED FOR pain, expecting the world to wrench sideways before dissolving around her. The pain was noticeably absent as she stepped through the world gate with as much ease as she'd step through any doorway.

That was where the similarities ended. Going from Ta Da'an to Ta Sa'Riel was like stepping from a warm pool into a hot sauna. The Mea'Ave at the planet's core surged, reaching up in an embrace that spoke of welcome and joy while at the same time overwhelming every one of Kira's senses.

This Mea'Ave wasn't like the one on Ta Da'an. It was ancient and powerful.

Processing the immenseness of it all was impossible. Knowledge hovered out of reach, threatening to submerge her mind under its weight.

Kira's mental defenses snapped into place, useless against the entity.

It was like being strapped to the underside of a hoverboard while re-entering atmo and getting hit with the bulk of the turbulence. It was intense and scary. Exhilarating and humbling all at once.

Kira made an inarticulate gurgle as she stumbled, suddenly breathless. Graydon was there in the next moment to steady her, his hands comforting as he kept her upright.

"Breathe. Just breathe." His chest rumbled beneath her ear as she fought to stay standing. "It's the planet welcoming you. Remember what we did last time."

The Mea'Ave at the planet's core rolled over like an eager puppy as it reached out to her, pouring through her senses. Kira was prepared, letting its energy flow through her before returning the energy to the planet in a clumsy attempt that nevertheless relieved the worst of the pressure.

Her legs threatened to give out before she steeled herself. She would not embarrass herself in front of these people. She refused to start off with a mark against her.

Gradually, the giant pressure sitting on her chest loosened and her ribs expanded, allowing her to suck in a grateful breath of air.

This was different than last time. More intense.

"This planet is older," Kira guessed with her eyes still closed. She didn't know when they had slipped shut.

Graydon made an approving sound. "Yes."

Kira opened her eyes as the Mea'Ave subsided, taking in her surroundings. She stood on a wide circular ledge, deep grooves creating lines running its width, meeting and bisecting it in places.

Before her, an endless ocean of turbulent gray stretched, its waves crashing far below, bringing with it the smell of salt and brine.

Behind her was the gate that connected this planet to Luatha's. Runes were written on its side as Silas stood in front of it, his hands upraised, and his forehead furrowed in concentration.

Teleportation. Or something so close to it that it didn't matter.

The Tuann had secrets humans never would have guessed. Technology her former people had only ever dreamed about in fiction.

Kira was surprised to see the gate was located midway down a tall cliff, ledges and staircases carved into the rock, leading both to the land above and to the ocean below.

Gone was the airy lightness and delicate architecture of the Citadel of Light. It was replaced by a world of grays and blacks, austere in a way that called to the depths of her soul.

To survive here, you'd have to be strong. Both mentally and physically.

It was simple, but there was beauty in simplicity.

The air contained a bite to it, fall giving way to winter.

She shivered slightly, the clothes Liara had given her—simple pants and a lightweight tunic—did nothing to keep her warm. The small pack of clothes that had been a gift from Liara during her time on Ta Da'an held none suitable for the climate.

The gate spat out several more people. Among them, Graydon's oshota.

Solal inhaled, tipping his face up to the sky and then exhaling. Kira knew that look, had seen it on countless soldier's faces. Solal had the look of someone coming home for the first time in a long time.

"You live here," Kira realized.

Graydon leveled a thoughtful gaze on her head. "Correct. How did you know?"

Kira nodded at where his oshota gathered, staring around them with happy expressions. "They're home."

Graydon smiled. "This is the capital planet. Almost all Houses have a presence here, including Roake."

"Luatha?" Kira asked.

Graydon made a small sound of assent.

"Why didn't they bring me here?" Kira asked, puzzled.

"Ta Da'an is their stronghold. Having you there guaranteed privacy," Graydon said.

Which had the added benefit of keeping her far from Roake's influence. Of course, it also restricted her access to the Tuann in case she presented a safety threat.

That made her wonder why hadn't Roake done something similar and taken her to one of the other planets?

"This is the Tuann's home world," Kira said, slowly looking around.

Graydon shook his head. "Our original world has been lost to us since ancient times. Ta Sa'Riel is one of the planets we sought sanctuary on when we fled our first world. The emperor calls this his home, which is why it's the capital."

"This doesn't look like House Roake," Kira observed.

"Of course not," Quillon said, stopping beside her. "Having the gate located in the fortress would present a great strategic weakness. An enemy could send a force through the gate and attack from the inside. House Roake would never risk itself in that fashion."

The mindset told her everything she needed to know about these new people. Paranoid. Militarily minded. Obsessed with security.

She'd be impressed if those same accusations hadn't been lobbed at her more than once.

Raider staggered out of the gate, looking slightly white. His face had that pinched look Kira always associated with fear.

"I don't like this form of travel," Raider said through gritted teeth.

Kira grinned. "What's wrong? You don't like breaking the laws of physics?"

"No, I don't." Raider cast a sharp look at the gate. For a moment, Kira caught a glimpse of the feral side Raider hid well. The one that made him so effective against the Tsavitee.

"If I can't kill Shandry, I don't think Roake would be happy about you blowing up their gate," Kira said lightly.

Raider bared his teeth at her but didn't respond. She smothered her laugh.

Blue bounded out of the gate seconds later, her eyes bright and enthusiastic. She spun in a circle, nearly toppling the Tuann stepping through after her. She darted toward Silas, questions pouring out of her.

"How does it work? I mean, I know the theory, but how really? Do you need two points connected via the gate to travel, or can you go anywhere?" She didn't give him a chance to answer, already peering closely at the gate runes while muttering to herself.

"Great. It's going to be a nightmare trying to keep her focused," Raider griped. He sent a look at Kira.

She shook her head. "Don't look at me. I'm not her commanding officer anymore."

Raider grinned, his expression sly. "Actually, that's not quite right."

Kira stiffened, her focus sharpening. "What are you talking about?"

"You never finished submitting your exit papers." Raider inspected his nails. "That means you're still a captain of the Space Force and as such, hold the highest rank of any here."

Kira's eyes widened. "Ah, damn."

Raider leaned forward, his smile gloating. "Welcome back to the fold, Boss."

Kira's eyes narrowed. She'd miscalculated. Raider was a chief petty officer; she was a captain. As the highest-ranking officer, it left her in charge. Somehow, she'd forgotten that, her interactions with Jace and the Curs on Ta Da'an lulling her into believing she existed outside the rank structure.

If the military could issue orders to her, it meant she still had rank. With rank came responsibility. And leadership.

All things Kira had no interest in anymore. She had no intention of allowing herself to get sucked back into the trap of being responsible for others.

"Corral your subordinate, Chief," Kira said through gritted teeth.

Raider's smile widened, and he snapped a salute. "Sir, yes, sir."

Kira growled as he stalked toward the other Cur. She didn't like this. She didn't like it one bit. If Jin was here, he'd have had some funny quip to annoy her out of her snit.

"Blue, leave it alone. I'm not getting arrested for you again," Raider said.

Whispers pulled Kira from her frustration of being maneuvered into a role she'd had no intention of taking up again. She glanced around, finally noticing Graydon and his people weren't the only ones present. Over a dozen Tuann milled around the edges of the ledge. They were a variety of ages, some not much older than Joule, others Kira's age or more.

They were dressed in a variety of styles, from simplistic to luxurious. Some were clad in a plain, lightweight armor, their vital spots covered but not much else. Not oshota, Kira guessed. Their armor lacked the slick sophistication of Graydon's warriors.

Bags were set at their feet. Travelers?

Kira's gaze caught on one who had a look of distaste on his face as he studied Raider and Blue. He was young. A human would have guessed around twenty-two or twenty-three. His face still held the unrefined edges of youth, and his build was slim but muscular. One day he'd fill out, rivaling Graydon for size and height.

He caught Kira looking at him, and his expression smoothed out, arrogance descending.

She raised an eyebrow, impressed in spite of herself. Not many could pull off that look so easily. He must have imbibed the trait with his mother's milk, or else he was taking lessons from Graydon.

Next to him was a boy, similar in age, his expression open and curious as he took in the platform and the ocean below. His hair was a curly mop on his head, and his limbs had a coltishness about them that said he'd yet to fill out. His clothing was less refined than the first Tuann, but it contained a quality that was unmistakable even at this distance.

Seeing Kira studying him, he waved and smiled. His companion murmured something. The boy's hand dropped as they exchanged several words, not even the other's rebuke seemed to dull his bright cheeriness.

"What are humans doing here?" one of those behind the two boys asked.

"They should go home," was the not so quiet response.

Kira observed the group, not exactly surprised at their reception. The Tuann had made their thoughts on humans clear more than once, by both word and deed. This lot was only echoing things she already knew, cementing the fact Jace had made a smart call sending Raider and Blue here.

Hate and prejudice flourished in ignorance. It was easier to believe a stereotype when you never had anyone to compare to your misconceptions. It was harder when you had a living, breathing person challenging them.

The headache that had started from the moment she stepped onto the planet surged, piercing in its intensity until it felt like someone was jabbing a red-hot poker behind her eyes.

"Are you all right?" Finn asked.

"Fine." Kira dismissed his question with barely a thought. "Who are they?"

Finn's frown deepened, but he didn't press. "They look like hopefuls, seeking to become initiates in Roake's House. A call went out yesterday announcing a trial for those interested in gaining an apprenticeship within Roake's ranks."

Startled, Kira took the newcomers in. "Like Joule?"

Finn inclined his head. "They'll likely be his peers. All from different Houses and backgrounds. Alliances and connections will be formed and broken over the next few weeks as they seek to advance their training."

Good to know. Kira left the strangers behind as she headed to where Graydon waited. Raider had finally corralled Blue and managed to herd her toward them.

With a sense of resignation, Kira took in the stairs and nearly groaned. Going up those was going to be a bitch and a half.

Graydon stepped close, bending slightly so only she could hear. "Show no fear. They take getting used to, but once you earn their regard, there are none more loyal."

Puzzlement settled on Kira's face. She saw the reason for the warning seconds later when a man stepped into view, seemingly appearing out of the rock. Kira jolted, adrenaline sending the throb of her headache to piercing levels. Her hand dropped to a weapon that wasn't there.

She growled at the lack even as Raider swore, dropping into a defensive crouch.

Blue yipped, her hands moving to her pockets.

Graydon and his people remained unmoving. Their postures were relaxed, their expressions calm. A friend then.

Kira reached out, grabbing Blue's hand before she could withdraw the device Kira suspected she had on her. If she knew Blue, it wouldn't look like a weapon, but it would hurt a person like one.

"Wait," she urged.

More than one perceptive gaze caught her action.

Blue grumbled, even as she subsided.

"Commander, it's good to see you again," the man in front said as he bowed his head.

Graydon nodded back. "As it is you, Makon."

The stranger examined those standing on the wide platform. His eyes met Kira's for a brief second, flickering before his expression smoothed into neutral lines.

Like most of the Tuann Kira had met, he seemed ageless. Neither old nor young. No beginning or end, just years stretching infinitely behind and ahead of him.

It made it impossible to guess his age. He could be Graydon's contemporary or his senior by centuries for all Kira could tell.

Authority was written on every line of his face. Despite that, he managed to seem almost serene. Reassuring even. He had the type of presence that made you want to confide and trust in him, like he'd listen to your woes and offer wise counsel.

His skin was the color of night, his hair cut close to his skull, exposing pointed ears. The golden amber of his gaze swept over the rest of those present.

He was tall with broad shoulders and a long, slim build of someone built for speed rather than power. Kira was willing to bet the enemy never saw him coming. He'd make a pretty good assassin, especially with that trick of appearing out of thin air.

Other Tuann appeared one by one on the ledges above.

The Tuann she'd mistaken as travelers stirred with unease at the evidence that they weren't alone and probably hadn't been for quite some time.

Camouflage. It had to be. It was some of the best Kira had ever seen, making the user indistinguishable from the rock.

Every one of the Tuann above wore the deep blue-black of House Roake's synth armor. More than one set of eyes lingered on Kira before taking in the rest of those assembled.

One man, in particular, drew her eye. He was tall, broad-shouldered, even more muscular than Graydon. He had the fierce countenance of a warrior who had seen and survived many battles. His hair was half pulled away from his face, a shade nearly identical to the wine red of her own. A vertical scar ran over one eye and down one cheek. Whoever had given him that scar had missed taking his eye by millimeters.

His stare was intense. Penetrating. A trim beard shadowed his jaw and above his lip.

This was a grizzled veteran, powerful and formidable. He was a tank, able to level any obstacle in his way. His hands were clasped behind his back, and his expression inscrutable as he took her in.

The man had a superb poker face. Better even than Liara.

Unlike Luatha, Roake didn't posture. They simply intimidated.

"I am the marshal of House Roake; I welcome you on our Overlord's behalf," Makon said.

Kira's gaze rose to meet the man above who had still not looked away from her. The Overlord she was willing to bet.

"You are our treasured guests and will be treated as such. Yet trespass against us, and you will die," the marshal said in that slow, controlled tone.

Raider let out a small scoff. "Quite a greeting you've got there."

Kira agreed.

What kind of host welcomed you in one sentence, then threatened you in the next? A dangerous one. Someone who didn't intend to give second chances.

Makon's smile was brief, barely touching his eyes. "We've learned it's best to be blunt. It cuts down on misunderstandings."

Raider grunted and cocked his head. "If you say so."

"Many of those present have answered our call in the hopes of being accepted for an apprenticeship that will prepare them for the *adva ka* and what comes after," the marshal continued as if Raider hadn't spoken. "But first you must pass the *uhva na,* the Trial of the Broken. Over the next few weeks, we will observe you. We will test you in many ways. Some will be obvious; others will not."

Makon's gaze moved over those assembled. "Those we deem worthy will be chosen for the trial. If they succeed, they will be paired with a *seon'yer* who will prepare them for the next phase. We wish you luck. The path you've chosen is not an easy one."

That was quite the speech. A real confidence booster.

"To begin, you must ascend. As is the case in most things, there is more than one path," Makon said.

He paused, and Amila and Noor, another of Graydon's oshota, grinned before sprinting straight at the wall. Amila reached it first and leaped, clearing ten feet before finding a ledge and jumping to the next one. Noor took a slightly different route. He landed on the wall, running up it like he had grav boots on.

Raider glanced at Kira and lifted his eyebrows as Joule made an admiring sound beside them.

She nodded. She saw it too. It would be tempting to dismiss Noor's feat as a tech they had never seen, if Kira hadn't once been able to do something very similar.

"This is your first test. There are many who come to us. Few are considered worthy of our attention and effort. To be accepted as an initiate, you must reach the top. You may keep anything you can carry." His lips tilted. "Choose carefully. Anything you set aside will be given to the sea."

Both Kira and Raider glanced up at the thousands of steps twisting above the marshal. Whatever they kept would likely feel like it weighed a ton by the time they reached the top.

"If you should decide this is not your time, the gate behind you will take you home," the marshal continued.

Kira's mouth pulled down. If only that was an option for her.

The marshal stepped aside and bowed his head. The Tuann behind them whooped, nearly a dozen racing for the cliff and the paths Noor and Amila had taken.

Their leaps weren't as high or impressive, though a few, including the tall youth who had tried to stare Kira down, managed to make it look easy. None took the stairs to their right.

Joule quivered at her side, staring at where the most talented had disappeared. It was easy to see he wanted to take that path.

"Twenty credits most of them gas out before they reach the midway point," Raider challenged.

Blue scoffed as she turned toward the stairs. "Nobody is foolish enough to take that bet. It's obvious they're weeding out the stupid and the arrogant."

As she spoke, there was a cry above them as one of the initiates faltered. They plummeted. Oshota, unseen until now, appeared next to them, catching them before they could fall to their deaths.

The oshota stepped off the cliff, the boy in his arms. He landed with a thump, setting the boy near the gate before turning and leaping to his post, where he almost faded into the rock.

Makon regarded the boy steadily. "Perhaps the next time you come to us, you will succeed."

The boy sent Kira and her friends a sulky look before bowing respectfully and striding through the gate.

"See, told you so," Blue taunted over her shoulder as she started up the steps.

Joule's eyes were wide before he grinned and raced for the stairs, passing Blue easily.

"I wish I had his energy," Raider grumbled as he bent and reached for his two bags.

Kira's headache intensified. Before she could think, she'd grabbed one of the bags, her hand closing on the handles at the same time as his.

She bared her teeth at him. "Thanks for carrying my bag until now. I've got it from here."

Raider's expression was careful. "Are you sure? It doesn't hurt to let someone help you every once and a while."

Kira's eyes narrowed. Who did he think he was kidding? "Sometimes, when people think they're helping, they're creating a bigger problem."

His smile was sharp and cutting. "Perhaps—or maybe it's simply that there are those who don't accept help gracefully."

Kira was conscious of the marshal, and no doubt countless other oshota hiding along the cliffs, watching the byplay between the two of them. It made her bite back her normal response. Instead, she said carefully, "I've carried it this long. I can carry it up a few steps."

If her voice contained a harsh edge and her expression looked mildly murderous, there was no helping it.

Raider raised his hands and backed away. "Whatever you want, Phoenix."

Kira straightened. If only that were so.

Raider hesitated at the base of the stairs. He switched to Japanese, a language she was reasonably sure those listening wouldn't understand. At least, no one from Luatha had understood it. "Don't kill anyone." He started up, saying over his shoulder as an afterthought. "Don't let yourself be killed either."

"If I were you, I'd be more worried about myself," Kira muttered.

His smile was cocky. "I'm not the one with the reputation."

Bullshit. His record was as bad as Kira's. Worse, in some ways, since he also tended to mouth off to people in authority. Hence, the reason he was still a chief petty officer instead of a senior chief petty officer. If he wasn't such a good pilot, he'd likely have been kicked out of the Space Force ages ago.

Kira's smile was saccharine sweet. "Enjoy your second round of basic."

Raider couldn't hide his grimace. Yeah, that's what she thought. No one who'd been through basic once wanted to go again. It was one of those necessary evils that remained with you long after you'd graduated.

"I'm going to be an instructor, not a recruit," he muttered.

Kira lifted an eyebrow. If that's what he wanted to tell himself. To her, it had sounded like he'd be a little of both.

"Try not to let what happened last time happen again," Kira suggested.

That shut him up. He sent a fulminating glare her way. She hid her snicker

He pointed a finger at her. "That wasn't my fault, and you know it."

He didn't wait for her rebuttal, jogging up the steps. He reached the first landing before starting up the next set at a slow, even pace.

The marshal waited until the rest of the initiates had disappeared before approaching where Kira and Graydon still waited.

"Do you often threaten guests with having their belongings tossed in the ocean?" Kira asked.

Graydon's grin was unrepentant. "It is our way."

Kira snorted. Why did she have a feeling that was a lie?

"Daughter of our House, I greet you. It is an honor to have you among us again." Makon's serene expression softened, and real warmth peeked out. "Though I sense your presence here is not entirely by choice."

"You could say that." Kira shook her head. "There are those who've convinced me to come here despite my instincts."

Makon dipped his head. "Then they have Roake's undying gratitude. While you may not know us or have any reason to trust us, we hope you will find kindred spirits among our people."

Kira tilted her head. "We'll see."

She knew they wanted more, but that was all she could promise. Her soul had been scarred, and her path set long before they found her. She honestly couldn't see that changing now.

The marshal straightened, wisdom in his gaze. "Then we will strive to prove ourselves." Makon spread his hands. "The Overlord has authorized me to offer you a choice. As a daughter of our House, your entry is yours by birthright. You may join us, and we will welcome you with open arms. You'll be treated with every honor we can bestow and have the best care as you heal."

Kira's eyes narrowed. It sounded too good to be true. "What's the catch?"

Makon hid his smile, approval in his eyes. "You will be considered a daughter of our House. That status comes with certain responsibilities. Leaving would be difficult if you so choose in the future. By accepting your role as a daughter of Roake, you submit yourself to our will. We will determine the course of your training and decide when—or if—you're ever ready for the warrior's path."

In other words, her future would lie in their hands. They could delay her advancement by years, if not decades.

"And the other?" she asked.

He nodded toward the stairs. "The same test; the same rules apply. All rights as a daughter of our House will be negated. Any position you gain will be through your own merit."

Kira considered. "And the healing I was promised?"

"Still yours, regardless of which path you choose."

At least that was something.

It seemed to Kira that the *adva ka* was the fastest way to independence. To get there, however, it had become clear she'd need the support of a House. From Joule's actions in seeking Graydon as a sponsor, she was getting the sense that she couldn't show up on trial day and hope to participate.

The Tuann placed a lot of stock on a person's allegiances and House. If she wanted her shot at the *adva ka*, first she needed to win Roake's confidence. That meant putting herself into the running for the *uhva na*.

Admittedly, it was a long circuitous path to her end goal. Much simpler to steal a ship and escape.

Kira had given up on short-term solutions for long-term problems. If she was going to coexist with the Tuann—and it was becoming increasingly obvious that was her only option—she needed to meet them on their level.

Even if she wasn't ready. Even if she'd rather spend her time healing rather than preparing for an unknown trial.

She'd manage. Somehow.

Maybe if she'd grown up among them, trusted them, then she could have taken option one. But she hadn't, and trust was something she'd never been good at.

There were too many ways a caveat like that could be used against her. In the way their society worked, she'd be powerless.

Something she'd sworn never to be again.

Makon hesitated. "It is my understanding your illness has weakened you. There is no shame in taking the time you need to heal. Some might even consider it the wiser course." He bowed and stepped back. "I will leave you to consider."

Mighty kind of him.

Kira studied the stairs. It was a long way up. Reaching the top wouldn't be as easy as it seemed.

The Tuann respected strength. It was evident in everything they did and the way their society was structured. Being able to defend yourself and others carried certain responsibilities, but it also meant it was more difficult to silence your voice.

The warrior's path he spoke of was her only option. When she finally left, her future dealings with the Tuann would come from a place of strength and independence. No one would question her abilities because she'd beaten them on their own playing field.

Graydon studied the stairs as his head tilted. "If you choose not to join the initiates, it'll be my pleasure to carry you up the cliff."

A challenge sparked in his expression. It was enough to startle a laugh out of Kira. It also knocked her out of her contemplation.

"Thanks, but I prefer walking."

His eyes glimmered with appreciation. "You're decided then."

She lifted a shoulder. Might as well. If the *uhva na* was her path to freedom, she'd walk it no matter the obstacles.

Graydon moved toward the cliff. "Well then, it looks like you won't be needing my services after all. I look forward to seeing you at the top."

Somehow Kira doubted that. Now that they were on the Tuann's main planet, she suspected he would soon be consumed by his duties.

This was likely goodbye. It wouldn't be long before he forgot her.

She knew she should be grateful for that, but she couldn't shake the ache in her chest.

Graydon walked toward the cliff at a sedate pace, breaking into a sprint when he was only a few feet from it. He was faster than a man his size should be capable of.

He leaped at the last second, shooting straight up. He kicked off the air, reaching a height that should have been impossible. He was out of sight and over the top in seconds.

Raider paused on a ledge as Graydon passed him, his mouth dropping open before he looked at Kira and raised his eyebrows.

She shook her head slightly. Show off.

Her gaze lowered to find the marshal observing her with a calculating look.

Kira tensed, her hand tightening around the bag handle, knowing if he attacked, she'd have a hard time fending him off. She was exhausted and hurting, not fully recovered from the events on Ta Da'an.

Perhaps all that talk earlier was simply that. Talk. Maybe Roake wanted the unknown nobody to go away permanently.

Kira was weaponless, whereas she suspected the marshal had more than one stashed in his synth armor.

She'd learned never to assume a warrior wearing the armor was unarmed.

That left the bag she'd taken from Raider and the one at her feet as her only defense. Already her mind was envisioning using them as a club, or tossing one in his face as a distraction so she could escape.

His lips lifted the slightest bit, and she got the feeling he'd guessed where her thoughts had gone in that moment.

"As an initiate, you're entitled to our courtesies, but there will be no special treatment for your blood ties. From here on out, they will be considered unimportant. All that matters is what you can do and what you can contribute to the glory of our House. None in Roake may help you conquer this phase. It must be done on your own," he said. "Will you still walk this path?"

It wasn't like she had much of a choice. It was that or death.

And she preferred to live. That meant making nice with House Roake and observing until she got to the point where she could survive on her own without their help. If that meant completing this silly test, so be it.

"I will," she said.

The slightest glint of approval shown in his eyes, there and gone in a blink.

"How long will this take?" she asked.

"Longer, if you don't take the first step," he instructed.

Hmph. Guess she should have expected that response.

"This path won't be easy," Finn said from behind her.

Kira gazed up at the obstacle in front of her. "Nothing worth doing ever is. Don't worry; I'm used to hard."

It was the theme of her life. An ever-present reminder. Nothing in her history had ever said she enjoyed easy anyway.

"Any tips?"

"Don't let go of your bags if you want to keep them," Finn said with a brief glance at the other Tuann. "They're serious about their threat. Other than that, it's up to you to figure it out."

Kira snorted. "Somehow, the planet changes, and yet things always remain the same."

Finn smirked. "I'll meet you at the top."

Like ghosts he and the other oshota disappeared the same way Graydon had, leaving Kira and the marshal standing alone, the gate at their back, the sea beneath them, and the stairs in front of her.

"Does it matter how long this takes?" Kira asked, staring at the twisting stairs as they threaded in on themselves.

"Only that you complete it."

"And if I don't?"

"Anything that falls is given to the sea."

Aw, the first trick. Falter, sit, and you were likely to get a little wet. Good to know. But he hadn't said you couldn't try again.

Kira considered the two bags. There was little chance she'd be able to carry both up the stairs.

She grabbed the one Raider had ceded to her. Why did she get the feeling that this was going to get more difficult the higher she climbed?

There was no way to tell without starting.

Kira set her foot on the first step and then started up at a controlled pace. If she truly didn't have a time limit, then there was no reason to rush. Slow and steady wins the race, as the saying went.

A few piddly little stairs weren't going to defeat her, the Phoenix, Scourge of the Tsavitee.

FIVE

GRAYDON MOVED THROUGH the place he'd once called home. The few Tuann he passed stepped out of his way, none daring to delay him.

Not with that focused look in his eyes, one that didn't invite casual conversation.

The place he'd once called home was ancient, steeped in tradition and paid for by the blood and sweat of generations. The fortress's design was brutally simple. Those who'd built the Fortress of the Vigilant had understood its purpose. Every brick laid was done to maximize its defense and increase its offensive capabilities.

Perhaps because of its simplicity, it was a place of minimalist beauty. Graydon had visited many strongholds, spent time on countless planets, yet Roake's fortress was still among the most stunning he'd seen.

Two oshota framed a massive wooden door at the end of the hallway. The door was functional, yet managed to be imposing, as if taking its cues from the man waiting behind it.

Once upon a time, Graydon would have found the sight of that door intimidating. It would have loomed like a specter. More than one Roake Tuann had faced that door and felt nerves eating away at their stomachs.

For Graydon, that time was over, his position and the intervening years blunting its impact.

"The prodigal son returns." The tall man on the left greeted him with a faint smile. His chest was wide, and he had skin that reminded Graydon of the *choko* trees in the southern tip of the continent.

"Veer." Graydon dipped his head as a sign of respect. "Is he in?"

"He is, but you might want to compose yourself before you enter,"

Veer cautioned, seeming all the more amused. "You know he won't respond well if your control wavers even a little."

Graydon held in his response. Outside these walls, he was feared, his reputation for swift justice and decisive violence well earned. He was respected, even as he was treated with wary caution. No one wanted to earn the enmity of the emperor's youngest Face.

In these halls, however, was a different story. Here, he was still the undersized whelp the Overlord's brother had taken under his wing and trained.

"Little Storm, you're not usually so off-balance." Indya was a tall woman with strong features and eyes that always seemed to be laughing. "Has the child worked her way so far into your heart?"

Used to it by now, Graydon didn't let the teasing distract him. Most of Roake's oshota had assisted in raising him after his parents fell in defense of their Overlord.

They'd acted as honorary aunts and uncles from the time he took his first step. In House Roake, every adult cared for the children like the precious treasures they were. That went double for the warrior class, where a parent might die at any time.

Indya had taught him how to hold his sword. Veer had worked with him on his *kattas*. The man behind that door had overseen every step of his training, pushing him when he would have faltered, forcing him to stand when he would have fallen.

He owed Harlow everything that he was. He wouldn't be the man he was without him.

Kira's uncle was a hard man. Formed by sorrow, hardened by battle. Everything Harlow was, everything he'd become, had been forged during the events of the Sorrowing when the previous Overlord— Harlow's younger twin brother—and his wife had been murdered, their daughter and countless other children of House Roake stolen.

Harlow had inherited a wreckage of a House, taken it and forced it to hold against all who would have tried to usurp it.

He had no primus form, but he'd managed to turn that into a strength. Graydon knew of no other who was as deadly as Harlow.

The current Overlord's example was a lesson Graydon had taken to heart. It didn't matter what skills or talents you had been born with if you didn't make the most of them, surpassing the limits others placed on you.

Kira reminded Graydon of Harlow in many ways. She contained

that same force of personality. She didn't let anything hold her back when she had set her sights on something. Perhaps that was why he had been drawn to her from the beginning.

"Little Storm, you've grown well," Indya said softly as Graydon moved past the oshota, pushing open the door.

As he had every time Graydon had entered this room, Harlow sat in a position of power behind his desk, studying the polymer screen that had dozens of streams of data scrawling across it. Some were live holovids, others stats or memos.

Harlow didn't bother looking up as Graydon entered. "You've come to take me to task."

Graydon shut the door behind him, careful not to slam it. "I'm simply here to ask why."

Harlow swiped a hand over the desk, dismissing the data and leaving the façade of ancient wood, nicked and scarred by time.

The Overlord settled in his chair, leveling that predator's stare on Graydon. The weight of thousands of years came to bear as Harlow dropped the reins on his control, letting Graydon feel the full might of his personality and power.

Graydon held firm. It might have been years since he'd experienced this, but even now the tiny hairs on his neck stood up, warning him of danger.

He ignored them with the ease of long practice, advancing across the room with a lazy stroll before slouching into a chair in front of Harlow's desk.

When he'd been under Harlow's command, he never would have dared. Everyone knew the chairs were a lure for the unwary. Sit in them without an invitation, and you would face repercussions.

Graydon gave Harlow a toothy smile as he lounged with deceptive ease. "The Trek of the Weary. Really? That is an old test even by House Roake's standards. I don't even remember the last time it was used."

It certainly hadn't been in Graydon's day.

The Trek of the Weary took its name from the beginning of the Tuann Empire's history, at a time when they had fled their first home world. It was said that their ancestors had crashed on a harsh world and had to walk hundreds of miles to find sanctuary. The journey had taxed the Tuann in ways they'd never experienced before. They could only take what they could carry. Anything they set aside was left behind.

It was said in their history books that was how the first affinities were decided. Pushed to the brink, barely able to survive, those first Tuann had unlocked the potential within. Helped in part by having no other choice.

The trek Kira was even now walking was meant to simulate a small part of what those first Tuann had gone through. The path was deceptive and meant to test an individual's perseverance and will power.

He did not envy her or the rest their journey.

"Why not simply greet her the way I know you want to? Why force her to make this decision now?" Graydon asked, genuinely at a loss.

"She's not one of us. You and Silas have made it clear she doesn't see her future in this House. She's already shown she responds well to challenge and adversity. I'm simply giving her the fuel she needs to succeed," Harlow said.

"You intend to trick her into accepting a place among Roake." Graydon knew his mentor well. The man did devious better than any other Tuann he knew except for the emperor. It was only luck that both men had a code of honor that was bedrock deep and had never found themselves on opposing sides.

"You, better than anyone, know what she faces here. There are those who will point to her beginnings and call her unworthy. By forcing her to prove her worth now, I remove many barriers she will face later," Harlow said.

"Are you sure that's what this is?" Graydon asked.

Harlow regarded him steadily.

Graydon shook his head. His mentor had always been stubborn. "Kira doesn't respond well to manipulation. If you're not careful, you'll make it so she hates you before the end."

She had been magnificent when routing the human admiral's agenda. She might not have wanted to cut ties, but she'd been willing and ready to when it became obvious they planned to use her status against her.

She'd done what she felt necessary to retain what she perceived as freedom. It proved the extent she'd go to when backed into a corner. Kira wasn't the type to surrender gracefully.

Harlow didn't seem surprised. "Her father was the same."

Harlow had worshiped Harding. The former Overlord had never had to worry about whether his minutes-older twin brother would come for his title because Harlow's loyalty, once given, was unbreakable. He'd been vicious when it came to Harding's safety.

"Then why test her?" Graydon asked.

He had no doubt that Harlow's loyalty extended to Harding's daughter. Otherwise, Graydon never would have manipulated events to bring her here.

Harlow's gaze was distant as he stared out the narrow window to the sea outside. "This way, she will live through anything. I need her to be able to survive. I won't lose another member of my family."

So that was what this was about.

The Sorrowing had changed all of them. In some ways, House Roake had never been stronger than it was today. They were small but fierce. Every member had some defensive training. It didn't matter their age or station, or what their affinity was. If you were of this House, you could fight.

It was the first of Harlow's many changes. He'd decided House Roake wouldn't be reliant on a handful for their safety. They would stand or fall together.

However, it had also made them reclusive and obsessive when it came to their safety. Harlow, as the Overlord, probably experienced those qualities to a greater extent.

By doing this he was ensuring Kira's future safety in the best way he knew how, even if it affected his current relationship with his niece.

"You know you won't be able to have much contact with her before she passes the *uhva na*," Graydon finally said. "There can be no evidence of favoritism from you."

Harlow's lips curved up the faintest bit as he leaned back. "I am aware."

Graydon watched him for several seconds. There was something more to this.

"What do you know that I don't?" Graydon finally asked. Because there was no doubt there was something. Harlow was too controlled to let fear sway him, and this action stunk of desperation.

Harlow tapped the desk and swiped his finger across it. A hologram formed above it.

Graydon sat forward. "Are those Tsavitee?"

"Two of their ships slipped through when the Luathan net went down. A third ship, origin unknown, also made it through. We lost track of them shortly afterward."

Graydon stood in an explosive movement, pacing to the window and staring at the sea.

That damnable net. Luatha's defenses protected the outer perimeter of Tuann space. With it down, the three ships had found it easy to slip into Tuann territory.

Tuann space was vast. In addition to the main Houses, there were hundreds of smaller Houses, many of which would have holdings on other planets.

None communicated well with the rest. The labyrinthian maze of feuds and alliances would make it difficult to track the ships. Each House protected its own territory and would be loath to admit an incursion.

It had been thousands of years since the Tuann had last united against a common threat. Even with the emperor's power to compel cooperation, it would take weeks, if not months, of sifting through the data to track the ships across the different territories. By then, the Tsavitee would have accomplished their mission.

"This is what the invasion was about," Graydon said, his mind already working.

It hadn't been about Luatha at all. It had been a feint, meant to distract them from the next prong of attack. Their real intention was to insert a few of their agents into Tuann territory.

"This enemy has proven unexpectedly cunning," Harlow rumbled. "Much more so than we had previously predicted."

"Do we know what they want yet?" Already Graydon's plans were shifting to take into account this new information.

Harlow shook his head. "Only time will show their true goal. I suspect my niece will play a role in the events to come."

Graydon gave him a sharp look. Harlow's assessment was accurate and fit with Graydon's perception.

The Tsavitee had shown a continued fascination with Kira. From what he'd picked up through conversations with her and his observations during the invasion, the two were connected. It was clear the Tsavitee wanted something from her. They either saw her as a weapon to be reacquired or a threat to be eliminated.

Either way, staying close to her would likely bring the Tsavitee plans to light.

"Kira isn't weak. She might not be an oshota, but her skills put her on par with them. She outran Baran in their human station. I have no doubt she would have escaped if the humans hadn't intervened," Graydon said.

"You sound admiring."

Graydon let a thin smirk play along his lips. His old mentor wasn't going to get any heartfelt revelations out of him.

"She took out a Tsavitee war drone in a simulation within thirty seconds. She can hold her own against nearly all of my oshota," Graydon finished.

To say nothing of the lower form Tsavitee she'd cut a bloody path through during the battle in the Nexus.

Kira might not have been raised Tuann. She might be weakened from her *ki* poisoning and lack of training, but underestimating her would be a mistake. She was a force in her own right.

"Has the Little Storm found his calm at last?"

"Would you object if I had?"

That canny old gaze was assessing. The corners of Harlow's lips tilted up. The only expression on the otherwise somber face.

That's what Graydon thought.

Harlow thought he needed to save Kira, but from what Graydon had seen, she rarely needed saving. It would be best if Harlow learned that sooner rather than later.

"What is your assessment of my niece?"

Graydon considered his words carefully. "She's strong. Stubborn. In that, she's exactly like both her parents. She has a strong martyr complex. She'll sacrifice herself for her humans without a thought."

"Loyal to a level that can be a detriment to herself."

Graydon grunted an assent. "I'm not sure what happened in the human's war with the Tsavitee, but it's marked her. I get the sense from her friends she disappeared for a time and is only now reintegrating."

"We're not built for solitude," Harlow murmured.

No, they weren't. The Tuann relied on social bonds, needing a connection with others, both mentally and physically. It's why they lived in Houses. Without those bonds, they withered and faded.

When others learned of the years she'd spent with only a drone for company, they'd point to it as evidence of a sickness of the mind.

Only the wanderers roved alone. Most were thought to be slightly insane as a result.

Graydon made to stand. "Now that I've returned, my duties to the emperor will take priority."

Harlow reached for a small disk, no bigger than a fingernail, and handed it to Graydon. "About that, this came for you."

Graydon frowned, taking the disk. It carried the insignia of the emperor, marking it as an official message. While it would look like an ornate coin to some, heavy and solid in the hand, it was anything but.

Encoded to Graydon's DNA and *ki*, it would open for no one but him. He pressed a finger to the top, unsurprised when the faint halo of the emperor's emblem flashed.

The message unlocked; he pressed the coin against a slot on the forearm of his suit. The emperor's message scrolled across his arm.

Graydon felt surprise spark through him at the information contained within.

"Interesting news?" Harlow asked, arching an eyebrow.

"When were you going to tell me the emperor's son was among the initiates?" Graydon asked.

"I believe I just did."

Graydon fought a growl. He'd forgotten how much Harlow liked intrigue. The disk on his arm drained of color, black spreading through it until it was no more than a lump of carbon again.

Graydon removed the disk from his arm and tossed it on the desk. "The emperor won't want his son's stay here advertised."

Harlow had likely guessed that, but it bore repeating. The boy's life couldn't be left to chance.

Harlow sat back, resting an elbow on the arm of his chair. "Given what happened to the boy's older brother during the Sorrowing, I can't blame him. The emperor has kept his youngest and only remaining child close to him—done everything in his power to safeguard his wellbeing, including limiting those who've met him or even seen his face."

Graydon waited, knowing Harlow wasn't finished.

Harlow speared him with a matter of fact look. "It's not possible to keep his presence here a total secret. There are those in my House who will recognize him, despite the emperor's precautions."

Graydon waved Harlow's concerns away. "He understands that and even expects it. This isn't meant to hide him entirely. It'll be enough if his presence here doesn't become common knowledge."

Harlow smiled. "That I can guarantee. It would do us no good to draw notice from the other Houses."

"Good." Graydon stood and prepared to leave.

"I'm going to assume this changes your plans."

Graydon stopped and aimed a toothy smile at his former mentor. "You would be right. I think perhaps I should stay close, after all. See for myself how the initiates' training is progressing."

Harlow leaned his chin on his fist. "That might be best."

*

"Couldn't have picked the easy way," Kira muttered to herself as she leaned against the wall and stared at the infinite stairs ahead. "No, you had to do things the hard way—as usual."

She'd thought this was the last landing. Not so much.

"When will you learn?"

She peered down the steps she'd traversed over the last several hours. Another person's spirit might have broken at the latest false summit.

"Not me, though. No, I'm too stubborn for that," Kira griped, setting one foot on the next step.

The Tuann and their stupid games. She was tired. Her body hurt. The headache she'd had since shortly after stepping through the gates increased with every step.

She yearned for Graydon's presence. Pushing him off a cliff would have gone a long way to improving her mood right about now.

She blamed him for this. If not for his maneuvering, she'd be sleeping in her bunk on a ship somewhere. Not testing her limits on a climb that felt like it would never end.

The bag she carried pulled at her arm. She paused, switching it her other shoulder before resuming her trek. One stair by laborious stair.

Kira glared at the bag in question, cursing the urge that had caused her to take it from Raider. She still wasn't fully recovered from her last fight, and carrying something that seemed to get heavier and heavier as time went past was severely taxing her resources.

She would have gladly left him to it if she hadn't been afraid the Tuann would search the bag when Raider reached the top.

"How are there so many damn stairs?" she grumbled.

There hadn't looked to be this many from the bottom. Nowhere close to this many.

It was like the air itself resisted, dragging on the bag and her body. A weight clasped her tight, pressing harder with every step forward until it felt like she was moving against a constant current that only grew in strength the farther up she went.

The other initiates had long since abandoned the vertical paths they'd started with, each making their way to the stairs. More than a handful had already quit, forcing Roake's oshota to recover them and escort them to safety via a dunking in the ocean below.

Kira's progress slowed as a thought occurred to her. It was possible this was not what it appeared. The Tuann had already proven they were masters of technology far beyond what humans could even grasp. To a level that shared a close resemblance to magic.

Perhaps this staircase that marched up a never-ending cliff didn't really exist. It could be an illusion meant to test her fortitude and willpower.

Kira made a face. Of course. That made sense. If she was training a group of warriors, she'd likely do something similar. Hell, she had done something similar to anyone looking to join the Curs.

You couldn't be part of an elite force unless you were the master of your own self. A person who could rise above their physical limits when the time came.

This was a gut check. Pure and simple. A way of seeing who would allow something as measly as a staircase to get in the way of their goal.

It made perfect sense.

The pain from the headache surged until it felt like a vise had ahold of her head. She made a small sound of pain as she staggered into the side of the cliff. She used the stone as a crutch. Mustn't sit down.

The marshal's warning had been clear. Sit down, and you're out. Set anything down and lose it.

She'd come too far to do either now. It might be a silly test, but she hated failing.

Call it stubbornness. Call it pride. She had no intention of losing here. Not to stairs. Not to her own body.

The pain increased.

"Son of a banter bot. I really should have made different life choices," Kira said through gritted teeth, her vision nearly gone.

Below, a bright mind snapped into shape. Rushing, rushing. Closer and closer.

A large form speared up from the deeps. Water sprayed off it, drenching Kira, so close she felt she could reach out and touch the serpentine body.

Blue scales shimmered in the light as it continued a path toward the sky. Its powerful body coiled as it reached the apex of its jump, already shifting to plunge into the ocean's depths.

Kira caught sight of horns curling from its head, its crest of feathers sleek and smooth to make the *lu-ong* as aerodynamic as possible. Long whiskers streamed from its snout, catching the wind.

Something akin to fear and awe trembled through Kira. She now saw how Graydon could call the last *lu-ong* she'd encountered a baby. This one was mammoth when compared to the one she'd met. Many, many times the size of Earth's whales.

Emotion threatened to overwhelm Kira. The wonder of the sight made her breath catch.

It plunged into the sea, its long, serpentine body following, only for its head to rise out of the water again in preparation for another jump. With its body stretched behind it, the *lu-ong's* length reminded Kira of a half-submerged mountain range, shifting and disappearing.

Its spirit brushed hers. Massive like the void of space—and just as wondrous.

Only when the *lu-ong* had moved into the distance and was a small dot against the horizon, did Kira start forward again. Her headache had faded while watching the *lu-ong*, but even without it, every step dragged on her.

It was a short time later when she stepped up one last time and nearly stumbled. She paused, startled to find flat ground. Kira lifted her head, weariness dragging at her.

No further steps waited for her. She'd reached the top.

She stilled as she took in the city before her. Its size and breadth dwarfed the Citadel of Light, even from this distance.

Five large fortresses rimmed the city, walkways extending from their walls like spokes on a wheel to a palace in the center. Each one as different from the last as night and day. Crests flew above them announcing the different Houses.

The city outside the fortresses' walls was made up of smaller, no less awe-inspiring buildings that filled the spaces between as it spilled toward the ocean below.

"I've seen a lot of places. Admittedly most of them were destroyed by the time I reached them, but this is definitely one for the history books," Raider said from a spot where he sat, leaning against his duffel. Sweat dotted his skin, making Kira glad she hadn't been the only one to find the test difficult.

"It's like a dream," Blue whispered.

Kira shook her head as feelings welled up, almost too big to contain.

We're home, something inside her seemed to say. She shook her head again, refusing its lure. No, she wasn't.

Her home was a ship currently docked at O'Riley Station. It was small and cramped, but it was hers.

"I'm sure we'll find a dirty underbelly if we look close enough," Raider said. "Places that seem too good to be true always have them."

Blue scowled. "Don't ruin it. Can't you see we're having a moment."

In this, Kira agreed with Raider. As beautiful as the city was, there was no doubt in her mind shadows existed within. It was best to remember that. Any instant connection she might have felt was an illusion, and she had no intention of letting it twist her goals.

The stairs had led them to a spot well outside the city limits. They stood on a ridge overlooking the vista below. The closest fortress wasn't far, standing stalwart and tall on the edge of the cliff on which it impossibly perched, its exterior walls creating a smooth drop to the ocean below. It was difficult to see the exact spot where the cliff and fortress met, so seamless was the integration between the two.

Kira's gaze was drawn inexorably to it. The stone that made up its structure seemed to absorb the light. Tall spires stabbed the sky's underbelly at its center, the strong walls of its defenses seemingly impenetrable.

In almost all ways, it was the Citadel's opposite. Imposing. Austere. This place seemed to care nothing of beauty, devoted only to one purpose—protecting those who resided within.

Kira turned her attention from the fortress, gazing at those around her.

It seemed only a handful of the initiates had made it to the top. Of those were the two boys Kira had seen at the bottom, a handful she didn't recognize and Joule.

"She was last," the friendly-looking boy observed to his peers.

The arrogant boy didn't bother to keep his voice down. "What do you expect from someone who keeps company with humans."

Kira grinned as Blue and Raider fell silent. She tilted her head, not able to keep herself from chuckling. Aw, they wanted to play mind games. How cute. And utterly pointless.

"This is familiar," Blue muttered.

Raider agreed, rising from his reclining position. "I'm too old to be playing an underdog."

When he finally straightened to his full height, it was like a mask had slammed down. His expression was cold and unforgiving. Cocky, one might say. A silent fuck you to all the naysayers.

"But you're so good at it," Kira couldn't help but tease.

"Shut it, granny. You're too old for this too," Raider snapped. Under his breath, he muttered, "And you suck at being the underdog. If you pick a fight because you're bored, I'm not going to have your back."

Kira smirked. "I thought I was the commanding officer of this little shit show. You'd leave me hanging? What happened to loyalty?"

Raider's expression soured as Kira's smile widened. He hadn't thought through his little power play earlier. It was now backfiring on him. He really should have known better. Kira had never been the type to let others take advantage. That hadn't changed much in the intervening years.

"Anyone think that climb was a little harder than it should have been?" Blue asked.

Joule joined them. "Roake is known for its illusions. The test was meant to strain our willpower while exhausting our bodies. The stairs were made of reiki stone, the properties of which drain our *ki* and sap our strength."

Raider's forehead furrowed as he thought. Admittedly, it looked painful. Raider was more suited to action than thinking. "What if you don't have *ki*?"

"Everyone has *ki*—even humans such as yourself," the arrogant boy from below approached, his expression cold and reserved. "It exists in all things. Humans haven't sufficiently evolved to perceive or manipulate it."

"Good to know," Raider said, eyeing the newcomer with interest. "Who are you?"

The boy—for that's how Kira thought of him, despite evidence he wasn't much younger than her—ignored the human, focusing on Joule. "Affinity?"

Joule jumped, scrambling to attention. Kira watched with interest. There was nothing obvious to point to the boy's greater status beyond the fact he carried himself with poise and an icy reserve. Still, Joule treated him with respect, as if the boy had the right to the information he'd demanded.

"Shield, Earth class," Joule said.

A muscle in the boy's jaw ticked. "Support."

Joule's expression wavered the faintest bit before he caught himself, his back straightening as if a greater height would protect himself from the dismissal implicit in the other Tuann's words.

Kira didn't quite understand what about Joule's response relegated him to a lower tier in the Tuann's eyes, but she did know the arrogant boy's words were shortsighted. They told her all she needed to know about his experience. He lacked a fundamental understanding of tactics or strategy.

Support might be less sexy or prestigious than infantry or other combat roles, yet it was no less important. An army didn't move without those in the support roles this boy had so casually dismissed. A soldier couldn't fire a weapon without bullets or fight on an empty stomach.

Her hoverboard would never have made it through a battle without the mechanics and engineers who performed regular maintenance on it.

Support got few accolades, yet a military force wouldn't make it far without them. Every role was vital. Dismiss it at your peril.

The boy faced Kira, a demand already in the arch of his eyebrow. She arched hers right back, her lips twitching as she waited, interested to see what his next move would be.

"We talked about this," Raider said in a sing-song voice. "No picking fights."

Kira ignored him. She didn't consider ignoring nonverbal demands picking a fight. That was just good sense.

The boy's face tightened. "Affinities."

Her amusement deepened at the demand disguised as a question. "And who is asking such a rude question upon first acquaintance."

There was a long pause as the boy tried to stare her down, his will trying to overpower hers. She cocked her head. This boy had nothing on Baran or Graydon. Resisting him was child's play.

The pressure he was trying to bring to bear on her relented, the faintest sheen on his skin exposing the effort the attempt had cost him.

His words seemed forced from him. "Devon of House Danai."

Her gaze dropped to Joule. "Another House?"

He nodded. "One of the five major Houses."

"How do you not know this?" the boy asked.

Joule straightened his shoulders. "Kira is the lost child of Roake and Luatha. She didn't grow up in a House."

The boy's eyes snapped to Kira, interest and something harder in his expression. Before he had been mildly combative, now an arctic front could roll off him, and Kira wouldn't have been surprised.

She couldn't quite name what she saw in him, but she suspected it was a close companion of envy. Or maybe suspicion. Sometimes it was hard to say.

This close, it was easier to see the details of his features. Surprisingly, they were familiar—especially the color of his eyes, a green the color of the land after a soft rainfall.

They tugged at a memory of another boy with the exact same eyes, a boy who had become her partner in all things and whose current absence was a thorn in her side.

Kira ignored the spark of familiarity, dismissing it as improbable, if not impossible. She was imagining links where they didn't exist.

The smile she aimed at Devon was bright and cheery. "As for your question, I have no idea. When Luatha tested my affinities, they found the test inconclusive."

Joule looked on the brink of speaking before he shut his mouth again, his face disgruntled.

It seemed he had learned something from her after all. Secrets were best held close to the vest until you needed them. The upper echelons of Roake's leadership no doubt already knew she had a primus form, but she saw no reason for those before her to know too. They'd either react with fawning admiration or deep suspicion. Neither of which appealed to her and would make blending more difficult.

Commotion interrupted before he could respond. Silas stepped from a small group of Tuann clad in synth armor, raising his hands, warmth radiating from his expression. He looked like a mild-mannered professor, an appearance at odds with the fierce warrior Kira had seen in action.

Those behind him had the look of battle-hardened warriors with the exception of one. The man stood out, and not simply because of his height and beauty. Like the rest, he held himself with a warrior's poise, aware of his surroundings.

However, his armor differed from theirs, vaguely reminding Kira of one of the warrior wizards in the fantasy games Blue used to force her to play.

A deep sapphire cloak trimmed in silver fur was clasped around his neck. Beneath, he wore a robe, close-fitting on top, the sleeves cut so the fabric revealed the midnight blue of his armor. A wide belt wound around his waist, a long piece of cloth dropping from the front, edged in a silver pattern.

He should have looked ridiculous. Yet somehow, he managed to project serenity and a sense of purpose.

His eyes met Kira's, a pleasant curiosity in them before he tipped his head at Silas, silently signaling she needed to pay attention.

Silas spoke, drawing Kira's attention away from the strange man. "I congratulate those of you who've passed the Trek of the Weary. I know it wasn't an easy task, and many failed along the way. To those of you who remain, I once again welcome you. I would like to say your path to the *adva ka* will only get easier from here. Unfortunately, I would be lying."

There were small sounds of amusement.

"All of you have passed the first hurdle. From here, you can expect many more as we assess your readiness to enter the Trial of the Broken. You've come to us for a chance at apprenticeship and to hone your skills as warriors. I want to thank you for your willingness to entrust your future to this House. Know we will push you as you've never been pushed before, but that the rewards are worth it. This is an honored rite of passage only a few ever complete."

Silas stepped to the side and gestured to two of the Tuann near him. "I'd like to introduce you to those who will be shepherding you through this phase of your training. You're to refer to them as *seon'yer,* though you're not technically anyone's apprentice yet."

The woman regarded them steadily. Her eyebrow quirked as if she found the sight of them too amusing for words. She wore little in the way of clothes. On her upper body, she wore only a breastplate that left her lean stomach exposed. The gauzy skirt around her legs was held up by slim chains, slits on either leg to mid-thigh to allow ease of movement. A handful of clunky bracelets clung to either wrist, and her feet were bare.

"Maida," Finn said softly, appearing next to Kira like a phantom.

She restrained her jump, now used to how quietly the oshota could move when they wanted to.

"She's deadly when she wants to be."

Maida flicked a half-undone braid that had slipped over her shoulder behind her as she regarded the students with a sultry gaze only marred by the disdain in her expression.

"Not sure I'd want to fight in that," Blue said. "Looks uncomfortable—and unsafe."

Blue had a point. The woman's outfit was stylistic, beautiful in its own way, but it wasn't ideal for combat.

"Synth armor would only slow her down and prove unnecessary. Her affinity allows her to change the composition of her skin, making it as strong and hard to cut as synth armor," Finn informed them. "She's not quite right in the head, but no one can argue with her abilities."

There were whispers as the second man stepped up, his expression cool and assessing.

"Wren," Devon breathed beside them. The Tuann's hero worship was unmistakable. "I thought he didn't take apprentices until they were fifty years past their *adva ka*."

"He's willing to make an exception if he finds an initiate worth his effort." Finn's face was neutral as he relayed that information. It was impossible to make any inferences from his tone.

That didn't stop Kira from trying. Whatever Wren's purpose here, it had better not have anything to do with her.

Silas wrapped up the introductions. "Over the next few weeks, we will be assessing your skills and abilities to decide which of you are ready for the *uhva na*. We will use these assessments to pair you with the best mentor. Good luck."

Excited chatter broke out among the initiates.

Devon's gaze was determined as it swung toward Kira. "Your ancestry means nothing here. Don't get in my way. I plan to beat the Face's record for passing the *adva ka*. I will eliminate any obstacle in my way."

Kira blinked at him. He was one to talk. Practically the first words out of his mouth had been his House affiliation.

That was the definition of using your connections to impress others. She didn't bother pointing that out, though. She doubted he'd appreciate or even acknowledge his hypocrisy

Besides, she had no intention of getting in his way.

"Good luck?" Her tone made it sound more like a question than anything.

His gaze narrowed before he spun on his heel and stalked off, following Maida and the others she'd gathered.

"Friendly guy," Kira muttered. If that was the sort of behavior she had to look forward to over however long it took her to heal, it was going to be a long few weeks.

"People will judge you based on your background. It's unavoidable," Finn informed her.

"Tell me something I don't know," Kira said, pushing the craziness of her shoulder-length hair, twisted and tangled from the ocean breeze, away from her face.

That seemed to be the story of her life. Why should the Tuann be any different?

Before Finn could answer, Silas and the strange man who looked vaguely like a genius wizard approached.

"Kira, this is Loudon. He is the *ki's* herald and an adviser to the Overlord. He's volunteered to show you around the Fortress of the Vigilant in my place. I'm afraid I have business to attend to." Apology colored Silas's words.

Loudon smiled at her, the skin at the corner of his eyes crinkling. "It'd be my pleasure."

"Thank you," she said as Loudon started toward the fortress of black stone that seemed to eat the light.

Raider and Blue shouldered their bags, catching up easily.

"Of course, your ancestral home would be the one that looks like it's straight out of a gothic, sci-fi, holovid," Raider muttered as they started along the cliffside path. "I don't know why I ever thought it would be different."

Neither did Kira, to be honest.

SIX

LOUDON'S PACE WAS sedate as he led them toward the hulking fortress in the distance, his hands clasped behind him like he was out for a Sunday stroll. Finn was several feet behind them, his gaze moving constantly as he assessed the area for threats.

"So," Raider started, breaking the silence that had descended. "Herald? Is that kind of like a priest?"

There was no hiding Raider's skepticism. Kira closed her eyes and shook her head. She'd forgotten how much he hated anything dealing with religion.

Most religions had survived humanity's spread through the stars. The distance between planets only serving to make it easier to practice an individual's faith.

In a few cases, particularly for those religions that had felt persecuted, they'd pooled their money to colonize their own planet, allowing only their beliefs to flourish on its surface.

Raider had grown up on one such planet. They'd been hardcore fundamentalists, his family the worst of the bunch. They believed you could only reach God if you were pure. Their faith came in the form of a stick and a rod, and they held no reservations about using them, especially on children.

Because of the planet's remoteness and his home's isolation—even from other fundamentalists—they'd gotten away with behavior that might have been considered criminal if it had happened anywhere else.

In the early days of space flight, Earth had come up with a codex of laws, one of which was that you couldn't interfere in another planet's recognized religion, no matter how abhorrent the spiritual practices were.

Then the war came—and not even his people's tightly held faith had saved them. Raider took advantage and used the opportunity for a new beginning.

He didn't often speak of his childhood, but from what little Kira had gathered, it had been harsh.

Loudon's expression was thoughtful as he considered Raider's question. "You could loosely interpret it that way."

Raider's lip curled slightly, but he held his opinions inside.

Nonetheless, Kira was careful to keep an eye on him. While she might have understood Raider's deep-seated suspicion of all things religious, she also knew he tended to sabotage himself.

The last thing he or Blue needed was to alienate their hosts. They had no idea how deeply ingrained religion was to the Tuann's daily life. On some planets, bad mouthing the faith could get you executed. On others, they'd take it in stride. Kira didn't know which category Ta Sa'Riel fell under.

Loudon glanced at the three of them. "It would be more accurate to say I am a guide for the Tuann's sense of identity."

Blue's face scrunched up as her attention focused on him. "What do you mean?"

Kira found herself interested as well.

Loudon's head tilted. "We don't believe in gods in the same way humans do."

Something in Raider relaxed. He listened rather than assumed.

"*Ki* is the building block that connects everything in the universe," Loudon said. "I interpret the *ki's* will. Provide counsel when needed and act as the keeper of our history."

Kira didn't get it, but she didn't need to. There was a serenity in Loudon as he spoke. It was enough to know he believed wholeheartedly. It wasn't her place to question or poke holes.

By then they'd reached the foot of the fortress, a tall curtain wall surrounding its exterior.

"Woah," Blue said softly, echoing Kira's sentiments as her head tilted so she could take in the imposing structure.

The perimeter wall stood impossibly tall; the towers of the fortress barely visible over its top. The surface was flat and seamless, with no evidence pointing to stones being stacked one on top of each other to create its structure. Unrelenting black stretched unbroken in either direction.

The only evidence of imperfection was regularly spaced, shadowy holes that Kira couldn't figure out.

"Where's the door?" Raider asked, breaking into her observations.

Loudon stepped forward and raised a palm. He touched his hand to the wall and spoke a word. An invisible force thrummed, stroking Kira's senses. A door appeared, revealing a courtyard on the other side.

Loudon stepped to the side, clasping his hands behind his back. "No matter how heavily guarded, a door will always be a point of weakness. We've found eliminating them to be the most expedient solution."

A squeak of glee escaped Blue as she moved toward the wall, her hand uplifted, and her expression blazing with fervid curiosity.

"Touching is not advised," Loudon informed her.

Blue drew back, just shy of touching, regarding Loudon with an interested frown.

He nodded at the wall. "This is our first line of defense. By successfully completing the Trek of the Weary, you're given admittance and are allowed to pass within. However, you will need someone from Roake to allow you to come and go. I wouldn't suggest attempting to climb the wall. There are defenses within to prevent anyone but one of us from gaining entrance."

Kira gazed at those holes with a newfound respect. They were a weapon of some kind. She was sure of it.

Knowing the Tuann, it would be deceptively powerful.

"While simply touching the wall once isn't likely to kill you, I am told the experience is unpleasant," Loudon continued.

Raider shifted his duffel bag on his shoulder. "I'm beginning to see the resemblance between you and these people. You both are paranoid and obsessed with security."

Blue nodded enthusiastically.

Kira didn't bother arguing, though she could make a case for Roake taking her paranoia to the next level. She couldn't help her admiration as she took in the perimeter wall. If a few human cities had defenses like these during the war, her job might not have been so damn difficult, and there might not have been so many casualties.

She took in the top of the wall. Then again, maybe not. The Tsavitee would likely have flown right over it.

"What happens if someone attacks from the sky?" Blue asked.

Loudon's lips curled, the devious smile making her question whether Tuann heralds were really that peaceful.

"They may try." He gestured to the door. "Welcome to the Fortress of the Vigilant."

"Yup, definitely seeing a family resemblance," Raider muttered as he moved past Kira. "They're as welcoming as you."

Blue quickly followed, leaving Kira, Finn, and Loudon bringing up the rear.

Kira paused as she got her first close view of the fortress. It was every bit as intimidating as her glimpse from a distance had suggested.

The fortress was massive. Its own city, much as the Citadel had been. What she'd thought was one structure turned out to be many. Wide at the bottom, countless smaller towers and buildings branched off the main one as it reached high into the sky.

Standing next to it, Kira felt small and young. The fortress seemed ancient and new all at the same time, countless ages steeped into its bones.

The door disappeared behind her as Finn stepped through. His expression was closed and set, his face a hard mask no hint of emotion could penetrate. He was even more reserved than typical as he took in Roake's home.

"This way," Loudon instructed.

Raider and Blue started after him as Kira stared up. They'd told her before that her father's family was an old one. She believed it now. Their ancestral lines, and by extension hers, were an ancient one. The proof was in this fortress, which would have taken countless generations to build.

"This is your home?" Kira asked as Finn paused by her side.

"It is."

There was a world of emotion in those two words. Loss and pain. Relief to have returned. Reluctance. All tangled together.

"Are you pleased to be back?" She couldn't help but prod.

Finn hesitated. "That's a difficult question."

Kira imagined so. If she'd grown up here as she was supposed to, would she have been willing to leave for any reason?

Knowing Finn wouldn't welcome an old wound being visited here and now, Kira started after the others, not wanting to get left behind. This place promised to be every bit as much a maze as the Citadel.

To her surprise, her first impression of the fortress's design turned out to be wrong. While it didn't have the artistic flourishes of the Citadel, there was still beauty here. Little touches here and there that managed to make it seem effortlessly timeless.

They were interwoven seamlessly with the defenses. Kira spotted eight cannons in the time it took them to step inside, and she had no doubt there were countless other weapons hidden in the event an enemy targeted the visible ones.

After showing them where they'd take their meals, Loudon took them on a quick tour, pointing out where they should report in the morning for training, and the parts of the fortress they were welcome to explore.

Kira couldn't help but be impressed with the structure's interior. It reminded her of an ancient castle, the architecture serviceable rather than ornate. The dramatic arched hallways and large rooms managed to save it from plainness as the group wound through the lower levels. The fortress's staircases became less wide and majestic the further they descended, until they ended up in an unassuming hallway lined with plain doors.

"These will be your quarters for the time being," Loudon told Blue and Raider. "Normally, guests are housed on one of the upper levels, but since you've expressed a desire to undertake Roake's training, the Overlord thought these would be more suitable."

As he spoke, Blue and Raider opened the doors indicated, entering sparse rooms; their only furniture a bed, desk and wardrobe for clothes. The space was narrow and tight, without a window to let in the light.

Raider looked around and shrugged. "These are more than enough. They're bigger than most of the berths I've called home."

Blue nodded. "I doubt we'll be spending much time in them anyway."

Loudon sketched a partial bow. "I'll leave you to get settled then. Every room in this corridor is equipped with chimes to tell you when training events start. Tomorrow, assemble in the Warrior's Hall at 0900 human standard time. You'll learn more then."

Raider and Blue nodded their assent as Loudon walked toward Kira, indicating she should follow. She easily fell into step with him, Finn shadowing.

"I apologize for the accommodations," Loudon said. "This is not how a daughter of the House is usually greeted."

Kira lifted a shoulder, dismissing the sentiment. "As Raider said, the rooms are plenty big enough."

Her room on the *Wanderer* was about the same size. She wasn't here to be pampered. She was here to heal herself and maybe learn a little about controlling her *ki* if she was lucky.

"Still, it can't be the homecoming you were expecting," Loudon said, his gaze sympathetic. "Your uncle is a hard man to understand, but he usually has a reason for doing things the way he does."

Kira had no doubt, but whatever his game, she had no intention of playing it. Her mission was simple. Heal. Pass the *adva ka* and achieve some measure of control before going her merry way.

Simple—even if the execution was not. Whatever politics or maneuvering her uncle or anyone else had in mind, she wanted no part in them.

Kira didn't bother explaining any of that to Loudon. It was clear he was her uncle's man. Even if he seemed sincere, he wasn't an ally nor a friend.

She made a noncommittal noise she hoped he would take as understanding.

"This is you," Loudon said, stopping beside a door several down from Raider's and Blue's.

Kira opened it, unsurprised to find a room even smaller and sparser—if that was possible—than her former soldiers in arms. Like theirs, there was little furniture. A bed made up with the sort of military corners and crisp lines a few of her past NCOs would have been overjoyed to see.

The bed and wardrobe looked worn out and well used, chips and dings obvious even from here. A hole had been punched into one wall. Kira raised an eyebrow, impressed. It would have taken a lot of strength to crumple the stone like that.

There were no rugs or decorations of any kind. Nothing to soften the austere interior. That suited Kira well enough. She hadn't grown up with such things, and even now, they were few and far between.

After Loudon's hint, she read her uncle's message loud and clear. He didn't care if she was here against her wishes. She'd be treated like everyone else. That was all right. She was used to making her own way.

"Home sweet home," Kira said with a look around.

"I'll leave you to get comfortable," Loudon said with a partial bow.

She murmured a quick goodbye as Finn lingered at the threshold, the faintest edge of uneasiness in his posture.

Kira said over her shoulder. "I don't think this room is big enough for you to watch me sleep as you did on Ta Da'an."

That had Finn straightening. "My duty is to protect you."

Kira gestured at the small space. "Not a lot of ways to attack me in here. You can guard me from outside."

His jaw ticked, his teeth clenching as he considered his argument, but quickly discarded it. Kira's words had been the truth. There was no other egress or ingress than the door in which he still stood. The quarters were comfortable for one, but two would be tight.

"Don't you trust Roake? They're your people," Kira challenged.

"Dangers can come from within and without." Finn's words were stilted.

True enough.

Kira crossed to the door, a distance of only two steps, as she grabbed the door handle. "I'll take my chances."

She shut it in his face before he could argue further.

Kira grinned and patted the door. "That was way more satisfying than it should have been."

She faced the room. "Now, then, let's take care of that other matter, shall we?"

She lifted the bag and threw it toward the bed, not bothering to be gentle.

It lay there as she folded her arms across her chest and frowned. "Are you really going to make me do this?"

There was no answer—not that she'd really expected one. She shrugged. "You never were good at making things easy on me."

That was fine. It was more fun this way.

A knock came before she could deal with the problem on the bed.

"Come in," she called.

Somehow, she wasn't surprised when the door opened to reveal Raider, Finn standing over his shoulder, scowling.

Raider sauntered in like he owned the place. His hair was damp, evidence of a shower, and he'd taken the time to change.

"Where did you get a shower?" Kira asked.

She hadn't seen any door leading to a bathroom in the brief glimpse she'd gotten of his room.

He indicated a plain part of the wall, before touching a small indentation. The stone façade disappeared as a doorway took its place.

"Huh, guess they really don't like doors in this place," Kira said.

It made her wonder if there were other hidden doorways around.

"Blue's the one who found it and then showed me," he said.

Somehow that didn't surprise Kira. Of all the Curs, Blue adapted the quickest, and her always restless mind had no trouble ferreting out secrets.

"It's good you're here. Maybe you can help me with something."

Raider raised an eyebrow. "Oh?"

She jerked her chin at the bed. Understanding settled on his face.

"When did you find out?" he asked.

She lifted a shoulder. "Does it matter?"

"I suppose not."

She let him see her irritation, not that it bothered him if his amusement was anything to judge by.

"Don't blame me. This wasn't my idea," he told her.

"You helped. This is your problem too." She pointed to the bag.

His gaze was unrepentant as Kira scowled.

Her shoulders relaxed as she nodded at the thin rod at his hip. She made a "give me motion" with her hands. With a sigh, he unclipped the rod and flicked his wrist, the asp baton unfolding to the length of Kira's forearm.

There was the slightest movement from the bag as he handed the asp over to Kira. Her grin was slightly maniacal as she faced the bag, lifting the asp before bringing it down with all her strength.

The asp whistled through the air as the door behind them opened. The bag jerked right, seconds before the asp connected. It rose, floating in midair as a strangled sound of disbelief came from the doorway.

Kira looked over her shoulder to find Finn's wide, disbelieving eyes on the tableau.

His hand dropped to the en-blade at his waist. "What is that?"

He didn't wait for her to answer, the en-blade clearing its scabbard in the next second.

"Would you believe it's a poltergeist?" Kira inquired politely as Finn stepped fully into the room, kicking the door shut behind him.

His presence was less than ideal.

Ah, well, beggars couldn't be choosers, and plans rarely survived first contact.

Finn's glare burned; his tone flat. "No."

That was really too bad. Things would likely have been so much easier if he had.

In the resulting silence, Kira's gaze fell to his en-blade. "Oh look, you've already primed a second weapon for me. How kind."

She grabbed the weapon from him, slightly surprised when he let her.

She didn't waste time, her foot already sliding back as she swung. The blade hummed in her hand, energy running along its length and assuring her it could cut anything she wished.

The blade met the bag, slicing cleanly through it as the acrid scent of burning fabric filled the room. The bottom half of the bag dropped to the ground as the rest darkened, catching fire and whisking away.

Jin rose from the ashes, his sphere glowing white-hot from the flames. "Surprise, bitches! Did you miss me? Don't lie. We both know you did."

Finn inhaled harshly, sounding like an angry tea kettle.

Kira's arm was still extended, the blade held as if it were an extension of her body.

Jin tilted, taking in the bag's remnants. "Really, Kira? You had to go there? You don't even believe in ghosts."

Kira allowed her stance to relax as she glared at her friend. "When you see a pest, sometimes you have to cut it down."

Jin sniffed. "How rude."

An angry sound escaped Kira. "Do you even understand what you've done? What are you doing here?"

Finn rumbled threateningly, looking seconds from attacking. Kira shuffled a step away so she could put distance between him and his blade, the only distance she could manage in her small room.

"You didn't think I'd let you do this by yourself? Did you?" Jin lowered onto the bed. "I'm angry at you, but I don't hate you."

"How kind," Kira said through clenched teeth.

"I'm evolved. I know. It's good you recognize that."

A small growl escaped her, and she handed Finn the blade, hilt first. Maybe the oshota should teach her friend a lesson in social etiquette.

"If you were so evolved, you wouldn't have smuggled yourself in a bag." Kira snarled. "You've put all of us in danger."

Jin shot up from the bed, zooming across the room.

"Come on. You're exaggerating." Jin hit the far wall and changed directions.

"Quiet, you. I counted at least eight defensive weapons after their perimeter wall." She chucked a pillow at him when he wouldn't stop circling, a clear sign he knew he was wrong but didn't want to admit it.

"Fifteen, but who's counting?" Jin sniffed.

"These people make me look trusting," she spat. "How do you think they'll feel when they learn I brought a military-grade drone into their home?"

Kira could be overreacting, but she didn't think their response would be nonviolent. She didn't really want a deathmatch right off the bat. She might have preferred to keep herself distant from these people, but they were still hers.

Raider sobered, the extent of the mess they were in registering. "How sure are you that will be their response?"

Kira lifted an eyebrow at Finn.

"Any other would face death. Kira might get a pass, but the humans wouldn't." Finn's expression was serious, his bearing that of one delivering a terminal diagnosis. This situation might as well be.

Kira knew her friend. He wasn't the type to fly under the radar.

"It's likely they would have forbidden him entry even if he'd come through proper channels," Finn continued.

"They did forbid him entry," Raider confirmed.

"Ha, I was right to smuggle myself onto this planet," Jin crowed.

Kira held up a hand. "Not. Another. Word."

"I'm mad at you," Jin protested. "You don't get to be mad at me too."

The three of them ignored him.

"What do we do?" Raider asked. "Come clean?"

Kira was reluctant to take that option. There were too many unknowns. Too many factors to account for. If Roake decided to kill them, Kira didn't like their chances of fighting their way free. Not when they lacked a proper weapon among them—Blue's smuggled device notwithstanding.

This wasn't like going against the Tsavitee or even humans. These people had the same strengths as Kira, only they were much better trained and weren't dying.

Escaping in the middle of the night while the Tuann's guard was down was doable. A straight fight that pitted the three of them against the still unknown numbers of Roake's military force, not so much.

"I need to think," Finn said. He moved to the door before pointing at Jin. "He doesn't leave this room."

"Aye, aye, Captain." Jin bobbed in the air as a salute.

Finn scowled, exiting and slamming the door behind him.

Silence descended.

Kira punched Raider in the arm. He jumped and cradled the injured appendage. "Ow. What was that for?"

"I expect this sort of behavior from him, but not from you. What were you thinking?" Kira hissed, feeling the urge to punch him again. "You don't even like each other."

Raider shrugged. "Not much choice. He would have found his way here one way or another. At least this way was less likely to draw attention."

Kira's shoulders slumped as she acknowledged the truth of that statement. Jin was nearly unstoppable when he got an idea in his head.

Raider patted her shoulder sympathetically as he made his way over to the door. "Let's be honest—he was never going to stay behind, no matter how mad at you he was."

With that, Raider took his leave, leaving Jin and Kira alone in the room.

Kira regarded her friend, an individual that had been in her life since she could remember. As dangerous as his latest antic might be to them, she couldn't bring herself to regret his presence.

The knot in her stomach that had developed when he'd left her to face Roake and Luatha on her own, finally relaxed.

"I'm glad you're here," she confided.

Jin snort was derisive. "Of course, you are. You'd be lost and lonely without me."

Kira shook her head even as she smiled. She should have expected his response. His arrogance was nothing if not consistent.

Jin settled onto her bed. "Man, this place is strange. I thought I was short-circuiting when we first crossed over."

Kira's head tilted, a few things suddenly making sense. "That headache was from you, wasn't it?"

She should have suspected as much. The nature of Jin's making meant they were irreversibly linked. Most of the time, that didn't mean much. He could ride her senses when allowed, experience things the same way she did. Only in moments of extreme adversity did the other's feelings or pain bleed over, as was the case in this situation.

Jin hummed in agreement. "I thought my number was punched. If that's how you felt on Luatha, I feel sorry for you."

Kira glared at her friend, not moving.

Jin spun to face her. "What?"

The question made her snap.

She grabbed him and spiked him onto the bed. "This is why smuggling yourself in a bag was dumb. Don't ever scare me that way again."

Jin sputtered before righting himself, electricity buzzing along his casing so Kira couldn't repeat the throw.

"You're always so violent," he complained.

She bared her teeth. "I'm about to show you violence."

Jin made a tsking sound before spinning in place. "What do you think it means, though?"

Kira calmed, considering his question. "I suspect you were interacting with the Mea'Ave."

"But why here and not on Ta Da'an?"

That was a good question. Kira could only guess.

"Maybe this is where you were born," she mused. It was a wild supposition at most. "Perhaps because I'm descended from both Luatha and Roake, I reacted to both."

It was a thin theory and would require testing. If she planned to stay involved with the Tuann, she would have delved deeper. As it was, she didn't know, and there was no one to ask without revealing Jin's unique situation.

Jin floated toward the ceiling as he made an unimpressed sound, seemingly losing interest in the topic. He was like her. He'd never had questions about their origins, never strove to find the people they came from. Such concerns were for dreamers. They had been too occupied with surviving to entertain such fleeting fantasies.

Kira didn't push. Tomorrow was going to be a long day. Getting cleaned up and then rest were the first orders of business.

*

A knock sounded at the door two hours before the warning chime.

Kira paused where she was doing pushups and sent a significant glare at Jin.

"All right, all right," Jin muttered, heading toward the bed. "I'm going to remember this, you know. It's going to take twice as long to earn my forgiveness."

"I'll keep that in mind."

Kira waited until he was under the bed and out of sight before approaching the door.

She paused to adjust her clothes, a pair of simple pants that were surprisingly easy to move in, and a top that hugged her figure. She'd found the two items and many others in the wardrobe.

She wasn't going to look a gift drawer in the mouth since the clothes she'd collected on Luatha were now gone—likely given to the sea if Makon was to be believed.

Finn waited on the threshold, his gaze darting to take in the room. Approval descended when he caught no sign of Jin. It was wiped away in the next second.

"What are you doing here? I thought I had until 0900 to report for training," Kira asked, puzzled.

His gaze dropped toward hers. "Quillon is expecting us."

He strode down the hall, not waiting for Kira's agreement.

"And good morning to you too," she muttered, feeling resigned.

Doctor's visits—especially those that came so early in the morning—made her cranky.

"Lingering isn't going to make this go any faster," Jin advised from under the bed.

She waved a hand at him and grimaced. She knew that. But it didn't make it any easier swallowing the fact that this course was necessary.

"Don't forget your promise." There was a vulnerability in Jin that silenced any argument she might have made.

"I know. I won't."

"Prove it," he ordered.

She fixed a hard stare on Jin. "Since when do I need to prove things to you?"

He was her oldest friend. They'd never had to be anything but what they were with each other.

"Since I found out you lied about something pretty damn important."

Kira's eyes flicked away. "I never lied."

"Omission is the same thing."

Kira released her breath. He was right, but how he'd gone about obtaining what he wanted was wrong. Something told her he knew it too.

"We're going to have words later about you manipulating me," she informed him.

Kira accepted her health was important to him. She was his link to the world. Without her, he'd very likely be alone.

A lonely Jin was dangerous. He might be slightly ridiculous, but he was brought up the same way she was. He was a killer, like her. For better or worse, his sanity hinged on her existence.

She'd let herself forget that. She wouldn't do that again, but she also couldn't let him overstep. They had boundaries for a reason, and not even he got to circumvent them.

"Good, because I'm still mad at you," he snapped.

Kira's smile was sharp. "Then we're in agreement."

Kira started out the door, Jin following. She paused on the threshold and arched an eyebrow at him. "Where do you think you're going? You heard Finn. You're to stay hidden, that means staying here."

Jin sputtered, looking like he was about to argue.

"I mean it. I see one electrode beyond this threshold, and I'm turning you into scrap metal," she promised.

"You can't leave me behind," he squawked.

Kira's expression was gloating. This predicament held a certain poetic justice. She planned to use it to its maximum potential.

"Maybe next time try using the front door like the rest of us," Kira taunted, stepping outside.

"You can't leave me in here all alone," he wailed as the door began to shut. "You know how I get when I'm bored."

"I have every faith you'll figure this out."

There was a crash, then angry grumbling that gradually faded as he moved further away from the door.

Kira shook her head, unsurprised. That had gone better than she expected.

The hell of it was, she did know how hard this would be for him. No one liked a bored Jin. He was dangerous if he didn't have something to occupy himself, but this time her hands were tied.

He couldn't come with her, and she couldn't stay in her room without arousing suspicion. He'd simply have to endure.

SEVEN

FINN WAS WAITING for her at the end of the hall. A fact which Kira was grateful for since she didn't want to wander around the massive fortress. She'd likely end up searching for hours and still not find her destination.

Seeing her, Finn started up the stairs, again not waiting for her. Someone still wasn't happy about Jin's presence here.

Kira mentally shrugged. There was nothing she could do about the past now.

Their journey was mostly silent, allowing Kira to take in the fortress's interior. There were only so many things you could notice at a time, and yesterday she'd been suffering from sensory overload after completing a grueling physical endurance test.

This morning she caught things she'd missed yesterday—like the stained-glass windows, not all of which looked outside. Some peered into other rooms.

It was beautiful and complicated in a place that seemed to have defined itself by its simplicity.

The contrast was unexpected, and if her companion's silence hadn't boiled with anger, she might have questioned him about it. As it was, she took note of things of interest even as she cataloged their route, storing it in a mental map of the fortress.

Perhaps the beauty of her surroundings was the reason it took her so long to notice the stares they were drawing from the Tuann they passed.

She glanced around, instantly on guard as one such Tuann stopped when she caught sight of Kira, her expression pained as if Kira's presence had ripped wide a wound that had barely sealed.

Another of Roake's people ventured over and hustled the woman away, but not before sending a glance filled with yearning toward Kira.

Kira became conscious of the whispers around them as they continued, the voices not quite hushed enough.

Very quickly, the weight of those inquiring glances, filled with more emotions than her presence warranted, became tiring. It didn't take long before Kira stiffened. Habit had her viewing them as potential hostiles. In her experience, good things never came with drawing attention like this.

Tension threaded through her as her hand itched for a weapon she didn't have. Her muscles coiled in preparation for action.

She stared at those they passed, her expression hard and unrelenting. Not antagonistic but not welcoming either. Several Tuann flinched from her, their gazes dropping as they hurried away.

"You shouldn't challenge them like that," Finn advised, finally speaking.

"Then they shouldn't be staring."

"Can you blame them?" he asked. "You're an impossibility they'd forgotten to hope for. They're bound to be a little curious."

It wasn't lost on Kira that Finn used the phrase "them" when referring to the Roake caught staring. It meant either he no longer identified with his former House or that he harbored enough pain that he was afraid to lump himself in the same boat.

Kira's posture shifted infinitesimally, enough that she no longer felt like she was on high alert for an attack. It had been a while since her instincts had led her to view everything and everyone around her as an enemy.

Kira supposed that as long as their curiosity didn't lead them to do anything stupid, she was content to let them watch from a distance.

Finn stopped in front of a large door. "We're here."

Kira hesitated on the threshold.

Like the rest of the fortress, the room had stone walls and floors, while still managing to seem homey and inviting. There were no windows, which in a way made sense. Everything Roake did showed a mindset focused on survival. Locating your hospital wing behind thick walls in the center of your stronghold made sense. It would allow healers to treat their patients without worrying a missile attack would breach their sanctuary unexpectedly.

Despite its lack of windows, it managed to appear light and airy without seeming artificial.

Kira wouldn't have minded knowing how they did that. The *Wanderer* could have used a little of this lighting. Even with UV lamps, she sometimes found herself missing the sun and natural light.

Far from being empty, the room contained more Tuann then Kira had expected. The healer worked briskly; her movements efficient as she tended to the Tuann sitting in the bed. The man was tall, his shoulders broad, his arms and torso corded with muscle. He had rough looking features and an unrefined air.

Next to him stood a woman clad in training leathers, frowning. Her arms were folded over her chest as she watched the healer clean a cut the length of the Tuann's bicep.

Both seemed younger than Graydon's oshota, but with the Tuann, it was hard to tell. For all she knew, they could be several centuries old.

Kira and Finn's entrance drew the trio's attention. The warriors glanced up, not bothering to hide their interest.

The healer remained focused on the man's wound, a five-inch cut, the edges raw and bloody. The instrument in her hands glowed as she moved it slowly over the wound, the jagged edges sealing themselves shut.

"I'll be with you in a minute," the healer called over her shoulder.

The words were said in Tuann, but even with her less than perfect grasp of the language, Kira understood.

Instead of answering, Kira stuck her hands in her pocket as she drifted around the room, taking careful stock.

It didn't resemble a human med bay, lacking the fancy monitors or equipment she normally associated with them. There was none of the sickly-sweet smell of antiseptic, nor was there a general air of desperation.

Only the healer working on the Tuann's wound and the faint coppery smell of blood suggested this was a working med bay. Well, that and the row of beds, which weren't nearly enough for a fortress of this size.

She studied the room with interest. If Kira had to guess, she'd say there were several tens of thousands of people living behind the fortress's sturdy walls. This small room couldn't possibly be big enough to act as their hospital.

Even judging by Kira's boosted immune system, there would need to be much more than this for a structure of this size.

Kira kept her questions to herself, conscious of the two warriors who were aware of her presence. They weren't being obvious about their attention, but she knew they were as conscious of her as she was of them.

The two traded glances but said nothing.

Kira clasped her hands behind her and settled in to wait, something she had grown used to. In the military, everything was a rush until it wasn't. Sometimes you spent hours waiting for action of any sort.

The *Wanderer* had been different. There, they could move at their own pace. She found she didn't miss the whole hurry up and wait mentality.

The woman sat back, throwing an irritated glance her way. Several lyrical words flowed from her.

Kira stared blankly.

The woman's voice turned sharp and cutting. A small smile crept across Kira's face. That was quite the dressing down. She was sure it would have been epic had Kira understood more than every other word.

The healer scowled, Kira's amusement not sitting well. Her voice rose.

Kira remained silent. How long would it be before the woman realized Kira didn't understand?

The two warriors traded a glance again before the one standing said something quick, her words precise and fluid.

Finn finally moved at Kira's back. His voice was rough as he spoke.

All three stared at Kira.

Quillon walked into the room right then, moving quickly. "Sorry I'm late, Kira. I had to finish briefing some of our people about what happened on Ta Da'an."

Kira inclined her head. "It's fine."

It really wasn't. Not when she would have very much preferred being anywhere else.

Quillon glanced at the other three, quirking an eyebrow as he took them in. He kept to human standard as he asked, "Did you have another accident during training?"

The big man's face was sheepish as he withdrew his arm from the healer's hold, answering in the same language. "Nothing so interesting."

"He was practicing one of those tricks he saw on the human holovids." The woman beside him scowled. "Only they don't work

87

quite so well with our technology. He lost his balance. This is the result."

Quillon made a thoughtful sound.

The woman's gaze darted to Kira's, and she slipped into Tuann, the words a waterfall of sound.

"I imagine he'll tell you what he wants you to know," Quillon said in standard with a hint of reproach. "Until then, return to the training hall."

"Of course, *aza*," the woman inclined her head before tapping her friend on the shoulder and nudging him toward the exit.

He lumbered to his feet. He flicked his wrists out, and his armor began crawling up his skin in panels, shaping around him in an impressive feat of technology.

The two weren't oshota, Kira didn't think. Their armor was different, but it looked no less formidable.

"You ready to finish this?" the man asked the woman in accented standard.

She grinned. "You're the one who bruised his poor little arm."

The man snorted as he padded toward the door, the woman trailing him.

"Do not strain my regen stitches, Blake. Rheya, keep an eye on him and make sure he listens this time." The healer shouted after them before muttering, "Paltry bruise, my ass. Nearly all the tendons were severed. It took me over an hour to get them reattached. They're worse than children."

"All warriors are," Quillon said as the woman put away the small tool that resembled a penlight. "I see Blake hasn't changed. He can still convince you to go against your better judgment." There was a pause. "And my orders."

The woman flushed, her gaze darting to Kira and away. "I'm sorry, *aza*. I thought I could be done before you arrived."

Quillon didn't respond to the apology, instead gesturing at Kira. "If you would have a seat, we will begin."

Kira didn't move for several long seconds, staring at the place where the two had disappeared. "That wasn't synth armor."

Quillon made an impressed sound. "Very good. Not many would have been able to tell the difference."

He pointed at the bed, making it clear he wasn't going to share anymore until she did as requested.

Kira was slow to move, trying not to betray her obvious reluctance as she hopped onto a bed. She was sure he saw through her. Quillon struck her as the quiet one between Silas and him. That didn't mean he wasn't observant.

She suspected he didn't miss much.

"Not a fan of healers?" Finn asked. "I'm surprised. I didn't think you were scared of anything."

"Everyone's scared of something." For Kira, it was less a question about fear than it was about trust. Not every healer had your best interests in mind. Sometimes they saw a puzzle that needed solving. It didn't matter who they had to hurt or what they had to do if it meant cracking the mystery that was her genes.

"Well put," Quillon said with a small smile, his hands pausing as they drifted over her middle.

Quillon took up the thread of what they'd been discussing. "If a House can afford it, they will often gift a set of *ural* armor to an initiate hopeful. It's not as high quality as synth armor, but it's still considered a mark of honor and evidence of a House's faith."

"I'm assuming a set of armor comes in handy for the type of training Roake uses," Kira guessed.

Quillon nodded, the corners of his eyes crinkling.

And if you didn't have one, you were at a tactical disadvantage, Kira concluded. The advantages of wealth and family were apparent even here in this alien society.

Kira's thoughts shifted to Joule. She hadn't seen any evidence of the armor the other two had worn with ease. He'd be one of those starting from behind at the beginning of the race. He'd have to work twice as hard to make up for the lack.

Quillon's forehead wrinkled as his gaze turned distant. He remained like that for several minutes, his frown growing more severe as the seconds ticked by.

His eyes snapped up to meet hers, his gaze piercing.

She waited, knowing what he'd probably found. It wasn't likely to be pretty.

Quillon's expression settled, no hint of his discovery on it as he shot Finn a censorious glance. "Most warriors, in my experience, are pains in the ass. They never think they need the healer until they've gone too far."

There was a small sound of agreement from the woman in the

corner, her eyes twinkling as she slid the oshota a sidelong glance.

Kira looked between the two, noting the synth armor that Quillon still wore and the healer's distinct lack.

Seeing the question on her face, Quillon raised an eyebrow. "Ask what you're thinking."

Kira took her time. "I thought the synth armor denoted your status as oshota."

Quillon's expression remained neutral as Kira looked between the two again.

"But you're a healer, like her," Kira said slowly.

Quillon's expression softened, and he shook his head. "Oshota is a very complicated concept. Primarily, they're warriors, but because of what they experience, it's often useful to have a healer among their number."

Like a medic inserted into an infantry unit. They were trained on the same weapons, to defend and protect like every soldier, but their focus was different. In battle, they'd return fire, but their primary mission was to care for the wounded.

Himoto always said medics were the most popular person in any unit because soldiers knew it paid to have someone who liked you willing to risk their ass to retrieve your bleeding, wounded body if you should fall.

"You're a healer," she said. Not an oshota like she had originally guessed.

"I'm both," he said with a slight glimmer of amusement. "Those called to be oshota are unique. They're not only skilled with every weapon, but they must demonstrate a desire to protect. Our primary function isn't as killers. We're lethal, but only in defense of the person we pledge ourselves to. I was a healer first before being called to become more. I followed my call."

"Does that mean she hasn't taken the *adva ka* either?" Kira asked, trying to understand.

Quillon's expression softened. "I think you misunderstand. One does not become oshota simply from passing the *adva ka*. It takes many years of training. The *adva ka* is the first step, not the final one. A person does not need to be a warrior to pass it; they simply need to conquer themselves."

"Of course, a warrior's skill makes that easier," the healer said dryly.

Quillon inclined his head. "That is not a surprise given how our society is predisposed to violence."

Considering the primus form crouched within Kira, he had a point. That creature was meant for war. Even before she'd used its form the first time, she had been prone to throwing herself into a fight. It was as instinctive as breathing.

"Now, I'd like you to tell me your symptoms," Quillon suggested. "If I'm to help you, there can be no secrets between us."

Kira managed to keep her snort internal. She wished him luck with that. She was made of secrets. They were her bread and butter, succoring her when times were tough.

Her gaze moved to the healer. "Before we go further, she needs to leave."

The woman straightened, protest filling her expression.

Quillon held up a hand, forestalling her words as he regarded Kira thoughtfully. "Elodie is highly skilled. Her input would be valuable."

Be that as it may, Kira needed to trust the people who had extensive knowledge of her weaknesses. The Tsavitee were still out there. She hadn't seen the last of them. Kira had no doubt they were gearing up for an incursion somewhere in settled space.

It was only a matter of time, and as Ta Da'an had already proved, they had their hooks in the Tuann as surely as they did the humans.

Kira wasn't willing to risk news of her health falling into the wrong hands. It might not be much, and might not even make a difference in the end since Lothos had insinuated they thought she couldn't access the burst anymore. Then again, it *might* matter. She'd take any advantage she could get in the fight against them.

She shook her head. "No, she goes, or I'm out."

Elodie straightened, her expression mutinous, insult in the jut of her jaw and clenched fists. Kira was sure the woman's honor had never been called into question. Kira didn't care. You didn't win battles by being nice or polite. You won them by doing what was necessary, despite the personal cost.

She could have let it go, be the nice person who never hurt anyone's feelings. That wasn't her.

Sometimes you had to speak up in your own best interests. No one was going to do it better than she could. If that meant the healer hated her, so be it.

"This is a highly irregular request," Elodie said. "I'm a fifth level healer. We take an oath. I wouldn't violate it."

"Can you tell me honestly that if someone asked you about my diagnosis that it would stay secret?" Kira asked.

Elodie paused, her eyes narrowing slightly. "It would be my duty to inform those in command if there is something concerning about your health, or if I suspect you're acting in such a way that jeopardizes you or others."

"And you?" Kira asked the man in front of her.

The corners of Quillon's eyes tilted up. "Only the Overlord or his marshal can compel me to reveal the results of your exam."

And they likely already knew the worst of it.

Kira shrugged. "Blame the doctors and healers that came before you. They taught me to be careful where I place my trust. There's no way I'm allowing you access to information I didn't even share with my friends."

Elodie made an angry sound, but Kira didn't budge. If she needed to, she'd walk out of here. She didn't want to do that. Dying held no appeal, but she would do this on her terms or not at all.

Quillon read the resolve on her face and nodded. "Very well. If that's what you wish."

Elodie shook her head and pointed at Finn. "I suppose the oshota is leaving too."

Kira's stare was thoughtful as she watched Finn hold up the wall, his expression a sea of calm. "He can stay. He's earned my trust."

The surprise in his eyes was stark. Kira stilled at the sign of naked vulnerability before he bowed his head and murmured several words in his own language.

Elodie's expression softened before she sighed, knowing when she was beat. "Kicked out of my own sick room. I can't believe it."

They were quiet as the healer made her exit.

When it was finally the three of them again, Kira focused on Quillon.

Reluctantly, she admitted, "I feel heavy. Slow. More tired than normal, but that could be a result of taking primus form."

The climb up the cliff hadn't helped.

It was the best description she could think of. For most of her life, she'd tried to ignore the power crouched at her core.

The tangle of thorny vines she normally associated with her *ki* lay quiet and dormant in her middle. For now, there was no pain, but that would change if she accessed her *ki*, the vines becoming razor sharp.

"We call it *ki* poisoning. It's exceedingly rare. I've only seen one other case similar to yours in all my years as a healer," Quillon said.

Not good news considering Kira had a feeling Quillon had been around for more than a minute.

"What causes it?" Kira asked, staying focused.

"It's difficult to say. Many conditions have to be in play for it to happen. I'm sure your isolation from the Mea'Ave played a major role. Couple that with what I suspect was sustained exposure to battle conditions and continued overuse of your *ki*, and you have a confluence of events that have led to *ki* poisoning," Quillon said.

Kira's jaw worked as she digested this information, all of which she'd long suspected—except for the Mea'Ave part. That was new.

"Did the other person who suffered from this survive?" Kira asked.

Quillon and Finn shared a glance, communicating silently.

It was Finn who finally answered. "Yes. Like you, he sustained heavy damage to his *ki* pathways in battle. It took many years, but he was able to recover. Since then, he has become a warrior of high status."

Relief filled Kira. If what he said was true, this didn't have to be a death sentence. Yes, the timing wasn't ideal, but she could work with this. She'd lived with the specter of the end for so long it was strange to have hope again.

"What's the treatment plan?" Kira asked.

Quillon shifted. "It is a two-step process. You'll need treatment from me every day in the beginning. As time passes, the treatment frequency will drop off, and I'll monitor your progress as you reconnect with your *ki*. I can help heal what you've broken, but making sure this doesn't happen again is another issue. That will be up to you to address."

"That's what I'm here for, isn't it? To learn how." Kira raised her eyebrows. Otherwise, her presence was pointless, and she'd go on her merry way after receiving treatment.

"I don't think it will be as easy as you assume," Quillon suggested gently. "My preference would be to start treatment and wait until your *ki* has stabilized before commencing training."

Seeing her instinctive protest, he raised a hand. "For reasons you have yet to share, you've chosen to press on with your agenda. I will do my best to make sure your body will withstand the demands you're about to place on it." Quillon speared Kira with a look. "But make no mistake, if the treatment fails, or your body continues to deteriorate, I'll recommend you be failed as an initiate."

Kira opened her mouth to protest but closed it when she caught sight of Quillon's resolute expression. He wasn't going to be swayed by any argument. Fair enough. She'd simply have to make sure it didn't become an issue. Easily doable.

Her nod of agreement was grudging.

Quillon's expression thawed, and he gestured for her to lay back. "We can begin now, if you'd like."

Kira complied. "Might as well. It's the entire reason I'm here."

Quillon raised his hands. One he positioned over her heart, the other over her solar plexus. "This might sting."

Sharp needles stabbed into Kira's middle. A pained grunt escaped her as those needles began to dig, scrambling her insides.

That fucking liar. Sting, her ass. This was agony.

The needles heated up until a white-hot burning sensation spread through her middle. It wasn't simply muscle and veins that suffered. The sensation went much deeper than that, to a place she knew existed but had only caught brief glimpses of until now. The place where the broken channels of her power hung. Neglected. Abused. Torn and tattered until they were barely recognizable as channels at all.

The brief glimpse told Kira why Quillon had seemed faintly impressed she had survived so long. The maze of veins sustaining her *ki* were tangled and disjointed. It looked like a pane of glass someone had taken a hammer to. Repeatedly.

Kira fought to hold still, knowing Quillon needed to focus. If this was what it took to be whole, she'd find a way to endure even if it felt like someone had taken a dull spoon and was trying to scoop out her insides.

The pain crescendoed as those needles began weaving, the broken pieces inside starting to move as they slid along each other. Nothing fit as it should, the damage was too extensive, but as Quillon kept working, she saw a pattern emerging from the chaos. It was still a mess, but there was hope where there hadn't been before.

Right when she thought she couldn't take a second more, the needles eased back, cool relief washing in to replace the fire of before.

"I think this is a good place to end today's session." Quillon's voice was shaky, his skin pale, effort and fatigue pulling the corners of his mouth down.

Kira forced herself up to a sitting position, her stomach feeling like she'd gone a few too many rounds with a core workout. Surprisingly, given the depth of pain she'd endured, there weren't many aftereffects.

Quillon crossed to a small table, removing an object and returning to Kira's side. "This is what we call a inhibiter. It'll help you modulate the flow of your *ki* until you learn how to do that yourself. This will keep you from re-damaging what I've started to rebuild."

Quillon held a wide bracelet. It was silvery and plain, looking more like a cuff than anything. He took Kira's hand, wrapping the bracelet around her wrist. The two ends fused together, not even a seam to show where it met.

Kira's ears popped, a metallic taste filling her mouth. The great weight she hadn't even known she was carrying receded. It was similar to pulling an eight-hour day in combat armor and then removing it when done.

She felt light and buoyant even as she still felt the press of *ki*, a hair's breadth outside her perception. She felt like she existed in a glass bubble hundreds of meters below the ocean, separated from its crushing weight by only the slimmest of barriers.

It felt wrong. There was an itch deep inside she would never be able to scratch.

She shook her head, dislodging the thought. Her wrist dropped, and she looked at the bracelet she now wore. Soft blue lines shifted and shimmered along its surface. Runes glowed before fading, leaving inert metal behind.

She felt adrift, cut off from her senses.

Quillon recognized her expression. "What you feel is normal. Many have likened the use of the inhibiter to losing a limb. Eventually, you'll start to feel lethargic and fatigued. I'm told it feels like an extreme case of a hangover for humans. Your body will adjust as you begin to heal."

Kira could already feel the difference. She wasn't sure she liked it. It left her feeling vulnerable and slow. Not exactly something she was accustomed to feeling. She'd better be prepared to learn fast if she didn't want to get used to the feeling.

EIGHT

THE MORNING DETOUR to Quillon's med bay meant Kira missed breakfast. Already behind, reporting to the Warrior's Hall took priority.

Finn managed to unearth a small pastry filled with meat that he called *kueper*, a protein-rich snack meant to tide a warrior over, kind of like a protein bar for humans. Only tastier. The spices burst on Kira's tongue; more vibrant than any quick meal bar she'd ever sampled.

If nothing else, she had to admit the Tuann had amazing food. It would be a shame when she left. Most human food didn't suit her taste buds in the same way.

The *kueper* was a faint memory by the time they reached the hall, a room much more impressive than she had assumed based on the name. Obviously intended for training, it, like the rest of the fortress, managed to seem ancient even while functional.

The ceilings were high, and voices echoed off stone walls.

Finn wasted no time leading her inside, sticking to the edge of the hall as they skirted the softer mats covering the majority of the room. Much like tatami mats of old dojos, the mats were meant to provide a softer surface for those who spent a lot of time falling. Handwoven and made from a fibrous substance, they added to the overall ambiance of the hall.

The familiar scent of sweat mixed with the slightest tang of blood filled the air as Kira moved along the wall, watching Tuann spar. Those initiates who had finished the Trek of the Weary were already present. Some sparred with their peers. Others watched with interest from the sidelines in the same way Kira was.

Blake and Rheya lingered a short distance from the new initiates, their gazes appraising. Interest sparked as they caught sight of Kira. She pretended not to notice as she moved on.

Areas were set up for simulations, their boundaries clearly marked. On one side of the hall, a wall was papered over with square banners. Many were a vivid blue, their lettering a stark white against the backdrop. Others had paled, time leaching the color out of them.

A Tuann warrior bowed his head in front of one, touching his first two fingers to his lips before pressing them against the white lettering.

It was a memorial, Kira realized. The reverence and respect she saw on the warrior's face as he strode away said it could be nothing else.

Kira moved closer, her gaze roving over the banners filled with characters she had no hope of deciphering without Jin's assistance.

She didn't need him to know what these were, however. She'd bet everything she owned these banners represented the names of the fallen.

A finger pointed over her shoulder at a banner, center mass and much larger than those around it. Unlike most, which jockeyed for an unobstructed place on the wall, this one stood alone in a place of clear honor. "That name belongs to your father, the previous Overlord."

Rheya stepped up beside Kira, bowing her head briefly. Her respects paid, her attention shifted to Kira, her gaze assessing.

A few feet away, Blake waited, his boredom evident as he studied the rest of the room. When he caught Kira looking, he dipped his chin in acknowledgment.

"I'm Rheya. That's Blake," Rheya said. "I know we met in the med bay, but you didn't look like you'd appreciate an introduction then."

Kira made an interested sound, only half paying attention. The majority of her focus was on Blue and Raider, where they lingered along the wall. Her former squad mates watched the sparring with deep interest, content to gather information before engaging.

Kira returned her attention to Rheya and waited, figuring the woman would reveal why she'd approached Kira soon enough.

An awkward silence ensued.

Rheya's hands fidgeted with the blade she carried on her waist, the only sign of her discomfort. "We're House Roake too."

Kira had assumed as much considering their presence with the healer.

"You'll have to forgive Kira; she's not big on talking to strangers," Raider said as he approached.

Caution settled on Rheya's face as Raider greeted Kira, the same distrust Kira had seen on other Tuann's faces when confronted with a human evident.

"You're late," he told her.

"Liar," she grunted. "I'm right on time."

He grunted and jerked his thumb at where a group sparred, their blows sending meaty thunks through the room. "I thought we'd seen the end of them."

Kira peered over his shoulder at Isla and Amila as they danced across the floor, their blades keeping a staccato beat as they clashed. The show they put on was impressive, leading more than one initiate to watch out of the corner of their eyes.

Amila swung at Isla's head, the blade whistling past as the smaller woman ducked before stepping toward Amila and striking at her torso. Amila danced back, narrowly avoiding catching the blade across her chest.

She grinned fiercely at her fellow oshota before lunging close, the two exchanging a flurry of blows in a demonstration that was as breathtaking as it was staged.

Solal, Graydon's first, barked instructions from the sidelines.

Kira gritted her teeth. If they were here, that meant Graydon was too.

As if sensing the direction of her thoughts, Graydon appeared at the entrance of the hallway. He paused, scanning those present. When he spotted her, he started toward her, his stride purposeful as those in his path cleared the way.

Kira fought the urge to groan as a high-pitched sound escaped Rheya. She didn't need to look to know there was a mixture of terror and excitement on the other woman's face. Graydon was like a rock star to the Tuann. His presence both intimidating and exhilarating.

The fact he'd fixated on Kira was as incomprehensible as it was troublesome.

"Don't you ever work?" she asked when he stopped, forestalling whatever remark he'd been about to make.

Rheya made a strangled sound as Blake dropped his pretense of boredom and watched Kira with reluctant respect.

Kira ignored them, interested in Graydon's response. As the Emperor's Face, he had a duty to his people. He didn't have time to waste lingering around like a lovesick fool. If he was here, it meant he had a reason. Kira found herself curious as to what it was and if it held the potential to impact her.

While his agenda might be his priority, Kira didn't fool herself. Graydon was a master manipulator, capable of achieving multiple objectives at a time.

"Outside interests have dictated my continued presence here," Graydon informed her.

Kira arched an eyebrow. "Oh, goody."

Graydon's smirk widened into a full-fledged grin, the expression that of a happy dragon toying with his prey.

Others in the room started to take notice until the focus rested on the two of them.

In the corner, Isla and Amila finished their sparring. Isla sent a respectful nod to Graydon and Kira while Amila covered her mouth to hide her smile.

So glad somebody found this situation amusing. Kira did not.

Rheya sketched a deep bow, Blake following suit. After a long moment, Graydon pulled his gaze from Kira, his expression softening as he acknowledged the other two.

"Rheya, Blake, I hear from the Overlord your training is progressing nicely," Graydon said.

Pleasure crossed their faces.

"I was about to ask Lady Kira if she would like a bout," Rheya offered.

Kira blinked.

"How unexpected," Jin crooned. "I wonder why she wants to fight you."

Kira held in her flinch at Jin's voice over her comms. Irritation flicked through her at being unable to respond without looking like a crazy person.

If Graydon hadn't been standing right there, she might have been tempted to do that. Unfortunately, Graydon had experience with the two of them. He'd see right through any subterfuge, making Jin's attempt at staying hidden pointless.

Seeing Kira's hesitation, Rheya explained, "The bouts are a good way to showcase your skills. Although the prospective mentors seem absent, they're likely observing." She pointed toward two spots on the longest wall, both appearing as stone. "There's a balcony the Overlord and the higher-ranking members of the House can use to observe training."

Jin made an admiring sound. "Now isn't that interesting? Another hidden doorway. I'm beginning to sense a theme."

Kira was too, and it wasn't one she liked.

Jin's voice was thoughtful as he mused, "It does present an interesting conundrum. How long do you think they've been watching you without your knowledge?" He paused. "Do you think some of these hidden doors are in our room?"

Kira didn't know, but Jin had better find out if he knew what was good for him.

"I wonder if I could steal that technology. It'd come in handy on the *Wanderer*."

He'd better not even think about it.

Kira considered Rheya's offer, trying to see the motive behind it. Rheya wasn't her friend. She had no vested interest in seeing Kira succeed, and if she was anything like other Tuann Kira had already met, she'd likely assume Kira's combat skills were low.

Graydon's expression was inscrutable. "I'm sure Commander Wren's presence is exciting for you. It's almost unheard of for him to agree to act as an instructor. I seem to remember you admired him at one point."

Rheya was unable to suppress her excitement. "Word is he plans to take an apprentice or two from those preparing for the *adva ka* if they impress him."

Ah, so that was it.

Rheya wanted to use Kira to make herself look good in front of her hero. Not a bad plan, except she didn't factor in that Kira was well versed in fighting. She wouldn't be the easy prey Rheya assumed.

Although, she could purposely lose, Kira supposed. Make sure the rest underestimated her.

"I fear your match will have to wait. The Lady Kira and I have a difference of opinion to settle from Ta Da'an." Graydon didn't wait for Rheya's reaction, guiding Kira away before she could protest or think of a reason to refuse.

"This is a bit presumptuous; don't you think?" Kira asked under her breath. Especially since she didn't recall a difference of opinion that needed resolving.

"You know you've been itching to see how your skills compare to mine. I thought I'd save you the trouble of asking." Graydon threw down the gauntlet, his lips twitching.

"He's got you there," Jin quipped.

Kira glared at a spot on the other wall, a retort for Jin on the tip of her tongue. She swallowed it back. Both Graydon and Jin had a point.

Kira had seen Graydon fight. He was impressive. Powerful, strong, and surprisingly quick for such a big man.

It was second nature for Kira to see a difficult foe and want to test her skills against them. Few could match her. Graydon was one who might, one she itched to test.

Until now, she'd throttled the urge, not wanting to reveal the extent of her talents. Her reasoning no longer held. Graydon and his oshota had gotten a good look at what she was capable of on Ta Da'an. Protesting the matter would only insult them both.

This had been inevitable almost from the moment they met.

"Besides, breaking the children won't endear you to Roake," he said with a purposeful look. "And this way, you can't purposely lose because you know I'll hold it over your head forever."

The anticipation that had been slowly filling her sputtered as Jin chortled. "I think I'm beginning to like the Mountain's idea of flirting."

A small growl escaped Kira, the only response she could make.

That only prompted Jin to cackle hysterically. "I take back my objection to being stuck in this room. I'm starting to see the benefits of remaining behind. I can say anything I want, and there's nothing you can do."

Maybe not now, but when she caught up to him again, she was going to rewire all of his circuit boards. Let him wait.

Graydon found them a small square of mat not occupied.

"This will certainly be a treat," Amila said, offering her blade to Kira. "I don't think the commander has found an opponent to challenge in years. Let's hope you're worthy of the honor."

"I'm probably not." Kira took the blade, swinging it a few times to test the grip and weight. Not bad. It was light, and the handle felt at home in her hand. Comfortable, the guard and pommel were perfect for both being wielded by one hand or two.

Matte black, the blade was slightly curved, its tip coming to a point. There was only one sharp side for cutting.

It was similar enough to other blades Kira had wielded that she shouldn't have any problems.

"Don't be so humble," Amila advised. "You forget I saw you fight a horde of Tsavitee."

Kira ignored the reminder, focusing on her opponent. Despite

Graydon's claim to the contrary, it was a given that she'd lose. Defeating the Emperor's Face, even in a simple practice match, would bring attention she didn't want, but that didn't mean she couldn't give those watching a good show.

He was right in that she couldn't half-ass this. Pride and her own competitiveness wouldn't allow her.

She raised her hand and frowned at the cuff. It would have been better to test her new limits prior to sparring with anyone. Quillon hadn't been lying when he said she would feel like she'd lost an important limb.

Reaction time. Speed. Endurance. All were question marks for now. Not the best strategy for facing a powerful opponent.

She dropped her hand and studied Graydon. Without the disrupter, his speed nearly matched Kira's, and he'd demonstrated a superior fighting ability.

Yes, this was going to be a challenge.

"Kick his ass, Nixxy," Blue yelled from the sidelines.

The rest of the training hall had given up any appearance of ignoring them. Kira grimaced at the idea of an audience.

Graydon raised an eyebrow. "Feeling shy?"

She made a dismissive sound in her throat as she settled into a defensive stance. "Let's get this over with."

The background noise faded away as her attention locked on her opponent. She exhaled, finding that sweet space in her head where nothing else mattered but figuring out what an enemy was about to do and countering it. The focus settled over her like a well-loved blanket. Familiar and nostalgic.

Graydon waited, his stance easy, no obvious holes in it.

Amila stepped forward. "As the younger opponent, you get first blow."

Kira arched an eyebrow. "How kind."

Graydon bared his teeth in challenge. "It's because you're considered weaker."

Kira's eyes narrowed, reading the jab for what it was, meant to prick her temper and make her come at him full strength.

It was working.

"In that case." Kira's stance altered. Normally she wouldn't attempt this move, especially right out of the gate. Her feet shifted until they were shoulder length apart, her knees slightly bent as she held her blade with both hands along her left hip as if sheathed. Slow this form might be, but it generated a hell of a lot of power. If he was giving her the opportunity, she was more than happy to take advantage.

Her breathing slowed. She exploded forward, the blade gripped in both hands as she swung it in a powerful diagonal line, aiming for his torso.

The sharp crack of blade hitting blade brought the conversation in the room to a halt.

Kira's shoulders and wrists ached as her sword vibrated from the power of his parry. He'd stopped her an inch from his torso.

Graydon regarded her from over his sword. "Good. You're already taking this seriously."

His stance shifted the barest bit, as his defense broke, letting her sword swish into the spot he'd just been. Kira whirled, taking his strike on the side of her blade. The next instant, she attacked, thrusting, then stepping to the side and pivoting for a swing.

Graydon's laugh was exultant as he blocked. His speed picked up; his blows suddenly more powerful. Kira forgot about losing; all she cared about was surviving.

His blade whistled past her ear. Kira saw an opening and took it. Her foot landed on his bent knee. She used it to launch herself up, scaling him like a tree. She punched the side of his face, gravity, and the unexpectedness of the blow lending it power.

Graydon stumbled, as those around them exclaimed.

"Nice one," Jin crowed.

Raider let out a guttural yell of encouragement.

Graydon's smile was dark as he wiped the trickle of blood from the corner of his mouth.

"First blow to Kira," Amila intoned. Approval gleamed in her eyes.

Graydon inclined his head. "Well done, *coli*."

Kira's chest heaved from exertion, sweat dampening her shirt as she remained on guard. Graydon wasn't the type to let something like that go unanswered. His next attack would be brutal.

Graydon roared, charging in the next instant. Kira met his intensity with her own. They came together with a crash that filled the room.

Graydon planted a foot and pivoted at the last minute, her blade missing and swinging through the empty air next to him. Kira fought to recover her balance, knowing she was already too late.

She braced as an invisible pressure gathered. He pushed out, a blast leaving his fist. Kira dropped, barely avoiding taking the full brunt of it. Her stomach quivered as she rolled to her feet in a smooth movement, putting distance between them.

Graydon straightened from his crouch, his smile dark and inviting. "That's not all you've got, is it? I'm barely warmed up."

She bared her teeth at him in challenge. He was welcome to end this at any time.

"Come, come. Amuse me for a little while," he told her.

They'd see who was amusing by the end.

Kira crossed the distance between them in three powerful steps; her attack glancing off his guard. They moved quickly across the space, their blades a blur, neither giving the other quarter.

Kira's breath came faster and faster, the weight of the blade dragging at her shoulders and arms. Graydon didn't pause, pressing harder as he backed Kira up.

She ducked, getting distance again.

He shifted with her, firing several *ki* blasts in succession. She dodged the first and the second, her body contorting to avoid them, even as her blade whipped up to protect her from Graydon's strike.

The last blast ripped through her guard, glancing off the tip of her sword to punch her in the chest. Kira staggered back, barely catching her balance.

Smug arrogance settled on Graydon's face as he waited, making a statement in how he didn't need to take advantage of the sudden break in her defense.

She glared as she rubbed her chest, even as she considered all that she'd learned so far. Most important of which was the blade had deflected some of the power of his *ki*.

Hm.

"If you're done, we can call it a day," he invited.

Not likely. She hadn't dealt him near enough damage to satisfy herself.

However, he did have a point. Her endurance was shit. She needed to end this before she gassed out.

Kira didn't respond with words, her attack answering for her. This time Graydon didn't bother defending, stretching out one hand, the *ki* blast already prepared.

She ducked under it, her blade scraping along his side in a solid strike.

He grunted. "Not good enough."

Too late, she saw his stance had shifted, his palm moving to point at her from under his sword. She had no time to dodge the point-blank strike.

Her feet left the ground as she flew back. She hit hard and lay there, trying to catch her breath. What the hell was that?

"Done yet?" he asked, arching an eyebrow.

Jin whistled. "Ooh, them's fighting words. If he had just kept his mouth shut..."

Kira leveraged herself up, ignoring the way her ribs protested. She was past playing nice, the inner demon inside lifting its head. Blood was in the air and she wanted to play. Consequences be damned.

Graydon grinned, telling her without words to bring it.

Kira found herself willing to comply. She was on her feet in the next second, attacking without thought or any sense of self-preservation. All that mattered was shoving those words down Graydon's throat.

"That's enough." The words cracked through the air. The weight of authority behind them brought all movement within the hall to a standstill.

Kira and Graydon broke off their attacks, snapping to attention as they faced the newcomer.

Wren watched them with an implacable expression, reminding Kira of a commander confronted with the indiscretions of his subordinates. Disapproval mixing with displeasure.

The slightest tinge of red stained Graydon's cheeks as Wren's gaze shifted to him. Kira blinked. Was that a blush?

Naw, it couldn't be.

"Commander, I believe you have duties elsewhere." Wren's reserve didn't mask his censure. His eyebrow lifted the slightest bit. "Unless you would like to do my job for me."

Graydon radiated discomfort, making Kira stare at him in surprise. She'd never seen anyone put Graydon in his place as easily as if he was a naughty child.

Who was this man? And could he teach Kira to do the same?

Jin's voice was hushed as he whispered. "That man is my new hero."

Kira couldn't help but agree. Anyone who could do that to Graydon with a few simple sentences was someone she'd do well to imitate.

"Pardon me, commander. I fear my sparring session with Lady Kira was too stimulating an experience to pass up. I apologize if it has delayed your schedule." He sketched a partial bow to Wren before doing the same to Kira.

Graydon's head lifted before he straightened. His eyes speared hers as his lips curved in a small, determined smile that said he looked forward to the next time they matched blades.

Kira was left with the sinking feeling this wasn't over. A pity since her body ached in places it hadn't in a long time.

Amila took her blade with a look of reverence. "This is the blade that scored a hit against the commander." She cradled it to her chest with a look of bliss. "I'll treasure it always."

Jin chortled. "I like her."

Graydon and his oshota left the room, leaving a charged silence behind them.

Kira caught the thoughtful look on Rheya's face. If Kira had hoped to fly below the radar, that hope was over now. Her battle with Graydon made it clear she was a force to be feared, even if she had little practice in fighting someone who could use air as a weapon.

Silas raised his hands, calling the initiates' attention. Maida stood at his side, a step behind Wren. Her lips quirked as she studied Kira closely before glancing over the rest of the candidates.

"We've placed you in groups," Silas said. "If I call your name, please step forward."

There was a rustle among the initiates, their excitement palpable.

Silas listed several names, Joule and Blue among them. The last name he called was Blake's before he gestured to Maida. "If you've been called, Maida will be your instructor for this phase of your training. Your *seon'yer*. It translates to teacher or guide for those unfamiliar with our culture. Blake, having advanced further in his training, will be her second."

Joule cast an uncertain look at Kira, his unease at being separated clear. Blue patted his shoulder and grinned. Whatever she said seemed to relax him.

"The rest of you will seek instructions from Wren," Silas said. "Your focus for these next few weeks should be on conquering yourself and exceeding your limits. I have faith you can do this. Listen and learn. Only your *seon'yer* can decide when you are ready to take the *uhva na,* the Trial of the Broken, and the first stepping stone in your pursuit of the *adva ka.*"

Blue's hand shot up. "What is the *uhva na*?"

"It is a trial and a test that we use to determine an initiate's readiness for the *adva ka*," Wren answered for Silas. "There you will face yourself. Only by conquering your inner demons will you proceed."

Kira wanted to ask how long before those present would be allowed to make the attempt but held back. She'd already created enough of a splash.

Blue didn't share her reserve. "How long until we're ready?"

"I can't tell you that. It differs for everyone," Wren told her, not even the slightest ripple in his stoic expression hinted at the aggravation he had to feel at being questioned by a human.

"Ballpark it for me," Blue challenged.

Maida stirred. "Typically, most initiates do not attempt the trial for at least four months after arriving here, depending on how quickly their training progresses. Occasionally, their preparation will stretch into a year."

Kira tensed. That was unacceptable.

Jin's hiss in her ear told her the same.

"However, exceptions have been made." Maida stared pointedly at the spot where Graydon had been earlier before smiling, the gesture slow and knowing. "It all depends on the initiate. Some of you have already received training from your Houses. Others gained experience elsewhere." Maida's gaze fell on Kira. "Both hold the potential for accelerating your timeline for entering the trial."

There was a rustle as those present seemed to guess the reason for Blue's questions. Kira didn't react, her expression remaining detached and impassive.

So, her goal was difficult but not impossible. Good to know.

It was a good thing she'd chosen to complete the first test. Otherwise, who knew how long it would have been before the Tuann deemed her ready to join the initiates? She could have been here decades.

Maida prowled away, saying over her shoulder. "Look alive, my pretties. There's much work to be done for today."

Those whose names had been called filed out after Maida, leaving the rest of them staring at Wren and Silas.

Raider joined her. "Looks like we're in the same group."

"Yippee," Kira muttered.

"I'll leave them to your care," Silas said, dipping his head toward

Wren before departing.

Wren's jaw flexed as he stared at those assembled. His expression was as unflappable and indifferent as it'd been when he'd stared Graydon down.

"Follow me," were the only words he spoke before padding out of the room.

Devon shoved past her, his shoulder knocking against Kira's. "Don't let the fact the Emperor's Face singled you out go to your head."

Kira stared at him, not letting him intimidate her. Raider's expression was careful as he watched the two of them, his hands twitching as if he was restraining himself from acting.

Devon arched an eyebrow. "No response."

"You didn't ask a question," Kira pointed out.

Jin crowed. "The Kira special. A remark guaranteed to send the recipient to Angerville, by way of Fury Road. I like your style, Kira Forrest. It gets me right in my tingly bits."

Jin didn't have tingly bits unless one counted his electronic circuit board. Not that rational arguments ever really affected him.

However, if he didn't shut up, she was going to find a way to reduce him to scrap metal when she finally returned to the room.

Devon's lips tightened as he leaned forward. "You're weak. You shouldn't be here." He flicked the disruptor around her wrist. "This practically announces you as a liability."

Kira's smile didn't reach her eyes. "There are many kinds of strength. If you don't learn to recognize that, you'll never advance beyond your current state."

Devon sneered before spinning on his heel and striding after Wren. Kira didn't relax, knowing others were still watching.

The Tuann she'd noticed during the test smiled and waved. "I'm Aeron."

Kira frowned. "Your friend is leaving you behind."

Aeron's smile dimmed with uncertainty. He hesitated before hurrying after Devon.

"I've always admired your ability to create enemies without even trying," Raider said. "It's good to see that hasn't changed in the intervening years."

"He's hardly worth considering an enemy," Kira said in distraction as she caught a glimpse of a broad back belonging to a man with the exact same shade of hair as hers as he strode away from the Warrior's Hall.

An annoyance? Yes. A distraction? Maybe. Someone to fear? Not really.

*

Raider staggered out of an archway; unhappiness written on his features. Runes flashed along the stone sides of the archway as another Tuann stepped through into the forest Wren had brought them to.

Kira didn't know how, but with a single step they'd gone from a courtyard in the fortress to standing in the midst of a lush forest, ancient trees towering overhead, a monolithic stone jutting from the mountainside behind them. It emerged above the trees like a leviathan breaching the surface. Tall and remote.

"Why do they keep insisting on breaking the basic laws of the universe?" Raider groaned.

Alarm colored Jin's voice as he shouted through the coms. "Where are you? Kira, answer me! Your signal disappeared."

The edge of panic creeping into Jin's voice meant Kira couldn't ignore him this time.

She lowered her voice and faced Raider as if the two of them were in the midst of a conversation. "Calm your jets, Tin Man. We're all fine. We went through a spot of teleportation, but that's it."

Raider looked confused for a second before understanding dawned.

Jin exhaled, audibly calming himself. "Right. Right. Teleportation. Why didn't I guess?"

Jin's consciousness pushed forward as he dipped into her senses. The experience of feeling like she'd disappeared—if only for a moment—must have been more disturbing than he wanted to admit, if he was riding her senses without asking first.

Kira let the trespass go, knowing being locked in the room while things were happening was difficult for her friend.

"I wonder why we didn't see these in Luatha." Kira glanced around. No one else seemed surprised or uneasy, which meant archways that enabled you to cross a large distance with one step were fairly accepted.

Finn's blank expression caught her attention.

Ah. They probably did. They simply hadn't shown them to Kira or the rest of the humans. Probably considered them too much of a security risk. She couldn't blame them for that.

The other initiates headed toward where Wren had taken up a position at the base of the towering monolith. He gestured at the surface behind him. "All of you failed to scale the wall during the Trek of the Weary. You will remedy that lack now. How you reach the top is up to you." He pointed at the trees. "For those who fail or whose *ki* isn't strong enough, we've set up nets. They'll catch you should you fall."

For the first time, he smiled, the expression hard and unyielding. "Let me be clear—you won't progress until you have passed this stage."

The pale, nearly invisible nets Wren pointed at weren't made of any material Kira recognized. They hummed with a nearly inaudible sound, beams of energy the likes of which Kira had never seen crossing and threading in and over one another.

"You may begin now," Wren said, stepping to the side.

Devon was one of the few who didn't hesitate, charging the wall without question. Much like he had during the trek, he leapt, his feet sticking to the stone as he ran up it. His fellow initiates followed; each person's technique slightly different.

Raider whistled. "I wonder what the purpose behind this is?"

It could be anything from testing their manipulation of *ki*, to increasing their stamina, to building their problem-solving skills. For all they knew, the task was designed to keep people like Kira and Raider from completing it.

"Does it matter?" Kira asked.

If Wren said they needed to reach the top, that's what they'd do.

"Suppose not, but it does make me curious," Raider said, looking up.

Aeron stood off to the side, shooting glances at them as he rubbed his hands on his thighs. He was one of those who'd taken the stair option during the trek pretty early on. He hadn't even made it twenty feet off the ground before having to switch. This task, no doubt, seemed monumental to him.

"Are you going to try the climb?" he asked them.

"Why wouldn't we?" Raider fixed him with a hard stare.

Aeron shifted in discomfort. "You can't manipulate your soul's breath."

Raider scoffed at his words. "Humans can't do a lot of things. That's why we find ways to modify the world around us. It might take a try or two, but I'll make it to the top."

"Too bad Blue's not here," Kira said. The other woman would likely already have jury-rigged a device that would make this task a simple one.

"It'd certainly be a lot easier," Raider agreed.

They shared a look.

That was probably the reason Blue was in the other group—so they couldn't cheat.

Kira followed as Raider started for the monolith.

Wren stepped into her path, blocking her. Raider paused, shooting her a look. She waved him on.

"Not you," Wren said.

Kira blinked, then blinked again, her head tilting.

Wren pointed to the forest behind her. "Your task is different."

Kira glanced between the forest and the monolith, confused.

Impatience crossed Wren's face. "Your bout with Graydon, while ill-advised, made one thing clear. Your endurance is lacking. Your strength is lacking. Manipulating *ki* takes both. Until you've built them up, you will run."

Kira's mouth clicked shut as a feminine laugh came from behind her. Rheya sprinted forward, flying up the monolith with ease.

Raider met her eyes, caution in his.

"Don't punch him," Jin advised.

The corner of Kira's eye twitched as Wren gave her his back, signaling she was beneath his notice. Her hands curled into fists as she took a deep breath, releasing it before taking another.

Raider's expression was sympathetic. "Want company?"

Kira shook her head.

He grunted before starting up the wall, searching out hand and footholds as he rose.

She watched him for several minutes before facing the forest beyond the arches. Finn was a steady presence beside her as she moved toward the trees at a sedate pace.

"Wait. Are you actually listening to him?" Jin didn't bother hiding his startlement.

"He has a point." Much as it pained Kira to admit.

Her bout with Graydon might have ended much differently if her energy hadn't flagged in the last half.

Kira moved below the trees' canopy, the leaves cutting her off from the faint warmth of the sun. Here, without its light, a chill quickly set in.

Kira didn't mind it. Once she got moving, she'd be plenty warm enough.

The path was dirt and well-trod, meandering through the trees until it twisted out of sight.

There was a menacing atmosphere to the forest. It felt almost sentient, as if thousands of eyes fixed on her as it waited. The trees rustled and whispered to each other. Trickery and deception lay here, waiting to beguile the unwary. It was the essence of every deep, dark fairy tale forest come to life.

Kira bent and clasped her ankles, stretching the backs of her legs.

"Well, yeah, he does, but when have you let that stop you?" Jin argued.

"When it serves my purpose," Kira told him, ignoring Finn as he waited several steps down the path, his expression inscrutable as always.

Wren's order played to her advantage. Right now, the best thing she could do for herself was to build up her strength and speed. Learn her new limits before she began pushing them.

Kira released her legs and straightened.

"My body feels different," Kira said. "I need to know what I'm capable of."

"I thought you were here to learn how to manipulate *ki*," Jin sounded querulous.

"We are, but Himoto always said you had to start at the base and work your way up."

Strength. Endurance. That was her base. They wouldn't let her down, even if her *ki* never reached the level of destructive power it once had.

"Besides, this allows us to get the lay of the land. Find out what's what while I regroup."

There was a short silence.

"That outlook is surprisingly evolved," Jin finally said.

Kira grinned. "Maybe I'm taking a page out of your book."

Jin snorted. "About time."

Kira finished stretching and straightened before setting out at an easy pace, conscious of the way her body felt. Finn was a silent shadow.

Kira was content to let him linger for the first mile. Only once she'd started on the second, did her pace quicken, picking up until she was sprinting. The distance between her and Finn widened as she caught him briefly off guard.

Good. The window wouldn't last long, but while it did, she needed to take advantage of it.

"Jin, I have a task for you."

"Oh?"

Already she could feel Finn closing the distance. She pushed a little harder, her breath coming quicker now.

"I need you to contact our little friend."

"What little friend? You have several."

Kira fought a growl. Now wasn't the time for him to play dumb.

"The little friend who might do something drastic if we don't turn up soon," she hissed.

"Aww, the impetuous and rash little friend," he said, sounding bored.

Kira huffed. He'd known who she was talking about all along.

"You know you can just refer to her by name," he suggested.

"I don't want any mention of her name anywhere. It might seem paranoid, but we've kept her safe this long. No sense exposing her existence to the Tuann through comms that might be intercepted."

Jin grunted. "I contacted her while we were still on Ta Da'an."

The tight ball Kira had been carrying in her gut loosened slightly. Their rash friend was still very young and hadn't quite grown out of the stage where she acted without thinking through all the consequences. The last thing Kira needed was for her to create an incident and expose her existence to dangerous groups who might want to use someone like her.

"Good. Did you also let the Allfather know we have the package?" she asked.

There was a long-suffering sigh in her ear. "What do you take me for?"

He didn't want her to answer that.

"Of course, I did," he finished.

"And?"

Silence echoed down the line.

"Jin?" Kira said, threat deepening her voice.

"I'll try again," he grumbled.

Kira didn't like the sound of that. Odin was almost never out of contact.

Footsteps pounded against the ground as Finn caught up. Kira thought she detected the slightest flicker of anger in his stoic expression.

"From here on out, I'm going radio silent," Kira said.

"Why?"

"Because it's sensible. I suggest you do the same."

"No need. I've encrypted my signal and piggybacked it off one of theirs. If they see it, they'll assume it's from someone on their side," Jin said.

"Your arrogance is going to bite you in your metallic behind one day." Kira's pace slowed, the brief sprint taking its toll.

"But it's not likely to be today."

She couldn't help the brief smile that crossed her lips at that rejoinder.

As angry as she'd been that he'd smuggled himself onto the planet, she was glad for his presence. Even in the darkest of times, he managed to create light. She didn't know if she'd have survived everything with her sanity mostly intact, if not for him.

Lost in her thoughts, Kira almost didn't notice as a tree root sprang up out of nowhere. She twisted in midair, only her quick reflexes saving her. She managed a semi-graceful landing on the other side of the root. She stopped and scowled at the root.

There was no way that had been there before. She was sure of it.

"Finn, can the forest move itself?" Kira asked.

The oshota was barely breathing hard, acting more like they were out for a lazy stroll than a challenging run. His only response was a silent stare. He arched an eyebrow at her. Kira took that as a yes.

She glanced around with new eyes, taking note of the way the trees seemed to have pressed closer to the trail, leaning ominously over it. Some of their roots had burrowed over the path she'd taken moments before, fully obscuring it.

Kira's lips curved up. "That's pretty cool."

"What? What is?" Jin demanded.

"I've never heard of trees that moved. I wonder if they would attack those they consider an enemy," she said.

Finn was predictably silent.

"Are you sure they're moving and it's not your imagination?" Jin asked skeptically.

Kira rolled her eyes before setting out again. Of course, she was sure. That wasn't the sort of thing she was likely to make a mistake on.

Jin grumbled, unhappy about Kira's silence.

"If I had known it was going to be like this, I would have stayed with Jace," Jin complained.

Kira didn't respond, picking up her speed while keeping an eye on the ground and trees around her. This time when one swung a branch into her path, she bounded lightly onto it, using it as a springboard to launch herself into the canopy.

A laugh escaped her as she hopped from branch to branch, executing random flips before landing lightly and finding her next foothold. She never broke speed, Finn shadowing her below.

Sweat gleamed on her skin, her breathing ragged by the time she dropped to the dirt path.

"Having fun?" Finn asked.

Her grin this time was unreserved. "A little; yeah."

NINE

KIRA'S DAYS QUICKLY settled into a pattern after that first day. Early morning was spent in the med bay, letting Quillon use his invisible needles to scramble Kira's insides. Afterward, Finn always shoved a quick snack into her hand before they reported to the Warrior's Hall.

Kira never did any real training with the initiates. Wren was nothing if not consistent in his assertion she needed to increase her overall stamina and strength before she embarked on learning to master her *ki*.

By the end of the first week, she'd stopped approaching him in the mornings, setting off for her run even before he opened his mouth.

Finn was her constant companion, accompanying her as her morning runs got progressively longer. If he resented being forced to tag along with someone not even deemed worthy of using *ki*, he never mentioned it.

Since Wren had never specified that all she could do was run, Kira used the opportunity to throw in circuit training, pushing herself as hard as her body would allow.

When she got tired of training, she'd use the forest as her opponent, learning to read its movements before it actually moved.

Her fellow initiates weren't much better off.

Wren had been true to his word, not allowing anyone to progress until they'd reached the top of the stone monolith, a challenge much harder than it seemed at first glance.

Stationary wind guns waited along the rock face to knock unsuspecting Tuann off its surface. If that wasn't difficult enough, camouflaged drones crouched in the crevasses came alive anytime someone strayed too close.

The drones always moved, never staying in the same place from day to day. It made it impossible for the initiates to map their location. A fact Kira knew frustrated Raider to no end. He seemed to have a talent for setting them off. This week alone, he'd felt their sting no less than seven times. The prior weeks hadn't been much kinder to him.

The monolith's traps weren't the only surprise the forest held. During one of her runs, Kira had stumbled across an obstacle course, much like the one on Luatha. It had taken some quick thinking to escape a swarm of drones and make it back over the fence with no one but Finn the wiser.

Since then, Kira had been careful to mark the edges of the course, delineated by the nearly invisible energy fence around its perimeter.

Finished with her run for the day, Kira headed for the arched gate she'd grown familiar with, the evening shadows deepening as she made her way through the forest.

Today, unlike other days, a small figure crouched at the base of the gate, nearly hidden where he sat.

Kira slowed as she and Finn traded a long look.

"I'll handle this," Kira said.

"As you wish." Finn paced a few steps away, giving them the illusion of privacy.

"Joule, I could be wrong, but your session with Maida finished hours ago," Kira said in greeting.

Kira had made it a point to keep track of when others were in the forest. Some of the things she was attempting would likely get her in trouble if others found out.

She'd learned early on that Roake wasn't the only House who used the forest. Other Houses sent people to train there as well.

Kira had gotten quite good at slipping through the trees unseen. It had become a sort of game, one Finn was happy to oblige her in, teaching her techniques to conceal her presence both physically and on the *ki* level.

Which was why Joule's presence was so startling. It wasn't the norm.

A pair of morose eyes met hers.

Kira knew that look. Things weren't going the way someone had thought they would.

"That's an awfully long face for someone who got everything they wanted. Things not working out like you hoped?" Kira asked.

Joule's jaw tightened, an angry kind of misery radiating from him.

That was a yes then.

Spotting a bottle of water in his hand, Kira nodded to it. "Is that for me?"

He looked at the water as if surprised before handing it over to Kira.

She took several sips, the water cool and refreshing. Only once she'd drunk half of it, did she nod at the gate. "Let's go. You don't want to be in these woods after dark."

It had only taken one late day for Kira to realize the danger. Nocturnal predators hunted here after sunset. They were big and deadly enough to consider even a Tuann fair game.

Joule started. "How do you know that?"

Kira scratched her cheek, her eyes sliding away.

"Someone just got caught doing something they're not supposed to," Jin said gleefully.

Kira pointed at Finn. "Sometimes, it's helpful to have a source of information who refuses to leave your side."

Finn was expressionless as he stared at the two of them, giving nothing away. Sometimes her unwelcome guard had his uses, like now when he made the perfect fall guy.

He hadn't told her anything about the forest, letting her experience its dangers for herself.

Joule didn't question her further, standing and dusting off his pants before touching the gate. His forehead furrowed as the runes shifted, and a path opened.

Since her arrival, Kira had learned the archways acted like a network. You could go anywhere as long as there was a corresponding archway on the other side that you had permission to access. Your *ki* had to be encoded into the archway before use, otherwise, the connection would fail to establish.

A sheen of color rolled over the middle of the archway, radiating a slight haze, similar to what you got when very hot rays of light hit a surface like sand or blacktop and reflected a shimmer.

Joule stepped through, Kira and Finn following.

The sound of the sea greeted her as the ocean stretched into the distance. Kira glanced behind them, unsurprised to find the hulking form of the fortress.

Joule didn't wait, continuing along the small dirt path, lined with long grasses on either side. Kira followed.

"What did you want to talk about?" she asked.

It was obvious something was on his mind.

His eyes remained trained on the horizon as they made their way to the cliff's edge, the chilly wind drying any lingering sweat on Kira's skin.

It was colder here, much colder than the forest, and not necessarily comfortable. Hopefully, whatever Joule had to say wouldn't take long. Kira already longed to retreat to the warmth of her room.

"I heard them talking," Joule finally confessed. "They called you an abomination and a coward. They said Roake should never have allowed you to become an initiate."

Kira took a slow sip of the water as she considered Joule. "That's it? That's why you look like the rug has been pulled out from under you?"

Confusion descended on his face.

Kira waved a hand. "Earth saying. It means you've had the balance knocked out of you."

Joule neared, his expression earnest. "You don't understand. If they think you shouldn't be here, they'll challenge you. The *seon'yers* won't be able to stop a challenge for those who haven't passed their *adva ka* unless it becomes life threatening."

Kira whistled. "Sounds scary." She glanced at Finn. "Anything to add?"

Finn's gaze was steady as he regarded her. "Initiates cannot kick someone out of the program. Officially."

Kira waited, knowing there was more.

"However, they can make life very difficult for someone they deem unworthy." Finn's lips twitched as if he was amused at the prospect they might try. "Unrelenting challenges are one method to obtain that goal."

Kira studied the water bottle. "Humans do something similar."

It was never pretty when it happened, but the training cadre usually turned a blind eye. People who were too different might not survive the sustained efforts of their peers to force them out. Things could easily get out of hand, which was why it was technically against military regulations to haze a fellow soldier. Despite that, it still happened.

"I'm surprised they haven't tried that with Raider and Blue." The other initiates, with Devon leading the charge, had made no qualms about voicing their dislike of the humans' presence.

Joule's eyes dropped.

Finn looked uncomfortable as he said, "I believe they've faced some difficulty. However, the other initiates underestimated the humans' stubbornness and ingenuity. I don't have all the information, but it appears the blue-haired one's retaliation was decisive—and impressive."

That surprised a snort out of Kira. "That sounds like Blue."

She was always resourceful and never willing to turn the other cheek.

"And Raider?" she asked.

"He's held his own so far," Finn said.

That was good. And unsurprising.

Kira gazed unseeing at the horizon, contemplating what Joule and Finn had shared. A lot had happened while she'd focused on herself. None of it could be helped. Blue and Raider had to establish respect for themselves, and it sounded like they were doing that.

Kira nodded. "Sounds like it's handled."

Done with the conversation, Kira started toward the castle. Joule jolted, hand upraised as if to stop her. "Wait, we need to talk about this."

Kira grabbed his outstretched arm, jerking him toward her as she swept his leg out from under him. He tumbled, jolting to a stop when she caught the collar of his light armor, one that was little better than leather strips over his vital area, likely the best he could afford given the state of his House.

His back toward the ground, he hovered, only her grip keeping him from falling. She lifted him a few inches toward her, the mask she normally wore gone. The carefree attitude, the cutting humor, all laid to the side.

Stripped bare, she gazed at him, letting him see her seriousness, the person who wouldn't let anything or anyone stand in the way of the pursuit of her goals. That was who he saw in that moment. The Phoenix. Someone who'd tasted loss and exacted the first phase of her revenge.

He swallowed thickly.

"Do I look like someone who gives a fuck what others think of me?"

Joule didn't answer.

Her lips parted in a snarl. "When you've experienced the worst life has to offer you, the little details no longer seem to matter so much. You choose what in this life affects you. What you will waste precious energy on. They want to belittle me? Mock me? I don't care. Let them challenge me. I'll win or I won't. The end. Everything else is details."

Joule touched her wrist lightly, naked vulnerability written in his face. Kira sighed and shook her head, lowering him until his butt rested on the ground.

She crouched before him. "Joule, you have a goal and a purpose. Focus on that. Forget about me, and don't let matters like these hold you back."

Joule swiped at his nose; his eyes suspiciously red as he avoided Kira's gaze.

Kira sighed, feeling like the lowest of the low. She hadn't meant to hurt his feelings or point out truths he wasn't willing to face.

"I thought we were friends," he finally mumbled.

He was so young.

"I'm awfully hard on my friends," Kira said, one hand rubbing her neck. "Ask Raider and Blue. They'll tell you how difficult a friendship with me is."

It would be tempting to think she was cursed. She didn't believe in such things. She was unlucky was all. Her standoffish nature and tendency to shoulder the brunt of any burden didn't help.

"I don't care," Joule said stubbornly. "You saved Ziva and me. You didn't have to, but you did."

"That doesn't make me a good person or a good friend," Kira pointed out.

His gaze held hers, unflinching. He didn't plan on letting go of this point.

"Is that the only reason you looked like someone had killed your dearest friend?" Kira asked finally, offering an olive branch.

His gaze slid away, his mouth setting in a stubborn line.

"Ah, I see," Kira said, hiding her smile. Joule might have wanted to warn her of the trouble brewing, but it wasn't the only reason he'd sought her out. "Having trouble?"

"It's different than I'd imagined it'd be," he mumbled.

"It always is," she murmured.

Achieving what people told you was impossible could feel like the greatest thing in the world. Miraculous and dreamlike. It could also leave you feeling empty—especially when reality didn't fit with what you'd envisioned.

"Does it make you want to give up?" she asked.

His gaze was sharp, the answer written on her face.

Kira's laugh was husky. "Good. I'd think less of you if it did."

A shy smile bloomed at the praise. Kira was glad to see it. Joule and Ziva had managed to burrow their way through her defenses. As much as she wanted to push them out, she didn't have it in her.

They reminded her she hadn't been broken by war and loss, their unwavering faith whispering to the parts of her she'd buried deep. The parts that insisted she had once been more and could be again.

It was humbling. Disconcerting, leaving her feeling vulnerable and off-balance.

It would be so easy to destroy their hero worship.

Kira stood. "Come on. You can show me the new things you've learned as we walk back to the fortress."

Hope lit Joule's expression. "Are you sure?"

Kira lifted a shoulder. "Not like I have anything else to occupy my time right now."

He bounded to his feet with an energy and grace only someone as young as he could manage.

He ran through the warrior forms Maida had taught him. Kira watched with interest, cataloging them to try later. She was glad to see his form had improved since she'd last seen him work. Whatever training Maida was putting them through was working. With practice, Joule would become a talented warrior.

"That's not all," Joule said. "She's been working on teaching us a shielding technique."

Joule fell out of his last stance, straightening. He inhaled, centering himself. His hands came up to meet at his chest, his palms facing each other as he left an inch of space between them.

The frown on his face deepened with concentration, sweat dotting his forehead.

The faintest flicker of power sparked to life between his hands. It built, the pressure causing Joule's hands to shake.

He held it like that, the flicker getting brighter. With a cry of effort, Joule ripped his hands apart, stepping back with one foot at the same time.

His left hand swept up in an arc, his right hand mirroring it as he drew a circle, his hands crossing as they finished the circle. Visible *ki* crackled in the lines he had drawn with his hand. His palms flipped to face out and he shoved.

Kira's ears popped as a dome sprung into being, accompanied by a soft glow. It wobbled then stabilized. Joule remained in that position for several seconds before dropping the dome.

Joule's gaze swung to Kira, his expression exhausted and victorious. "Well?" he asked.

Kira didn't say anything for several seconds, and uncertainty crept into Joule's posture.

"That is badass," she finally told him.

"Indeed," Finn agreed. "Holding a *ki* shield as complete as that at your age is impressive."

Joule basked in the oshota's praise before the happiness drained. "It's only good for defense. Not as impressive as a primus form."

Kira knocked him lightly on his head. His expression was incredulous as she pointed a finger at him. "Something like that might save lives one day. Listening to the nonsense of others or comparing yourself to them will only serve to hold you back. Develop the talents you have until you know every facet of them."

He was letting the attitudes of others influence him. If he couldn't see past *what was* to *what could be*, he'd never make it to the position of Overlord.

"Yes, it's helpful to have offensive talents, but I can think of a dozen ways something like what you showed me can be used effectively in battle." Kira's tone was harsh. "Your imagination and adaptability will stand you in far greater stead than something like a primus form."

Joule's hand dropped, and he stared at the ground for several seconds before meeting Kira's gaze. "I understand. I won't think like that again."

Yes, he would. It was inevitable. But as long as he didn't get stuck in that kind of thinking, he had a chance to exceed the limitations life had put on him.

Not that she should blame him. In this, she had a bit of an advantage on him. She'd seen skills like his before. Seen their creative application until they barely resembled the original intention behind them. If Joule had even a fraction of that person's creativity, a talent like that would stand him in good stead.

Not that she could tell him that. Trust was a valuable commodity, and some secrets weren't meant to be shared.

*

Several pairs of eyes shifted to focus on Graydon as he stepped into Harlow's office. Graydon paused in the doorway, observing the scene with the same scrutiny he would if it was a battlefield, and he needed to determine the best strategy for victory.

The analogy wasn't too far from the truth. Over the past few weeks, Graydon had begun to feel like a caged animal, hemmed in by his duties and responsibilities, his skin too tight and a coiled tension sitting in his middle.

Tuann weren't meant to sit idle for too long. War and fighting were bred into their bones. Inactivity only fostered aggression and trouble. All the discipline in the world would only delay the inevitable.

"Look who deigns to join us," Caius said from where he lounged with an insolent slouch.

Like the rest of those present, Caius was a senior member of Harlow's council. A warrior and commander of Harlow's forces in the sixth quadrant of Roake's territory.

He looked like a playboy with his hair roguishly styled, sharp cheekbones, and a cockiness that seemed to appeal to many women. The only mark that marred his perfect features was the faintest nick in his eyebrow.

Graydon throttled his desire to plant his fist in Caius's face. For one thing, it would be pointless. Caius wasn't physically there, despite appearances.

He looked as tangible and real as Graydon, but if you were to touch him, your hand would fall right through his body.

"Caius, still alive? I thought the *fendrik* would have killed you by now and split your body into pieces to decorate their homes with." Graydon's tone might have been mild, but his expression was not.

Caius threw his head back with a roar of amusement. "Little Storm, your mask is slipping." He shook his finger at Graydon in mock rebuke. "Someone needs to spend more time on the front lines. You're getting a tad cranky."

Graydon grunted.

He wasn't the only one. All of his oshota were showing the strains of forced inactivity.

Their presence in Roake might have been necessary, but it hadn't made the intervening weeks any easier. For warriors used to being in the thick of things, it was a difficult adjustment—especially since they had to be on their best behavior while in another House.

Roake might have once been Graydon's home, but it wasn't anymore. A certain decorum was expected.

Wren didn't have to move to draw the attention of everyone present, making it clear without words it was time to get to the reason why they'd been summoned.

Graydon quelled his impatience and moved into the room.

Silas, Makon, Maida, and Quillon all nodded respectful greetings as Graydon took a position among those of Harlow's House that the Overlord trusted most.

Although two were missing, no doubt attending to pressing matters that couldn't be put aside, these were the men and women tasked with decisions that played a pivotal role in the House's future. All of them commanded their own people, each focused on helping Harlow oversee a House of this size.

"How are the little birds doing?" Caius asked, directing his gaze toward Maida and Wren.

Maida propped her chin on her hand. "There are several who show great potential. Others who will be lucky to be accepted into a House's lowest tier of soldiers."

Wren inclined his head in agreement.

Caius arched an eyebrow, his gaze meeting Harlow's. The Overlord showed no reaction, his expression remote.

"And what is your assessment of the person we're all likely thinking of?" Caius asked.

Wren touched a spot on the wrist of his synth armor. Numbers scrolled into sight above the Overlord's desk.

"Oof, those numbers are terrible," Caius muttered.

Indeed. They were. Astonishingly so.

"Wait. There's a pattern in the numbers," Maida said, leaning forward.

Of those present, Graydon wasn't surprised Maida spotted it first. Her affinity made her a difficult opponent to defeat, but her ability to recognize battle tactics and ferret out patterns in an enemy's strategy were the real threats.

Maida focused on Wren. "Is it a code?"

Wren was a man given to stillness. He didn't fidget. He never lost his poise. As a result, he was one of the most difficult men to read Graydon had ever met.

He was also a contemporary of Harlow's. The two men had served in the same pod. Similar to the squads the human military sorted themselves into, a pod was a unit. The size could vary, but it was always made up of an uneven number of those with complementary talents. The bonds between a pod were considered nearly unbreakable.

Graydon's own oshota consisted of two pods of which he was the commander. It meant when they fell into a situation suited for battle, they would act as a single unit, their cohesion guaranteed.

That's why it was so surprising to see Wren shift, the movement small and almost unnoticeable if it had been any other. This was a man used to commanding. His self-possession rivaled Harlow's. To see it disturbed meant the puzzle had been more difficult than Wren had anticipated.

"I thought so too," Wren finally admitted. "Which is why I approached the humans. Neither seemed surprised, nor were they willing to reveal its meaning."

The revelation was a startling one to those present.

"Loyalty. Who would have thought it from humans," Caius mused.

"I've witnessed the evidence for myself several times," Graydon rumbled from his spot near the window. "Somehow, she has managed to secure their loyalty, though the presentation of its depth can often take a surprising form."

From first glance, the humans seemed to have an antagonistic attitude toward her, but when it counted, they moved to provide support when needed and protection when warranted.

Graydon understood from his oshota, both humans had faced multiple challenges from the other initiates. Neither had sought out Kira for assistance in dealing with the matter. The male went so far as to intercept those who might push her for a fight, making himself a target. He did this through a combination of cutting remarks and cocky bravado.

Raider had acquitted himself quite well for someone with his limitations. The initiates were coming to understand *ki* wasn't the overwhelming advantage they'd assumed. Raider met them head to head, winning decisive victories almost every time.

Caius propped his elbow on something unseen, his expression unconvinced. "Are we sure we're not seeing things that aren't there?"

Finally, Harlow stirred, nodding at Graydon.

Graydon touched a spot on his forearm, flicking the data package at Harlow's desk. "These are a few clips my oshota have taken over the last week or so."

Caius stirred, focusing a gaze on Graydon that saw far more than his enemies ever gave him credit for. "And what are your oshota doing keeping an eye on the lost daughter of our House?"

"They've taken a liking to Kira." Graydon's smile barely touched his eyes. "I fear once she has progressed to the point where she can take a pod for herself, they will desert me for a chance to pledge their loyalty to her."

Surprise touched Makon's face. "High praise considering your oshota are among the elite."

Graydon dipped his head. "Praise she's earned." He glanced at Silas. "Unless you disagree."

One side of Silas's mouth twitched up. "There was more than one reason I chose to intercede when it seemed she would retreat to human space."

Caius wasn't one to be deterred, his expression faintly suspicious as he stared at Graydon. "I find it interesting you've chosen to linger on Ta Sa'Riel. It's not like you."

Graydon wasn't fazed by the abrupt change of subject, brushing it aside with the ease of long practice. "My oshota and I have been away for too long. I decided it would be wise if we reacquainted ourselves with home."

Not even Caius could argue that point. Graydon represented the emperor's interests. He'd served on consecutive front lines in the protection of his agenda.

Sometimes he was a mediator. Sometimes he was the executioner. It meant long periods away from the safety of the main planet.

Caius's expression was grudging as he let the matter drop.

The rest of them took in the image that had formed over Graydon's desk. Kira held a practice en-blade in her hand, her outfit disheveled, trees surrounding her. Her eyes were narrowed at something off-screen. Even through the holovid, it was impossible to miss the overwhelming focus in her stare.

She burst into movement between one second and the next, her form fluid as a drone dove into view, firing a barrage.

Maida leaned forward in outrage. "Is that one of my *kattas*? Where did she learn that?"

"Joule likely showed her," Graydon murmured. "The two are close."

"Even so, for her to have mastered it to this extent..." Maida trailed off.

Few could. *Kattas* took an instant to learn and a lifetime to perfect. Kira flowed through them with the ease of someone who'd practiced them relentlessly.

Her primus was one thing. It was powerful, but like all things, it had its weaknesses. Most Tuann with a primus became overly reliant on the form. They had incredible power while active, but it only lasted so long. When they reverted, it left them vulnerable and weak. More than one primus had been killed in such a moment.

This, though, pointed to hard work. Dedication. Years of sacrifice as she trained her body above and beyond.

"She watches. She learns," Graydon ignored the impatient feeling crouched in his middle. These people hadn't spent as much time around her as he had. They thought she was a child, her development delayed and hampered by her history among the humans.

They needed to adjust their thinking before Kira force-fed them their misconceptions. While he suspected that would be amusing to watch, Graydon didn't have the time to wait, nor did he think Kira would be willing to stick around after she was done.

Two more drones launched into view, quickly surrounding Kira. She evaded, a whirlwind of motion as she lured the drones into her trap, the practice blade almost hanging forgotten at her side unless needed—which was rare.

"That's not a beginner's *katta*. She's mixed in at least two mid-level and one high-level," Wren murmured.

"I haven't shown my initiates any of those," Maida said, her eyes glued to the image. "They're not quite the same as mine, but they're a good approximation."

Irritation and admiration mingled in her features. Graydon could practically see the other woman taking notes, already itching to get out and try some of the *kattas* Kira was demonstrating and see how they compared to her own.

Abruptly, Kira planted a foot on the side of a tree, propelling herself into the air. She spun like a top landing three precise strikes and disabling the drones.

They fell to the ground around her as she landed. Her balance wobbled, her eyes widening before she tumbled ungracefully to the ground.

Muttered curses could be heard as she picked herself up, her movements jerky as she knocked dirt and debris from her clothes. It was obvious this wasn't her first fall.

"Yes, yes. I know it's pointless unless I stick the landing," she growled.

Loudon frowned, speaking for the first time. "It's concerning the way she talks to herself. This isn't the first time I've caught evidence of such. Isolation madness would not reflect well on our House."

Graydon's temper, already short before the meeting started, threatened to ignite at the implication. "She spent many years with humans as her role model. I'm told this is a common trait of theirs."

Isolation madness was a condition rare to the Tuann except in the case of those exiled from their Houses, who were left to roam alone. Tuann didn't often isolate themselves. They were too reliant on the bonds they formed with those of their pods and families. Those who did, occasionally went mad from the lack of companionship.

Loudon didn't retreat, his expression apologetic. "Be that as it may, she will need to be monitored closely. We don't know her history or what was done to her. It could have effects we've not anticipated."

Graydon reined in his ire. Loudon wasn't saying anything others hadn't already pointed out and would continue holding against Kira.

Harlow waved his hand, dismissing the image. "I've seen enough for now." The Overlord leaned forward, steepling his hands in front of him as the rest of them waited.

His tone was considering as he said, "As it stands now, Rheya and Blake have already passed the *uhva na*. They're only waiting for their official *seon'yers* to be declared. It is our job to determine whether there are others among the initiates who are also ready and meet the criteria necessary for advancement."

Silence descended as they considered the Overlord's words. Such a request was out of the ordinary. Many Houses would have been overjoyed at having two pass Roake's *uhva na*; to ask for more could be considered greedy.

Maida shifted, worry lingering in her eyes. "There are a few whose capabilities stand out, but I don't want to rush. Normally, we would have several more weeks before we considered advancement."

Harlow leaned back slowly, one finger tapping against the surface of his desk. "In the normal course of things, I would agree." He gestured at the image of a frozen Kira. "But circumstances aren't normal. We can't pave the way for one, no matter how talented, without offering the same opportunity to the rest."

Wren's stare was penetrating. "You're so sure she's ready?"

Of them all, Wren understood the challenges of what Kira faced best. Probably better than even Quillon.

Like Kira, the channels through which Wren's *ki* flowed had been shattered through grief and circumstances.

The rest of those present went still and silent at the reminder of that dark time. Wren had been broken, held together only by will and fortitude.

If he decided it was too dangerous for Kira to progress, not even the Overlord would overrule him.

That would be a mistake. Graydon knew Kira well enough to know she wasn't likely to linger if she felt coddled or held back. She would find a way to her ship and disappear.

Graydon had every intention of making sure that didn't happen.

"Quillon?" Harlow asked.

Quillon's expression was calm and remote. "You know I cannot share the particulars of a patient's progress."

Caius scoffed. "How predictable."

A flicker of irritation tightened Quillon's jaw. "I can, however, advise that there is no reason to delay Kira's progress unless her *seon'yer* truly thinks she isn't ready."

Wren didn't speak, his gaze faraway as he considered Quillon's words.

"Speak, Loudon. I know you want to." The Overlord's voice was wry.

Like Wren, the two had a long history. They were boyhood playmates. Loudon had been part of the twins' first pod and had remained close to them even when the pod split to pursue separate paths.

"It's obvious she possesses amazing potential, but her motives and upbringing remain an unknown. It would be wise to delay her progress until we are assured it is safe," Loudon said. "I can't help but feel we would be making a mistake in allowing her to progress."

Graydon crossed his arms against his chest and regarded the man who acted as the *ki's* herald. "The only mistake would be in letting our preconceptions destroy her faith in us."

Loudon's smile was gentle but firm. "Little Storm, I can respect the fact the child has caught your eye. Like her mother before her, she has a bright presence that draws us. However, you have no say in her future. She is a child. It's our responsibility as the elders of her House to ensure she remains on the proper path, despite any wishes she might have to the contrary."

Graydon held in his words by dent of will. Speaking unwisely now would damage his credibility, no matter how satisfying it would be in the short term.

"Loudon, you overstep," Maida chided as she sent Graydon an apologetic glance that was full of wry frustration.

Graydon wasn't the only one who occasionally found the herald annoying.

Harlow's intelligent gaze watched the drama, taking everything in, but as usual, he was slow to provide his own counsel. He preferred they do the arguing for him. Only once he saw all possible outcomes would he weigh in on an issue.

"This question can be tabled for now," Harlow said. "We still have time before a decision must be made."

Loudon sat, pacified for now, but there was no doubt in Graydon's mind the Tuann would pursue this line of thinking again.

Harlow focused on Maida and Wren. "The Haldeel have called a quorum."

Silence fell, the issue of Kira's future forgotten in the wake of the news. It had been more than fifty years since the Haldeel had last called a quorum. Humans hadn't even been a player on the galactic stage then.

The quorum was a highly anticipated series of events in the Haldeel's culture. Holding more in common with the Olympics of old Earth, it took place over ten days and nights. It consisted of physical events as well as difficult puzzles. Any could compete. Those who did won favor for their cause.

It was said a House's or empire's fortune or fate could be won or lost during a quorum. The amount of political maneuvering that took place during one was astonishing.

That they had called a quorum now couldn't be a coincidence. Not with the Tsavitee beginning to move in the shadows.

"Have the humans received an invitation?" Makon asked.

Graydon was the one to answer. "They have."

Surprise echoed in the room. No one had expected the humans to be extended such an honor. That they had been would be something to keep an eye on.

It also answered the question of why Harlow was considering shortening the training of those who showed talent. Roake was smaller than many Houses and wouldn't be able to send many to the quorum without sacrificing their security. Nor could they abstain from attending.

"I don't have to impress on you how important it is we present a strong showing," Harlow continued. His gaze shifted to Maida and Wren. "Begin incorporating the groups. Learning each other's strengths will be important when it comes time to deciding their readiness. We have time before the quorum takes place but not much."

What went unsaid was having initiates who'd already passed the *uhva na* would be extremely useful in such a situation.

Harlow regarded them steadily. "Dismissed."

His council stood, acknowledging the order with a wordless assent.

Caius's attention settled on Graydon, a sardonic smile tugging at his lip. "Should you find yourself bored, know that you and your oshota would be welcome on my battlefield any time."

Graydon inclined his head in acknowledgment. "I'll keep that in mind."

Caius's threw his head back, his laugh warm and carefree.

"Any news on the unidentified ships I sent you?" Graydon asked.

Caius sobered and shook his head. "I've had my people checking into it. None of the planets in my sector have been visited by the Tsavitee. Nor have any of Roake's other commanders seen any suggestion of an incursion."

"Then we still don't know their destination," Harlow said.

Caius hit a few buttons on his armor before sending the data through. "Not in a way that is meaningful. However, a few of mine were able to analyze likely trajectories."

Harlow brought up the information Caius had sent, his expression darkening as he put it in the holovid. The planet of Ta Sa'Riel shimmered into being.

"You think they're coming here?" Graydon asked.

Caius's expression was serious as he nodded. "My person isn't often wrong. It won't get you proof enough to have the emperor launch a full-scale search of all Houses' territories, but it can give you an idea of what you're dealing with."

"The Tsavitee are here," Harlow stated, sprawling in his chair.

"The question is why and what do they want?" Graydon said.

Caius shook his head. "I'll leave that for you to discover. Try not to die, won't you?"

With that the commander signed off, leaving Graydon and Harlow to sit in silence as they studied the information Caius had sent

"I will inform the emperor of this. Caius was right in that it isn't enough proof to justify trespassing onto House territory, but he can put some of his own resources on this," Graydon said, standing. "I trust you will do the same."

Harlow nodded. "In addition to Caius, I have a few people I can place on this. See if we can pinpoint where they landed. If they've infiltrated our House, we will find them. The same can't be said if they've infiltrated one of the other Houses."

"Leave that to the emperor. He has contacts he can reach out to. It's not a perfect solution, but tensions are already high because of Ta Da'an," Graydon said.

"Before you go, there's one last matter I want to discuss," Harlow said, tapping a button on his desk.

Information scrolled above it.

"Care to explain this?" Harlow inquired.

Graydon's frown morphed into a scowl. "I'm not sure, but I'm going to find out."

Harlow gaze held Graydon's for several long seconds before the corner of his mouth twitched. "I expect you will."

Graydon was on his feet and out the door in the next instant. He had a certain woman to track down and demand information from. This time he planned to get it.

TEN

KIRA DANGLED UPSIDE down, patiently waiting as she basked in the crisp morning air that contained more of a bite than normal. Snow was in their future.

She shook her hands and cupped them to her lips, blowing on them as she trusted the cable attached to the harness around her waist would hold her. The movement caused her to twist slightly, changing her view from the rock face of the monolith she hung next to, to the forest stretching below.

"I don't know how you can be so calm with only a few pieces of wire to hold you up," Jin grumbled in her ear.

Kira's grin was brief. This from a being whose antigravs enabled him to reach heights much higher than her current one.

"It's safe enough," Kira assured him.

"Tell me that again after you've been splattered into a pancake," he snapped.

Kira touched one foot to the cliff, halting her rotation. "If the nets work the way Wren said they did on the first day, it shouldn't be a problem."

Jin blew a raspberry, his lack of faith in Tuann technology unmistakable.

"I don't understand your fascination with heights," he said.

"They make me feel free and remind me that limitations can be circumvented."

Movement came from below, and Kira placed a second foot along the wall, straightening her legs until she stood parallel to the monolith's surface as she faced the ground and those below.

Kira noted with interest Wren's initiates wouldn't be the only ones attempting the monolith today as Maida and her little lambs, Joule among them, joined the group.

Jin continued to grumble. "Only spiders lurk like you currently are. Disgusting, terrifying creatures. I can't believe humanity has reached the stars and still not eradicated those annoyances."

"Spiders play an important role in the ecosystem," Kira murmured, her gaze caught on a familiar figure, one taller and broader than the rest, arms folded over his chest as he frowned at those present. "What's he doing here?"

"Who?" Jin said, sounding alert.

"Graydon."

"Hmm. Maybe he's bored," Jin pointed out. His tone shifted. "They're not necessary on space stations or ships."

Kira paused, puzzlement crossing her face. "What aren't?"

His sigh was gusty. "Spiders."

Kira's head tilted as she considered. "I guess that depends on if you have a bug infestation or not."

People would be surprised by the tiny critters that managed to stowaway in goods shipped through merchant ships. Some of the planet critters were downright terrifying. All the safety protocols and clean rooms in the universe hadn't managed to solve the problem.

Jin hummed in thought.

"Looks like they're starting," Kira said.

Those below were warming up as they began to prepare for their ascent. This time Wren's initiates weren't the only ones, Maida's were doing the same on their side of the field.

Jin chortled with glee. "This is going to be so much fun."

Kira agreed.

"Remember the plan," she told him.

He grunted in confirmation as the first of the initiates started up the wall. Kira wasn't surprised to see Devon and Rheya sprint to the front, competing against each other, their movements bordering on reckless as they left the others behind. There was a distinct lack of coordination or teamwork present.

Humans might be a lot of things, but they understood success in battle often depended on your weakest link. Rarely your strongest. Cut it and you could strike a strategic blow to the enemy.

Kira started bouncing against the wall, the cable keeping her in place. "This is going to be too easy."

"I'm ready when you are," Jin said.

While Kira would do most of the heavy lifting, Jin would decide the flow of the next few minutes. He was a shadow in Kira's mind, riding her senses and using what he picked up to parse information about the world around her.

In addition to seeing out of her eyes, he'd also had her place several sensors around the base and top of the cliff that fed him data. They were as ready for the coming battle as they could be.

"They're spread out, it should make it easy to pick them off," Jin said, analyzing the situation. "There's one drone ten feet below. As long as you don't touch the wall within five feet of it, you won't wake it up."

"Understood," Kira acknowledged.

"Prepare to drop," he told her.

Kira pushed off lightly.

"Drop."

The harness released, the cable spooling out as she descended rapidly.

"Drone is behind you. You're good to go for the next twelve feet."

Kira planted a foot, changing her trajectory. The contraption controlling the cable clicked over with her, allowing her to run down the cliff instead of being pulled to her original spot.

"Jump away from the cliff," Jin ordered.

Kira did; the horizon of the forest shifting before the cable and gravity brought her back to the cliff.

She landed in a crouch above Devon. Shock descended, his expression almost comical as he froze.

She grinned at him. "Hey, there."

"Move," he snapped, coming out of his stupor.

Kira made a tsking sound. She didn't think so. "Do you know what you're doing wrong?"

It was a rhetorical question. If he did, she wouldn't be there.

She didn't wait for him to answer, pouncing. She hammered both feet into his chest, knocking him off the cliff with ease. "Guess you'll have to try again."

He tumbled, his body hitting Aeron and sending both careening into a grav net. It sagged under their combined weight, before slowing their descent.

"Two strikes for the price of one," Jin crowed.

Kira bounced in place on her toes. "That was fun. Who's next?"

"Rheya is coming up on your left side. She'll pass you in five seconds."

"We can't have that, now can we?"

His laugh this time was diabolical. "No, we most certainly can't."

Kira raced horizontally across the cliff, spotting Rheya several feet above. When she was directly below the other woman, Kira exploded away from the cliff, executing a twirl as the cable caught Rheya and yanked her free. She sailed past Kira with an angry shout.

Kira's feet landed on the rock again, where she began to bounce, occasionally flipping or twirling at the apex of the move.

"Look alive, Raider and Blue are on the move," Jin told her.

She glanced down, spotting the last two. "Looks like Blue made a few modifications to her mag boots."

"I don't think anybody has thought of that application for them before," Jin said, sounding interested.

"You can ask her about it after this," she promised him.

Kira studied the Curs closely. They would be a more difficult foe than the other initiates. With Blue, they were guaranteed to have a trick or two up their sleeve, and their teamwork would make them that much more dangerous. And they'd seen the others fall to her machinations.

Kira bared her teeth in a crazy grin; one echoed on the faces of her former companions. She wasn't the only one anticipating the coming confrontation.

"Our fearless heroine on one side and her worthy foes on the other. Who will come out the winner?" Jin's tone adopted that of a race announcer, playing up the drama.

Kira crouched. "Us. Always us, Tin Man."

"Ten-four, Phoenix."

Kira breathed deep, springing forward as she exhaled. She propelled herself at the two in the blink of an eye.

Raider straightened from the cliff, his boots clinging to the stone. He reached for Blue, a tracery network of azure lines sprang into existence between the two of them, crackling with electricity.

"Now," Blue shouted.

Raider heaved. Blue's feet left the cliff as he slung her toward the top.

"Oh, that is clever," Kira said as Blue passed her. "But not clever enough. Jin."

"Already on it."

The cable whirred as Kira raced up the cliff as if she was running, chasing Blue. Raider appeared at her side, a maniacal grin on his face. "Not today, Phoenix."

"Now," Jin cried.

Kira stopped, grabbing the wall and finding a toe hold as she hit the release on her harness. It popped free. She grabbed the wire and slammed it into the rock face.

Startlement registered on Raider's face at the unexpected action. It quickly changed to understanding as camouflage leaked out of a drone seven feet above Blue's new position.

"Shit," he hissed.

Blue jerked back as the drone fired. A short squeal accompanied her plummet to the ground.

Kira leaped, landing on Raider's back, one arm wrapped around him below his armpit, the other over his shoulder. Her hands met in a fist at his chest.

"I expected the initiates to have trouble with his challenge. I'm more surprised you haven't figured out the secret of it yet," Kira said into Raider's ear.

"What?"

Kira didn't respond, planting a foot against the wall and shoving off, taking Raider with her.

His protest was drowned out by her laughter as they followed Blue down, Jin singing a song of victory the entire way.

*

Graydon stared in disbelief at the woman who was entirely too pleased with herself as she hit the grav net and bounced. She grabbed the edge, using it to flip herself up and over, hitting the ground in a crouch.

"Suck on that landing," she muttered.

"Kira!" Raider shouted as he fought his way over the edge of the net.

"Uh oh." She sounded slightly guilty as she stuck her hands in her pockets and started to amble away.

It wasn't going to be that easy, *coli*.

Graydon folded his arms over his chest and settled in to watch the scene unfold, anticipation curling through him.

Raider wasn't the only one of Kira's victims to lock onto her. Devon and Rheya not far behind.

"Abort, abort," she muttered, picking up her pace slightly.

The rest of the field watched with varying levels of interest. Graydon's oshota were amused, having come to expect the unexpected from their former charge. They had the luxury of feeling such since they weren't humiliated so thoroughly.

Graydon expected the lesson she'd taught the initiates was liable to sting, especially since he knew they viewed her with varying levels of pity or disdain.

From here on out, they'd forget the challenges they'd been throwing at the humans and focus on the real threat in their midst. Kira.

"I don't think I've ever seen anyone so thoroughly circumvent your test," Solal remarked to Wren.

The other man grunted; his gaze focused on the monolith as he tried to figure out how she'd managed her ambush.

"What was that?" Devon demanded, cutting Kira off.

She cocked her head, her expression one of innocence. "Were my actions unclear? I can always demonstrate the lesson again if you'd prefer."

Joule lifted a hand, his shoulders shaking suspiciously. Despite being one of those Kira had knocked off the cliff, he seemed to be taking his fall with good grace.

Rheya shoved closer. "You had no call to force us to fail."

Kira raised an eyebrow. "Is that what I did?"

Their glares were fulminating.

Kira speared each of the initiates with a penetrating look, her resemblance to her uncle clear enough in that instant that it was startling.

"Or did you do that to yourself?" Her voice was hard, her stare flat.

The humans traded a look, communicating with unspoken words. They weren't the only ones who caught her hint. Joule glanced up at the monolith with a puzzled look. His face cleared seconds later as his lips parted, and his attention swung back to the spectacle.

"Hmm. He's not bad at reading a situation," Maida murmured, her gaze locked on the young Tuann.

"Of those present, he and the humans are the ones who've acquitted themselves best this morning," Amila agreed.

The rest of them were silent as they watched the initiates deal with this latest development.

The test of the monolith wasn't only meant to test the initiate's manipulation of their soul's breath. It was also meant to force them to recognize that there were some hurdles they weren't yet ready to face alone. Its purpose was designed to get them to work together and figure out a way to best utilize each other's talents.

What none of those present realized was that none of them would be deemed ready until *all* of them had reached the top.

"What's that supposed to mean?" Devon demanded.

An angry exhale escaped Kira, her patience visibly evaporating. "It means you need to learn to listen to what is not being said as closely as you do to what is being said."

Wren's gaze locked on Kira as she pointed at the monolith.

"When did he ever say this was a solo mission? Why haven't one of you tried working with the rest to conquer that piddly wall?" Each word came out forcefully as her voice raised so everyone could hear her. "You would have been done weeks ago if you'd bothered to capitalize on each other's strengths."

Devon looked ready to spit, unwilling to retreat. Rheya held herself stiffly, not any more inclined to listen than him.

Both looked seconds from challenging Kira, a fact the humans seemed to be aware of as they stepped up to stand shoulder to shoulder with her.

A pinched look settled on Rheya's face as the odds tilted out of her favor. She visibly swallowed her anger, her stance easing.

Devon didn't show the same inclination, aggression in his posture as he took a threatening step forward.

Kira stiffened, her eyes flattening as she stared him down. "If I were you, I would rethink whatever is in your mind right now."

The words barely made Devon pause, a formal challenge forming on his lips.

Graydon prowled closer, danger rolling off him. That was enough of that. The boy showed promise, but if he challenged anyone in full view of the *seon'yers* and oshota, he would find his tenure in Roake cut short.

While those past the *adva ka* rarely interfered in the challenges of their juniors, there was a time and place for such things. In full view of two pods of oshota while in the midst of training was not it.

That the boy didn't understand that fact said he still had a long way to go—no matter how developed his skills.

"Trouble, Kira?"

His words seemed to have the effect of an electrical whip on Kira as she stiffened, invisible hackles rising as her gaze swung toward his.

Ah, there was his little *aksa*. Her resemblance to a fist-sized animal of this world whose stubbornness and bloodthirsty viciousness were in direct disproportion to their smaller size was unmistakable.

Kira held in her instinctive remark. Pity. He would have been interested in her unfiltered response.

Instead, Kira arranged her face in what she no doubt thought was a pleasant expression but didn't manage to hide a speck of her irritation.

His oshota struggled to keep straight faces as Kira stared at him balefully. "Nothing that concerns you, commander. Just a friendly challenge among friends."

Lazy interest curled through Graydon as he moved his eyes over the others. "I confess I wouldn't mind seeing that."

It would be a diverting entertainment seeing her handle herself among those who should be her peers. Almost as diverting as another bout between them. Something that had been on Graydon's agenda since the moment Amila brought the first recording of Kira battling drones.

Devon and Rheya both straightened, coming to partial attention at the hint of threat in Graydon's tone.

Kira batted his words away. "As much as I live to amuse you, I have better things to do with my time today."

Graydon's head tilted. "Oh? Do share."

Devon shifted, his impatience at Graydon's interference obvious.

Graydon's gaze speared his, the façade of lazy entertainment dropping as the full force of his personality overwhelmed the younger Tuann. "Careful, *zala*. I won't be as merciful as she was."

Kira's intelligent gaze moved between them. "What does *zala* mean?"

"Infant," Joule said into the quiet.

Graydon ignored them, the predator inside staring down the two initiates who'd already embarrassed themselves enough for one day.

"Knowing when it is time to retreat and regroup is as important for a warrior as knowing when to stand and fight," Wren said into the strained silence.

Devon relented. "Rheya, Aeron, let's go. We'll never reach the top standing here." He paused, his gaze lingering on the humans. "You too, if you think you have something helpful to add."

He didn't wait for their response, aiming a curt nod at Graydon and Wren before striding toward the monolith.

Rheya's expression was outraged as she stomped after him.

Kira blew out a puff air. "Look at that. He *can* learn if he tries."

Raider shoved her shoulder with his as he followed in Devon's wake. "I forgot how brutal your teaching methods are."

Kira made a dismissive sound at the humans' backs, watching as Devon organized the initiates into teams before the group started up the rockface, their teamwork shoddy but existent.

Kira started as if suddenly realizing she was now surrounded by oshota and the *seon'yer*.

"On that note, I'll return to my own task," she said, backing away.

Finn peeled away from the tree line, following as she broke into a slow jog that held the distinct air of one beating a hasty retreat.

Graydon didn't think so. Any boredom or pent up aggression was now gone, washed away in the wake of a new prey, one that held every bit of his attention.

His chuckle was deep as he loped after Kira, his powerful stride eating up the ground between them.

*

It occurred to Kira after she'd been running for several minutes that Jin had been conspicuously absent during the confrontation with the initiates. No sarcastic quips. No distracting sideline conversations.

Kira stopped abruptly as she considered the ramifications of his atypical behavior. For the past few weeks, he'd been a constant, irritating companion. She'd taken it as a sign he was obeying the rules.

She should have known better.

"Jin. You there?" she said in a low voice as she made her way through the forest.

Silence echoed.

"Answer me, Tin Man," Kira cajoled. When a response never came, she continued, "What? No rejoinder about Tuann flirting habits?"

If anything got his attention, that would.

Kira waited.

Nothing.

Kira mentally cursed as she kicked the nearest tree. Damn his short attention span and propensity for boredom. She'd hoped the excitement of what they'd done would distract him. No such luck.

Kira started for the archway and the gate that would lead to Roake's fortress. Her tussle with the younger initiates would have to suffice as a workout for the day. She had a drone to corral.

"You'd better not have put one electrode out of that room, buddy, or I'm going to turn you into a pile of scrap metal," Kira threatened.

A hint of a presence tugged at her senses, and Kira went still, suddenly aware Finn wasn't her only companion in the forest.

Graydon glided out of the trees with a dangerous prowl.

Adrenaline flooded Kira as she calculated the chances he'd heard her. Graydon was the last person she wanted overhearing her. If so, any hope of keeping Jin's presence a secret was up. Graydon wasn't the type to write off the unexplained. He'd ferret out the information with a bloodhound's obsession until he knew every last detail.

Kira considered and discarded several responses before settling on, "I could have handled the puppy."

Graydon didn't even pause as he approached. "Of that, I had no doubt. Your way of solving the challenges your friends have been fending off was a creative one."

Kira grunted, unsurprised he'd guessed her motivations.

"Walk with me," he invited.

Kira reluctantly complied, despite the sense of urgency pressing her to find her wayward friend and anchor him to her room.

She shot a look over her shoulder, trying to find Finn. Maybe he could do what she no longer could. The effort was in vain. Catching his eye proved impossible.

The only bright spot in this was that the direction Graydon had chosen led them directly to the gate.

"Fine group of sharks, you've landed me among," she told him.

He paused. "That is a large water predator, is it not?"

She hummed an agreement.

Graydon's expression was considering. "That is a surprisingly apt description. We've always been a predatory race. Jockeying for position and status is as natural as breathing to us. There is always a drive to achieve more."

They reached the gate, and Graydon stepped up to it. The pathway opened, and he walked through, Kira following. His oshota and Finn kept a respectful distance, allowing them the illusion of privacy.

"That's one thing I can't get used to," Kira said, watching them. "You're never alone."

"Not always," Graydon aimed a roguish smile at Kira.

She rolled her eyes at his innuendo. Nice try, but she wasn't falling for it.

The difference in power between them was too stark. Trying to hold onto Graydon would be like grasping a balloon while standing outside in a category five hurricane—an exercise in futility that would only end in disappointment and heartbreak. Yet, it didn't stop her from wondering about what was beneath his synth armor, how his skin would feel against hers, his limbs tangled with hers during passion.

Kira pushed the thoughts away. She had no business thinking about that right now.

Instead, she focused on their surroundings. He'd brought her to a section of the fortress she hadn't explored yet. By her estimation, they were several stories below the surface, but it didn't feel like they were underground. Long narrow windows looked out on more walls. Light reflected from above.

The room was a cavernous chamber, the floor rough-hewn and uneven. Like the rest of Roake, the walls were black.

Along one side of the room, life-sized statues of Tuann clad in synth armor holding various types of weapons stood sentinel. Kira noted a lance and mace among them, along with several weapons that had a more futuristic look.

"We recognize there is strength in numbers," Graydon explained as they moved through the length of the room. "Even the strongest warrior can fall when faced with a big enough force. My oshota have my best interests at heart, and they will always come to my defense should I need it. Their loyalty is assured; they won't divulge anything they learn in my company, not even to the emperor. To do so would be to betray one of the founding tenets of our society."

"Even if they thought you had lost your way?" Kira asked.

Many would have pushed her question to the side, saying such an event would never occur. Not Graydon. He gave it the serious contemplation it deserved.

"That is one of the rare instances where they might break my trust. Our history is riddled with such occurrences. None take that step lightly because those who do are often treated as pariahs afterward. It's not unheard of for those who have broken faith to commit suicide shortly after." Graydon's eyes met Kira's. "It's why an oath of that magnitude isn't undertaken lightly. They tie their fates to mine, and we rise or fall together."

It was a pretty concept, deceptively seductive. To have people who were so loyal to you that you knew they would always be in your corner.

The only flaw was reality. Sometimes people weren't who you thought. Sometimes, they changed and evolved.

"Can they leave your service?" Kira asked.

Graydon paused. "Yes, but usually only under certain circumstances. It is rare."

"Even if they find the fit isn't right?" Kira asked.

Graydon inclined his head.

Kira grimaced. "Life is too short to waste in service to someone you deem unworthy."

Graydon's big shoulders shrugged. "I agree with you. Our people are incredibly long-lived and can be exceptionally stubborn. We don't change our loyalties or views easily—even when it's warranted and in our best interests."

"Where have you brought me?" Kira asked, looking around.

Besides the statues, there was a smooth wall with circular lines carved into it, many intersecting in different places until it resembled a model of a foreign star system.

The rings it was made up of each had smaller circles attached to them, representing planets. Only instead of a sun at the middle was the carving of a coiled *lu-ong*, its crest flared and fangs bared.

Graydon gestured to the room. "This is Roake's Hall of Ancestors."

Graydon stopped in front of the last statue. This one was newer than the rest, the stone lacking the patina of age.

"These are the previous Overlords," he said.

Kira stiffened as she realized why he'd chosen to linger in front of this particular statue. Almost as if drawn by a magnet her eyes shifted until they were resting on the statue's face. Her father's face.

Echoes of her features had their origins in his. The line of her nose, the shape of her lips.

He seemed almost amused, as if on the verge of laughter.

Graydon moved away, stopping in front of the wall. He touched one carved line reverently, the deep blue of Roake's colors spreading from the spot he touched, marching around and around until the solar system stood in stark relief.

"You're determined to pass your *adva ka* as soon as possible." Graydon's hand fell, and the wall vanished, revealing the beginnings of a carved passageway. Despair and grief wafted out of it. "This will be your first challenge. Before you can be deemed ready to advance to the next stage, you must pass the Trial of the Broken."

The wall snapped back into existence.

Kira stared at it, tucking her shaking hands against her sides. Whatever that place had been wasn't natural. It had felt like every one of her deepest, darkest fears waited within its depths.

"What is that?" Kira whispered.

Graydon walked toward another set of statues. At first glance, it would be easy to assume they were of Tuann. That assumption would be wrong. Upon closer examination, Kira found the limbs a hair too long. Their eyes bigger than any human's or Tuann's.

Their beauty was unearthly and alien. Cruelty and amusement were stamped on their faces as they looked out at the world.

Their armor wasn't synth armor, which was Kira's biggest clue.

Graydon paced along the statues. Every other statue was of a monster, no two alike. Some crouched and snarling, others upright on two legs.

"Not all of the Mea'Ave can be considered welcoming. It has its darkness like all things. What you just felt is a small sample of that. Roake uses it to determine a person's inner strength, how well they will stand against temptation and self-doubt. Admittedly, it can be rather brutal, and Roake is one of the few who still use the Trial of the Broken on its young. Passing the *uhva na* will mean your integrity is virtually unassailable," he told her.

"Why go to such lengths?" she asked.

He nodded at the statues in front of them. "The enemy of old. The ones who bred our race to fight their endless wars. I suspect ancient Tuann were much like your humans. Fragile and only half aware of the deeper secrets of the universe. The enemy of old forced us to evolve. Our stories tell us unspeakable wrongs were committed against us in the attempt."

"What happened to them?"

"They're extinct now." Graydon's expression darkened, cruelty stamped on his features. "The Tuann may have played a large role in their fate."

Kira's gaze lingered on a statue's features. They were disturbingly familiar. They starred in her oldest nightmares from a time when pain and fear were her daily companions.

Graydon's enemy of old was the same one who used to visit the camp where Kira and Jin had spent their youngest years.

Realization rocketed through her. She was staring at the Tsavitee's masters. More surprising was the knowledge that the Tuann had once been their servants.

"Why are you telling me this?" Kira asked, still distracted by her discovery and its implications.

No wonder the Tsavitee had turned their attention to the Tuann. Their masters weren't the type to let their toys escape their control.

Kira had intimate knowledge of the extent they'd go to return a wayward toy to their care. Could the reason for everything be so simple? Her parents' deaths, her childhood in the camp, the war against humans?

One thought stopped her. Why would the Tsavitee's masters make their move now? From what Graydon had said, the Tuann had escaped thousands of years ago.

What had changed?

"If I expect information, I should be willing to share in return." Graydon's focus was searing, startling her out of her contemplation. "Would you like to share why your ship has left O'Riley?"

Shock made Kira slow. Her expression went blank in the next second. She hoped Graydon hadn't caught her surprise.

"My ship has built-in security systems. If we don't access it in a certain time frame, it will disengage from whatever station and use autopilot to fly itself to a remote part of space where it will remain until I activate my beacon," Kira heard herself saying as if from a distance.

There was no hint Graydon had caught her slip as he regarded her steadily. "I can see many ways such a feature could come in handy."

A strangled sound of agreement was all Kira could manage.

While plausible—and worth making a mental note so Jin could rig the ship to do exactly that in the future—it was also a bald-faced lie.

"As interesting as this lesson has been, I have more training today," she said, making an excuse to escape.

The corners of his lips tilted up, the smile not quite reaching his watchful eyes. "I wouldn't want to stand in your way."

Kira's nod was jerky as she took her leave.

If the *Wanderer* wasn't at O'Riley, it meant someone had stolen it. There were only a few people who had the capabilities to bypass the ship's defenses.

Of those, only one Kira could think of who would devote the time and effort to such an undertaking. It was not a person she wanted flying her ship.

*

Graydon watched Kira's hasty retreat, pondering what the conversation had revealed. Next to him, the shadows parted as Solal stepped away from the line of statues.

He joined Graydon. "She doesn't know who took the ship."

A "hmm" was Graydon's only response.

No, she didn't. Her moment of unguarded reaction had been brief. There and gone in an instant. Had he not spent time observing her and her mannerisms, he might have missed it. Because of that, she couldn't hide her surprise at the news of her ship's disappearance.

"What do you think it means?" Solal asked with a hint of a frown.

Graydon shook his head. "I don't know, but I think we need to find out."

ELEVEN

KIRA APPROACHED HER room at a quick clip. Jin had better be there. If he wasn't, there were going to consequences—extreme ones.

She threw open her door and stepped inside, her mouth already opening on his name when she came to an abrupt stop.

The room was occupied—but not by the person she'd been hoping to find.

A woman in a long green dress straightened from where she was fiddling with Kira's closet. Her half-done braid slipped over her shoulder.

Kira dropped into a defensive crouch. "What are you doing in my room?"

Thoughts of assassins raced through her mind as she tensed.

Finn was beside her in the next moment, holding his arm in front of her. "Wait."

Disgruntled and still slightly off-balance from finding a stranger going through her things, Kira straightened. She wasn't happy about his order, but she also knew he wouldn't put her in danger on purpose.

She'd trust his judgment. For now.

Finn dipped into a short bow. "Lady Odelia, we thank you for your kindness."

There was a frown on Kira's face as she gazed between the two. Of all things she'd expected Finn to say, that wasn't it.

Her gaze caught on the half-opened drawers of her dresser, a stack of shirts neatly folded inside. Kira's eyes narrowed. She'd only had one clean shirt left this morning and had thought she'd have to find somewhere to wash the few clothes that had appeared in her dresser.

Now, it appeared, she wouldn't have to.

"You're the reason new clothes keep appearing," Kira said slowly.

149

It was the only obvious explanation. The woman wasn't a warrior, and Kira doubted she was a cleverly disguised assassin. Most assassins Kira knew didn't first provide a new wardrobe for their targets.

A tentative smile crossed the stranger's face. "Along with a few others."

Kira tapped her fingers against her thigh as she studied the woman. "Why?"

This woman didn't know Kira. They'd never met before. There was no reason Kira could see for her to go to such lengths.

"Your oshota made it clear you had little. This was something we could do for you," Odelia said.

Kira frowned. "What happened to no one being able to help me during this process?"

Odelia's face softened. "There are many ways to help someone that don't involve breaking the rules. We found one that allowed us to provide a needed service to you."

Kira released a long breath, sneaking a look at Finn's face. The oshota had relaxed, his expression almost kind—or as kind as it ever got.

"You know I'm not the child you lost, right?" Kira finally said.

Rather than take offense, Odelia smiled and dipped her chin. "I do, and so do the others. That's not what this is about. Not entirely."

Kira folded her arms and leaned against the doorframe. "Then what?"

Odelia was quiet for several seconds as she considered. Her expression was serene and kind when she said, "You're not our child, but if you were, we'd hope someone would do the same for them."

Kira had nothing to say to that. She had half expected recrimination for being the one to survive or a fawning clinginess that couldn't help but demand something from her.

Not this. Something so simple and done without any expectation of return. If Kira hadn't blundered into the room when she did, she likely wouldn't have ever met the woman who had made sure her time in Roake was a little more comfortable.

Kira could survive without clean clothes. However, it would be uncomfortable and likely have led to conflict with her fellow initiates.

No one wanted to be known as "the stinky soldier".

When Kira didn't say anything, Odelia took that as her leave and dipped her chin, grabbing the small bag she'd brought from the bed.

Kira moved to the side, letting Odelia skirt past her.

"Odelia," Kira said at last.

It was tempting to let the Roake woman walk out without saying anything. Kira couldn't do that. Kindness deserved to be acknowledged.

Odelia paused and looked over her shoulder.

"Thanks." Kira tipped her head toward the wardrobe filled with clean clothes. "For this and everything. It was a kindness I didn't anticipate."

The woman's smile transformed her face, banishing the weary grief that seemed embedded in every line of her face. "You'll find Roake is full of such things if you look hard enough."

Kira was beginning to see that. Now, if only she could convince herself she was deserving of such regard.

*

The unmistakable feeling of being watched pulled Kira from a fitful sleep of being chased by a terrifying shadow. Her eyes fluttered open, adrenaline flooding her as she caught sight of an indistinct shape lurking over her.

Her body reacted without thought. She grabbed a pillow, flinging it at the shape.

Jin darted out of the way, making a strangled sound of protest as the pillow barely missed him.

"What the hell, Kira?" he asked in outrage. "That's not how you're supposed to greet friends."

Kira didn't think, grabbing another pillow and sending it his way.

He dodged that one too. "Are we playing that game again?"

Her glare could have incinerated him. "Don't even think about it."

Jin must have judged her serious because the object he'd levitated using his antigravs dropped to the small desk in the corner. "Spoilsport."

"Where have you been?" Kira demanded.

When she'd returned to the room after her conversation with Graydon, Jin had been nowhere to be seen. Rather than set off on a fruitless search, she'd settled into wait. That had been hours ago.

"If I tell you, you're not going to be happy."

Her smile was icy. "I'm already unhappy."

There wasn't much he could do or say to make it worse.

"You know that place they called the Nexus on Ta Da'an?" Jin started.

Correction. She was wrong. Things really could get worse.

"What did you do?"

"I thought knowing where such a place was could come in handy if we needed it," he said.

Kira closed her eyes.

This was her fault. Jin wasn't equipped to handle boredom. She should have seen the signs. Maybe then she could have prevented this.

"Why didn't you answer any of my coms?" she asked, wondering how often he'd been making these little excursions over the past few weeks. She had little belief this was his first time out of the room.

"It seems Roake's paranoia extends to their Nexus as well. I ran afoul of a defense system that knocked me offline for a brief span."

Kira's eyes closed as her chin sunk toward her chest. Why her?

"Did they discover you?" Kira asked, her tone one of careful control.

"Nooo," he said, drawing the word out.

At least that was something.

"But they know someone tried an incursion. I barely came back online and managed to find a hiding spot before they came looking," Jin confessed.

Kira cursed.

This was not good—especially with Graydon in the mix. He was already suspicious because of the ship. This would only add to his belief she was hiding something.

"What were you thinking?" Kira asked.

Jin wasn't dumb and he wasn't usually this careless.

"I didn't want to tell you because I didn't want you to worry, but our little friend missed her last two check-ins. She's been radio silent since I contacted her from Ta Da'an," Jin blurted. "Odin too. I haven't heard from either one. There's not even a message on any of the forums."

Kira touched the dermal data patch on her forearm, all too aware of the danger it posed. The Tuann might forgive her a lot, but taking advantage of a crisis to steal starmaps? Even they had their limits.

With every day that passed, the chance of discovery grew greater. Handing the patch off was the best solution, and had she returned to her ship as originally planned, that's what would have happened.

There was also the small fact that Luatha could discover she'd accessed the maps at any moment.

"I thought if I could patch into the Nexus's systems, I might be able to get through," Jin confessed. His tone made it clear he knew how badly he'd screwed up.

Not that it mattered now. They had to hope for the best and pray Roake didn't decide to launch a search for the mysterious intruder. Or if they did, that they wouldn't discover a certain annoying drone was the culprit.

Kira's hand dropped away from her arm. "I know where our little friend has wandered off to."

"Where?" Jin asked, perking up.

"She's stolen the *Wanderer*," Kira said grimly.

"That's bad. Very, very bad."

Kira's thoughts exactly. She fixed him with a look. "What exactly did you tell her about the reason we missed check-in?"

Jin was silent for several seconds. "The truth?"

Kira exhaled. She could see that being a problem. Their friend was young and impulsive. She didn't always consider the full extent of the consequences of her actions.

"There's nothing we can do about it now," Kira conceded.

Right now, she was more concerned about Odin's radio silence. While Odin had shown a propensity for going dark in the past, Kira didn't see her friend doing that now that the piece they needed to complete their goal was in their hands.

Leaving Ta Sa'Riel to track the two down wasn't an option either.

"Odin will turn up eventually. Until then, all we can do is wait," Kira finally said, trying to convince herself as well as Jin.

"I did warn you Odin could be unreliable," Jin informed her.

Kira fixed a dark look on him. He was one to talk. He made a grumbling sound as he caught her meaning.

Kira swung her legs over the edge of the bed, pulling the covers into her lap. A thought occurred to her. "Did you know some of Roake's members were slipping new clothes into my dresser?"

Jin froze. "Ah, about that. Yes."

Kira shook her head at him. "Why didn't you say anything?"

"It seemed to fill some need in them, and I didn't see the harm," he said. "I kept an eye on them anytime they entered. They never tried

153

anything suspicious, so I left them alone."

Kira grunted. Well, that settled any remaining suspicion—not that there had been much.

"While you were gone, I made a few discoveries," Kira told him, changing the subject.

Jin listened as she recounted what her excursion with Graydon had revealed, including the fact the Tuann's history included the Tsavitee's masters.

Jin whistled. "That's an unexpected development."

Kira grunted.

He circled the room. "Although, if you think about it, it makes sense. What better way to reestablish control of the beings you created than to kidnap their offspring? It would take years of observation to determine how their time away from their masters might have changed the Tuann."

It also allowed them time to find weaknesses to exploit if they were thinking of conquering their former slaves.

"I'll have to consider this new information," Jin said. "Does Blue or Raider know?"

Kira shook her head. "I'd have to explain too many things, and I don't think it wise to let humans know of the link between the Tuann and Tsavitee."

Jin's voice was grim. "You're right. Humans have a tendency of vilifying those they consider different. There's already negative sentiment toward the Tuann because they didn't play a bigger part in the war."

The two shared a look. If the Tuann's history with humanity's scourge got out, it would devastate any hopes of a continued alliance. Humanity would be ripe pickings for the Tsavitee in the event that happened. It could start a domino effect, ending with the Tuann returned to their master's control.

Kira scrubbed at her face. "Why do things always have to get complicated?"

*

Music blasted in Kira's ears, drowning out any distractions as she pelted along the trail, her mind still preoccupied with the previous day's revelations.

So many things to digest. So many ways her life had become more and less complicated.

In the end, she decided to set the Tuann and their mysterious enemy of old aside. There wasn't much she could do about the information. All she had was a child's memories, taken from a turbulent time in her history.

Nothing could be done at this point. Baseless speculation would be more likely to cause harm than good.

The morning held a crisp chill, the temperature perfect, a runner's dream. Not too hot that you felt like you were swimming in sweat, but also not cold enough to steal your motivation.

Kira's breath plumed in front of her as she picked up her pace, Finn stretching to match.

She planted a hand on a fallen log, using it to spring over the obstacle, Finn flipping over it with an effortless grace she couldn't help but admire.

They both noticed a shift in the atmosphere at the same time. A slight thread of wrongness that didn't belong. Danger lurking in the shadows as if it had a right to be there.

Kira and Finn slowed to a stop, sharing a glance as they focused on what had set off their instincts.

The trees practically quivered with tension.

Even Kira's basic grasp of *ki* and its nuances told her something was wrong. The currents she'd begun to sense in the world around her were disturbed. Something deadly had made an appearance.

Yodeling howls split the silence.

"Are those—" Kira started.

"Yes, *tala* dogs," Finn confirmed, sounding grim.

The *tala* dog was one of those predators Kira warned Joule hunted the forest at night. A cross between a wolf and a boar if they'd been sired by an armored tank—the *tala* dog was dangerous, hard to kill, and surprisingly cunning.

They were also nocturnal. For them to be hunting during the day and this close to the Tuann training courses was unusual.

"Stay here," Finn ordered.

Kira snorted, already racing after him. Yeah, like she was going to do that.

He shot her a hard look but didn't pause to argue.

Together, they ghosted through the trees. For once, the forest didn't fight against her as she eased through it, branches teasing her hair as they bent to make way instead of blocking her path.

Not a single twig cracked underfoot, the barest rustle of leaves was inaudible, nothing to announce their passage to the foe ahead.

As if they'd done it a hundred times, Kira and Finn split from each other, the distance between them widening as they worked through the forest.

A wail of pain changed into a roar of rage that shook the trees.

Kira stopped. That wasn't a *tala* dog.

No, this sound was one she recognized, though she'd never experienced it while in this form.

Finn came to a halt, using the trees as cover as he stopped to observe the scene. Kira did the same several feet away, peering at the dirt running path she usually used.

Right now, it was far from empty.

Two *tala* dogs circled their prey, their heads lowered as they fixed hungry gazes on their target. The *tala* dogs were massive, their shoulders reaching Kira's chest. Armored plates protected their vital spots and tusks curled out from their mouth as furry ears pricked and rotated as they communicated with each other.

To the right, Kira caught sight of several bodies, red dotting them.

A primus stood between the *tala* dogs and the initiates, his lips parted as he showed his fangs. Larger than Kira's primus form by at least a foot, he was built for power.

Runes and swooping lines covered skin the color of ebony. Bright yellow eyes stared out of a face that no longer looked entirely Tuann, his change more drastic than Kira's. He had a blunt nose, his lower fangs more pronounced so it looked like he had an underbite. His hair was shaggy and long, almost a mane.

And he had a tail.

That was all Kira had time to observe as he burst into movement, grabbing one of the mammoth dogs and flinging it aside. A high-pitched yelp left the creature as it hit a tree and crashed to the ground.

Impressive.

Her primus might have been able to kill the *tala* dogs, but it wouldn't have been able to fling them around like they were children's toys.

The creature's mate attacked, leaping onto the primus's back. It used claws and tusks to try to maim the primus, who was having none of that. He reached around, grabbing the dog and slamming it into the ground.

Kira remained motionless, thinking it was over.

Muffled sobbing reached her. She stiffened as the primus went still, his head lifting, those yellow eyes with slit pupils focusing on something to her left.

Kira shifted, her stomach dropping as Joule's terrified face came into view. His arms quivered as he fought to hold a *ki* shield in place. Visible cracks ran through its surface, testament to the blows he'd already fended off.

Blake lay on the ground at Joule's feet, unconscious and with his right side covered in blood. Aeron and Rheya stood at Joule's back, their faces bloodless from the same fear that covered Joule's.

It wouldn't be long before Joule's strength failed him, and the shield collapsed, exposing those inside it to the primus.

"Jin, we have a slight problem," Kira whispered.

The primus took a step forward.

Determination settled on Joule's face, the shield growing brighter as he pumped more *ki* into it.

She'd say this for the kid. He was brave. One day, when he grew up, his people would be lucky to have him as their shield. Until then, it was up to her to make sure he survived.

"What do you mean there's a problem? I thought you were supposed to be running." There was a pause, Jin's suspicion crackling through their link. "You did go running, right?"

"Yes," Kira growled, her eyes not leaving the primus as he inched closer.

"What's the problem then?"

"Primus."

There was a beat of silence. "Say that again. I couldn't have heard what I thought I heard."

"You're not hearing things."

Jin swore, his curses accompanying the primus as he stalked toward the initiates. "I don't suppose you could leave it be?"

"No."

Jin's muttered curses were unmistakable as the primus launched into a sprint.

No more time to wait.

"Finn, make sure the *tala* dogs are taken care of," Kira ordered, leaving her cover.

She didn't wait to see if he agreed, her mind already on what needed to happen.

Her field of focus narrowed. In seconds, she cataloged possible weaknesses.

Taking it head on would be foolish, if not impossible. Which meant she was going to have to be smart and fast. And very, very lucky.

"I take it from your sudden silence, elevated breathing, and increased heartbeat, you've decided engaging the primus without a proper plan was the way to go," Jin snarled.

Kira was too preoccupied with not dying to give him an appropriate response.

Best way to get a primus's attention was through pain.

The distance between them narrowed. Fifteen feet. Ten. Five.

Warning filled Joule's face as he caught sight of her. She ignored him, already mid-leap.

She landed on the primus's back, throwing her weight to the side. They tipped, the primus falling. She let go, hitting the ground and rolling before landing on her feet.

A bellow of surprise left the primus.

"Come on, big guy. Let's see what you've got," Kira snarled, facing him.

Take the bait. Come on.

"Oh, that's smart. Let's anger the big, dangerous beast," Jin groused.

The primus shook his head. Confused eyes came up to find Kira's.

She didn't know how much of the world registered for him. During her transformation, it was like a haze descended. She was still her on some level, but every primal instinct was dialed up to the max.

It hadn't always been that way. The first time she took primus form, she'd blacked out, only piecing together what happened from other's accounts and snippets of memories that came to her much later.

Judging by Joule's and the other initiates presence, she was betting this Tuann didn't have a lot, if any, experience with the form. He was likely one of the initiates who'd been attacked by the *tala* dogs, fear and pain catapulting him into the form.

His control would be nonexistent. Without something to fight, he'd attack randomly. She needed to get him away from the rest before that happened.

The primus's lips lifted in a snarl, and his head lowered. He charged. Kira spun out of the way, sharp satisfaction filling her as he careened head first into a tree.

Not the brightest of lightbulbs.

Primus form came with increased power and strength. It was ideal for war, but she knew it took trial and error to use effectively.

Kira waited as he lumbered to his feet, smashing his fist into the tree that had offended him. It splintered.

If his primus was anything like hers, his prey drive would be all-consuming—especially since she'd thwarted him once. He'd fixate and be drawn into the hunt. He wouldn't be able to help it.

Kira's grin held anticipation. *Well, buckle up, buttercup, this was going to be a frustrating experience in delayed gratification.*

A puff of air escaped him, his hands opening and shutting as if anticipating burying his claws in her flesh.

Kira's wave was taunting as she sprinted for the trees, calling over her shoulder. "Let's play follow the leader, shall we?"

The roar of a predator denied its prey proved her gamble had paid off.

Her smile fell from her lips as her pace flattened into a sprint. Now that she'd gotten its attention, it was time to see how fast he was.

Kira didn't let concern over the rest distract her. Finn would take care of them—or he wouldn't. Either way, their fate was out of her hands. All she could do was hold up her end of things. That was the only thing you could do in war. Do your part while hoping the next person down the line did theirs.

Underbrush cracked and rustled behind her. He was gaining.

Kira maintained her current speed. Getting too far in front of him would be risky. If he got distracted or stumbled on another Tuann, the situation could turn deadly.

Baiting. Whoever thought she'd be on this end of it?

The number of times she'd lost control of the primus form could be counted on one hand. You didn't even have to use all your fingers.

The concept was familiar as it was for all Curs. It only had to happen once for them to institute a protocol. Of course, it hinged on being on a warship where airlocks could be used as traps, and a berserker Kira could be spaced if it looked like she was going to compromise the integrity of the ship.

Sadly, no handy airlocks lurked in these trees.

"Do you have a plan or are you going to run around all day?" Jin asked.

While his tone was sarcastic, Kira could hear the tightness in Jin's voice.

"Working on it."

"Work faster. He's closing on you."

The smallest whisper of instinct warned Kira. She planted a foot, using it to launch herself sideways. The primus tore out of the bushes, his claws tearing into the trunk of the tree where she'd stood seconds before.

He whirled, swiping at her, his claws nearly cleaving her head from her shoulders. She dropped, rolling and gaining her feet in the next instant.

Reaching for her *ki* was instinctive—and misguided. Her vision narrowed, black eating away at the edges. Her head throbbed a warning as she rebounded off that glass wall.

"Kira!" Jin screamed, his voice sounding like it was coming from a distance.

Instinct took over. She ducked, then raced forward, running two steps up the tree before pushing off, flipping in midair and kicking the primus in the head.

She landed several feet away, chest heaving as he shook his head as if batting away a fly. His tail thrashed. Good to know her blow hadn't even budged him. More evidence a physical confrontation wouldn't end well for her.

"What the hell was that?" Jin demanded.

Kira thumped her bracelet. "I tried to use *ki*. It didn't work."

"No shit. You haven't been able to draw *ki* since Quillon put that on you."

Not for the first time, frustration ate at her. Weakness had never been something she accepted. That she had no choice at the moment, galled.

The primus attacked in the next second, leaving her no further room for self-pity. She was too preoccupied with surviving.

"Find a way to get this off me," Kira ordered, evading. She used the trees as obstacles, putting several between her and the primus.

She ran toward one, using the trunk to propel herself higher. She caught a branch and swung herself up.

"No dice. You don't have the time. You'll have to figure another way out of this," Jin said.

Kira made a grumbling noise, going still as the primus crossed under her position.

He sniffed the air, his eyes lifting abruptly to meet hers.

"Don't think you're special," she told him. She held up the arm with the bracelet. "If I didn't have this on, I could do that too."

There wasn't even a glimmer of reaction in his gaze. It was like speaking to a mindless beast.

"Oof, you really are gone, aren't you?" Kira said.

Even when lost to madness, no one had ever compared her to a beast. Her primus form was never stupid. It possessed a diabolical cunning, making her difficult to bait. It was also what made her such a threat to the enemy.

The primus inhaled, its mouth dropping as a roar filled its chest. A slow rumble built, deeper and deeper, a freight train barreling toward her. The pressure in the air condensed, spearing away from the primus in a blast. The tree branch Kira perched on splintered as she leaped away from it.

Kira tumbled to the ground, barely landing upright.

"What was that?" Jin shouted.

She didn't get the chance to answer as the primus charged. There was no time to dodge. Kira threw her arms up to block as its fist smashed into her, desperation exploding out of her.

The air millimeters in front of her forearms shivered, the faintest existence of a *ki* shield taking the brunt of the blow. It popped, and his fist landed on her arms. Kira flew, her spine hitting a tree. She stumbled, somehow managing to remain on her feet.

The primus panted as its yellow eyes glared.

Kira shook her arms out, pain running their lengths. The *ki* shield might have protected her for the most part, taking the majority of the force, but she'd still felt that blow.

A shiver worked through her. If she took one of those head on, it would shatter her bones.

"Good news and bad news," Kira said, not taking her eyes off the primus. "I finally used *ki*. Bad news—he can too."

"How is that fair?" Jin asked in outrage. "That form is already dangerous enough without being able to use *ki* too."

The primus rushed her; claws extended as if it planned to dig out her guts by way of her stomach. She slid to the right with a light laugh. "Better luck next time, little puppy."

"Are you purposely trying to enrage it?" Jin snapped.

Kira took off, the primus following close behind. "I need it mad. That'll keep it entirely focused on me."

"Well, good job. You succeeded."

Yes, she had. Now she had to figure out what to do with it.

Kira darted through the trees, the primus only feet behind her, as she considered her options. Luring it to anywhere populated was a no go. At this point, escaping to leave it wandering the forest was also impossible. She doubted she'd be able to outrun him.

Gradually, the scenery grew familiar. She swerved right, already knowing what she'd find. Her feet touched a section of the running path she didn't normally bother with since it led right to the section of the forest filled with drones.

Kira grinned, a plan forming.

"Where are you going?" Jin asked. "The archway and safety are in the opposite direction.

"I'm not going there," she told him.

He was silent several seconds as he worked through her logic. "The course?"

She grunted.

"Is that wise?"

"Probably not, but I don't have a better idea, do you?"

Silence crackled over the line.

"You can do this, Kira." There was certainty in Jin's voice, even if she detected a trace of fear.

Fear was okay. It kept you sharp. Made you faster. Letting fear overwhelm you was not good. Panic made you miss things.

"If you could hack the course, that would be great," Kira said.

"You think the drones can slow the primus down," Jin guessed.

He didn't wait for her to answer, already thinking out loud. "The settings the last time you ran one of these were too low to do more than irritate it. I think I can boost their power."

Jin went quiet as he worked.

Kira rounded a bend in the trail, trees rushing by as the shimmery haze of air marking the boundary of the course came into view. Whatever Jin was going to do needed to happen fast.

"I'm in the system. Programming the drones to a higher setting will be easy, but I'll be locked out of their controls as soon as the course starts. It will be extremely painful, possibly debilitating if you're not fast enough to evade their fire."

Kira allowed herself a bloodthirsty smile. She loved it when a plan came together.

The simple gate of the course appeared twenty feet away, the welcome sight of it marred by the presence of Maida and her initiates next to it.

Kira raced toward them, considering and discarding her options. Trying to change course now ran the risk of the primus fixating on those in front of her. Maida might be able to hold her own, but Kira didn't know the other woman well enough to say for sure.

Confusion crossed the initiates' faces until they caught sight of the primus chasing her.

Maida screamed, "Shield."

The initiates hesitated for only a second before *ki* shields popped into existence.

Runes around the gate lit up as a chime sounded, announcing the course's start. Maida's eyes widened in realization, her gaze moving from Kira to the course. She cursed, whirling and yanking a practice blade out of the closest initiate's hands.

Kira drew closer, only feet separating them.

Maida twisted, tossing the sword at Kira. It tumbled through the air, almost in slow motion.

Kira snatched it up.

The primus's presence grew larger behind her, until she could practically feel his breath on her neck. Some instinct warned her.

Kira sat, sliding through the gate as the primus sailed over her. He tumbled to the ground and rolled.

The gate snapped closed, the intangible barrier around its perimeter hardening until it was impermeable, locking the primus and Kira inside. There would be no escape until she crossed the gate on the other side of the course, a good three miles away.

All around her, drones woke up, coming out of their hiding places, one goal in their mind. Seek and destroy.

Kira tested the sword's weight before eyeing her foe. "Let the games begin."

TWELVE

THE PRIMUS CLIMBED to his feet, thunder filling his throat.

Kira watched him carefully, even as her senses detected faint flickers of movement as the drones started toward them. There was a swarm of them forming, many more than the last time she'd stood on a course like this. Their nearly inaudible buzz shook the leaves as they started their run.

"Be careful, Kira," Jin warned. "Death is unlikely but possible."

"I'll manage."

Somehow.

There was no other choice. She didn't want any further unnecessary deaths on her conscience. If she had to suffer a little pain, so be it.

The primus pounded over the ground toward her.

Kira let him come.

Ten feet. Five. Three.

A drone drifted from the shadows; its weapons already locked on the primus. Laser fire arced toward him, hitting his torso from three different directions.

It was the distraction Kira needed. She dodged the two bolts aimed at her, breaking off for the trees. The ground dissolved under her feet. She propelled herself to the side, barely grabbing onto a stump. She pulled herself up and took off again, never settling in one place long enough to fall afoul of the traps, never pausing for the drones to target her.

Attracted to his commotion, the drones swarmed the primus, ignoring the howls of fury and the repeated attempts to destroy them.

They were unrelenting, even when the primus leaped, catching one and using it to club another until it was nothing but scraps of metal.

Still, the drones came.

Whatever setting Jin had chosen, it was a doozy.

Even Kira had trouble, every bit of her attention and skill going to avoiding being turned into a pincushion.

The drones' sizes varied. Some as small as her fist; others as big as a beach ball.

Not all flew. Kira nearly got tagged by two as they snaked across the ground, their movements somewhere between a centipede and a snake.

Kira jerked back as one dangled in front of her, its lower body curled around an upper branch. Light rippled across its smooth sightless head as its mouth opened, spewing a web.

Kira's blade flashed up, knocking it aside. She changed course, barely avoiding the laser fire of its brethren.

She streaked through the trees, finding her way into the canopy. Danger brushed across Kira's senses. She twisted sideways as red lanced from a hollow in the tree. She wasn't fast enough, the laser catching her upper bicep in what would have been a flesh wound had this been real.

A cry of agony tore from Kira, pain searing her flesh.

"Damn, that felt like a Tsavitee fire lance," Kira panted, swallowing any further sounds as she gingerly touched the arm, half-expecting blood and a gaping tear. To her surprise, the flesh was whole, except for a single red mark where the laser had grazed her.

"You really outdid yourself with these." Kira rested her head against the tree trunk as she took a moment to catch her breath. She hated to think what a full hit would do to her.

"I calculated based on your primus's known tolerances," he told her.

Probably a good call.

Pained bellows from beneath drew Kira's attention. Where she had relied on stealth and the path of least resistance to make her way through the trees, the primus had decided on brute strength.

The drones had acted accordingly, sensing the primus as the bigger threat.

Kira was more than happy to let them do the work for her. She made her way through the canopy, relying on instinct and experience to tell her when danger was near.

Unsurprisingly, Kira found the primus had been overwhelmed by the swarm of drones. He was going to lose. It was simply a matter of time.

Kira straightened, careful not to draw the drone's attention. It was time to find the second gate and make her way to safety.

A low moan of pain and a heavy thump had her pausing as the primus collapsed face down into the dirt. His form dissolved to reveal Devon.

The drones' laser fire didn't abate, despite his change. Strike after strike landed on unprotected flesh.

Kira hardened her heart against empathy. Better him than her.

Ahead lay safety. Below, pain. The smart move—the only move—would be to find the exit while the drones were still distracted. Out there, she could shut down the course.

It'd likely be painful for Devon, but sometimes pain was necessary.

"Kira, I'm reading you as stationary. The exit is right there. Get out."

A broken moan of agony drifted up from below.

Kira closed her eyes.

Walk forward. You don't have to help. Jin said death was unlikely. Take the chance.

Leaves rustled as a drone took position behind her, her inaction giving it an opening.

"Jin, play me some music. Something with a powerful beat," Kira said, backflipping over the drone as it opened fire. She fell toward the ground as the rest moved in for the kill.

Kira landed in a crouch on one drone, her sword spearing through it. Music blared in her ears as electricity crackled, the sparks illuminating the dark interior of the forest.

Kira ripped her sword free in the next instant, flipping off the drone to place herself between it and Devon.

The rest paused, assessing the new and unexpected threat.

Kira's grip tightened on the sword, her gaze on the drones as they reconfigured.

This was going to hurt. A lot.

Kira bared her teeth. "Bring it."

Between one breath and the next, the drones lit up the forest. Their lasers swam through the air, a merciless storm of fire. Kira's body moved without conscious thought, acting on muscle memory. The blade cut the air as she parried, over and over again, catching and knocking the lasers away from her and Devon.

Patience crouched in the back of her mind. Panic had no place here.

She'd do what she could and wait for her opportunity.

Right now, she was pinned down—defenseless—but all she needed was the smallest of windows. That would be when she struck.

Until then, her mission was to survive and protect the man behind her with everything she had. Standing between him and the brunt of the drones' full attack.

Her movements were sharp. Crisp. Not even a single gesture wasted as the blade spun.

Behind her, Devon stirred.

She caught an energy bolt with the flat of her blade, shouting, "Can you move?"

Devon glanced up, his eyes widening in confusion as he took in the swarm of drones. He fought to push himself upright, fear mixed with stubbornness on his face.

A drone strayed close, breaking formation. Kira lashed out, slashing it in two. The pieces shot apart, striking two other drones. They exploded.

Fierce satisfaction filled Kira at the destruction. More drones lined up, replacing the three she had destroyed.

"Not going to let this be easy, I take it," Kira told them.

That was all right. She was used to no-win situations.

A glance at Devon told her running was out. He'd be lucky if he remained conscious for the next few minutes.

"Get under the tree roots," she ordered. They'd provide a little protection at least, make it so she only had to defend herself and not the both of them.

Devon moved to comply, for once not arguing. Kira struggled with impatience at his slowness, knowing he probably couldn't crawl any faster.

A bolt hit the sword, accompanied by a splintering noise. A large crack ran up the length of wood as the energy she'd deflected finally exceeded the practice blade's capacity.

Kira cursed, grabbing one broken piece and flinging it into a waiting drone.

Weaponless and out of options, Kira settled into a defensive stance, bracing as she raised her arms to protect her vital spots, ducking behind them like a turtle in a shell.

Energy bolts hammered into her unprotected arms, pain shredding her nerve endings and stealing her breath.

Still, she didn't waver. She didn't fall.

She stood there, and she took it.

"I am Kira Forrest, and I do not break so easily," she told them.

Tough words when it took everything she had to remain standing.

Kira locked her knees, leaning into the laser fire, chanting an old mantra. Embrace the pain. Make it part of you. Yearn for it like you do a good cup of chai on a cold day.

When the body threatened to collapse, sometimes the mind had to step in and give it a swift kick in the ass.

She held on, fire eating away at her arms. Her mind gibbered an endless litany of "it hurts, it hurts, it hurts."

Kira didn't care. She would not fall, not while there was a speck of life in her body.

In that moment, she was no longer standing in a forest on a planet her ancestors had claimed. She was in another place, defenseless young behind her. The drones wore the faces of her enemies—and they were hungry.

Falling meant losing the people she loved. Too much had already been taken from her.

Just when she'd been forced to her knees under the onslaught, she sensed the opportunity she'd been waiting for.

There—a break in the pattern as the drones closed in, intent on the kill. Victory was at hand.

They inched closer and closer, their bolts containing the force of a tank. Still, Kira waited, gathering strength, coiling it deep inside as she waited with the patience of a spider whose victims had neared her web.

Not yet. She'd only get one chance at this.

Now.

Kira sprang, one hand lashing out to catch the first drone. Its electric defenses flared, her hand going numb. She winced but didn't let go, grasping its side and turning its weapon on the rest.

The smell of burned flesh reached her, and still she didn't relent as she took aim at her previous hunters, now the prey.

Drones exploded, short-circuiting in quick order.

The drone in her hand buzzed. Kira heaved it at another, not even pausing to watch the two destroy each other before leaping up to find another prey.

Seconds later, the clearing lay still. Smoke curled along the edges. Drone carcasses littered the ground. Kira panted, unable to drop her guard, waiting for the next attack.

None came.

Her breathing slowed, and she allowed herself to start to believe it was over. By some miracle, she'd managed to win.

The world stilled, the faintest hint of a presence dropping out of the trees where it'd been hiding.

Kira twisted, her hand flashing out as she flung the remains of the sword hilt at the last drone.

A dark shape flew from the side, and an en-blade split the drone in two as her broken practice sword embedded itself into the drone's casing.

Graydon's chest heaved, a feral look in his eyes as he removed his blade from the drone.

"You're late," Kira told him.

Rage flashed across his face before being buried. Graydon straightened, danger rolling off him, carrying an almost tangible kiss of steel.

This was a man very much in touch with his inner monster. The primus she'd faced wasn't anywhere near as terrifying as Graydon as his gaze lingered on the welts dotting every inch of exposed flesh.

Kira was too exhausted to move or even pretend she was in better shape than she was. Every part of her throbbed. Fine tremors shook her hands.

At long last Graydon inhaled, shaking himself slightly before aiming a dangerous smile her way. "I didn't want to take your spotlight."

Kira couldn't even summon the ghost of a grimace to pretend at disdain. She was glad to see him. This fight had been close. Much closer than she wanted to think about. She'd danced along the abyss's edge and barely escaped.

If the pattern hadn't broken, she wasn't sure Graydon would have arrived in time to save anything.

"I look forward to experiencing the form your gratitude takes for saving your ass," Graydon told her, his pleasant expression not touching the darkness in his eyes.

Finn arrived, appearing out of the trees like a ghost. He took in Kira's state, a heavy look dropping over his face. She could practically read his thoughts, feel his self-recrimination that she was hurt on his watch.

"The kids?" she asked.

"Safe. I killed the *tala* dogs and summoned help for the injured."

The tight feeling in her stomach that had been there since she'd left Joule behind loosened. Her nod was sharp, conveying her gratitude.

"Thanks," she told him. "I couldn't have done this without you."

He might not like that she'd drawn the primus off, but his actions had likely saved the initiates. That was well worth any harsh feelings he might have.

His expression thawed the faintest bit, and his nod was slow. Graydon's oshota appeared out of the trees, Maida and several from Roake at their side.

With effort, Kira gathered herself, straightening with an internal wince. She might want to collapse into a puddle on the ground, but what would that say to her audience?

Right now, she looked like a badass. The evidence of her abilities strewn all around her. No need for anyone to see how much this had cost her.

Always keep them guessing, as Jin would say.

"You destroyed one drone," she told Graydon. "Don't go getting a big head about it, or else I'll point out all the ones you didn't destroy."

Those who'd joined them looked at the truth of her words. Kira knew how she must look, her skin covered in red welts, her clothing torn and dirty, broken drones all around her like a scene out of a holovid science fiction nightmare.

Now to seal her badassery for the ages. Walking toward Graydon was an effort every bone and muscle in her body protested, her vision going gray along the edges, her head feeling like it was stuffed with cotton.

Graydon remained motionless as she pulled abreast. "We're going to have a long conversation about this later."

Kira had hit her wall, not even those dire words could summon more than faint alarm. "But not now."

The skin around his eyes tightened. "No, not now."

Good. Whatever had put that look on his face could wait.

Walking out of here was going to be a bitch and a half.

Disbelief and awe were on the faces of those she moved past.

Kira wavered, almost toppling as she forced her feet to move. Finding a deep dark hole where she could rest and regain her strength had become a priority.

Willpower only took you so far, and she'd just hit the end of hers.

Graydon's hand settled under her elbow. "Don't spoil your little demonstration by collapsing now."

"Easier said than done."

Graydon raised his voice, speaking to their audience. "Clean up this mess and get Devon to the healers." To Kira, he murmured, "So you do have a limit; how very human of you."

Kira snarled silently. She forced one foot in front of the other, then did it again and again. The tree line closing with agonizing slowness.

Finally, they were there. Kira made it two steps into its cover before her legs collapsed.

Graydon caught her as she fell, lifting her to cradle her against his chest. "Good girl."

He strode through the trees, his pace fast as her head lolled on his shoulder. She was too spent to give a token protest. She'd make sure to do that later when she could move her limbs again.

Over his shoulder, Kira caught the concerned look Finn and Amila shared, worry written on their faces.

The path she'd taken through the trees had seemed so short with the primus chasing her, but now it felt never-ending as Kira struggled not to lose consciousness.

Graydon jostled her when her eyes closed for a second time. She blinked slowly up at him.

Concern and anger warred in his expression. "What possessed you to take on a primus?"

She forced herself out of the darkness's embrace. Tempting as it was to slip away and escape the pain radiating through her body—her very cells feeling swollen and tender—she couldn't. Not until she was safe.

Her lips lifted in a halfhearted grin. "I don't think I did so bad, considering I can't reach my *ki*."

Graydon's pace increased, not quite running. Her old drill instructor would have said he was moving with a purpose.

Kira nodded off, waking herself at the last second.

"Not far now," he assured her. "That course is meant to be taken with two oshota pods. Not by a single woman with suicidal impulses."

"I see the conversation you wanted to have couldn't wait," Kira observed, her eyes drifting shut. Her words slurred. "I got skillz."

Graydon bounced her in his arms, jarring her awake. "No, you don't get to fall asleep now. Stay awake."

Kira moaned. So annoying.

"At least this time, I saved you. I think I deserve a reward," Graydon said, his voice tight.

Kira knew what he was trying to do. He wanted a fight.

It worked. From somewhere, she summoned enough strength to fix him with a glare. "Bullshit, you killed one. I destroyed nearly two dozen."

"In battle, it doesn't matter how many you kill if the last enemy still gets you," Graydon taunted.

A thin growl escaped her. "I would have had it. You didn't need to interfere."

He raised an arrogant eyebrow. "Are you sure? Because it looked to me like you needed saving."

"You should take off those goggles you're wearing. They're impeding your vision," Kira said, disappointed to find her words lacked the appropriate bite.

"I'd like to know how you managed to reset the parameters while being chased by an infuriated primus," Graydon said in a silky voice.

"I thought we weren't doing this now."

His smile held teeth. "Soon then."

Her head sagged. No amount of taunting or will power was going to keep her upright much longer.

"We're there." He set her on her feet.

"Oh goody," Kira muttered. Resignation filled her.

They moved out of the cover of the trees, Kira taking those last few steps on her own, her pace slow and measured.

"See the conveyance," Graydon murmured. "Make it there, and you're done."

She could do that. She'd pay for it later, but she could do it.

The trek across the small distance felt interminable. The edges of her vision were fading as Graydon snapped a few words. The Roake near the conveyance moved, opening the door and stepping back.

Graydon was careful not to touch her during the forced march.

Kira reached the conveyance and stopped, staring at the two stairs standing between her and blessed unconsciousness. They might as well have been a mountain guarded by a fast-moving river, that was how much of an obstacle they presented.

"One step at a time," Graydon murmured.

One step at a time. Like everything else in life. Focus on the next thing. Only then could you look up.

Kira didn't know how she made it up the steps, her vision entirely gone, her head spinning. Finally, she collapsed inside, Graydon crowding in after her. She was past caring who saw or judged. Her body was done.

Darkness reached up for her; she reached back.

*

Kira groaned on her return to consciousness. Her body hurt, but not to the extent it should have. Before, it had felt like she'd burned off a couple of layers of skin. Now, she felt better than she had any right to, not good as new, but close.

She blinked up at a strange ceiling.

"Jin, we're going to need to talk about what you term non-lethal," she muttered.

She sighed when he didn't answer. She wasn't surprised since the comms had gone dead somewhere in the middle of that last barrage, the energy coursing through her system from the laser fire probably shorting them out.

Kira shifted in the comfortable bed, taking in her surroundings. This wasn't her tiny, dark room in the initiates hall, nor was it the med bay.

She'd been an unwilling guest of too many a hospital room not to recognize when she was in one. None of those had looked anywhere near as inviting as this.

The walls were stone, the furnishings comfortable and of obvious quality. Narrow windows marched along one wall, and a fireplace took up one corner, the fire within bringing the comforting smell of burning wood as it chased away any lingering chill.

Unlike Luatha, which seemed to prefer bright whites, the room had a color palette that was warm and welcoming. Homey, for lack of a better word.

This was the sort of place you'd look forward to coming home to at the end of the day.

It was someone's room, Kira decided as her gaze found the man sitting in a cozy-looking chair next to the bed. He stared at something in his lap.

Kira almost didn't recognize him without his synth armor.

She started to sit up but didn't make it far before the pain that had been absent upon waking made itself known.

"I'd take it easy," the man said, not looking up. "The healers did a lot, but it'll take more than twenty-eight hours of rest for you to heal."

Kira relaxed into the bed and stared at the man, her gaze roving over familiar features, ones she saw in the mirror every day, ones nearly identical to the statue Graydon had showed her of the previous Overlord.

This man was older than the one who'd posed for the statue, the rigors that came from living a hard life stamped on his face, but the line of his jaw was the same, the set of his eyes. Hair so red it was nearly black was pulled away from his face, exposing the harsh lines of his features and the neatly trimmed beard he wore. She suspected that hair was nearly as unruly as her own.

A scar bisected one eyebrow, missing the eye, before continuing on to his cheek. Another smaller scar was visible on his forehead.

The man was huge, giving Graydon a run for the name Mountain. His long sleeves had been pushed up, exposing forearms corded with muscle. His chest was broad, his legs the size of tree trunks.

"Not even going to ask who I am?" Tawny, golden-colored eyes met hers.

Kira made herself more comfortable. "I know who you are."

The hair was a pretty good giveaway.

"And who is that?" the man asked calmly.

"The Overlord. My uncle."

And the orchestrator of current events. If not for him and this House, she'd be on her ship. Of course, she'd also still be slowly dying, so you couldn't win them all.

When he didn't speak, Kira continued, "Is this where you give me a speech about how you love me because I'm a child of your House and want only the best for me?"

Because if so, she'd pass.

"You're certainly your father's daughter," the man, whose name she still didn't know because he hadn't bothered to introduce himself, mused.

Kira didn't say anything, settling to watch and wait. Often people felt the need to fill the silence, their inane chatter revealing more than they wanted.

Kira preferred to let other people hang themselves with their words.

Usually, it worked. Not so much on this man who seemed to have taken a page out of her rule book.

The silence between them deepened.

"You're certainly as stubborn," he observed. It didn't sound like a compliment.

"What are you here for?" Kira asked.

This Overlord would be more difficult to manipulate than Liara. He wasn't an untried youth. He'd held his House together in the face of tragedy. Trying to deceive him would be like dipping a bleeding finger into a tank full of piranha. Dangerous and liable to end with her missing an arm before the end.

No, this man had more in common with Himoto. Circling in the shadows, arranging and pushing until events took the shape he wanted.

"Don't bother trying to pretend it's because I'm the daughter of your brother, and you want to give me a good life." Kira was many things, but a fool wasn't one of them. She had a hard time seeing the man before her as sentimental. Those emotions were often the first thing to go when faced with hardship. She had no doubt he had dealt with his fair share of that.

"My brother was the most important person to me in this world. Ensuring his daughter has a future is the least I can do for his memory," the man said.

"If you really care about my wellbeing, arrange passage to my ship," Kira challenged.

His lips curved. "You know that's not happening."

Kira lifted a shoulder. It was worth a shot.

"How long do you think you can keep me here?" Kira asked.

"I've already beaten Luatha's record by several weeks. Most would agree I'm not doing too bad."

Kira's eyes narrowed. He had a point, but in all that time, he had not once made any effort to see her. If he really cared about her because of her relation to his brother, you'd think he'd want to introduce himself. Maybe try to get to know her.

He hadn't. So, either he was lying, or there were things she didn't understand.

"I've been thinking about why you chose the warrior's path, and I think I understand now," he said after several moments.

Kira waited.

"You think passing the Trial of the Broken will get you what you want," he said.

"And what's that?" Kira asked.

"The respect of the House and sponsorship to the *adva ka*," her uncle said.

Kira wasn't concerned he'd guessed right. Graydon had done the same. Even an idiot would be able to see her motives.

"It's not a bad plan," the Overlord said, settling in his seat. "But the *uhva na* is simply the first hurdle on the way to the *adva ka*. If you pass, you'll be appointed a mentor. They will determine when you advance. Passing the *uhva na* won't solve all your problems."

"It's a start." That's all she needed.

Tuann law was clear on this point. Those who passed the *adva ka* achieved a certain level of freedom not available to those who hadn't. They could choose their course. Whether that was to pledge themselves to their old House or find a new one was up to them,

"As long as your path leads you to the Tuann," he said softly. "Right now, you think you will be able to leave and never return. That is a fallacy."

"Oh?" There was danger in Kira's tone. She didn't like threats—especially when they came from supposed family.

He shifted, his expression relaxing as if her response had assured him of something important. "The humans have something called an energy vampire in their myths, yes?"

Kira stared at him, not answering.

He continued with an air of finality. "It is as good an example as any. Tuann are dependent on our links with others and the Mea'Ave. One of the reasons your *ki* started to poison you was because you had no access to the Mea'Ave when grief broke your few connections. Spend too long away from the Mea'Ave or your brethren, and it will start happening again."

An instinctive denial filled Kira. "Quillon said it was because I used too much *ki* too quickly."

"He is right, but what he no doubt hesitated to tell you was that trauma starts the process," her uncle said. "Devastating loss coupled with an explosive release of *ki*. You never replaced any of those relationships, did you?"

Kira's gaze shifted away from him as she stared unseeing at the wall.

"Deprived of the emotional and physical links to others can cause a Tuann to fade. The Mea'Ave sustains us as we sustain it. You'll always be tied to us. Accept it as your due and adjust your goals to take that into account," he told her.

Her gaze snapped to his. "I'm ninety-two. For a human, that's not half bad."

He studied her, judging her seriousness. After a moment, he shook his head. "No, you're not the sort to give in. You've seen too much of death to be any other way." Hie expression filled with certainty. "You'll keep fighting because to do otherwise would dishonor those you've lost."

Quiet fell between them.

"Tell me I'm wrong," he challenged.

"You're wrong." There was no hesitation in Kira's answer.

"Liar." His chin dipped as a faint smile touched his lips.

Kira's jaw flexed, hating he knew her that well. He was right. She could no more let death take her than Jin could resist a challenge.

Her uncle reached out and touched the disrupter. "This can help you learn to manage your *ki*, but it can't change reality."

Kira held his gaze, unable to hide the stubbornness that refused to accept his words.

He sat back. "I'm sure you'll need time to come to terms with this."

There was no coming to terms. Kira wouldn't let her life be derailed. Even if what he said was true, she'd find a way around it. If she had to make regular visits to Tuann worlds to get her dose of Mea'Ave that's what she would do.

Her uncle's face was thoughtful as he considered her. "You've caused a stir. No one, not even an oshota, has ever attempted that course alone and walked away. You took a risk. The drones might not cause death, but they can burn out your mind."

"Maybe now you and yours will stop treating me like I'm a child in need of saving," Kira suggested.

His lips twisted. "I'm nearly two thousand years old as humans measure it. You'll always be a child to me."

Kira blinked, unable to compute the magnitude of his age. He looked maybe middle-aged, if she stretched it. The only clue to his long years was the press of experience hiding in his eyes. The sort that said he'd seen and done everything and lived to tell the tale.

"Didn't expect that, did you?" He seemed amused by her surprise. "The Tuann are an old race. Our children are rare and precious because of it."

The way he said it caught Kira's attention. "How many children did you lose to the Sorrowing?"

Harlow didn't answer, a blend of rage and pain, sorrow and sadness lingering in his expression. It was a cocktail Kira knew intimately.

"All of them," he finally revealed. "Every child we had. Over seventy in our House alone. The other Houses weren't as hard struck as ours, but they suffered losses as well. Until you were found, we thought all the children had died shortly after they disappeared."

No wonder they refused to let her go. To do so would be like reliving the Sorrowing all over again.

"Your father was so happy when he learned your mother was pregnant with you," Harlow said.

Kira quelled her instinctive desire to leap on his words and demand more. Her parents were little more than figments to her. Not quite real. Stories about fictional people that had little to do with Kira.

Despite that, she couldn't help wondering who these two strangers were. What they had been like.

"He called you his little miracle." Harlow's expression held a faint note of reminiscence. Memories of her father were happy ones.

Harlow focused on Kira. "Neither of your parents expected to fall in love with each other. Their union was a political match, arranged by the emperor to foster peace between Luatha and Roake."

"Did it work?" Kira asked.

Harlow's head tilted. "After a fashion. Liliana's sister, Leigha, was the Overlord, and from what I saw the two loved each other dearly. Leigha wouldn't have lightly considered an action that would have led to putting your mother in danger."

Kira read that as Leigha would act in the best interest of her House against her sister's new husband, even if it made her feel like crap inside. Such was the responsibility of being a leader. You didn't always get to act according to the needs of your heart.

"I'm guessing they managed to fall into something," Kira said.

Harlow inclined his head. "Against all odds. My brother and Liliana were a surprisingly good match. Harding was the gentler soul of the two. Not to say they weren't both warriors. Liliana was surprisingly well versed in the art of the blade given she came from a House comprised primarily of artisans."

"She was your friend," Kira guessed. The way he talked about her was too familiar for that of a near stranger, brother-in-law or not.

Harlow's lips quirked. "That surprises you."

Kira lifted a shoulder. "Roake hasn't exactly struck me as a warm and welcoming sort of place, and from the way you talk, it's obvious she would have had difficulty fitting in here."

"You'd think, but Liliana had a way about her." Harlow's gaze sharpened. "She dumped your father on his ass during their first meeting."

That startled a laugh from Kira, interest sparking.

Harlow put an elbow on the arm of the chair. "I thought Leigha was going to kill Liliana for that stunt. I've never seen an Overlord so torn between pride and fury. When Leigha told her to apologize, Liliana got this stubborn look on her face and refused. Said he'd got what he'd deserved."

"What had he done?" Kira asked.

Harlow paused, then shook his head. "I'm not even sure I know. That was Liliana, though. She had a code that only she understood. If you crossed it, she was always quick to let you know."

"I'm surprised your brother married her."

Harlow got this secretive smile on his face. "I'm not. Harding always said Liliana made him look at the world in a different way. She was his balance, and he hers."

Harlow focused on Kira. "He got her back in the end for dumping him on his ass. He spread *piri* dye on the handle of her en-blade. She managed to leave several streaks all over her face before she realized. It stayed there for nearly a month."

Sounded like something one of her old squad would have done to get back at someone.

"Harding used that time to work his way into her heart. It didn't stop the pranks, however, which became legendary," Harlow said. "They were both extremely competitive. Neither was the type to let something go."

"How long were they together?" Kira asked.

"Nearly a century."

Kira raised her eyebrows. She tensed as a thought occurred to her. "Did they have other children?"

Did she even now have a sibling running around Roake?

Harlow's gaze was steady as he considered her. "No. As I said, children are rare and precious for us. Since we live a very long time, there often isn't a strong urge to procreate. It's not uncommon for a couple to wait centuries before attempting to have children."

Kira plucked at the sheet covering her legs as she debated continuing this line of inquiry. There were questions she could ask. Questions she had thought often about, if she were honest with herself.

But, did she want the answers? She still didn't know.

"My name—" Kira stopped.

This was one of those things she waffled on. She had been Kira Forrest for so long. It was a name she'd picked for herself. A way of claiming her identity from those who'd tried to strip it from her.

Her younger self had thought the name Kira meant rebirth. An attractive sentiment to someone who had grown up in hell.

It was only later that she realized she'd added an r and changed the meaning entirely.

"Did they have a name in mind for me?"

Harlow's gaze was enigmatic. After what felt like an eternity, he inclined his head. "They did."

Kira squeezed her hands together, the question hovering on the tip of her tongue.

Harlow waited, letting her set the pace. If she wanted this piece of her past, she would have to claim it.

Before she could decide one way or the other, Graydon appeared in the threshold, breaking the moment between her and her uncle.

Kira slammed the lid on her questions, her walls coming up.

Good thing too, as Graydon filled the room with a roiling mass of emotions Kira struggled to decipher. Anger was there. Relief. Rage.

He observed the two of them with an implacable expression, finally offering, "I can come by later."

"You're here now; you might as well stay." The Overlord stirred, waving him inside. Graydon stepped into the room, the door closing behind him with a decisive thump.

The Overlord focused on Kira and changed the subject to one no less emotionally fraught. "The Emperor's Face tells me you were recovered from a camp. Did any other children survive?"

Kira was quiet for several beats. She needed to be very careful in how she answered this. For all that the Sorrowing happened decades ago, the wounds from it were still fresh. She had no desire to reopen them.

"I was the only child rescued by Himoto and his team that night,"

Kira said carefully.

The Overlord's face tightened as if he'd taken a blow. All expression smoothed out. "That's regrettable. Many of our people were hoping for a miracle."

Kira had nothing to say to that.

"Little Storm, I assume you have news," Kira's uncle said, addressing Graydon.

Kira couldn't help peering at the commander in interest. That was an unusual nickname. She never would have attributed it to him if not for hearing it for herself.

He stared impassively back, not betraying by even the flicker of an eyelash embarrassment for the name. Kira found she liked him better for it. Those who took themselves too seriously crumbled and broke in the end. You had to remember the good even when the bad was at your doorstep.

"Devon will make a full recovery," Graydon revealed. "I spoke with the other initiates. They all agreed if he hadn't taken primus form, the *tala* dogs would likely have slaughtered them. He's shaken but mostly unharmed."

"Do we know why they ventured so close?" the Overlord asked.

Graydon shook his head. "My people are investigating. There is evidence they were driven from their normal hunting ground, but it's circumstantial."

The Overlord nodded and rose. "I'll leave you two to talk. There are other matters requiring my attention."

Graydon murmured an agreement as the Overlord made his way to the doorway. He paused before opening it, fixing his attention on Kira. "I hope you'll consider what I said."

Kira lifted her chin, not answering. She'd do that, but she doubted he'd like the conclusion she would draw. People rarely did.

Harlow seemed to read that in her, nodding as if he understood what she didn't say. "When you're ready for the answers to the questions you're afraid to ask, I'll be waiting."

With that, the Overlord made his way out of the room, the door shutting behind him.

Graydon faced Kira, fury on his face. "We're going to have that talk now. Then we're going to discuss the military-grade drone gadding about in Roake's territory."

THIRTEEN

ALARM CHASED ACROSS Kira's face, disappearing as quickly as it had come. Nonchalant ease replaced it seconds later.

"What are you talking about?" she asked, managing to strike the perfect balance between confusion and bravado.

Graydon showed his teeth in a dangerous smile, catching the barely perceptible flinch before she could hide it. *That's right,* coli. *You're caught.*

There was no escaping it this time.

"Where. Is. He?"

Kira blinked innocently at him.

Graydon stared back. Not many tested him when he was in this mood. Most feared what he would do. Even if they hadn't been wary of the power he wielded as the Emperor's Face, they would have still considered him dangerous on a physical level.

He was the youngest chosen Face for a reason, and it wasn't because he was good at diplomacy.

Kira opened her mouth, a lie already forming. Graydon lifted a hand, cutting her off with a sharp gesture. "Careful, *coli*. Lying right now would be inadvisable."

He knew the drone was here. It had contacted him shortly after Kira started the course. The drone's warning was the only reason Graydon reached her in time. Even then, he'd been too late to prevent the ordeal she'd endured.

The reminder of his failure threatened to send his thoughts into a very dark place, and he felt a deep-seated rage building all over again.

Surprise lurked on Kira's face. Guilt. But no fear.

Graydon's mouth quirked unwillingly, the anger easing slightly. A good liar, she was not. It made the fact she'd built an entire life on deception and subterfuge all the more puzzling.

"Bring him out," Graydon said, unnervingly calm.

"Graydon," Kira started.

That snapped the thin tendril of patience he'd been holding onto. He shoved forward, ignoring her flinch.

He wasn't an untrained initiate she could run circles around or lie to without expecting severe repercussions.

He was the Emperor's Face, the highest position a Tuann could achieve except for Emperor. He wasn't someone to trifle with.

"Bring. Him. Out."

All expression on Kira's face leaked away.

"Jin. You might as well come out," Kira said emotionlessly.

Graydon didn't drop his guard. It would be dangerous to make the mistake of thinking she had been defeated.

Kira might have conceded for now, but soon enough, she'd return to challenging him on the simple basis that she could.

Silence thickened the air as they waited.

A rustle came from under the bed, the sheet hanging over its side stirring.

No one said anything as Jin revealed himself, rising until he hovered at eye level.

"Hey there, big guy," Jin said with an awkward laugh. "Long time, no see."

Graydon sent Kira a flat look. "You couldn't be this stupid."

Her mouth pulled up on one side. "I'd like to argue, but current company points to the fact I am."

Graydon's lips thinned and tightened. This was a disaster on so many levels.

"Do you have any idea what you've done?" Graydon asked Kira.

"I'm beginning to get the idea it isn't good," she said dryly.

Graydon stared at her, sending her a look that said "you think?"

She winced, reaching up and rubbing her forehead before her hands settled in her lap. She slumped, looking tired.

"He wasn't supposed to be seen." She sent the drone a hard look. "He had orders to remain in the room."

Jin hummed. "You're lucky I broke cover and sent the big guy your way. That last drone almost had you."

Kira opened her mouth to argue, and Graydon cut into the brewing argument with a hard look. "I don't care how I found out. I care that he's here where he isn't supposed to be."

"To be fair—Kira didn't know about my presence until it was too late. I did it all on my own," Jin said.

"Not helping," Kira shot at him.

"Maybe in your mind, but I think I'm being super helpful," Jin grumbled.

Graydon scrubbed his face, ignoring the interaction. If only he had walked away on Luatha, his life would be so much simpler.

"Does anyone else know about this?" he asked.

Guilt crossed Kira's face. He guessed what she was going to say before she said it.

"Finn."

Graydon found himself surprised the oshota had kept Kira's secret. Then again, considering his history, maybe not. The man would not willingly give up another of his charges unless circumstances were dire.

"And Raider," Kira finished.

Graydon stood in an explosive movement, prowling the length of the room and stopping at the window to stare out. The two behind him were quiet, leaving him to his thoughts.

If Graydon was smart, he'd inform Harlow and Roake of Jin's presence immediately. His credibility would be damaged, but he'd likely not suffer too much from this debacle. From this point on, he would have no plausible deniability. If Jin was discovered and Roake decided to take issue, Graydon would be treated as a traitor. Everything he'd worked for gone.

The whispered argument taking place behind him brought his attention to the troublemakers.

He faced them. Kira's mouth snapped shut as she regarded him with a mingling of defiance and understanding.

She expected him to tell Roake, he realized.

Nothing was ever easy with this woman. Perhaps that's why he found her endlessly fascinating. She was complicated, with cracks that made her even more beautiful for their presence. She'd make him work for every inch of progress.

But the reward would be worth it.

"You're going to owe me for this," Graydon informed her.

Wary distrust filled violet gray eyes he could lose himself in. "What are you saying?"

His smile this time held cunning. The expression wasn't nice and it wasn't easy. He found himself chuckling internally when her suspicion deepened.

"I'm not going to reveal his presence to Roake," he said.

"Why?"

He shook his head. Oh no, she wasn't getting that. He might not want to see her pretty head separated from her body, but that didn't mean he was going to trust her.

"My reasons are my own."

Kira's eyes were steady as she held his gaze. "There are many things I regret in this life. Jin isn't one of them."

Graydon was starting to see that. Had the drone been flesh and blood, their relationship would be admirable. That he was a machine made her reliance on him worrying, but that was a problem for another day.

Graydon approached the bed, running a finger along one of the faint red marks on the exposed skin of her shoulder. Kira shivered, unable to hide her response.

"You took a chance with this," Graydon informed her.

Stubbornness filled her expression. "I couldn't leave Devon."

And that was why Graydon found himself breaking a law that had been in place for centuries. Devon hadn't been especially kind to Kira, yet she'd stayed and protected him anyway.

Her selflessness was inspiring. All the more so because not many would have bothered.

"No, I suppose you couldn't," Graydon agreed.

Graydon made to rise, Kira's gaze lifting to follow him.

"Make sure he stays out of sight," Graydon informed her.

"And this thing I owe you?"

His grin flashed. "You'll find out soon enough."

He suspected she wouldn't be happy about the cost.

*

Kira waited until the door shut before whipping the nearest object at Jin. "What the hell is the matter with you? You told him?"

Jin spun out of the way. "What did you expect me to do? You were up against a primus. You might not know how terrifying it is to face one, but I do."

Kira's glare didn't ease. "You know he's going to use this as leverage to make us stay."

185

Jin let out a scornful sound. "Of course, he is. That's Tuann etiquette 101." Jin circled the bed, making sure to stay out of the range of any more missiles. "Just like I know you'll find a way to use this situation to your advantage."

Jin had a point. Some of Kira's anger drained away, and she slumped.

Graydon, for reasons of his own, had decided to keep her secret. It left them room to maneuver and plan.

A corner of her mind whispered she knew why he had chosen not to reveal Jin's presence. It was one she ignored.

As attractive as she might find Graydon, he wasn't for her.

Kira threw her legs over the bed, tentatively resting her balance on them until she was sure they'd hold her weight.

"What do you think about the *tala* dogs' role in this?" she asked.

Jin snorted. "I think it's pretty convenient a nocturnal animal decided to leave its territory to hunt prey in an active section of the forest. They might be a deadly predator, but they don't normally challenge Tuann."

His assessment fit with hers.

"Is it paranoia or fact when you see Tsavitee machinations around every corner?" Kira asked him.

Jin played devil's advocate. "You could be seeing things after Graydon's history lesson."

Kira nodded. Very true. Not every plot or accident in her life led to them.

"But then, it's happened before. More than once," Jin said.

Also true.

"What do we do?" Jin asked.

"I'm thinking on it."

Jin   sighed.   "That's   what   worries   me."

*

Kira hovered at the edge of Quillon's med bay, torn between crossing into his domain and leaving. Her daily treatments had ended shortly before her encounter with the primus, and there was no real reason for her presence here.

It had been over a day since she'd woken up with Harlow keeping vigil.

Since then, she'd decided she had questions. Many, many questions. Somehow, much to her surprise, Quillon had become one of the few she trusted to give her the answers she needed.

"If you're going to linger, you might as well do it inside," Elodie said from the end of the hall.

The healer continued toward her, brushing past Kira and Finn with barely a glance.

The healer's presence gave Kira the incentive she needed to cross the threshold. She followed as Elodie headed for a table with the bag she was carrying. The healer reached inside, pulling out several delicious smelling containers of food and setting them on the table.

"I didn't realize you had a treatment, so there isn't much. You're welcome to what food we have," Elodie said without looking up.

"I don't have an appointment today. I don't expect you to feed me," Kira said, one finger tapping restlessly against her thigh.

Since the first confrontation when Kira had insisted Elodie not be privy to the details of her diagnosis, the healer had made herself noticeably absent during Kira's morning treatments.

Elodie finally looked up. "In that case, Quillon should be here soon. I'm sure you'll want to wait until he returns."

Kira nodded, drifting around the room as Elodie sat and began serving herself a spoonful of the many dishes she'd unpacked.

Finn waited next to the door, his expression typically blank.

"It was brave, what you did for Devon," Elodie said after several minutes. Her eyes lingered on the inhibitor still locked around Kira's wrist. "Stupid with that hampering you, but brave all the same."

"You're not the first person who has said something to that effect," Kira admitted.

Elodie snorted and sat back. "I can imagine. They do like to harp on a person."

Kira sent a look at the healer, surprised to hear such a sentiment echoed by one of Roake's members. She'd thought they all happily toed the same line.

Elodie laughed. "I'll admit it's not always easy to live with these people, having them critique your decisions like a bunch of overprotective siblings."

"Then why do it?" Kira asked.

Elodie sobered. "Because the alternative is far worse. To be alone? To have no one care enough to call you on your bullshit? I'll take the small irritations this lot gives me any day over such a bleak existence."

Kira considered her words. "Fair point."

Solitude—true solitude—wasn't easy. It preyed on the soul, filing it down to the bare bones. Lucky for Kira, she wasn't alone. She had Jin. Always.

"Did you ever consider following Quillon's path?" Kira asked.

Elodie snorted and busied herself with the food. "No."

"But you could—if you wanted to."

This time Elodie speared her with a look, a frown wrinkling her forehead as she studied Kira. "I could. If I indicated a leaning toward that direction, I could submit myself to the Trial of the Broken and request a *seon'yer* who would prepare me for that life."

"But you don't," Kira said slowly, trying to understand.

"No, I don't."

"Why?" Kira asked.

Elodie released a deep sigh. "By now, you should have realized the path you've chosen is hard. Even if you pass the *uhva na*, you face a difficult road. Training is designed to break the weak. Doing and seeing things that the rest of us don't have to. It's a calling and not one to be undertaken lightly."

Elodie glanced at Finn. "Ask your oshota. He'll tell you."

Finn stared at the healer for a long moment before lifting his eyes to Kira's. "She is correct. There is great honor in being deemed worthy for the *adva ka*, but there is a lot of hardship as well."

Elodie took a bite of her meal, chewing and then swallowing. "The *uhva na* has killed those it deemed unworthy. Call me crazy, but I have no desire to chance that fate."

Kira pondered their words.

Elodie sat back and crossed her arms over her chest. "Is that it? Is that why you came here?"

Before Kira could answer, Quillon stepped inside the med bay, coming to an abrupt stop as he caught sight of Kira.

Elodie placed a piece of bread-like food on her plate and dusted off her hands. "I'll be going. I'm sure you'd like a little privacy for your conversation."

Kira hesitated. Her instinct was to let the healer go, but for some reason, she found herself saying. "Not yet. This next part isn't sensitive."

Surprise crossed Elodie's face. After a moment, she settled in her chair as Quillon lifted his eyebrows at Kira.

"I'm surprised to see you," he finally said. "You've made no attempt to hide how much you dislike coming here every day. I thought once your preliminary treatments were up, I'd have to find someone to drag you here."

The corner of Kira's mouth quirked in wry acknowledgment. "I can't say I would be here now if not for Elodie's interference."

Quillon slid his fellow healer a look. "Then I'm glad you two had a chance to talk."

As was Kira. She still wasn't comfortable with the other woman, and unreserved trust was a long way off, but Elodie made her pause and consider a different perspective.

In the healer's place, Kira wouldn't have handled being kicked out of her own territory with nearly as much grace. That Elodie had, said the woman was someone worth knowing.

"What have you come here for?" Quillon asked.

Kira folded her arms across her chest, uncomfortable. It had never been easy for her to ask for help, less so when it came to doctors and the sort.

The confrontation with the primus, however, had made it clear she couldn't keep trying to do this alone.

"Affinities," Kira finally said. "I don't understand them—and I'd like to."

The two glanced at each other. Quillon's expression gave nothing away, even as Elodie looked slightly confused.

"What about them?" Elodie asked.

"How do they work? Why are they important?" Kira asked.

The two exchanged another look.

"What makes you ask?" Quillon finally said.

Kira screwed her mouth up, unsure how much she should reveal. "Devon. He used *ki* while in the primus form." She hesitated, before adding. "I never have. At least not in that way."

Tear things apart with her bare hands? Yes. Go on a killing spree that left dozens dead? Of course. Use her soul's breath? Not once that she knew of.

Elodie stood without a word and strode to a cabinet, rustling inside while the rest of them watched.

She returned with her arms filled to overflowing with stones of all colors and shapes. They clattered to the table she'd been using for her meal as she moved quickly to set the food aside.

"This is a test we give every child to see what form their soul's breath takes. Since you didn't grow up among us, it might be a good place to start," Elodie said, her hands moving quickly as she laid out the stones.

Kira watched as they took on a familiar pattern. "I've taken this test before on Luatha. No affinities revealed themselves."

"Most Houses typically test for those skills prevalent within," Elodie explained. "Though you have Luathan blood inside you, you're also Roake. It's possible your affinities lie more with us."

Quillon stirred, "Each House cultivates the affinities that are most beneficial to them."

Kira bristled. "And how do they do that?"

Quillon's eyes crinkled. "Nothing as bad as you're imagining, though there are some who do choose mates based on their affinities and strength. However, that is not the primary way Roake introduces new affinities into our bloodlines."

Kira relaxed. The idea the Tuann would arrange breeding lines to boost their abilities was a disturbing one. It smacked too much of the camps and what they'd been willing to do for power.

"The best way we've found is through accepting applications from those who wish to join our House," Quillon said. "The affinities are naturally introduced into our bloodlines after that since most tend to marry within their House, unless it's for an alliance."

Seeing the question on Kira's face, Elodie drew closer. "Cuts down on the questions about loyalty."

Kira paused before shaking her head. She wasn't going to get into that. "So, either of you can choose to go to a new House?"

"Not quite," Quillon said. "It is more common for those with warrior potential to change Houses when they are an initiate."

Kira cocked her head. "I assumed all of the initiates would return to their House once they were through with the *uhva na* and the apprenticeship that comes after."

"Most will—but not all," Quillon agreed. "Some will apply to remain with our House. The Overlord accepts those who he thinks might be of benefit to us."

Hence the introduction of new affinities to a House.

"Elodie could still change Houses if she chose to walk the path you're on. My path is set," Quillon finished explaining.

"You can never change Houses then?" Kira glanced at Finn. That wasn't the impression she'd been given.

Quillon opened his mouth, then paused as he noticed where her attention had gone. "Few choose to leave because of how difficult it can be. The Overlord has to release you from service. Finding another Overlord willing to let you join their House is the next obstacle you have to conquer. If you don't, you become Houseless. Not many want to chance that fate."

"But you did it?" Kira directed her question to Finn.

He inclined his head. "I did, but as you can see, I wound up in my birth House anyway."

"Why leave then?" Kira asked.

Finn hesitated, his expression vaguely uncomfortable.

Elodie snorted. "A woman."

He flashed her a hard look. Her mouth flattened, and she looked down, nudging the stones into an order they were already in.

"I felt there was little for me if I remained," he said, not elaborating further.

Kira left the matter, returning her attention to the stones. "Even if I have an affinity, I still don't understand its point. The others are being taught how to use their soul's breath, their *ki,* but the outcomes are often similar."

Elodie's tone took on the cadence of a teacher's. She held up her hand, her forehead furrowed in concentration. "*Ki* moves through and over everything. It is raw power."

Her hand lifted as the air stirred beneath it, ruffling Kira's hair and tugging on her clothes.

"It comes from within and without. Some have vast stores of the soul's breath waiting inside them. Others, a very small amount."

The wind settled, and Elodie's hands rose, sketching the rune for a shield. It popped into existence.

"However, the skill to manipulate it into different forms depends on a person's affinities. This is my version of the *ki* shield, one of the first things taught to initiates," Elodie said, her forehead wrinkled in concentration. "Finn, would you care to demonstrate the difference."

Finn's lips quirked as he stepped forward. His hands flowed through the gestures impossibly fast. His gestures looked markedly different than Elodie's to Kira's untrained eye.

When his shield burst into existence, Kira thought she saw what

Elodie had been speaking of.

Finn's shield was larger than Elodie's and carried with it a substance, whereas Elodie's shield looked small next to it and almost fragile. Very little force would be needed to puncture it.

Of the two, Kira was willing to bet Finn's would deflect a much stronger attack.

"The way we get to an outcome differs," Quillon instructed. "Elodie used a *katta* more suited to her abilities. Finn, a different one."

With a grunt, Elodie's shield vanished, and her hands dropped. After a moment, Finn's shield disappeared as well.

"Elodie's affinity is more suited to precision and control. It's why she's a healer," Quillon said. "Whereas Finn has devoted his life to protecting others. His affinities suit that drive."

"I think I am beginning to understand," Kira said slowly.

"A person's affinity determines what skills they are most suited to learning," Elodie said. "You can try to refine and perfect what you have, but trying to learn an opposing affinity would be like a blind person learning to see."

"Not impossible, just very, very difficult," Finn said.

"Why the gestures and symbols when using the *ki*?" Kira asked. She had always been able to use the soul's breath without them.

"They help our *ki* flow into the form we want it to take," Elodie explained.

"Visualization is the starting point of any use of *ki*. We're taught the *kattas* to give us a form through which the *ki* can flow." Quillon's fingers flicked and a shield formed around him. "It's possible to force your soul's breath into the form you want without it, but it's much more difficult."

"The *kattas* make things easier," Finn said.

"How do they work and where do they come from?" Kira asked.

Elodie shrugged. "I'm sure the theorists could give you an explanation. Most of us simply learn the forms. As to where they came from, that's a history lesson for another day."

Kira stepped closer to the table. "And you think this will help me?"

Elodie lifted a shoulder. "I think it will give you more information. That's what you're here for, right?"

She wasn't wrong.

Elodie gestured at the table. "Hold your hand over the stones."

Kira complied, feeling a little foolish.

"Now, concentrate on which of these call to you," Elodie said. "Feel the soul's breath moving through you."

There was only one problem with that. The inhibitor was supposed to prevent her from touching her *ki.*

How could she feel it when there was a glass wall between it and her?

Kira held her hand above the table, but like at Luatha, she didn't feel pulled in any one direction.

Her hand started to drop when a small feeling rippled through her. She hesitated, her eyes pulled to a sapphire stone, one dwarfed by the rest.

She picked the stone up. "What does this one mean?"

Elodie frowned and took it from Kira. "I don't think I've ever seen anyone pull this one before. Quillon?"

His gaze lifted from the stone to Kira's, his expression neutral. "It denotes a rare affinity, one that is not much seen anymore."

Kira waited, hoping he'd expand.

His forehead creased, and he gave a slight shake of his hand. "I'm afraid the test will be inconclusive with the inhibitor still on. Any results you get are likely to be faulty."

Elodie's expression dropped as disappointment crossed her face. "I should have considered that. Sorry, Kira; I wasn't thinking."

Kira rolled the stone in her hand, the odd attachment she'd had to it fading. "I learned something, and that was what I came for."

She set the stone on the table. She still had questions, but after Elodie had gone to so much trouble, she didn't feel right about asking the healer to leave again.

She'd have to wait until next time.

"How about I see you out?" Quillon offered. He stepped aside and gestured for the door.

Kira stepped toward it then hesitated. "Thank you, Elodie. You were very helpful."

Elodie's head lifted, her expression momentarily surprised before pleasure washed through her expression.

Kira dipped her chin before heading out of the room, Quillon keeping pace beside her as Finn trailed them.

They walked for several minutes in silence before Quillon spoke. "I sense there was more you wanted to ask, but that you wanted privacy for it."

Kira slid him a hard look. "How observant of you."

His lips lifted the barest bit in a faint smile. "I have my moments."

They walked several more feet before Kira lifted the wrist with the inhibitor. "This is supposed to block my *ki*, yet I was able to create a small shield. Why?"

If something was wrong with her treatments, she needed to know—even if it was bad news. Especially if it was bad news.

If her gamble of coming here didn't work, she'd need to make other arrangements. Put into motion plans that would see that Jin and others were taken care of if her disease ran its course.

Quillon's head tilted. "You misunderstand the inhibitor's purpose. Yes, it is to block your *ki* to give you a chance to heal, but as your channels strengthen, so will your access to your soul's breath."

Kira stopped and faced him. "What does that mean?"

Patience filled Quillon's expression. "It means you're healing. The *ki* poisoning is slowly reversing. The stronger your channels get, the more of the soul's breath you will be able to access."

Kira's breath stuttered in her chest, a desperate hope fluttering through her.

"You still have a long way to go, but this is a positive step," Quillon explained.

Kira started moving again, her thoughts churning. As welcome as Quillon's words were, it didn't change the fact that the inhibitor was a glaring weakness.

"I need to know how to get it off in the case of an emergency."

Quillon blinked at her. "Absolutely not. You'll undo all the progress you've made."

Kira scowled at him. "Progress that will be meaningless if I die first."

This time it was Quillon who stopped. "If you'd known how to remove the inhibitor when facing Devon, you would have, and you'd be in the same state you'd arrived in, only worse. I won't help you commit suicide."

Kira struggled with patience, knowing the oshota healer was doing what he felt was best for his patient.

His face softened. "You found a way to win even without your *ki*. You wouldn't have if you'd been able to take the easy way out."

"Next time, I might not get the chance," Kira pointed out.

The universe was a dangerous place. Being on Ta Sa'Riel didn't change that. If anything, it probably placed her in more danger because she was unfamiliar with the culture and customs. Who knew when she would trespass against someone she shouldn't have?

Quillon raised an unimpressed eyebrow. "There's an easy solution to that."

Kira raised her eyebrows expectantly.

"Don't go running headlong into danger."

Kira's frown was dark as he straightened with a small smile.

He tilted his head toward Finn. "That's what your oshota is for. It would be best to leave the heroics to him. For now, anyway."

Finn snorted quietly but didn't say anything. He didn't have to; it was clear he didn't hold much hope of that happening.

Yeah, Kira didn't either.

FOURTEEN

HANDS CLASPED OVER her stomach, Kira watched clouds pregnant with rain drift over the spot she'd chosen for her afternoon nap. Hard shingles weren't the most comfortable of beds, but the smell of salt and ocean and the chance to be outside made up for the discomfort.

The steady drone of young Tuann learning what it meant to be Roake kept Kira company.

It had been several days since the incident with the primus. Quillon had been serious about her taking it easy.

He'd put his foot down, forbidding her from any physical activity. Surprisingly, Wren had agreed, making it clear that if he caught wind of her not following the oshota healer's orders she could pack her bags and go.

Her time as an initiate would be done. Her path to the *uhva na* closed—perhaps permanently.

Finn's near-constant presence made testing the ultimatum impossible. Since the incident, he'd been more overprotective than ever. To the point she wasn't sure he was even sleeping. More than once, she'd opened her door in the middle of the night to find him standing in front of it, practically daring her to try to sneak past.

She might have taken him up on the unvoiced challenge if she hadn't also agreed with Quillon's restrictions. Her body needed rest. The wise thing to do was to let it.

It wouldn't be long now before she could resume training anyway. Her mind might still expect to see wounds when she looked at her arms and torso, but all evidence of her standoff with the drones had healed. The welts fading as strength flooded into her muscles.

"I finally caught you Ms. Shammer Mcshammerson of the

Summerset Shammertons," Blue called.

Kira looked up, finding the woman leaning out of a window from one of the towers overlooking her napping spot.

Blue didn't wait for Kira to reply, disappearing only to reappear moments later as she backed carefully out of the window. She descended the ten feet to the roof before picking her way over to where Kira rested.

"I've never heard that version," Kira observed as Blue collapsed beside her, spreading her arms and legs out in an impression of an oversized starfish.

"Made it up myself," Blue admitted, her eyes closed as she smiled up at the sky. "Thought it had a certain cachet."

It was certainly creative.

Kira didn't think she'd ever heard such an official title attributed to the time-honored tradition of soldiers going out of their way to avoid work.

Shammer. Skater. Sandbagger. Kira had heard many in the course of her time in the military. Sometimes the names were said with derision, other times envy. You couldn't help but admire some of the more creative ways people chose to evade work.

"I see you haven't managed to lose your shadow yet," Blue said, cracking an eyelid and glancing to where Finn scanned the area for threats.

"Despite my best efforts."

Blue propped herself up on her elbows, looking around with interest. "How did you manage to land such a sweet gig while the rest of us are being run ragged?"

One side of Kira's mouth tilted up lazily. "You too can have this. All you need to do is go a thousand rounds with about a million drones."

Blue grimaced. "No, thanks."

Kira snickered, not blaming Blue. Kira would rather have bowed out too.

"Training is that rough?" Kira asked.

Blue groaned, flopping to the shingle. "I don't know who is worse. Wren or Maida. They're relentless."

Blue popped up, her gaze wide and indignant. "Last night, I fell asleep in the middle of reconstructing a grav hook. Me! I never do that."

Kira couldn't help the chuckle. "Are they worse than me?"

Blue looked away, grumbling. "That was different. You were trying to prepare me for war in the event I ended up in the thick of things."

Kira arched an eyebrow wryly. "If you're better for the experience afterward, I'd say the momentary discomfort is worth it."

Blue's agreement was grudging as she sat up, wrapping her arms around her legs and looking out at sea. Distance crept into Blue's gaze as silence fell between them.

Kira waited patiently, figuring Blue would reveal the reason she'd sought Kira out eventually.

Kira was content to let the simple peace of lying there fill her. This was nice. She didn't often let herself exist in the moment, and she found it more restorative than a thousand treatments with Quillon.

"This place is interesting, isn't it?" Blue asked, pulling Kira out of the beginnings of her doze.

"How so?"

Blue considered it. "Their technology outstrips ours in a way I can barely fathom. In many ways, it's so advanced it resembles magic."

"That's not new," Kira pointed out. "The Haldeel are like that too."

Blue nodded. "You're right. Yet unlike the Haldeel, their society shares similarities to a feudal one with a warrior class and an almost military-like hierarchy. One might even say an oshota's duties resembles that of the knights of medieval Europe or the samurai of feudal Japan. The Overlords only answer to the emperor, and I'm not even sure he controls them."

Blue paused, her expression puzzled as she considered the different implications of such a conclusion.

Kira let her think. This was how Blue worked. She bounced her ideas off others, learning and adjusting based on their responses. Once, she'd done this regularly with Kira every time she had a problem she couldn't solve.

It was nostalgic being in this position again.

"Each House exists within an intricate network of alliances and grudges. The very fact that they have no homogeneous identity should make them chaotic and disorganized, almost unheard of in a society as advanced as theirs obviously is," Blue continued.

Kira suspected she could guess why. Graydon's revelation in the Hall of Ancestors provided answers Blue had no way of obtaining from her position as an outsider. Unfortunately, Kira couldn't give them to her, not until she understood for herself the full ramifications such knowledge would have.

"Then there's humanity's history," Blue trailed off.

"What are you talking about?"

"Myth and legend have long been how humans made sense of the world," Blue pondered. "Most are nonsense, their origins lost in history, but where there is fiction there is often a seed of truth hidden within. When you take these stories and then see certain patterns emerge across many cultures who would have had no opportunity to interact, it makes you question certain things."

Kira tried to follow what Blue was saying. "You're going to have to break this down, because I'm not following."

"What if the reason humans have so many different stories about strange, mythological creatures is because the inspiration for those creatures once visited Earth."

Kira sent her an unconvinced look. "You think the Tuann visited ancient Earth."

Blue's excitement brimmed in her expression. "Why not? They have the technology for it. In Germanic mythology, elves were said to have pathways to other worlds. We've seen something very like that already. Who is to say the Tuann never used their world gates to visit? It would explain why we've seen human symbols here and why they're so dismissive of us as a race."

Kira's mouth opened in preparation for shooting Blue's theory down. She paused when she caught Finn looking at them with something approaching alarm.

His expression smoothed into one of hard implacability in the next instant, leaving Kira questioning whether she had seen what she thought she had.

She shook herself, bringing her attention to Blue who hadn't noticed Kira's distraction.

"You're saying you think the wizards are the basis for myths of elves and fairies and the like," Kira guessed.

Blue nearly buzzed with enthusiasm. "I do. I think their history with humans goes back much further than anyone has guessed."

Kira hummed. "The Tuann are an ancient race, I suppose it's not outside the realm of possibility."

Kira rubbed a finger along her chin. Her knowledge of mythology was shaky. Such matters hadn't seemed as important as ones that might directly affect her survival. Kira seemed to remember stories of monstrous creatures whose only desire was to prey on humanity.

Take Blue's theory one step further and consider the Tsavitee. A race humans often compared to the demons of one of their main religions.

Perhaps the Tuann weren't the only ones who'd visited past Earth.

It opened up a whole world of possibilities that no one had likely considered.

"If you think about it, it makes sense," Blue pressed, her words passionate. "They could have come to Earth and stayed long enough to leave some of their influence behind."

"For what purpose? Why not conquer us?" Humanity, at that point in history, would have still been slinging rocks and sticks at each other. They wouldn't have put up much of a fight.

"I don't know," Blue confessed. "And we never will if we don't ask the questions."

Kira shook her head. So that's what this was about. As interesting as Blue's theory was, its real purpose wasn't determining if the Tuann had once visited Earth. All she wanted was an excuse to get closer to the world gate's technology.

Blue was a good soldier. Smart. Dedicated. She contained a curiosity that far surpassed most. She had a genius-level intellect and could extrapolate concepts Kira could never dream of. Once she got her teeth into something, it was damn hard getting her to leave it.

Kira had forgotten how much Blue tended to fixate.

She'd do anything—justify anything—if it served her purpose.

Kira sat up, dusting off her arms, and shook her head, unable to hide her disappointment. "A thousand different things on this planet, and you're focused on the one thing they've refused you."

Blue leaned forward. "Do you know what a gate like that could do for us if the Tsavitee come back? Forget ships. We could be anywhere nearly instantly. Entire planets evacuated before they even hit the atmosphere. The ability to send reinforcements without worrying they'll be shot down before they ever touch down."

"So now you don't want just one gate; you want many," Kira observed.

"Why are you fighting me on this?" Blue asked, sounding exasperated. "You, more than anyone, understand what we're up against."

"I could ask you why you're fighting so hard for this," Kira shot back.

The Cur closed her mouth mutinously.

It wasn't hard to guess. Blue was here to absorb as much information about Tuann technology as she could. This joint training operation was another name for spying.

Kira was okay with that. She'd been prepared for it.

What the Tuann didn't understand was that humanity was at a constant disadvantage. They were the underdog of the galactic stage. It meant they sometimes had to get creative.

Kira had written a book full of tactics exactly like this one.

What she had a problem with was when they pushed beyond the set boundaries. When they ignored common sense and common decency in their pursuit of progress at all costs.

She'd seen too many victims strewn on that path. Been the victim one too many times to somebody else's ambition. It hurt to see Blue espousing those same ideals.

"It's easy for you to say that," Blue accused. "You're not the one who is going to be on the front lines of the next war. You've made that quite clear."

Kira ignored the lance of pain Blue's words caused. "So now I'm the villain. Because I won't give you what you want?"

Blue's gaze dropped, but not before Kira caught the flash of defiance.

"Tell me, *Friend*." The last word held a vicious bite. "How many wars must I fight for you? How many friends do I have to lose before you consider it enough?"

Blue didn't answer. An angry scoff escaped Kira as she rubbed her forehead.

"I can guess your reason for being here, but why Raider?"

Blue's jaw worked. "You're smart. I'm sure you can figure it out if you try. You always were good at knowing a person's motivations."

There was bitterness in her words.

Kira looked out at the ocean. "The *adva ka*."

Blue lifted a shoulder.

"You think if a human passes the *adva ka*, it'll open doors that are currently closed to you."

It was an elegant solution to a complicated problem. If humans demonstrated the discipline and tenacity it took to overcome one of the Tuann's most difficult rites, it would lend them credibility they currently lacked.

Kira suspected this brainchild came courtesy of Himoto or Jace. It had their fingerprints all over it. Both men would prefer a solution that worked within the confines of Tuann society. Use their own culture against them, and not even they could deny a human's place beside them.

Raider was the most logical choice. Physically, he was among the top five percent of humans, and his history with Kira would mean he had an advantage where another wouldn't.

Kira focused on Blue, her voice hard. "The Tuann told you the world gate was off-limits. I expect you to listen."

Blue tapped her fingers against her knee. "It's been a long time since you were my captain. I no longer have to follow your orders. You abandoned us."

"Ah, there it is. I was wondering when this would come."

"What's that supposed to mean?" Blue asked.

"It's your MO. When denied the newest shiny thing, you go on the attack. You did it in Atlas. You're doing it now."

Blue scoffed. "That's rich coming from you. The moment you face the tiniest bit of pain, you take off."

The peace Kira had managed to obtain lying on the roof popped like ephemeral soap bubbles. Pleasant while they lasted but gone all too soon.

"I needed you after Rothchild," Blue confessed. "We all did. We were family, and you left us. Jace told me you were in a coma for several years, but we both know you walked away long before that. You were going to do it again if Himoto hadn't hung up on you."

Kira stilled. She hadn't realized Blue knew about that.

"Jace told me," Blue confessed. "He thought I should know."

"He doesn't want you getting attached." Kira's chest tightened at the betrayal and hurt in Blue's face. She hated knowing she was the one who put it there. It reminded her of the first time she'd met Blue, hiding in a dumpster, a stuffed bear clutched to her chest, more feral than human. Everyone Blue knew had been long dead, and she'd spent weeks surviving in a city overrun with Tsavitee.

Blue wasn't the only civilian Kira had saved that trip, but she was the only one who'd stuck like a burr to Kira's side and refused to let go.

"I understand why you left," Blue said, calm again. "I never blamed you for it. You needed to heal, and it was impossible to do that with constant reminders of them."

Kira's mouth tightened. Blue was half right. She had needed time and space. Something in critically short supply during a war. The flow of battle didn't always leave you able to take time to heal your psyche. Sometimes you had to push through even when you were broken. Even when a large part of you wanted to lay down and not get up for the next few decades.

She'd left the Curs, but she hadn't left the war.

That had to sting for those she'd been closest to. People like Blue. And Raider.

"What else did Jace tell you?" Kira asked, her attention fixed on the ocean.

Blue paused. "That you're not coming home after this."

That meant he hadn't told her about the possibility of a mole in the highest echelons of the military and government, or the fact that the mole was likely responsible for everything that had happened on Rothchild.

Kira didn't know whether to be happy or disappointed he'd chosen to keep secrets from the people he trusted most.

She hadn't wanted that for any of them.

"You could, you know," Blue said, her expression earnest. "Come back. I think even Raider would be happy to have you in the Curs again."

That surprised a laugh out of Kira. "You haven't changed. You always see the good side of people."

"That's not a bad thing," Blue pointed out.

Kira's gaze was soft as she clasped Blue's shoulder. "You're right. The universe needs more of that. Not less."

"I find myself in agreement," Silas said from behind them.

Blue started as Kira glanced back, unsurprised to find him there. She'd sensed him a while ago, and she'd been waiting to see how long he'd wait before announcing his presence.

Silas's expression was wise as he took in the view. "This is a favorite spot for many in Roake. Perfect for ocean watching. It's good to see you have things in common with us, fight it though you must."

Kira watched him carefully, unsurprised at the news. He was right; the spot was perfect, the towers providing a windbreak and the height allowing you to see for miles. Sitting here, it was easy to imagine yourself far from the clamor of people, all while never stepping foot from the safety of the fortress.

Silas looked at them. "I'm here to inform you there will be a class this afternoon."

Blue perked up, the intense conversation already forgotten as she found something new to focus on. "Tactics and battle strategy, right?"

Silas inclined his head.

Blue faced Kira. "I guess they finally deemed us ready for more than running around a forest while getting our asses handed to us by their damn drones."

"You need to be there. I don't care what it takes," Jin crooned. "I'm going to do so much information gathering."

Kira rose, dusting off her hands and pants. Even if Jin hadn't chimed in, she probably would have gone anyway.

Blue's startled gaze followed her. "Where are you going?"

"Class."

"But—" Blue scrambled after Kira as she headed toward Silas.

"You're here to learn as part of a joint training operation, aren't you?" Kira sent the other woman a significant look. "You can't exactly do that sitting on a rooftop."

Besides, Kira had a feeling if they stayed, the conversation would deteriorate again. Blue had a lot of pent up feelings surrounding what she saw as Kira's abandonment, and Kira couldn't explain why she'd acted the way she did.

Avoidance might not solve their issues, but it would delay them. Blue might have had a point when she said Kira avoided dealing with emotional pain.

For now, Kira was fine with that.

Silas led the way into the fortress, scaling the wall with the ease of long practice. Mentally and emotionally, he might seem ancient, but physically he was as spry as any of the initiates.

Kira climbed through the window, reaching back to help Blue, who either didn't notice the helping hand or was still mad from earlier. Kira's hand dropped as Blue finished crawling in by herself.

The tight expression on Finn's face told Kira he'd seen the other woman's slight. Unlike Kira, he didn't seem willing to give her the benefit of the doubt.

They walked through the fortress, following Silas as he led them through long corridors and twisting passages.

"How are you liking our home so far?" he asked.

Blue was the first to answer. "It's beautiful. I don't think I've ever seen anything like it."

Earth might have had a distant approximation if many of its cities hadn't been razed during the war. Buildings that had stood for centuries had been destroyed. The Tsavitee didn't care about the cultural history of the people they sought to destroy. They were locusts, consuming the resources without care or concern for future generations.

All of the other planets were too young to have anything as steeped in history as the fortress. Their cities hadn't been built with defense in mind and while their architectural details might be fascinating depending on where you were, they didn't carry the same impact as a church built in the medieval or renaissance period.

"The Fortress of the Vigilant was one of the first structures built when we came to Ta Sa'Riel," Silas said.

"When was that exactly?" Blue asked, trying to seem nonchalant. Her studied disinterest wasn't fooling anyone as she fiddled with her ear nervously.

Amusement deepened the corners of Silas's eyes even as the rest of his expression remained serious. "A long time ago."

Blue didn't relent, prodding. "By gate?"

"No."

Kira leveled a dark look on her friend. "We talked about this."

Blue spread her hands, innocence on her face. "It's a simple question."

Kira knew better than to believe her. She'd seen that exact expression on Blue's face one too many times to be fooled now. It was the same look she used to get when she tried to convince Kira to overlook her latest disaster.

It hadn't worked then; it wasn't going to work now either.

"The gates are among the oldest relics in our worlds," Silas said into the silence that had descended. "No one knows how they were built."

"Why not study them, then?" Puzzlement settled on Blue's face. She genuinely didn't understand why the Tuann wouldn't investigate such a powerful artifact.

Silas's expression was polite, if firm. "Some things are better left to the past. The world gate is useful, but it is also dangerous. It serves our current needs, and that is enough. We have no interest in tearing it apart in the misguided notion it will give us more power."

Kira concealed her smile at the mild rebuke. It seemed Silas had been listening longer than she thought.

The view highlighted the biggest difference between the Tuann and humans. The Tuann were much more accepting of things as they came. They were more likely to make decisions based on tradition and the ideas of the past.

The Tuann were so used to being the biggest and baddest on the galactic stage, so secure in their superiority, that Kira feared what might happen to them because of their arrogance.

Humans were their opposite. They fought for more, even against great odds. They were bound and determined to progress, containing a constant thirst for evolution.

That desire to grow and evolve had led them down many a dark path. It made it easy to justify acts that were wrong on the most basic of levels. Left to their own devices, they held the potential to destroy themselves. Several points in their history were marked with events where they had nearly done that.

Neither race was right. Neither was wrong. Instead, they were a little bit of both. Perhaps Himoto was wiser than Kira gave him credit for. If humans and Tuann could learn to coexist, learn from each other's weaknesses, they could find a path forward where each flourished beyond their current limits.

Unfortunately, Kira thought this endeavor was more likely to end in failure and hard feelings rather than success.

FIFTEEN

SILAS STOPPED IN front of an ornate door, gesturing inside at a large room with an amphitheater-style setup that would have rivaled any university classroom. They must be able to fit all of Roake's top brass in this space, Kira realized. Convenient when planning a military offensive, and you needed all your leaders for a briefing.

The different tiers contained desks and chairs, allowing their occupants an easy view of the speaker no matter where in the room they might sit. On the bottom floor, where the speaker would stand, was a heavy stone table that seemed out of place in the space.

Silas pointed to one side. "Initiates sit over there."

Kira glanced in the direction he'd indicated, finding several familiar faces. Blue spotted Raider in the next instant, taking off in his direction without another word.

Joule sat one row down but directly in front of Raider. Her gaze moved past him to linger on Devon, where he surprisingly sat by himself.

His fellow initiates had placed several rows and seats between them and him. It was a marked shift from the last time Kira had seen him.

"His primus came decades early," Silas told her. "It's set him apart from his peers."

Kira studied the group across from her, noting the careful way the initiates darted glances that held admiration and a hint of fear in Devon's direction.

For his part, Devon held himself carefully as if afraid moving too quickly might tip him into another transformation.

The young man had always struck her as a bit arrogant. Now, she could see the struggle in his face. He was afraid of himself.

He wasn't the only one, she realized. There was a thread of unease running through the initiates that had its source in Devon's presence.

They might revere the primus form here, but they feared it as well.

She knew what that was like, to have the people who'd shared meals with you, laughed and joked with you, to suddenly see you as the monster. It wasn't an easy thing to experience.

Silas's gaze was thoughtful and knowing as he studied Kira. "I'll leave you here."

She narrowed her eyes at him as he moved to the other side of the room where Roake's oshota had arranged themselves. Sly old dog. Why did she have a feeling he wanted her to sympathize with Devon? Perhaps he hoped she understood what he was going through.

Maybe so, but Kira had done all she planned to do for Devon. At least he wouldn't have to live with the knowledge his primus had killed one of his friends. That would have to be enough.

Graydon quirked an eyebrow at her from across the room from his position next to Harlow. He seemed to be inviting her to take a seat with them.

Kira shook her head and started for where Raider and Blue sat.

A hushed silence fell over the initiates as several shot furtive glances her way. Kira paused. Ah, so Devon's status wasn't the only one that had changed.

Now Kira saw why Graydon had beckoned her. Any thoughts she might have had of blending in with the rest were over now. She'd done her job of distracting Devon's primus a little too well.

She glanced his way again, to find him staring at his desk.

Ah, well, she couldn't exactly take it back now. She'd done what was necessary.

"Big crowd," Kira said, taking a seat beside Raider.

A smirk spread across Raider's face as he made a show of looking her up and down. "Well, look who deigned to show up. Did you catch up on all your beauty sleep?"

"I did, yes, thank you," Kira responded. She made a show of stretching. "It was lovely. You should try it some time."

Raider snickered as he shook his head.

Kira caught Joule craning his neck to get a look at her. "Kira, you're back!"

She grinned at him, slinging her arms around his neck in an impromptu hug. He held still.

"Are you still upset about being support?" Kira asked softly.

Joule made a soft, muffled sound, emotion clogging his throat.

Kira cupped his cheek with one hand, her smile proud. "If you hadn't held your ground, I never would have gotten there in time. Some of you would have likely died or been so damaged it would've taken years to put you back together."

Joule looked afraid to believe her.

Raider nodded, spinning the stylus he held. "She's right. I saw the video. You did good. If this Overlord thing doesn't work out, I could use someone like you in the Curs." He jerked a head at Kira. "She's shit at those shields."

"They only think that because they're humans," someone muttered below. "Anyone can cast a *ki* shield."

Joule stiffened.

"But they didn't," Raider said with a nasty smile. "They stood there like fish in a barrel. Only you cast that shield, and you held it."

Kira glanced at him, a thought occurring to her. "What videos?"

His grin spread, turning wicked. "Evidently, the forest has an entire surveillance system wired into it. Some enterprising individual accessed the feed and then shared it so others could see. You're heavily featured."

Kira grimaced. No wonder the initiates were treating her differently.

Raider cast her a sideways look. "It's pretty impressive. I especially like when you threw your broken blade at a drone."

"I was improvising," Kira grumbled.

Not her best plan—throwing part of her weapon away—but it had bought her a little more time.

Joule slid a small coin on her desk. "Ziva wrote you a video letter and asked me to give it to you."

Kira picked up the coin and rolled it through her fingers, slightly befuddled on what he expected her to do with it.

He grinned and pressed her pointer finger and thumb along the edge.

A tingle rippled across her skin, and then a small hologram of Ziva appeared above the coin.

"*Seon'yer*, I hope this message finds you well," the little girl started.

"Joule, why is Ziva calling me *seon'yer*?" Kira asked calmly.

The boy's gaze dropped, and he mumbled something indistinguishable under his breath.

"Joule?" Kira's voice deepened with threat.

"She's decided she's your apprentice," he said, looking guilty.

Kira shook her head and didn't stop. "No. That's not happening."

Joule didn't answer, steadily avoiding meeting her gaze.

"How can she decide something like that?" Kira asked. "I'm not even past the *uhva na*. I'm in no place to be someone's *seon'yer*."

Joule lifted a shoulder. "Ziva is stubborn. Once she's decided on something, it can be very difficult changing her mind."

Kira studied him with narrowed eyes. Something told her Ziva wasn't the only one.

She picked up the metal disk again and pressed the two spots Joule had shown her. Ziva's message resumed.

"I have undertaken training with Luatha as you instructed." The girl's mouth screwed up in a grimace. "They're not as skilled as you, but it's a good place to start."

Raider's shoulders shook beside Kira.

"Your advice to find allies was wise. I've made a few acquaintances. Two of them will make good additions to House Maxiim when the time comes. They're refusing to join us right now, but I have plenty of time to change their minds," Ziva said, looking serious.

Kira's eyes widened as she stared in horror at the recording. Raider's shoulders shook harder. Blue didn't even try to hide her laughter.

"That's not what I advised at all," Kira said in dismay. Her gaze swung to Joule. "You know that, right?"

He nodded slowly, not looking very convinced.

Raider clapped Kira on the shoulder. "Congratulations, your pupil shows the same diabolicalness as a certain drone we both know. I'm sure the two of them have much to learn from each other."

Kira shook her head and raised her eyes to the ceiling. How had things managed to spiral so quickly?

"At least she's making friends—even if she's planning on eventually luring them from your aunt's House," Blue said.

Wren stepped into the center of the room, cutting short any further discussion. Kira slipped the metal disc into her pocket. She didn't even know how to begin addressing Ziva's misconceptions on her advice. She was afraid to even try for fear Ziva would do the same again.

Wren's presence had an immediate effect as those in the audience fell silent.

"You have all done well to make it this far." Wren's deep voice rumbled through the amphitheater. "I want to commend you on your tenacity."

The initiates sat up straighter.

"There are those among you who have risen to the challenge, surpassing the limits you've placed on yourself and overcoming every obstacle." Wren paused, his attention shifting to where Harlow and Graydon sat. "Which is why the *uhva na* has opened."

The initiates below stirred, their whispers breaking the silence. Even Devon was unable to hide his interest.

Below them, Wren held up his hands, demanding quiet. A hush fell as the initiates sat forward in their seats, anticipation electrifying the air.

"You know what an honor this is. The appointment of a formal *seon'yer* isn't something we do lightly. Once you pass the *uhva na*, you will be acknowledged as a warrior and will gain Roake's sponsorship to the *adva ka* when it opens," Wren said. "We've been monitoring you since your arrival to determine who is ready and who still needs more time. The next few days will be your last chance to change our minds."

Kira sat back as the initiates erupted into chatter.

"A word of warning—I know passing this phase seems like a given with how far you've come, but I warn you, it's not easy. There is no shame in waiting until you're ready." Wren's eyes lingered on Kira.

She stared placidly back. He could warn all he liked, but if she had the opportunity, she was taking it.

"I caution you to know your limits," Wren continued. "The trial has claimed lives in the past. Once you are in its depths, not even we can easily save you should you stray."

The lights in the room dimmed as Wren stepped to the head of the stone table, touching it. A hologram formed above it, a planet and stars glittering as they came into focus.

"Now, let's begin the day's lessons."

Those around them rustled as they tapped the desks in front of them, bringing up holoscreens as they began to take notes.

It quickly became apparent why Wren was so revered by the initiates and why Rheya had seemed so interested at the prospect of an apprenticeship under him. He held a strategic mind, his observations of long-ago battles insightful and revealing.

The Tuann, it seemed, were no strangers to conflict. Their Houses showed a propensity for descending into war over what, to Kira, seemed like inconsequential matters.

"What have you learned from the engagement during the fourth feud between House Danai and House Asanth?" Wren asked, finished depicting a pitched space battle between the two Houses.

"Not to leave your supply bases unguarded?" Aeron said with a lilt in his voice, making his statement a question.

Wren nodded. "That is one conclusion. What else?"

The initiates looked at each other, none willing to volunteer their opinions. Wren was a harsh critic, more inclined to point out the fallacy of a comment than praise it.

His gaze found Kira's. She tensed, knowing what he was going to do before he did it. "Kira, you've been quiet."

Raider hid his snicker beside her. Blue's shoulders shook suspiciously on Kira's other side as she ducked her head, pretending to take notes on the tablet in front of her.

"Perhaps you have something to add," he said.

Kira was quiet for several seconds, her gaze lingering on the battle simulation that was still running. "I suppose you could also conclude that any decision you make needs to make sense in both the short and long-term. What might be advantageous today may lead to your defeat in the future. Long and short-term planning are necessary for the survival of any combat force."

Wren's face was expressionless, his gaze flat. After several seconds, he inclined his head. "Very good. Now, can we think of any other battles that demonstrate this concept?"

Rheya held her hand up. "I can."

Wren gestured for her to take his place. She stood and walked over to the stone table, spending several seconds fiddling with her wrist unit.

Her eyes met Kira's.

"This should be good," Raider muttered.

A hologram began to form over the table, a familiar planet and moon surrounded by an armada of ships.

Rheya took a deep breath, her chin lifting as she indicated the hologram. "I think the battle of Rothchild, where humans lost nearly a quarter of their ships for a non-crucial target, demonstrates this concept."

Raider looked down. "Well, fuck."

A pin dropping could have been heard as all eyes swiveled toward Kira, checking her reaction. Her expression was blank, numbness spreading through her.

She hadn't expected them to take this tactic as a means to hurt her. Rheya was smarter than Kira had given her credit for. And more ambitious. Kira would have to remember that.

"I take it from Raider's reaction, she chose an emotionally charged battle," Jin guessed.

His presence in her mind was muted, which meant he wasn't seeing out of her eyes.

"It's Rothchild," she whispered.

There was an audible indrawn breath.

"Oh, Kira. I'm sorry," Jin finally said.

Kira didn't respond. She couldn't; her throat was thick with heartbreak. Shards of ice expanded across her chest, deadening everything it touched.

She was right there again, a Tsavitee war party appearing out of nowhere. Her friends too far away for her to help. Knowing there was nothing she could do to change what was coming.

Feeling the ship's internal screams as the *CSS Vega* broke apart, watching the moon disintegrate from a plan she'd put into action, its debris shredding their ships along with the enemies'.

Kira inhaled slowly, forcing herself to count to three before exhaling. When she'd finished, she did it again and again until she'd stuffed all those emotions in their boxes.

Rothchild was a very long time ago. How long would it take until a simple mention of its name no longer affected her this severely?

"That's it, Kira. She wants a reaction. Don't give her one," Jin coaxed.

Kira hummed softly, letting Jin know without words she appreciated his support.

She focused. The woman shifted nervously, suddenly not seeming so confident under the hostile gazes of the two at her side as she had moments before.

Wren waited, his body tense. When Kira didn't do anything, he relaxed. "Rheya, I assume you have data to back up your conclusion."

She nodded, recovering a modicum of her confidence. She gestured, and the scene shifted, the ships starting to move. "Human media claims this battle was the turning point of their war. I don't understand why. I've created a simulation of the battle based on reports and footage I found."

She expanded the planet, clicking through so the audience was treated to several shots of its terrain. Snow-covered mountains, continents threaded with thousands of rivers.

Rothchild had seventy-four percent landmass. The primary form of water came from snow caps and the glaciers that riddled its poles.

A humble city took shape, the buildings simple, most not even topping three stories. The planet was still in the early days of settlement. They hadn't bothered with beauty and form when building their cities and towns, more concerned with function and efficiency.

"From what I could find, there was little in the way of strategic resources that needed protecting. There was no obvious tactical value in this colony," Rheya continued.

The hologram expanded to the moon and the armada of ships. Four destroyers, each housing nearly a thousand soldiers, escorting one large carrier craft.

"What about the lives of three million souls?" Blue challenged.

Rheya paused. "Humanity claims they were in a fight to prevent their annihilation. Three million lives do not justify crippling your fleet, no matter how difficult a decision such as that would be."

It was easy for Rheya to say. Three million lives of her own people hadn't been at stake.

In the simulation, five dots separated from the human ships, streaking across space away from the planet and its moons. Shortly after, several Tsavitee warships, all elite or superior class, moved into view.

Kira's hand clenched on the desk as she took a slow breath, knowing what would happen next.

Two of the destroyers moved out of formation, one taking the lead as they raced for the dots.

"Rather than tightening their formation, several of the human ships broke away, weakening their defenses." Rheya tapped one of the dots, expanding it to reveal a humanoid figure clad in military-grade body armor, standing aboard a device that shared a resemblance to the surfboards of humanity's past. Bulkier than Tuann synth armor, the military combat armor insulated the wearer against space while providing a thin protection against projectiles. It wouldn't stop most missile armament, but it might deflect shrapnel, proving useful when in close combat.

The board looked like a bristling hedgehog, rail guns and rockets strapped all around it, containers housing ammo rounds on its underside.

It was a crazy way to fight, yet surprisingly effective against the Tsavitee. Life expectancy for a waverunner pilot wasn't great, but there had been no shortage of volunteers willing to risk their lives on them.

"I can only conclude their actions were to protect these five," Rheya said. "Though why you would send five craft of this size up against a Tsavitee warcraft, I can't guess."

"They're waverunners," Blue informed her. "In the early part of the war, our single craft fighters were getting slaughtered. They weren't maneuverable enough or fast enough to be effective against Tsavitee ships. The waverunners gave us a fighting chance. Because they're so small, they're harder to lock onto, and their boards can be used as a battering ram for an insertion force."

"After that, it's a matter of planting a few bombs in critical areas and then bugging out before the ship blows," Raider added.

"Clever," one of the oshotas from Roake said.

"We thought so," Raider said.

Not to mention they were useful when dropping into atmo for a space to ground insertion. It was easy to hit one big target. Much harder when trying to hit hundreds.

It was a hell of a ride down, though.

The simulation resumed with the Tsavitee ship firing. Debris flew from the ship on the right. The *McNeil*.

Unlike in holofilms, ships didn't typically explode immediately upon taking a hit. They were built to withstand a lot. When the survival of those inside depended on the air and atmosphere staying where it was, it made you a tad paranoid in the design.

There were redundancies built into a ship in the event of hull puncture. It was always the vacuum of space that got you in the end. Punch enough holes in a ship's hull, and it didn't matter how good the design, you'd suffocate in seconds if you weren't wearing a pressurized suit.

That was demonstrated seconds later as the Tsavitee launched scatter bombs, which detonated a hundred feet from impact, the shrapnel shredding the ship's port side.

The *McNeil* listed to one side.

"They should have retreated at this point," Rheya said. "It was obvious they were outmatched."

Silence fell as one by one, eyes turned toward Kira.

"Blue, give me your tablet," Kira said calmly.

Blue flicked a glance in question toward Raider. He hesitated before nodding.

Blue handed the tablet over. Kira bent, her fingers flying across the screen. A short time later, she smiled. She should have known Blue would have all the mission reports, every piece of information she could get her hands on, stored in her files. It made sense. The Curs had been her family too.

"Jin, a little help," Kira whispered.

"Got it."

Kira flicked the information away. Jin took it and put it on the same device Rheya had been using for her little presentation.

"What you didn't take into account was the fact that this was the single most important moment in human history," Kira told her, rising.

In the midst of the three ships that had remained close to the moon, a Haldeel diplomatic vessel took shape.

"That day, we were in the midst of talks regarding a treaty." Kira descended the steps, her pace slow and unhurried.

"We couldn't retreat because the Haldeel's ambassadors were planetside. We knew if the Haldeel lost any of their diplomats because we turned and ran, we could kiss any possibility of support goodbye." Kira's lips quirked up on one side, the half-smile not touching her eyes. "Though, I'll admit the prospect of abandoning three million never really occurred to us. I doubt it would have occurred to Roake either, if it had been their people down there. We'd already lost so much. They were ours, and they deserved our best even if the sacrifice was more than we wanted to pay."

Kira's attention moved to the hologram as she studied it. She thought Rheya had controlled it like this. Kira made a gesture, and the scene rewound.

"The waverunners were sent out to investigate a stray comet. The Tsavitee war party was using it to hide their ship's signature in a move they learned from us."

Humans hadn't been able to fight head to head so they'd gotten crafty, using any and all techniques to even the odds. It was one of the reasons the runners had been sent out. The command team had known exactly how a comet could be used to hide unsavory surprises.

Turns out, they were right to be worried.

The battle resumed as the *McNeil* began to break apart, venting atmosphere and water that froze instantly, creating a giant plume around it.

"You have this part right. The *McNeil* falls early. Its death serves as a warning to the rest of the fleet," Kira said, circling the table, her gaze fixed on the battle taking place above her head.

"Outgunned and outmatched, they only have minutes to decide on a course of action." Kira stopped, facing Graydon. He listened; his thoughts unreadable. "The commander of the *Vega*, Charles Berry, decides to lure the Tsavitee into a trap."

"How?" one of Roake's oshota asks.

"Only a few species of Tsavitee display executive functioning skills. Most are a slave to their desires. Enrage them. Distract them, and they're easy to manipulate."

"They wouldn't leave a force of that size to one of the lower forms," another oshota said.

"You're correct. A higher form always accompanies a force of this size. Sometimes it's a general; or it can be a mantis, skyling, or yellow, as we call them. The commander opens a channel to the lead ship and offers them something they've wanted for a while." Above Kira, the *Vega* slowly breaks off its attack, heading toward the moon.

Soft murmurs break out among those watching as the Tsavitee ships followed.

"On the moon was a temporary mining camp of a mineral called Smaralta, a compound known to be dangerous when combined with hydrogen. If exposed to heat, it will explode. The more heat, the bigger the explosion," Kira said. "While the *Vega* and the *McNeil* buy them time in the battle, the miners start flooding the shafts with hydrogen. They set charges throughout in the hopes of creating a big enough explosion to damage the Tsavitee ships."

The *Vega* circled to face the Tsavitee warships.

"Unfortunately, no plan ever survives contact with the enemy. Those on the waveboards would have been in the path of the resulting debris. Exposed. Defenseless. Their armor would have been little protection; the debris would have shredded it. However, if they veered away to try to escape, they would have alerted the Tsavitee to the trap."

They weren't the only ones in the path of destruction either. The *Vega* also stood between the moon and the approaching force.

Above Kira, the moon exploded, a quarter of it disintegrating as a great plume of debris shot toward the ship and waverunners. Everything was destroyed.

Kira touched the small icon hovering in front of her. The battle scene faded, replaced by hundreds of photos with names under them.

Rheya stared at them in confusion.

"I thought you should know the faces of the people whose sacrifice you were so dismissive of," Kira said.

There was a frozen look on Rheya's face, as Kira walked away, the colored lights from the hologram playing over her as she stepped through two of her fallen friends. She felt almost brittle as she made her way to the door, past caring what anyone might think of her.

Jagged glass coated her throat as she fought to swallow dangerous emotions.

She needed be away from here before she did something she might regret.

*

The individual photographs scattered to reform into one large group photo. This one was different than the others, unposed. The people in it were relaxed and comfortable, their postures saying they were familiar with each other. Taken on the flight deck of a human destroyer, there were cargo containers and mechanic tools scattered all around.

That wasn't what drew Graydon's eye, however. It was the devil may care grin spread across Kira's face as she posed with a group of eight others. They looked happy—carefree, despite the rigors of war.

They wore uniforms, but were clearly individuals.

Raider had his arm slung around a woman who was half turned from the camera, a hat on her head, the only thing visible the curve of a wide smile. Blue stood on top of a crate holding a blow torch, her gaze directed at a man beneath her. Two others stood next to Kira, caught in mid-laugh.

"The Curs," Raider said with a sharp smile. "They were the ones who didn't turn away despite knowing it was likely to cost them their lives. The only reason Kira wasn't with them was because of an injury and dumb luck. It was her plan that led to the moon's destruction, the death of her squad, and seventy percent of the *Vega's* crew," Raider said.

Rheya paled, understanding and guilt creeping into her expression.

Had Kira been raised Tuann, she would have been within her rights to issue a challenge over the ambush Rheya had launched. She could have demanded recompense. That she had annihilated Rheya's argument with simple words only served to highlight the maturity and wisdom she carried herself with.

Rheya was nearly mute as she shook her head. "I didn't know. I swear."

"How did you survive?" Indya asked.

"We weren't there," Blue said. "Raider had a short-term assignment on another ship in transit to one of our military bases. He was supposed to rendezvous with them after the treaty with the Haldeel. I had already left for training."

Across the room, Graydon caught the faint echo of conversation from the humans.

"Two guesses what she offered to get them to change course," Blue muttered.

Raider sent her a hard look. "We don't have to guess. We know."

Graydon wasn't deceived by Raider's easy manner. The human hid it well, but he was furious. The kind of anger that tasted like acid as it ate you up from the inside out.

Kira wasn't the only one this discussion had touched a nerve in. Judging by the hostile way those two were examining the Tuann around them, neither was particularly happy with what had just happened.

Raider struck Graydon as someone who sought control in all aspects of his life, much more so than most probably realized. It made him a dangerous enemy. Right now, he was cataloging the different ways he could hurt those around them and judging whether the risk was worth the reward.

The woman beside him wasn't as contained, stabbing at her tablet with anger.

Graydon's head cocked. Such interesting individuals Kira chose to surround herself with.

He could see why she showed a reluctance to abandon them. Despite Harlow's hopes, she'd never fully embrace Roake. The humans would always hold a piece of her. Unless the Tuann could claim a piece of her as well, their hopes of tying her to them would be in vain.

Graydon hid a sigh as the hologram caught his notice again,

acknowledging Kira had ample reason to be upset. Not many oshota he knew could have spoken so matter-of-factly about the events which led to their pods' deaths.

Whether she'd meant to or not, Kira had earned points with the oshota of Roake. They would remember her poise when confronted with such a devastating memory. He had no doubt many of those in the seats beside him would ask Harlow for a chance to serve at her side.

Kira might not wish it, but she'd just cemented herself as Roake. They claimed those they loved and were loath to part with them. They wouldn't easily give her up.

Graydon relaxed into his seat. This was an interesting development. All the more so because it hadn't been planned—at least on Kira's part.

Wren pulled his gaze from the door where Kira had disappeared, a thoughtful frown on his face. He stood, addressing Rheya, "One of the hardest things to learn is to see what isn't obvious. You made assumptions based on faulty data. Next time you will know to look below the surface to the motivations that aren't so easily discerned."

Chastened, Rheya returned to her seat as Wren took her place before the table.

"Now, I'd like to discuss the Thratni engagement," he said to the initiates.

Graydon quelled his impatience, knowing going after Kira at this stage would tip his hand. He had duties here, and as much as it might chaff, there was no getting out of them.

He forced himself to relax. She had Finn with her. Of any Graydon knew, Finn would have the best chance of breaking through to her right now. He had experienced something similar and knew what she was going through.

SIXTEEN

KIRA MOVED QUICKLY through the halls, uncaring of her direction as she fought to hold herself together. The diamond-hard shell she'd built around memories of that time was beginning to show hairline cracks, the emotions she'd buried deep seeping from its crevasses.

The sense of loss, the feelings of guilt over her part in their deaths, the soul-crushing sadness. It would be so easy to lose herself to their murky depths.

Logically, she knew the Curs would never have wanted her to feel this way. They would have been furious with her that she was still allowing this to fuck with her mind.

What had happened had happened. No amount of protest or argument would change things now.

It was war. Someone was always going to die. It was just their bad luck they were the ones to go.

Her Curs were dead. The majority of her family—the ones she'd carved from a harsh world—were dead. Misfits and the disenfranchised who'd found a home with her. All gone.

Sometimes she wanted to rage thinking about it. To rend and tear and destroy.

For a while, immediately after the war, she'd done exactly that. She'd tracked down any hint of Tsavitee presence and eradicated it. Picked fights with people and organizations she had no business antagonizing.

She wasn't proud to admit she'd been on a path of self-destruction, glorying in her descent.

Jin was the one to bring her around again.

He'd convinced her no amount of death or sacrifice would return their family. He'd been the one who'd made her see there were other ways of honoring their sacrifice.

She'd created her mission from the ashes of the old, clung to it during the nights when her demons had threatened to destroy her.

Having her failures thrown back in her face was insulting. It galled her on a level she could barely comprehend.

It was difficult resisting the urge to return to the class and exact retribution on Rheya. Kira knew the kid didn't deserve it. She'd seen an opportunity to knock the humans down a peg and exploited it. Exactly as she was no doubt taught.

Except this time, she'd gone after an open wound.

Kira's footsteps slowed as she came to a stop, staring at the empty hallway in front of her.

"I know you're there," she said, not bothering to look around. "Might as well come out."

Silence echoed. Kira waited with a restraint she didn't feel.

Finally, she turned, knowing what she'd find even before she did. Finn waited patiently; his expression carefully blank. A good thing given how fragile Kira felt. She couldn't have guaranteed she wouldn't have tipped the situation into violence if he'd looked at her with sympathy or pity.

She looked away, her mouth screwing up. "I don't suppose you'd agree to go back the way you came."

He didn't answer, which was answer enough.

"It's too bad. I could use some alone time right about now." There was a shakiness in her voice that said she was at her limit.

Finn read that, moving to take a place at her side. He stared out the window she'd unwittingly stopped in front of. Finally, he moved. "Come on. I have a place to take you."

Kira didn't bother hiding her suspicion. Finn and Kira had come to a compromise of sorts, but it wasn't the sort of thing that made them friends. This smacked of caring, the sort you might apply to someone you were friendly with.

His smile was brief, lightening his eyes and revealing a glimpse of the man he might have once been. "Don't act so suspicious. Not everyone is out to get you."

"Says you," Kira threw at him. "My track record says otherwise."

*

"This is where you wanted to bring me?" Kira asked skeptically.

They stood outside a bar located on the edge of the city, close to the fortress's walls. Housed in a cozy-looking building of stone and stucco, the inside was filled with a sea of synth armor, deep blue the dominant color.

Wide-open windows looked out on the city below and the ocean beyond it.

A long bar curved through the middle of the room, its surface polished and bright.

The place smelled clean and fresh. A murmur drifted through the space, the Tuann inside not paying any attention to the newcomers. Many hung out in alcoves; gauzy curtains pulled to hide the identities of those inside.

There was none of the electric hum of depression or desperation that she'd become accustomed to from the station bars she normally frequented.

This space spoke of elegance and comfort.

"You never struck me as the type to drown your sorrow with alcohol," Kira said, sending Finn a sidelong look.

Warmth lit his expression. "You looked like you needed to get away for a while. This place fits that need, while exposing you to another side of life with us."

Kira hummed in interest, taking in those around her. Roake's colors may have dominated, but she caught glimpses of the armor of other Houses as well.

Kira moved toward the bar, leaning against it as she people watched.

"Do you guys ever take your armor off?" Kira asked.

Of those she could see, almost all wore some type of armor. Not all were synth, but the majority were. Those who were dressed normally were mostly behind the bar or moving through the room with trays. Less than a handful of the patrons themselves were out of armor.

"Rarely outside of House walls." Finn signaled a Tuann at the end of the bar. The man pouring a drink lifted his chin in acknowledgment. "There are exceptions. Most of those are like Maida, who can reinforce her skin, but the rest wear the armor with the pride it deserves."

The bartender made his way toward them. As tall as Finn, he had a similar build. He moved as if any moment the floor might jump up and bite him. Kira had seen other soldiers move like this, as if prepared for the shit to hit the fan. Usually, it took several tours in hostile environments to develop that type of response to your surroundings.

There was a surliness to his expression, like showing any other emotion was too much effort. His hair was shaggier and more unkept than most Tuann she met. Eyes of light amber lightened infinitesimally as he approached.

Finn clasped the man's offered forearm with a nod that was downright friendly for the dour oshota. "Brother."

Kira glanced between the two of them as the bartender settled his forearms on the counter.

A slow smile dawned as he looked Finn up and down. "It's good to see you in the armor again."

Finn touched his armor, his motion almost surprised before he dipped his chin slightly.

"Again?" Kira asked.

The man's gaze shifted to her, his look guarded. Finn might be his friend, but he was withholding judgment on her. Fair enough. He wasn't the only one.

"Talon, this is Kira. She's my current sword."

The man's eyebrows lifted as his gaze sharpened. "The lost Roake heir I've been hearing so much about."

Finn nodded before addressing Kira. "We call the people we serve swords. Oshota are their protective shields. It's custom when a sword under your care dies to put away your armor until you find a new sword or have redeemed yourself in battle."

The stilted way Finn said this made her think he wasn't happy about having to reveal this odd Tuann idiosyncrasy.

It made her think his last sword, as he called it, had died under less than ideal circumstances.

It was hard to tell if the distance between Finn and those in Roake was because of his reserve or theirs. It was likely he'd played some role in this person's death, even if she still didn't have all the details.

"Doesn't make much sense to me, but many things about the Tuann don't," Kira admitted.

Talon's smile was slow in coming. "I like this one."

She arched an eyebrow at him, saying dryly. "I'm flattered. Really." She pointed at her chest. "It gets me right here."

He threw his head back on a roar. "Much better than Brianne."

Seconds later, he set two glasses of amber liquid in front of them.

"Welcome to the *Sirav Rytil.*"

"It means—"

"Second Chances," Kira finished for Finn. Seeing his surprise, she lifted a shoulder. "I may know a little more Tuann than I let on."

It was true enough, but it also helped to have Jin constantly in her ear translating what others were saying around her. It had allowed her to pick up a few interesting tidbits. You could find out a lot about a person based on what they said when you weren't around—or at least they thought you didn't understand.

"Smart," Talon said with admiration.

"I try."

Kira picked up her drink as Talon looked at Finn, tilting his head in a clear invitation for conversation.

"Talk to your friend," she told Finn when it looked like he would hesitate. "I'm sure you have a lot to catch up on."

Finn didn't move, reluctance in his posture.

She made shooing motions at him with one hand. "You brought me here so I could clear my head. Let me."

Kira took a sip of the drink she was holding, nearly coughing in surprise as it burned all the way down.

Finn didn't quite manage to hide his chuckle at her reaction.

She eyed the drink in her hand with suspicion. "What the hell is this?"

Talon smirked. "I take it you've never had *keeva* before."

She took another hesitant sip. This time the burn wasn't as intense, and the flavor was spicy and warm, like a jumped-up version of chai. "I grew up with humans. We didn't have anything like this."

"Humans have alcohol. We have *keeva*," Finn said, glancing at Talon. It was obvious he wanted to talk privately with his friend, and just as obvious that he was reluctant to do so because of her.

"We both know I can take care of myself," she told him.

"Yes, but isn't it nice sometimes to have someone watch your back?"

"Perhaps, but this isn't one of those times. Go. You'll be close enough if I get into trouble," she said.

Finn moved off reluctantly. Kira watched until he and Talon settled into conversation before putting her back to the counter and studying those around her.

For the most part, she went unremarked. Those in the bar seemed more interested in each other than Kira. It was a refreshing change from the fortress where she seemed to draw attention wherever she went.

Here, she was one of many. Kira felt herself settle a little, pushing away the sting of her memories.

She watched for several minutes, sipping on her *keeva* as the conversation ebbed and flowed around her, comforting in its steady hum.

A person entered the bar, drawing Kira's notice because of the way they seemed to stick out without even trying. Shorter than any adult Tuann Kira had met, they were also shorter than even Kira. Clad in a cloak, the person had their hood up, obscuring their face.

If that didn't say suspicious, Kira didn't know what did.

The steady drone of conversation dropped at the person's presence before resuming. Kira didn't miss the way several of the patrons kept an eye on the individual as they made their way toward the bar.

Kira tensed as they slid into the spot next to her, Finn doing the same from his position a few feet away. She shook her head at him. He settled back, his eyes glittering and his body tense.

Kira was careful not to look directly at the stranger as she observed the person. Finn wasn't the only one ready for action. Kira had been in too many bar fights not to be instantly on guard by the stranger so close to her.

"I thought for sure after the shenanigans on Ta Da'an you would be halfway into human space by now," the stranger said, not lifting their head.

Kira stared at the hood in surprise, her body locking up as the stranger signaled for a glass of what Kira was having.

Talon prepared the drink, shooting a look at Kira, asking without words if she needed help.

With a resigned sigh, she shook her head. No. They were past that.

The stranger took the *keeva* and downed it, exposing a smooth jaw and fingers that were a shade longer than any human's.

Finally, the stranger faced Kira, peering up out of the hood with a sly smile. An eye patch covered one eye, the other an emerald so bright, it looked like the green of spring after a week's hard rain.

The person's features were androgynous. Neither entirely feminine or masculine but a perfect blend of both. Their skin was the color of almonds, and they had hair shorter than Kira's.

The stranger slapped Kira on the shoulder before heading to the booths. "Come on, Nixxy poo. We could use a little privacy from big brother."

Grimacing, Kira mouthed Nixxy poo as she followed the cloaked figure.

"Kira, you won't believe this, but I think I finally found Odin," Jin crowed.

"You don't say," Kira drawled.

"I found a message." There was a pause before Jin grumbled, "I don't know how Odin dropped it into my cache, but when I find out, I'm going to skin that annoying brat."

Kira hummed as she took a seat in the booth in front of the stranger, noting the earring dangling from the person's ear.

Jin's voice dropped to a whisper. "Odin is here."

Kira's mouth quirked. "I know."

Jin choked. Several seconds passed before he screeched, "What do you mean you know?"

"She dropped by for a visit. I'm looking right at her."

Odin grinned, her expression mischievous. The earring was Kira's clue as to which gender Odin was leaning toward today.

Odin had told Kira that her species didn't experience gender the same way most humans did. They were all and neither, a benefit of having minor shapeshifting capabilities.

Often when they reached maturation, they leaned toward one or the other, but they didn't have to remain the one they chose.

Odin liked flipping between genders as feelings dictated. The earring was her way of letting those who knew and cared for her which gender she preferred at the moment.

Today she might be female; tomorrow male. The next day she might choose neither, instead using her species' gender-neutral form.

Even as Kira studied Odin, she could see her friend's features taking on a more feminine caste. Her lips were a shade plumper, the line of her jaw softer. It was a minor difference, but there nonetheless.

"What do you mean you're looking right at her?" Jin demanded.

"How many other ways can that statement be interpreted?" Kira asked with irritation.

Jin exploded. "This is why I need eyes and ears on the ground. Stuck in here, I'm limited to what you see. I might as well be blind."

"Stuck there is exactly where you had better stay," Kira ordered in alarm. "I mean it, Jin. No wandering off again. You've already tipped Graydon to your presence. Let's not make it worse."

Stubborn silence answered her.

"Jin," Kira said in warning.

Odin's grin widened, her feet kicking as she slurped up her drink.

Kira slapped the table. "I mean it, Jin. I will dismantle you."

Jin scoffed. That was the trouble of having a best friend who'd known you basically your whole life. They no longer believed your threats.

Kira ignored the sinking feeling that told her no amount of threats would get Jin to listen, instead focusing on the problem she could solve. "I thought it was too dangerous to be seen together. Your rules, remember?"

Odin's smile was impish. "Indeed, I do, but I thought I'd take a page out of the great Kira Forrest's book and break a few rules."

"How did you get past the defense net? And why are you here?" Kira asked, not letting herself get distracted.

Odin's presence was concerning on a number of levels. The least of which was she'd managed to pierce a system the Tuann seemed to believe couldn't be penetrated.

If Odin had managed it, who was to say the Tsavitee hadn't as well?

Odin's shrug was casual as she reached for her drink. "I have my methods."

Kira's hand landed on her wrist. She squeezed gently in warning. "Explain."

It wasn't that she didn't trust Odin—well, Kira didn't trust anyone really—so that wasn't entirely true. She'd learned to be cautious. She didn't like it when people acted outside of the norm. This was unusual behavior for her friend.

Except for their first meeting, Odin had always been careful to only communicate with Kira via the forums and message boards. She felt— and Kira agreed—it was too dangerous to chance meeting out in the open too often. Their shared goal of finding the Tsavitee home worlds was dangerous. Too many people would have loved to get their hands on that information, or even the various possibilities.

Suspicion deepened in Kira's stomach. She opened her senses, hunting for the telltale mental scent of Tsavitee mind meddling. Odin felt normal, metallic with electricity zipping along her thought patterns.

Odin's gaze darted to Kira's ear. "Let's say a little birdie was very helpful."

"Jin?" Kira questioned.

"I didn't, Kira. I swear."

Kira believed him. Jin's loyalty was unquestionable.

"Not on purpose anyway." Odin's smile widened, revealing pointed teeth.

An inarticulate sound escaped Jin, equal parts rage and denial.

"Did you hack my encryption?" he demanded.

Odin's mouth pulled down in a pout. "Was it supposed to be difficult?"

Jin's gasp was outraged. "Did you stick one of your nasty little bugs in my code? You did, didn't you?"

A chortle slipped out of Odin.

Jin fell quiet as he went hunting for the stray code Odin slipped in.

Kira groaned and scrubbed a hand over her face. She was going to hear about this later. "You really know how to leave an impression. He's going to be paranoid for months now."

And Kira would be the one who had to deal with all his neurosis. Last time Odin had performed this stunt, Jin had been insufferable with his security protocols.

Odin slouched in her seat, not the least repentant. "But it's such fun, and I needed him distracted so we can talk. Don't worry. I left him a few toys to make up for the teasing."

Jin was going to need more than a pretty bauble to take out the sting of having his code compromised.

Kira was never going to hear the end of this. He'd blame her because she was the one who found Odin.

The only good thing about being planet-side was he couldn't use climate control to mess with her.

Odin set her chin on her hand. "It's good to see he hasn't changed at all since the old days."

"Not everything is the same," Kira said, sending a significant glance around the room. It was a far cry from the accommodations of their last meeting.

"No, it isn't," Odin said with a wistful sigh.

Kira caught Finn casting them suspicious looks. He was not happy with her new companion. Not that she blamed him.

"Do you think if I drew the privacy screen, he'd try to remove me?" Odin asked idly, noting where Kira's attention had gone.

"Probably," Kira guessed. "You're welcome to find out."

Odin snorted as she reached into her cloak. "Perhaps another time when the stakes aren't so high."

Odin pressed her thumb on the button of the small ball she held. Kira's ears popped, the murmur of the bar falling away.

Kira sat forward. "What did you just do?"

"We need privacy for this conversation. I simply insured we got some," Odin said.

Kira tensed. Finn wasn't stupid. His paranoia made Kira's look reasonable. If he suddenly couldn't hear them, he was going to know something was wrong. That would lead to him checking on them, which would inevitably give rise to questions. Questions Kira couldn't afford to answer.

"Are you insane? Tech like that will draw notice," Kira hissed.

Odin waved a dismissive hand. "Please, I'm not stupid."

That was an understatement. Odin tested genius level on every aptitude test Kira had ever come across. She made Jin look slow in comparison. Blue would have sold her soul to be able to grasp even a tenth of what Odin understood.

"To anyone outside a two-foot radius of this device, it will seem like we're talking about the city sights. Just keep your face pointed away so he can't read your lips, and we'll be fine." Irritation colored Odin's voice.

"You're taking a dangerous risk," Kira said.

Odin shrugged. "It's my risk to take."

Not when Kira was the one who would pay the price. The Tuann didn't trust her. They might want her there. The yearning in their gazes when they looked at her was clear, but they were keeping their distance.

Her time in the camps had marked her. Sometimes she wondered if the Tuann smelled the wrongness that clung to her like a miasma that wouldn't go away.

"Not when it puts my mission at stake," Kira said in a hard voice.

Odin was pivotal to their plan. She had to decode the information Kira salvaged from the Tsavitee wreckage. Without Odin, finding the Tsavitee home worlds would be nearly impossible. Kira would be reduced to throwing a dart at a star map and hoping she landed on the right solar system.

Odin reached for Kira's arm, her fingers lightly brushing over the dermapatch there. Odin plucked the patch off Kira's skin, attaching it to her own in a casual movement Kira knew even the sharpest of observers would have trouble seeing through. The patch mimicked her coloring, becoming undetectable.

Odin folded her arms before her on the table. "Happy now?"

Kira fixed Odin with a flat stare. "Thrilled."

Odin's smile was brief as she stared out at the Tuann. "Fascinating, aren't they?"

Kira didn't answer.

Odin kicked her feet under the table as she set her chin on her folded arms. "I've found it interesting how similar the Tuann primus form is to a general. They're nearly identical, wouldn't you say?"

Kira grunted. "Except for the whole glowing symbols thing."

Runes and lines didn't appear on a general's skin during battle, and they didn't have a second form like Kira.

"True." Odin's attention shifted to Kira, her stare piercing. "Your blue-haired friend sees a connection too."

Kira stiffened, her blood turning to ice. "What do you know of Blue?"

She couldn't help the dangerous rumble in her voice.

Odin's lips quirked up playfully. "Only that she's sticking her nose in places people don't want her to. If she's not careful, someone might cut it off."

Kira was quiet as she considered Odin's warning mixed with a subtle threat—though whether it was Odin doing the threatening was the question.

Odin liked nuance. She rarely said everything she meant or meant everything she said. She might be warning Kira that Blue's curiosity was bringing her to the attention of some very dangerous people rather than saying Blue was stepping on Odin's toes.

Odin straightened, taking a moment to stretch. "You've landed in a very good place. I hope you decide to stay."

Kira's gaze was sharp. "What does that mean?"

Odin's eyes were wiser than they had any right to be since she didn't appear much older than a human in their very early twenties. "More than any of the others, you've always searched for a place to belong. For a while, you thought that place was with humans."

"And you think I've found that place here?" Kira didn't bother to hide her skepticism.

"I think, if you let yourself, you would find happiness." Odin's lips curved. "Maybe even allies for your more ambitious endeavors."

Kira narrowed her eyes. "Is that what this is really about?"

Odin looked away, thoughts moving across her face. Her head sagged, and she withdrew a mini viewer from another cloak pocket. She clicked the side, and a screen popped up. On it, the photo of a woman caught in profile appeared.

Kira sucked in a breath, reaching for the viewer and pulling it closer. "When was this taken?"

Kira's gaze lingered on the woman's features—ones as familiar to her as her own.

"Three weeks ago."

Kira looked up sharply. "Two weeks after my encounter with the generals."

Odin inclined her head. "They're trying to draw you out."

Of course, they were.

Honestly, Kira should have expected this reaction. They would know she'd do nearly anything to find Elise, and this tactic guaranteed she'd come to them, practically hand-deliver herself into their trap.

"Where was this?" Kira asked.

Odin's hesitance was marked. Kira leveled a hard glare on her. She could see why Odin might want to withhold the information, not wanting Kira to run off and destroy years of planning, but that wasn't how this partnership worked.

"Near Osiris."

"That's in Haldeel territory," Kira said, unable to hide her surprise. What would Elise be doing there?

Kira's fingers drifted over the person's features. They were nearly the same as they had been. Perhaps her face was a little thinner, maybe Kira imagined the haunted expression in her eyes, but overall, that was the woman she'd thought dead because of Kira until she realized Elise's fate had been much worse.

The urge to find the first ship off-planet was nearly overwhelming. Kira hadn't been this close to Elise since Rothchild.

"Do you have a plan for when you find her?" Odin asked. All trace of playfulness had faded. "A real plan?"

Kira's silence held a note of stubbornness.

Odin jabbed a finger at the picture Kira still cradled. "You'll be up against a planet filled with millions of your greatest enemy when you're nowhere near top form."

Odin tapped the disrupter, her expression meaningful. "They know by now that you're coming. Your burst is gone, and you have no allies except one insane drone and a hacker. How exactly do you think you're going to save her?"

Kira sat back. "From the looks of things, I won't need to find their planet. She's out in the universe again. Much easier to find her out here than there."

Odin lifted an eyebrow. "And what if she fights you? I don't see any Tsavitee chains on her, do you?"

Kira's expression darkened at the implication. Her gaze dropped to the photo. Odin had a point. The Tsavitee had perfected mind control. The fact they'd let Elise out meant they were confident in her brainwashing. It was doubtful she'd escaped on her own. If she had, she would have wasted no time contacting Kira. Jin would have told her if he'd found activity on any of their old message drops.

Kira's stare was stony. "It wouldn't be the first time I've faced impossible odds."

"You weren't alone then," Odin pointed out.

"I'm not now either. I have Jin."

Frustration chased across Odin's face. "You're not usually this obtuse."

Kira fixed her with a dry look. "Usually the people I trust don't make an end run around me after I've taken considerable risk getting information they said they needed."

"Perhaps I don't want to watch you commit slow suicide. Because if you take on the entire might of the Tsavitee horde, that's what it will be."

Well, when she said it like that.

"If you fail, they'll have both of you. You know what that would mean," Odin said.

It was a nightmare that haunted Kira's dreams. The Tsavitee were merciless, but their unseen masters were worse. They lacked a sense of right and wrong.

They were deceptive. Deadly. With a thirst for power that would consume the universe if left unchecked.

For some reason, they found Kira's genetics fascinating and believed it held some mystery they wanted to unlock. Kira was just as invested in making sure they failed.

"The others don't wish to see you die either," Odin said carefully.

Kira's gaze was cool. "They're welcome to lend a helping hand."

Odin sent her a reproachful frown. "You know why they won't."

Kira looked away. Yes, she did. Most days she didn't even blame them. They had safety in anonymity. With childhoods as traumatic as her own, she couldn't begrudge them the peace they had found.

"You have options they don't have, anyways," Odin said.

"You know why I don't."

Odin's sigh was grudging. "I guess I do."

Commotion at the door caught Kira's attention. Her eyes widened as Raider pushed his way inside. He paused, scanning the room before his gaze fell on hers.

"Crap," Kira breathed.

Odin twisted. She caught a glimpse of Raider and spun around. "This isn't good."

No, no, it wasn't. Their only saving grace was Odin had never lowered her hood. Good thing too, because Raider would have known exactly who she was—or at least who she used to pretend to be. Any attempt at subterfuge would be over then.

"I hope you have another way out of this place," Kira murmured.

Odin was already scooting out of the booth. "Think about what I said."

Kira didn't get a chance to respond as Odin walked past her, moving without an ounce of hurry. She was just another Tuann going about her business, in a cloak, while taking a back exit to avoid being spotted.

Kira fought the urge to sink her face into her hands.

Raider's narrowed gaze moved from Odin's retreating form to settle on Kira. There was a marked pause before he started her way.

She took a hasty sip of her drink as Raider joined her. She swallowed its warmth, as he stopped next to her table.

Kira was the first to speak. "I trust I didn't damage relations too badly."

Raider lifted a shoulder. "No worse than they already are."

And there was the crux of the problem. The Tuann were suspicious of outsiders, which meant the possibility of a lasting alliance was an ephemeral dream at best.

"Actually, some interesting things happened after you left," he said.

Kira waited.

"I don't think Rheya's ploy worked out the way she intended. If I read them right, the oshota of House Roake seemed almost impressed that you didn't try to knock her head off her shoulders," Raider said.

Kira swirled the liquid in her drink. "That would be a first."

He grunted in agreement.

His gaze was thoughtful as he considered her. After several seconds, he slapped the table as if reaching a conclusion. "Come on, I know what we should do."

He didn't give her the time to ask questions, heading toward Talon and Finn.

Kira watched through narrow eyes as the three exchanged words before Talon reached beneath the bar, pulling out several glasses and two bottles of liquor.

Raider faced Kira and tilted his head to a table in front of one of the bay windows overlooking the harbor. Reluctantly, Kira heaved herself to her feet, curious in spite of herself.

"What's this?" Kira asked, meeting Raider at the table as he started setting slim glasses the length of her pointer finger in two neat rows.

"Do you remember that dive bar we visited on O'Riley shortly after our first battle as Curs?" Raider asked.

Kira paused before smirking. "I remember Courtland getting so drunk he couldn't see straight and walking into a door. He had a black eye for weeks."

Raider paused and pointed at her. "Oh yeah, we all got put on extra duty for a week because of that."

Extra duty was used as a punishment in the military. Most shifts were a determined length of time. Sometimes eight hours, other times ten or twelve. Whatever the length, extra duty took place after normal working hours and on days off. Sometimes it was cleaning the flight deck. Other times it was swabbing the head—or bathroom as civilians called it.

"That was the first night we remembered the fallen." Raider took a seat and grabbed a familiar-looking tequila bottle. He started pouring the liquid into one row of the shots. "You said as long as we told stories about them, they'd never really be gone."

Tired of standing over him, Kira took a seat. "I know what I said."

"That night, we drank to each person we'd lost." Raider capped the tequila bottle and reached for one she suspected held *keeva*. "We still do that, you know. Every year on the anniversary of the war's ending, we remember them."

Pain ran through Kira at the evidence of another aspect of her former life she'd been absent for.

"What I remember most from that night is you ending it shirtless while wearing a pair of boxers on your head," Kira said, pushing away the bad feelings.

Raider paused in pouring the *keeva*. "I never did figure out whose those were."

"They were Walker's," Kira said. "He dared you to do a triple flip off the bar. When you only did a double, he gave you them as your penance."

Kira snickered at the look of horror on Raider's face.

"That bastard. He always swore he didn't do it."

"Elise tried to warn you, but you refused to listen. Said something about how no one would malign your skills."

Raider pulled a face. "We were all so young."

With no idea of what was coming.

Raider finished pouring the *keeva* into the last of the glasses. He picked up one and gestured for Kira to do the same. "Tonight, we'll create new memories. I think it's time we put our brothers and sisters to rest, don't you?"

Reluctantly, Kira reached for the first glass. "We're nowhere close to Rothchild's anniversary."

Raider downed his first shot. Kira followed suit, warmth spreading through her veins.

"Who do you want to start with?" Raider asked, slamming the shot onto the table.

SEVENTEEN

"YOU KNOW I always hated Bates," Raider said hours later, slamming his latest shot. Outside, the world had deepened to a golden hue tinged with blush and azure. "He was a pretentious know it all. Always telling us about the origin of a word or term. Used to drive me crazy."

"I don't think you were the only one," Kira said.

"Elise always called him Brainy Bates," Raider confessed, startling a laugh out of Kira.

"She didn't."

Raider nodded. "She did."

"I didn't know that," Kira said, her laugh fading. "That name used to drive him crazy, and I never could figure out where it came from."

This time Raider's grin was cagey as he swayed in his seat. "She was always proud she was able to keep that tidbit from you. Thought it was a game."

Kira snorted, not surprised in the least. Elise had taken great joy in her pranks. She and Jin had had a long-standing prank war that had made Kira the unsuspecting victim too many times.

"He died a hero though," Raider said in a soft voice.

Kira's nod was slight. "That he did. Drew that eel even knowing there was no way he'd outrun it. Saved a lot of lives in the process."

Raider's eyes were shiny as he raised his glass. "At least it was quick. More than I can say for Ranger and Park."

Kira hid her sadness. Ranger and Park had had the misfortune of living through the battle for Paxus, only to waste away from substandard care, as toxins ate away their nervous systems. The two had been bright and funny. Sometimes when Kira dreamed, she could hear the jokes they used to tell each other.

Kira played with her glass as Odin's advice rumbled through her mind. There was something she needed to tell Raider. Something that was long overdue.

Maybe if she hadn't split from the remaining Curs and hidden herself and her secrets for the last few years, this would be a non-issue. Only she had and it was.

"Did you ever think about having kids?" she asked instead of what she'd planned to say.

Raider froze in the act of picking up another shot. "What the hell brought that on?"

Kira lifted a shoulder. "Just a question."

He studied her. "Is this that whole fear I'm going to die alone again?"

Kira rolled her eyes, knowing he was referencing the conversation they'd had when she'd been high on one of the things Luatha's doctor had given her after she'd been injured.

Evidently it had made her very talkative. Raider and Jace told her she'd shared a whole bunch of interesting factoids—including that she thought Raider was going to die alone as a grumpy old man.

"Never mind, it was a stupid question," she said.

He grunted in agreement before downing his shot. He set the glass down. "No, I didn't."

Kira frowned. "Not even with Elise."

"It was war. You know what our lives were like. Nothing was safe," he said. "Why would I bring a child into that?"

She did know. It was why she'd kept Blue close to her after she'd found her in a dumpster. The kid had lost everyone and everything. Kira had pulled major strings to keep her on her ship. It helped Blue had been useful when it came to repairing things.

"Besides, Elise didn't want kids. She was adamant about it," Raider said.

Kira took a sip of her drink. She did know that. Any child Elise had would have been hunted. The child would never have been safe. Same with any child Kira had.

"You could have one now," Kira pointed out.

Raider considered her words for half a second before shaking his head. "I'm a lifer at this point. I don't plan on changing that."

They sat in silence for several moments.

"And you? Do you want kids?" Raider asked.

"Jin is enough of a child." Kira shook her head. "I haven't thought about it. Until recently, I didn't know how long I had left."

Raider tipped his glass at her. "Whole new future for you."

Blue appeared beside them in the next instant, cutting off any response Kira might have made.

"I finally found you," Blue said in exasperation.

Raider lifted his head slowly, a dull surprise flitting across his face. "Little Blue, there you are."

Blue scowled at him. "Don't give me that, old man. I've been looking for the two of you for hours."

Raider swept his arm out, indicating the table strewn with empty glasses. "Here we are."

"I can see that," Blue said, dropping the scowl and eyeing the table with consternation. "What are you doing?"

Kira lifted her glass. "Toasting the fallen."

Blue's expression softened. "You know you need more than two people for that."

She wasn't lying. With as many dead as Kira and Raider had between them, they needed an entire squad. Even then, they'd likely end up regretting it in the morning.

"That has become very clear." Kira aimed a significant look at where Raider swayed.

Blue hooked her foot on a chair at the next table and pulled it over. She snatched a glass from the table and downed it in a single gulp. "Who is next?"

Raider raised his arms and cheered.

Kira sighed. "Bayside, right?"

Raider's nod was careful, as if the copious amounts of alcohol he'd consumed might escape if he moved too quickly.

A sound of surprise left Blue, her glass lowering as she shot the two of them a disconcerted look. "How long have you been here?"

Raider and Kira shared a look, saying at the same time. "Long enough."

Shaking her head, Blue threw the shot back, grimacing at the taste. "The thing I remember most about Bayside was that he hated peppers. Used to complain anytime he got them in an MRE. Said they were an offense to food everywhere."

"Oh yeah, didn't he also have a habit of trading them for the cheese?" Raider asked.

Kira nodded. "Used to drive me crazy because he always came after mine first and then would pout if I didn't give them to him."

Blue's laugh was bright. "He didn't even like the cheese in the MREs."

Kira scowled. "Yes, he did. Used to get them from everyone."

Blue shook her head. "He always gave them to me because he knew they were my favorite. He said that if he couldn't have what he wanted, he didn't plan on letting you lot have it either."

Kira gaped. "That asshole."

Blue burst out laughing. "How did he even get that name anyway? Bayside? He never would tell me."

Raider was the one who answered. "He showed up wanting to be called the Butcher. Thought it was badass. Elise found out he was from a coastal city and started calling him Bayside. It stuck."

Kira snorted. "Like we were ever going to call him the Butcher."

Blue's face sobered. "We had a good family."

Raider clinked his glass against hers. "That we did."

"I miss them," Blue confessed.

Raider's eyes met Kira's, sadness there.

"We all do," Kira said, ignoring the prickling at the back of her eyes.

Finn's gaze caught hers from where he still sat at the bar. Kira ignored the understanding reflected there as she focused on her friends.

Shaking off the sadness, Raider reached for another glass only to have his hand knocked away as Blue got there first. She held up a hand at his protest. "Stow it, old man. I have some catching up to do."

With a harrumph, Raider sat and folded his arms.

Kira's response was forestalled as newcomers entered the bar. They lingered in the entrance as they looked around with cool, almost derisive glances. Only one of those present wore synth armor, fiery flames of orange emblazoned on his chest, accents of the color woven throughout.

The rest wore simpler versions of the synth armor, declaring them as initiates from well-to-do families, much like Rheya and Devon.

The group headed toward the bar as Talon moved to meet them, the same surliness she'd seen on their first meeting present. His movements were rough and abrupt as he served them, something in his manner saying the newcomers weren't exactly welcome. A fact Kira had picked up on when the rest of the patrons quieted, the looks being cast at the newcomers not exactly hostile, but definitely not friendly either.

Raider and Blue argued as she studied the Tuann, wishing Joule was here for a lesson.

One of the strangers glanced their way, nudging his companion before several of them made their way toward Kira and her group.

"Hostiles incoming," she muttered into the glass.

Raider and Blue quieted as they watched the three approach.

Raider squinted at them with a fierce frown that might have been more effective if he wasn't actively swaying in his seat. Blue sipped her tequila, her eyes meeting Kira's as one of her hands lowered under the table to clasp the weapon Kira suspected was hidden along her thigh.

Kira aimed a grin at the floor, proud of the person Blue had become. She was someone to trust at your back.

The three had already dismissed Blue and Raider as nonthreats, focusing entirely on Kira.

"What do we have here?" the first asked with an arrogant twist of his lips, looking like he smelled something nasty.

"It looks like a pair of humans and a human lover," the woman behind him answered.

Blue scooted her chair back a hair, angling it so she could stand easily.

Kira flicked her fingers at Finn, signaling for him to stay put. "This is a private moment among friends. I'd appreciate it if you three took yourselves away."

There—diplomacy designed to deescalate the situation.

Raider made an impressed sound as he gave her a small clap.

The look she sent him was irritated. He wasn't helping matters.

"I think I recognize her," another of the three said. "She's House Roake's mad heir." He leaned into Kira's space. "They say you have to be insane. No Tuann could have survived so far from home, or brethren, for so long."

Kira stared into the man's eyes. She waited, holding his gaze, not speaking, watching as uncertainty filled his expression. "Are you done?"

He drew back slightly, glancing at the man Kira pegged as being in charge.

Kira's smile was hard. "As I said before, this is a private party. We'd appreciate you leaving."

The leader settled a heavy hand on Kira's shoulder. "How about you be the one to leave?"

"Uh oh," Raider said, alarm snaking through his expression.

He had a right to be concerned. Kira had a thing about uninvited touching, and this Tuann had crossed her invisible bubble in a big way.

"If I were you, I'd take your hand off my shoulder before I break it." Kira was no longer as concerned with playing diplomat. Quickly she calculated the possible consequences of starting a fight, for once wishing Jin would chime in with his thoughts and opinions. He'd studied Tuann law. He'd likely know the possible repercussions.

Quiet fell, spreading throughout the bar as the patrons focused on the unexpected drama. Kira spotted Rheya and Devon among those present and stuffed down the part of her that would like nothing more than to start a bar fight.

"I'd watch your mouth, mongrel. You and your humans are a travesty. They should have put the lot of you down. It would be a mercy." He raised his voice so the rest could hear. "I question Roake's strength if they accept one such as you within their ranks."

Tension filled the air as no one moved.

Kira's lips quirked. "Raider, do you hear yapping?"

He stuck one finger in his ear and jiggled it around. "Yeah, it's kind of high pitched. Sounds like one of those little toy dogs—or maybe a puppy. It's hard to be sure."

Blue's shoulders shook with an inappropriate laugh she couldn't quite hide. She wasn't the only one as those around them followed suit.

It was not the reaction the Tuann in front of her were expecting if the flush that tinged their cheeks was any indication.

Kira picked up another shot glass, dismissing the three. "Now, where were we?"

A sharp crack rent the air. Pain bloomed on Kira's cheekbone and jaw as her face turned with the force of the blow.

Raider and Blue were on their feet, their chairs screeching across the floor as Kira touched the painful spot.

"You try to be nice," she muttered to herself, dropping her hand.

Kira studied the other three, her gaze assessing. These idiots weren't the ones she was worried about. It was the man in the synth armor still standing at the bar and the four beside him.

"Last chance to walk away," she warned them.

The first man sneered. "You're a disgrace."

"I'll consider that a no."

Pity.

"You'll be the one leaving," he told her as he reached for her. His fingers were bruising where he grabbed her shoulder.

"Mistake one," she whispered.

Her other arm swept up, breaking his hold. She rose, yanking him forward and slamming his face into the table. Glasses jolted, several falling to the floor with a crash.

Raider and Blue threw themselves forward, blocking the others. Raider rammed the chair he'd been using into one, pinning him against a wall.

Blue withdrew a marble and squeezed it before tossing it at his companion. It touched the armor, and the woman jerked, her eyes rolling up before she hit the floor.

Kira easily held her quarry against the table as he struggled to rise. "Underestimating us was your second mistake."

She leveraged his forearm higher, hearing the joint stretch and pop.

She glanced over her shoulder to find Devon and Rheya, their backs to her as they faced four of the man's fellow initiates as they stepped away from the bar.

The two's show of support was surprising, a fact Kira forced herself to ignore as the Tuann clad in orange accented synth armor stepped forward.

Finn was quick to meet him, casually inserting himself between the oshota and Kira.

"Move," the oshota ordered.

"The day I accept orders from House Dethos is the day I hang up my blade," Finn said mildly.

The other man's lip curled. "If you can't control your mongrel, I'll be forced to do it for you."

Kira snorted from where she still held her prey against the table. She'd like to see him try.

The oshota's cold, furious eyes found hers. She was sure it was meant to be impressive. Unfortunately, the effect was lost on her. She'd never learned to fear people who sent the inexperienced to do their work for them.

"I will break his arm," Kira warned him.

It wasn't personal, though she'd be lying if she said she wouldn't get a certain amount of satisfaction from the act. It was simply smart business—incapacitate an enemy so she could move onto the next.

Maybe it would make the oshota rethink this course of events. Probably not, but Kira still had to try.

"Dethos, you know what to do," he rumbled.

Resolve snapped into the four facing Devon and Rheya. Seconds later, they surged forward. Devon and Rheya braced to meet them.

Blue whooped and charged forward. "Show them the gristmill! Show them hell!"

Kira cursed, yanking on the man's arm. His shoulder joint popped amid an agonized cry. She lifted his head and smashed it into the table, stepping away as he slumped to the ground, unconscious.

Raider whipped the chair he was holding back before crashing it over his assailant's head. The man's eyes rolled up in his head before he hit the ground with a thump.

Raider plunged past Kira with a wild grin. "Just like old times."

Kira didn't let herself linger on the truth of that statement, following on his heels as he darted into the fray.

A woman in the training armor of Dethos stepped into her path, a dangerous glint in her eyes. She swung, and Kira ducked, nearly getting a knee to the face. She twisted, stepping into the woman's space and hammered an uppercut into her stomach. Air left the woman in a rush as she staggered.

Kira grimaced and shook out her hand. For training armor, that stuff was surprisingly sturdy.

The woman's lips twisted in a snarl, her hands coming up in a stance Kira recognized as the air bubbled and a rune started to take shape.

"No, you don't," Kira muttered. One hand swept up, knocking the woman's hand away so she couldn't finish what she'd started. Unused *ki* crackled, nipping at Kira's skin and lifting her hair away from her head.

Kira thrust with her palm, hitting the woman's chest and catching her off guard. A grunt left her as she swayed, tripping and falling to the ground at Graydon's feet.

He regarded the woman with an amused twist to his lips before his gaze rose to find Kira's. "I didn't know we were at the gift-giving stage of our courtship. I confess I didn't get you anything."

Kira leveled an unamused stare on him.

"Or perhaps this is your way of inviting me to take part in another practice bout." He bent in the barest of bows. "I accept."

Kira ignored him, focusing on the woman at his feet. "*Ki* only works if you're faster than your opponent."

Unfortunately for the woman, Kira was used to people far quicker—one of which was currently standing over the woman.

There was a snarl on the woman's face as she struggled to rise. Graydon got there first, pressing a hand into her shoulder and pushing her down. "She's right. You're not prepared to go up against someone like her. You should stay down."

The woman twisted, a retort already on her lips before she caught sight of Graydon. Her eyes widened, and a gasp left her instead of the harsh words she'd planned.

Her shock had a ripple effect, Graydon and Wren's presence causing the fight to peter out as the rest became aware of the two.

Graydon straightened, flicking a coolly entertained gaze over those assembled. Rheya and Devon disengaged, panting as they snapped to attention.

Both looked disheveled but happy, their expressions caught between pride and chagrin. Rheya was sporting a red mark around her eye that hadn't been there before the fight. No doubt it would be black by the time morning rolled around. The skin around Devon's knuckles was bruised and busted, his opponent carrying the evidence of how they got that way.

Out of the confusion, Raider sauntered over to Kira, handing her a piece of armor. "Here."

She bobbled the unexpected package, before cradling it to her chest as she looked to Raider. What exactly was she supposed to do with this?

He read her unvoiced question and shrugged. "It fell off the unconscious guy when you dislocated his elbow. Thought you might want it as a memento."

How thoughtful—and complete bullshit.

That piece of armor was a slap in the face against their attackers. Every soldier knew you had to take care of your equipment because one day that equipment might save your life. To be relieved of a critical piece of armor in such a way implied the wearer was untrained, or worse—lazy and negligent.

Raider knew this.

He had always been a vindictive bastard. It seemed time hadn't changed him.

Kira tossed the piece at the woman. "Here. This is your friend's."

The woman caught it, her expression caught between humiliated and furious.

At Graydon's side, Wren observed the chaos. His thoughtful gaze landed on Blue and the unexpected weapon she held in her hands. One part looked like a slingshot, the other was a two-inch narrow energy beam like the ones Kira had seen the Tuann use with a weapon that looked like a bow, the beam acting as the arrow.

"Lady Blue, I see you've made use of your off-time to make a few modifications to a standard Tuann *zuipi*," he commented.

Blue blushed, the energy beam dissolving as she lowered the slingshot, putting it behind her back as if to hide it. Raider and Kira fixed her with similar expressions of disbelief.

Blue shrugged at them. "What? I got bored."

Graydon's lips twitched before smoothing out. "Would someone like to tell me what is going on here?"

"Nothing that concerns the Emperor's Face," a strong voice said out of the crowd.

Kira caught sight of Finn next to the strange oshota, his guard up and looking vaguely homicidal. It looked like the initiates weren't the only ones who had come to blows.

Graydon raised an eyebrow, his attention settling on Dethos's oshota. "Nial, why am I not surprised to find you in the midst of this?"

Nial ignored the statement, his expression stony. "Even you can't interfere in a challenge."

Graydon looked around, noting the way Dethos outnumbered them and the interested expressions of those surrounding them. "Is that what this is?"

Nial's posture was ramrod straight. If Graydon's question intimidated him, you wouldn't be able to tell by the way he held himself.

Graydon stepped forward, managing to seem threatening from that one motion. The skin around Nial's eyes tightened saying he wasn't entirely obtuse, reading the danger he was in.

"Because the emperor himself decreed the Lady Kira couldn't be challenged by those outside her House," Graydon said through bared teeth, his smile that of a dragon who'd cornered its prey.

"He said she couldn't be challenged; nothing about her doing the challenging," one of the initiates chimed in.

The oshota's jaw flexed, even as he held his silence.

Graydon fixed a dangerous look on the initiate. "Why am I not surprised to find House Dethos obeying the letter of the emperor's decree rather than its intent?"

Silence answered him.

A heavy sigh gusted from Graydon as he focused his piercing gaze on Kira. "And did you challenge them?"

Kira started to speak only to find Talon already talking. "Dethos struck first. Even by the loosest of definitions, the part of challenger would be considered theirs." His gaze flicked to the oshota. "If you wanted to instigate a challenge, you probably shouldn't have picked a place heavily frequented by Roake."

The oshota's jaw worked as he ground his teeth.

"It is possible my initiates got a little overzealous greeting the lost daughter of House Roake." The words seemed ripped out of him.

Graydon arched an unimpressed eyebrow. "I'm sure." He ran a gaze over the rest. "It seems this scheme backfired on them. I have no doubt half the city will learn your initiates got their asses handed to them by a few humans and a woman you have a distressing tendency to refer to as insane."

Nial didn't respond to the taunt, his movements jerky as he headed for the door, barking over his shoulder, "Let's go."

Slowly the rest of House Dethos filed after him as they shot fulminating glares at the rest of them.

Kira stopped next to Graydon. "I didn't know you were itching for another round in our bout."

His smile came, slow and wicked, tugging at Kira's insides. "Anytime, anywhere, *coli*. It was the highlight of my week."

His words brushed along Kira's senses, sparking a warmth inside. Call her strange, but fighting Graydon was like having all her senses ramped up a thousand-fold. It was exhilarating and thrilling because she never knew if she'd win—not that she planned to let him know that.

Kira made her way to the table where Wren stood, gazing at the half-destroyed glasses. Surprisingly, a few still stood.

"I expected better of you all," Wren said as she approached.

Raider collapsed into his seat, snagging a shot and drinking it down.

"Don't know why," Raider said, pointing the hand that held the glass at Wren. "I think we cleaned up pretty well."

Especially since one of them appeared to have had more alcohol than they should have, Kira thought with a spurt of amusement.

She was surprised at the feeling of nostalgia and regret that the night was over.

How many bars had she and the Curs closed out? How many times had one of them gotten into a fight only to have the rest step up to protect their back? A unit even when they weren't on the battlefield.

"This shows a critical lack of judgment," Wren continued as if Raider wasn't even speaking. His attention was locked on Kira, letting her know who was the real recipient of this lecture. "You're unfamiliar with this world and its customs. Drinking until you're intoxicated puts you at a disadvantage."

Graydon picked up the glass in front of her seat, taking a sip and grimacing. "Not as much as you might think."

He handed the glass to Wren, who sniffed it. His forehead wrinkled, and he took a small sip. "What is this?"

Graydon's eyes seemed to glitter with amusement. "You weren't really drinking, were you? At least not *keeva*."

Raider straightened out of his slouch, his dismayed gaze shooting to Kira's. "No."

Kira winced.

"You wouldn't mess with tradition," he said in a hushed whisper.

"Technically, tequila *is* tradition," she pointed out.

He pounded on the table. "Getting drunk is the tradition. That's why I got the *keeva*."

"If it's any consolation, I switched our drinks on the third shot so neither one of us would get too drunk," she told him.

He stared blearily up at her as his head started shaking and then kept shaking. "I thought we were sharing a moment." He flopped back in his chair. "I feel so used."

Consternation filled Kira. "At least I thought I switched them."

"You did," Finn assured as he joined them. "*Keeva* can be intoxicating for humans as well."

"Oh boy," Kira said, staring at Raider with new eyes. She'd thought he was pretending to be worse off than he was. Turns out she was wrong.

She scrubbed a hand over her face. "He is going to be so mad later."

Blue appeared at her side. "Yup. As soon as his hangover subsides, he's going to be gunning for you, Nixxy."

Great, just what Kira needed, a vengeful Raider.

She clapped her hands. "All right, let's get you out of here. I think we've done enough toasting for one night."

Raider shrugged out of Blue's grip, grabbing one of the only upright glasses and holding it up. "Not yet. There's one more toast to be done."

Kira hesitated. She had an idea of who she meant, and it was the last person she wanted to toast. "Maybe some other time. I think we've both had enough."

"No," Raider insisted. He swayed, nearly toppling over before righting himself again. "No, you toast her death. You've never done that."

Even as drunk as he was, Kira could see the resolve in his face. She wasn't going to get out of this. Not this time.

"I don't want to do this," she warned.

He grabbed one of the intact glasses that had fallen onto its side, righting it before pouring *keeva* into it. Finished, he shoved it into her hand.

"Prove to me she's dead." He lifted his glass in front of her.

This entire night had been leading up to this. All the drinks, the trips down memory lane, the names of their dead, all so he could maneuver her into this moment.

Her gaze met his, anger licking her insides, her control slipping.

He knew what this would cost her and didn't care as long as he got his result.

Her chin lifted, and she swiped the glass from the table, downing the contents in a single gulp.

Fuck him.

She slammed the glass down. "The Elise you knew is gone. The next time you want to toast our fallen, maybe don't do it as a power play."

The fierce light in his eyes faded, the hope she had failed to see snuffed out as loss and grief crept into his expression. Kira's stomach sank, regret curdling her insides. The impulse to offer comfort hovered on her tongue, swallowed before it could leave.

He wouldn't want her platitudes, and offering them would likely undo the necessary blow she'd struck him. The conclusion he'd drawn was dangerous and placed many lives in jeopardy. He needed to believe Elise was dead, even if it killed her to put that look in his eyes.

The glass slipped out of his fingers, crashing to the table and bouncing off with an air of finality. Kira barely held in her flinch as he shuffled past, the forceful spark of personality he threw at the world subdued.

Blue stopped in front of Kira. "That wasn't nice."

"What do you want from me, Blue? He asked, and I delivered." Kira felt exhausted.

Emotion. It would suck the energy out of her every time.

"Right," Blue said, not hiding her skepticism as she shoved past Kira. "You were always a terrible friend when it counted."

She left Kira standing there, staring out the window at the ocean. Self-hatred and the taste of bitter regret lingered on Kira's tongue. She couldn't even argue with Blue's statement. The truth hurt, even if it was unavoidable.

She was tired of the deceptions and the lies. The expectations.

So tired.

As much as the night had felt like coming home to family after a long time away, she needed to remember she had no family anymore. Blue and Raider were pieces of her past. A few drinks and the sharing of memories weren't going to change that.

Light reflected off a mirror in a pattern Kira recognized. She squinted at the tower window in the distance, realization making her curse silently.

Odin. Always pushing the boundaries as usual.

"We'll escort the two of them home," Rheya said hesitantly when Kira continued staring out the window. She and Devon filed in the Curs wake, shooting glances at Kira as they did so.

Graydon's heavy gaze lingered on Kira as he watched the ocean with her.

Finally, he stirred. "Let's go."

"Not really in the mood, Graydon," Kira warned.

He arched an eyebrow at her. "You've already started one fight and alienated your closest friends. Do you want to go for a third fight tonight?"

Her glare was hard, which made his smile widened as he moved away.

The urge to do exactly that tugged at her, even as she ignored it. Fighting would make her feel better in the short term, but later, when morning came, she would regret her lack of control.

No need to make things worse than they already were.

Wearily she trudged after Graydon, pausing beside Talon as she took in the destruction she and the rest had caused.

"I'd offer to pay for the damages, but I'm afraid I don't know how the Tuann monetary system works," Kira said. That regret burrowed deeper. Talon didn't deserve this. "Unless you accept human credits?"

"They're not worth much here."

She grimaced. She had a feeling.

"Don't worry. Seeing you three knock Dethos down a couple of slots was worth it." He clapped her on the shoulder. "Besides, House Roake will pay for this."

Even worse. Kira's debts kept rising.

Talon gestured at Finn with his chin. "Take care of my friend."

Kira regarded Finn for a long moment. "Do you know the story of the Phoenix?"

Talon studied her. "It's a human myth, right?"

She nodded. "I got the name because of my habit of rising from my own ashes." She started walking away. "They never bothered to warn me that those who stood next to the Phoenix tend to get burned in the same fire."

EIGHTEEN

KIRA FOUND GRAYDON staring in the direction the light signal had come from. A small gesture from him sent Amila loping toward the tower with an easy gait.

Kira mentally cursed Odin's propensity for stirring up trouble. The hacker had better have gotten out. If she got caught, Kira planned to let Jin make good on some of the threats he'd made over the years.

For now, there was nothing Kira could do. Any action she took to prevent or delay Amila would only serve to further arouse Graydon's suspicions.

Graydon's hands were clasped behind him as his eyes met hers.

She clamped her mouth shut; her expression blank.

Graydon might look like a handsome brute, but his attractive façade hid a devious mind.

She recognized her match in him. He was a survivor, like her. Someone willing to put in the hellish amount of work needed to protect what was his.

He was every bit as deadly as she was. Maybe even more so, which was why if they ever ended up enemies, she'd come for him from the shadows and only when victory was assured. He wasn't the type you fought fairly. Not if you planned on winning.

"Come," Graydon said again before walking away.

"I'm not a dog," Kira muttered. To Solal, who stood partially hidden in the shadows, she asked, "Any idea what he wants?"

"Only one way to find out," he returned.

Kira exhaled. She'd had a feeling he was going to say that.

Kira bowed to the inevitable. If they didn't do this now, Graydon was likely to force the issue at a time that was inconvenient for her.

Reluctantly, Kira followed him through the city, over cobblestone streets and by cute houses. The architecture here showed a marked difference than that of the fortress's. The two couldn't have been more different if they'd tried. The only similarity was the fact both appeared built from stone.

The city reminded Kira of the ones in old Europe. Ageless, quaint history mashed together with modern convenience. Their buildings were decorated with natural hues, allowing them to blend in with the nature all around them even as the fortress was a hulking form in the distance.

"I'm surprised Finn took you to Talon," Graydon finally said, breaking the silence.

"Why?"

Graydon looked at the ink-dark sky above. "Talon and Finn used to be pod mates. They served the same sword."

But no longer. It was on the tip of Kira's tongue to ask why.

"If he took you there, it means he trusts and admires you," Graydon said.

Kira snorted, unable to help her disbelief. That was stretching it.

Graydon's lips twitched. "What do you see when you look at this place?"

"Blind corners. Easily taken streets. An enemy would find it easy to march through this city," Kira responded immediately. On the other hand, the locals would be able to slip through any net the enemy sought to secure, the same disadvantage working against the enemy as well.

"Most would have commented on its beauty," Graydon pointed out. "However, you've only focused on the flaws in its defenses."

There was a reason for that. When your safety depended on the defensibility of your surroundings, it taught you to look at everything through a certain lens. It was a difficult habit to change.

"Are you implying I'm broken?" Kira asked.

Graydon chuckled. "Never. You're invested in protecting yourself and others. There's no shame in that."

That seemed like a nice way of saying something inside of Kira was broken.

"Do you know what separates an oshota from a sword?" Graydon asked.

"No."

And not from lack of trying.

As far as she'd been able to piece together, the person they called sword received much the same type of training. It didn't seem to be determined by birth either. Graydon was evidence of that.

"Perception," Graydon supplied.

She frowned at him, not understanding.

His chin dipped. "That's all it is. Someone perceives your strength and asks to lend theirs to yours. Sometimes that strength is physical as it is in my case; other times, it's because they recognize something deeper. A strength of soul or nobility of spirit. No amount of force or scheming can elevate you to that position. It is something that needs to be earned through your actions."

Kira's gaze fell on Finn as a dismayed look settled on her face.

"You don't seem pleased with this knowledge," Graydon said.

"I never want to be in charge of anyone else's life besides my own, again." Her words revealed much more than she intended, but she couldn't take them back now.

The truth of them reverberated in the air between them.

"You inspire loyalty in those around you," Graydon said as they approached the edge of the city before it dropped to the sea. A waist-high wall ran along the cliff, and Graydon leaned muscular forearms against the stone. "I doubt your fallen would appreciate you using their deaths as a reason to hide."

Kira couldn't help her weary huff. "You're right about that—but then the dead don't get to choose."

That blessing and curse lay solely with the living.

A pair of youths, not much older than Ziva, frolicked along the wall's edge, catching Kira's attention. She watched the excitement and innocent joy on their faces as they played a game that looked like an energetic version of tag.

They held an innocence that was missing from her young friend. The horrors of life had touched Ziva and Joule, marking them indelibly and forever changing them. They'd tasted the dark parts it had to offer; they'd known loss, and there was no way to wipe away its sting again.

"Do you remember what it's like to be young?" Kira peered at the ocean far below and the lights that glittered and swirled under its waves.

"A little," Graydon said, allowing the shift in topic. "My parents were often busy, but I remember the games my father played with me and the way my mother laughed at the two of us."

"I don't remember ever feeling young," Kira confessed. "My

childhood was pain and rage. The closest I came to joy was during the height of the war with the rest of the Curs."

They'd steadied her. For the first time, she'd felt like she belonged somewhere. She'd been good at something. There had been difficulties, sure, but it had felt worth it.

She missed that sense of purpose, even as she knew there was no returning to those days.

"Do you regret not ever having what they had?" Graydon asked, nodding toward the two.

Kira considered. "Regret isn't the right word. I wonder what it would have been like, to grow up assured of my parents' love, to know they would do anything to keep me from harm."

A hum rumbled from Graydon. "I can't help but notice the distinct lack of questions you have regarding them." He slid her a look. "And I can't help but wonder if that is by design."

Kira allowed herself a brief smile. She should have known he'd see through that. "You can't exactly manipulate someone's desires if you never know what those desires are."

"And yet you'll never learn anything if the questions are left unasked," Graydon returned.

She leaned her chin on her fist. "Right now, I'm more interested in Wren's story."

The man held her immediate future in his hands. She needed to get through him for a shot at the trial and later the *adva ka*. It was all one giant stepping stone, and he was the gatekeeper.

"You remind him of painful things," Graydon said, shooting her a look that said she wasn't fooling him. For now, he was going to let her dodge the subject of her parents, but not always.

Kira waited, hoping Graydon would continue.

He sighed and shook his head as he gave in. "He and Loudon used to serve Harlow as oshota. Both men lost much in the same attack that took the lives of your parents. Wren lost a daughter; Loudon, a wife."

Kira's head lifted. "Obviously, they responded differently to tragedy."

Graydon grunted. "Loudon threw himself into studying the Mea'Ave and its will. It meant he could no longer serve as an oshota because no sword would ever eclipse his loyalty to the Mea'Ave. Wren became one of the best military commanders the emperor and Roake has ever had. He used his grief as fuel to ascend to the next level. It took him beyond being an oshota and made him more. Now, he's one of the most respected among the warrior class. He almost never takes apprentices."

"So, the fact he's here says something," Kira concluded, her eyes narrowed.

Graydon shrugged. "You'll have to ask your uncle or Wren about that. I had nothing to do with it."

For once.

"Why?" Kira asked.

"If I had to guess, it's because Wren is the best. Your uncle is many things, but I have never doubted his devotion to his brother—and by extension, you."

Kira cast him an arch look. "Is that why you sold me out to him?"

Graydon pressed a hand to his chest. "Such harsh words, but we both know in my position you'd do the same." He lifted a finger and pressed it into her forehead. "Like it or not, you contain the potential to be a devastating weapon. No sane person would allow that weapon to be turned against them. There was also the small fact of your health." He dipped his chin, staring at her from under lowered brows. "Or are you going to try to convince me, you're not using this opportunity to your advantage."

Kira avoided his gaze, staring stubbornly at the sea. Maybe so, but that didn't mean she had to be happy about the part he'd played in matters.

His shoulder nudged her. "You forget I saw you drop the initiates off that cliff. You had fun. I know you did."

Her answer was forestalled as one of the youths lost his balance. Kira jolted forward as they teetered on the edge, knowing she would never be in time.

Graydon remained motionless behind her as the youth plummeted. Several seconds later, a splash sounded, and then a voice shouted up at them.

Kira watched open-mouthed as the second youth laughed before backflipping off the cliff.

Two heads appeared in the waves below as they swam along the cliffs.

"The *adal.* Loosely translated, it means the reckoning," Graydon mused, joining her where she peered over the edge. "I remember doing something similar when I was their age. Tuann on the cusp of adolescence often challenge each other to dangerous undertakings. As challenges go, this one is relatively safe."

"Relatively?" Kira stared at him in disbelief.

Did he understand how far below the ocean was? If they hit it wrong, they could break a limb. At the very least, they could knock the air out of their lungs and make surfacing difficult. She'd known hardened soldiers who would have hesitated at such a jump.

Graydon grinned, his expression suddenly sly.

Kira took a step back. "Don't even think about it."

Graydon was already climbing onto the edge. "You wanted to know what it would have meant to grow up Tuann."

Kira lunged, trying to grab him. Too late as he tilted, letting gravity drag him over the edge. He dropped into a headfirst dive.

"You're still wearing your armor," she shouted after him.

It was no use. He was already gone.

Kira shot an angry glance at Finn and the rest of Graydon's oshota. They stared placidly back.

Kira growled before clambering onto the wall. At least she knew where she got her lack of fear about heights from. It seemed her species were nearly as crazy as her.

She stepped away from the wall, not allowing herself to second guess or think about all the things that could go wrong. Things like hitting rock instead of water, of getting sucked down by an undertow, drowning, breaking a limb. Nothing mattered except the thrill of falling.

The rush she got as air swept by her was familiar.

Kira crossed her arms over her chest and pointed her toes an instant before she hit the water.

Its icy embrace closed over her head as she held her breath. When her descent slowed, she opened her eyes and started to swim for the surface, the lights she'd seen playing on the waves all around her, emanating from everywhere and nowhere at the same time.

Kira's ascent paused as she stopped to study a fleck where it bobbed next to her. She reached out to touch it and withdrew in surprise when it winked out.

Her curiosity thwarted, and her lungs burning, she kicked, propelling herself toward the surface. The first gasp of blessed air was a welcome relief.

As soon as she could breathe properly again, she shouted,

"Graydon, you bastard. You'd better not have drowned."

A warm chuckle sounded in her ear seconds before arms wrapped around her. Kira had enough time to mentally curse and suck in a lung full of air as he sank beneath the waves, taking her with him.

She wiggled free, using his torso as a springboard as she made her escape. They surfaced at the same time. Graydon remained mostly submerged, only his eyes and nose peeking above the water.

It was surprisingly mischievous—and disturbingly adorable.

A wall of water hit her from the side, nearly drowning her in the process.

Kira coughed and choked when she finally surfaced. "How is that fair? I can't use *ki* to exact revenge."

He smirked at her. "The strong know you have to make your own justice."

He wanted to play like that, did he? He had no idea what he'd started.

The smile that flared on his face said he did and looked forward to the battle.

Kira dove before he could grab her, cutting through the water with the efficiency of a shark. She might not have spent much time planetside, but she'd always loved the water, spending as much time in it as she could.

Unburdened by armor, Kira found herself with the advantage. Graydon was fast, but here, she was faster. She grabbed his leg, yanking him down, disengaging before he could retaliate. She was already swimming away, disappearing into the inky darkness.

The water grabbed her, an invisible current dragging her toward the surface and above where she hovered a foot above the ocean as Graydon laughed.

With a sly grin, Graydon released his *ki,* and Kira splashed into the water, going under.

Graydon was waiting for her with a taunting smile as she surfaced. "That's not all you've got, is it? I must confess to being disappointed if it is. I was looking forward to a challenge."

Kira snarled, whipping the water off her face.

"Now, what are you going to do, *coli*?" he said, his voice wrapping around her like decadent silk.

She was going to conquer.

Before she got the chance, waves, disobeying the laws of physics, swamped her, sending her spinning. She grinned as she tumbled through the water. It wasn't going to be that easy.

She reached out with her senses, her heart leaping as the faintest trickle of *ki* answered her. It was nowhere near the tsunami that had once flooded her, but after weeks of nothing, its presence felt like the first battle cry of victory.

As it flowed through her fingers, Kira considered her best options. She couldn't compete head to head with Graydon, not with *ki*. Not yet.

However, there were other ways.

Kira started to swim away from him, letting him think he'd won, and she was trying to escape. A chuckle rumbled from him as he sliced through the water toward her.

That's it. Come to mama.

The *ki* trailed out from her, gossamer-thin strands barely visible in her mind's eye as Graydon cut through them. Sweat popped on her forehead as she coaxed more of those strands out of her, faster and faster, tangling them to create a deceptive web, one that looked fragile but wasn't.

Those threads wrapped around Graydon's limbs, creating a lasso that tightened the more he moved.

She flexed that internal muscle she associated with the *ki,* and the lasso tightened, halting his movement.

Surprise reflected off Graydon's face, and she chortled at his shock as he was yanked beneath the surface of the waves.

That was her chance. The web she'd spun with *ki,* creating dozens of wire-thin currents to impede his progress, wouldn't delay him long. Kira sliced through the water toward the shore, reaching for every bit of speed she had.

Her feet touched bottom, and she stretched, victory within reach.

He yanked her back, murmuring in her ear. "Nice try. Give up yet?"

"You should know by now, I don't know the meaning of the word," Kira taunted. She drove her elbow into his face, a victorious grin chasing across her face at his muffled curse as he dropped her.

That'd teach him not to take victory for granted.

She sloshed forward, feeling the *ki* build. She tried to hurry, the water fighting her. He barked a word and a wave crested, sending her tumbling. She scrabbled at the seabed as it dragged her backward, dumping her at Graydon's feet in waist-high water.

She burst from the water, aiming a punch at the arrogant angle of Graydon's jaw. His head shifted as one hand changed the trajectory of hers. "I believe this is my win."

"Not yet," Kira snarled.

She thrust the heel of her palm into his chest, much as she had the woman from House Dethos. Unlike the woman, Graydon barely budged as pain rocketed through her wrist and palm.

Graydon's hand was gentle as it cradled hers where her hand still rested on his chest. "Was that a love tap? I barely felt it."

Kira bared her teeth. Love tap, her ass.

She kicked out, aiming for his knee. Graydon stumbled sideways, recovering in time to block the two punches she aimed at the side of his head. He grabbed one of her arms, twisting. Kira twisted with it, unprepared for him to shove her away.

This time she was the one to stumble, barely defending against him as he hammered a blow against her side. She caught it with a side block, her grin bloodthirsty and vicious. Another man might have retreated. Not Graydon. His answering grin invited her to reciprocate.

Normal ocean waves battered at them, making footing difficult.

Kira thrilled at the challenge, whipping a feint at his head before dropping and hammering both fists into the side of his knee. It collapsed, a grunt of pain leaving Graydon.

Was that love tap enough for him?

She didn't get the chance to dwell on her victory as he followed up with his own feint and lunge, forcing her to back away. They fought like that, each gaining and losing ground as they battled.

"What's wrong? A little tired?" he asked, his chest moving from his exertions.

"Please, this is nothing," she returned, as out of breath as him.

They leaped toward each other, coming together with a crash. Pain blossomed along Kira's side and arms. She ignored it, returning the favor seconds later when Graydon's guard dropped.

He shoved her back, using his bigger mass and greater strength as a battering ram.

Kira cursed as a wave nearly sent her under. The same wave caused his balance to wobble.

She moved before he could recover, latching onto his arm and attempting a judo throw. He let his balance fall forward, changing his grip at the last minute and taking her with him.

She felt her balance reach the point of no return and sucked in a breath as they both went under. Graydon wrapped her in a bear hug and rolled them away from shore.

She brought her legs up, planting them against his belly and shoving. He resisted, and for a split second, she feared she wouldn't get free. She strained, putting more force into her legs. She popped free, her spine hitting the sea bed.

She floated up, blinking into the oddly lit water. Finally, noticing how bright it had gotten. Small balls of light coalescing around their bodies until it looked as if they were glowing.

Kira forgot their battle, pushing herself toward the surface.

Graydon rose with her, hovering an arm's length away as she touched the small glowing balls with wonder. What sort of creature or plant created such things?

She laughed at the gentle sensation brushed against her skin, like something was mouthing it to get her taste. It felt astonishingly like thousands of silky hairs brushing along her fingers and hand.

"They're *feilli*," Graydon rumbled, his eyes soft as he watched her interact with the glowing balls. "They're symbiotic. Their preferred food source is the *lu-ong*, but our *ki* will work too. With the *lu-ong* being this close to shore for the first time in years, we've had a better than average nightly display."

"Are they dangerous?"

"No. Feel," he instructed.

She did. The slight zips of energy weren't only one way. She could feel it flowing into her as well, a constant feedback loop, strengthening and healing. All around them the *feilli* lit up, creating a river of light under the water as they led into the wide ocean. In other places, smaller groupings of dots floated along the waves. For a moment, Kira let herself get lost in the wonder, fancying the stars above had come down to dance with the ocean.

"I've never seen anything like it," Kira breathed.

Her eyes met his. The moment stretched between them, a magnet slowly and inexorably drawing them together.

Their bodies brushed, the movement of the waves bobbing them up and down. His lips found hers, soft and firm. She reached up, her hands landing on his shoulders as he pulled her body tight against his.

Her legs wound up around his waist as he fed at her mouth. The glow around them grew, the *feilli* burning brighter as if in response.

"This is a bad idea," Kira said between kisses.

"I don't care.

She didn't either, too busy glutting herself on him. Adrenaline transformed to desire as his hands moved along her back. A bright sensation, almost too intense to bear, stole her breath.

Her fingers scrabbled at his armor, wanting to touch bare skin. Frustration hummed through her when they met hard resistance.

One of his hands landed on her breast, his clever fingers swirling over her nipple. She forgot about his armor, arousal shooting through her as her head fell back. Graydon's lips left hers to travel along her jaw and then the sensitive side of her neck.

His expression was feral, possession and anticipation crouched in his eyes. Challenge glittered in hers.

Graydon was the temptation she kept trying to resist, his presence a drug.

His lips moved over hers, his hands cupping her ass as he pulled her more fully against him. Kira wiggled against his armor. She squeaked as it peeled back, leaving bare skin for her to explore. She didn't hesitate, her hands moving over muscle, squeezing, unsurprised at his hardness. His physique showed the commitment to his cause, developed over years. Right now, though, it existed solely for her pleasure.

Her tongue flicked out, tasting salt on his skin as a breath shuddered out of him. She smiled against him. She was glad she wasn't the only one who had trouble thinking in these stolen moments.

"Come to my room," he demanded as she trailed her lips along his jaw, nibbling on the side of his neck in a mirror of what he'd done to her moments before.

"Can't."

"You keep saying that," he growled.

Her fingers dug into his waist as she fought to resist the arousal coiling in her belly. It was harder than it should have been.

If he'd been just a pretty face, she could have walked away without a backward glance. He wasn't. His mind was as intriguing as his body.

"That doesn't mean it isn't true," she told him.

"Face it, you find me irresistible."

Surprisingly, she found his grumpy arrogance charming. More so as he dropped another kiss on the side of her neck right below her ear.

Her eyelashes fluttered shut. She cleared her throat. She was on the brink of giving in. She wanted this so much more than she could admit.

The word "yes" hovered on her lips, swallowed as a presence on the shore caught their attention. Graydon's armor crawled across his skin, cloaking his vulnerability as a harsh exhale left him, visible irritation replacing the anticipation that had been there.

"What?" he growled.

"A communication came in from the emperor," Solal said, amusement in his normally staid voice.

The sound Graydon released held a lot in common with a snarl. "I'll be there momentarily."

The look he fixed on Kira nearly made her laugh. He reminded her of a child denied a treat, pouty and sulky. She smoothed a hand over his cheek, the twin feelings of regret and relief twisting her insides.

"Duty calls," she said.

It was a needed reminder. Graydon might be attracted to her and she to him, but he answered to a powerful master. One who would no doubt destroy Kira if all her secrets ever came to light.

"We're going to finish this one day," Graydon informed her.

"Promises, promises."

Graydon pushed the hair from her face, his gaze intent. "You'll see."

Kira unlocked her legs and dropped to her feet, the water rising to chest level.

She took the opportunity to duck under the waves so she didn't have to see Graydon go. The chilly embrace of the water dousing some of her passion and providing clarity.

Kira was last to reach the shore. She found Solal with his head bent toward Graydon as he relayed the message.

Graydon held up a hand, halting him as Kira lumbered out of the waves, feeling considerably less powerful and graceful than she had during their mock battle. She shivered as a breeze touched her, conscious of the cold in a way she hadn't been with Graydon's heat beside her.

"I look forward to tomorrow," Graydon said.

"What's tomorrow?"

His teeth flashed. "You'll see."

Graydon walked away, leaving her gaping after him.

"I'll see what? Graydon?"

A wave over his shoulder was his only answer as he headed toward a small opening in the cliff Kira hadn't seen before now.

That wasn't enigmatic or anything.

Kira caught Solal's stare, his expression disturbingly neutral. She scowled at him, not fooled. The amusement was there for someone who had spent any time with him.

Her scowl made his lips twitch.

Solal dipped his chin in a respectful nod as he finally followed his commander.

Finn's shadow detached from the cliff as he moved to stand beside her to watch Graydon and his oshota's retreat.

"I don't want to hear it," she finally said.

She was well aware this had been a serious error in judgment. Something about the combination of the moon and Graydon made her lose her head. It worked magic on her senses, luring her into situations that could only cause trouble in the long run.

"I haven't said anything," Finn said neutrally.

"You're thinking it. Loudly."

Kira sensed rather than saw his small smile. "Perhaps you're projecting."

Kira glanced at him. "Pretty sure I'm not."

If only she could believe it.

NINETEEN

KIRA SLOGGED TOWARD the spot where had Graydon disappeared, hoping it led to the city above. From there, she could find her way to the fortress. Otherwise, it was going to be a long climb.

She ignored the way her shoes squished and squelched after their submerging in the sea. Already sand was beginning to make its way into them, rubbing at the soles of her feet and along her heel. Happily, Graydon had left the access to the tunnel open for them.

"For someone determined not to form attachments, you have shown a certain proclivity for them," Finn observed.

Kira didn't respond. This was a well-known weakness of hers. It'd been the same with the Curs. She'd only intended to form a team capable of combating the Tsavitee. It hadn't been long until they developed into a makeshift family.

She hoped she wouldn't fall into the same trap here.

Kira came to a sharp stop as the tunnel abruptly widened into a large cavern, walls sloping up to meet an arched cathedral ceiling, paintings the like of which she'd never seen decorating it. The colors were vibrant and saturated, almost too intense. Gold separated the different panels, leading Kira's eye through a story she didn't quite understand.

She had a feeling she could sit there for hours and still find something new to discover in the paintings above.

"What is this?" Kira asked.

In the center of the cavern, a massive crystal cluster drew her attention. What she at first assumed was a natural phenomenon, she soon discovered wasn't. The column formations were entirely too uniform, pointing to the Tuann's hand in their design.

The crystal shimmered, flecks of rose and gold seeming to dance and move, almost like a fire flickered within its depths. Vaguely diamond shaped, the crystal cluster had dozens of columns branching off the large geode in the middle.

Kira moved closer, the feel of water splashing underneath her foot drawing her up short. Abruptly, she realized a thin layer of liquid covered the smooth floor surrounding the crystal cluster.

Kira caught movement as scattered Tuann kneeled in the water, touching a column and bowing their head.

The atmosphere of the cavern was somber. Almost holy.

Small candles bobbed on the water like offerings. Flowers floated near them, some on the surface, others submerged beneath.

Finn's voice was hushed and filled with respect. "We call it the *etheiri*. It's a place of remembrance."

"Like the banners in the Warrior's Hall," Kira guessed.

Finn's head cocked as he thought. "Similar, but different. The banners represent those who fell in service to House Roake. This is for anyone who lost someone in the Sorrowing."

Kira took in the crystal cluster. As a memorial, it certainly made a statement. It was surreal and beautiful. Peace and serenity seemed to fill the space.

"Kira, how kind of you to visit," Loudon said from a few feet away.

He wore the synth armor and ceremonial robe and vestments similar to the ones she'd seen him in that first day, though the colors were different—and unexpected. They looked like a sunrise, deep orange at the ends transitioning into a golden color toward the middle.

On Loudon's face, he'd painted runes on both cheeks and his forehead, connecting them with a complicated pattern of swirls and lines. The effect was startling. Stare too long, and the slightest bit of dizziness would creep in.

"Have you come to visit with your father?" he asked.

Kira's forehead wrinkled. Her father was dead—or so people kept telling her. What did this place have to do with him?

"I'm not sure what you mean."

"Come, I'll show you." Loudon walked toward the cluster, leaving Kira with no choice but to trail behind him like a lost lamb. She bid her plans of finding her bed and changing out of her wet clothes a grumpy farewell. Annoying as Loudon's presumption was, she found herself curious and knew this place would only torture her with questions if she didn't follow.

Loudon's step was confident as he circled the crystal cluster, careful not to step in the water as he gave Kira a brief history lesson. "The Tuann believe no one is ever truly gone. Their physical bodies might wither and decay, but as long as we are connected to the Mea'Ave a piece of us lives on. In a sense, this place is a graveyard."

Kira looked at the cavern with new eyes.

"The Mea'Ave responded to our overwhelming grief during the Sorrowing and created this. Each column houses the memory of someone we lost," Loudon instructed.

He stepped over the small, narrow channel separating the water from the rest of the cavern. The faint trickle as it cascaded over the lip of the ledge echoed in the space. Kira was a bit surprised the candles and flowers didn't float over the mini waterfall, but perhaps that was because the gap separating it from the rest of the room was only a few centimeters wide.

Loudon's steps were soundless, ripples spreading out from each foot in ever-widening rings as he walked toward the cluster.

Kira hesitated on the edge, before glancing at Finn. His blank, emotionless expression wasn't exactly a surprise. He did that a lot when others joined them, especially if it wasn't someone he knew or particularly trusted.

Since Loudon was House Roake and likely familiar to Finn, she suspected it was the latter. Still, the fact Finn hadn't already tried to stop her said he didn't think whatever Loudon wanted to show her was dangerous. That was something, at least.

Finally, Kira took a step, freezing as soon as her foot touched the water. It was like stepping into a pool of mild electricity. Her shoes were no impediment as she rode the line between discomfort and pain. A stinging awareness pricked her as her senses were thrown wide, every part of her on high alert.

She wavered between the need to step back and the desire to move forward as she wrestled with the uncomfortable sensation.

After a brief battle of wills, she forced herself forward, inching toward the cluster.

Once she neared him, Loudon inclined his head to her. "I apologize. I forgot the effect the *etheiri* can have on the undisciplined mind."

Kira wasn't sure how to react to that statement. While his tone had been kind and understanding, his words suggested an insult.

In the end, she chose to do nothing, more interested in what he had to share than his hidden motivations.

"Here. Feel." Loudon set his hand on the small growth, his eyes sliding shut as his face relaxed, happiness and bliss on it.

Kira reached out, barely touching it. Warmth spread through her, a tight sensation in her chest gripped her heart as it overflowed with feelings.

Behind her eyelids, she caught a glimpse of a woman, her smile soft, love in her eyes as she glanced over her shoulder with a mischievous grin. Her hair was a riot of curls, reaching to her waist. It framed a heart-shaped face with a button nose. On both cheeks, symbols were painted in blue, seeming to add to her beauty rather than detract from it. She wore a loose, flowing dress that exposed the skin of her shoulders and arms before ending inches above her bare feet.

"Marielle," he whispered. His longing was easy to hear.

The feelings were too much. Kira stepped back. Her cheeks wet as she fought to untangle the riot of emotions, none of which were hers.

Loudon didn't move for several long seconds, still lost in the memory. Kira used the time to compose herself, her breathing returning to normal, and some of the emotions from the memory fading as he withdrew from the crystal.

His eyes were glassy with unshed tears as he folded his hands behind his back.

"My wife," he said in answer to the questions on Kira's face. "She was taken from me the same day your parents died."

"I'm sorry for your loss," Kira murmured. She gazed up at the crystal cluster, a grim feeling settling in her stomach. There must be thousands of columns. "Do these represent all those who died that day?"

Loudon nod was somber. "The Mea'Ave helps us remember the things that affect the collective. In time, when the sting of events fade, the columns will merge into one."

Kira gazed around the room, finally noticing other columns interspersed throughout the great cavern, their surface smooth, light refracting off them.

"Other times of tragedy for the Tuann," Loudon supplied, noticing where her attention had gone. "I wouldn't touch them, however. Their memories are chaotic. Only those who have practice can sort through them."

"People like you?" Kira asked.

Loudon inclined his head. "One of my duties is to interpret the histories written in our memories. It can take years to build up the discipline needed to unravel the tangled threads."

"Interesting," Kira said, gazing around.

She didn't know how she felt about the cluster and the memories encased within. On the one hand, being able to revisit a moment with your loved one would be a priceless gift. On the other, how were you to heal when constantly confronted with the memories of what you'd lost?

"Would you like to find your father's memories?" Loudon asked, his gaze shadowed.

Kira exhaled. "Somehow, I don't think that's a good idea."

Especially not in Loudon's company. He'd done nothing to arouse suspicion, but everything inside Kira rebelled at leaving herself so vulnerable in front of another.

It was surprising the depth of yearning she had for memories of a man she'd never met and never would. She'd thought she was over the phase where she wished for a family that would never come.

She liked to think she was strong. Resourceful. She didn't need a mother and father anymore. Either way, she doubted a few memories would fill the ache of their absence, anyway. They'd simply remind her of what had never been hers in the first place.

"You remind me of him," Loudon said.

Kira snorted. "Of my father? People keep telling me that."

Loudon tilted his head. "I was thinking more of your uncle."

Kira's attention swung toward him.

Loudon smiled. "Did that surprise you?"

"A little, yeah."

Loudon stared up at the cluster in thought. "Your father was considered a great man. Fate was kind to him."

"What do you mean?"

Loudon looked down as he clasped his hands in front of him. "Did you know your father and Harlow were twins? And that Harlow is the older?"

Kira thought it was safe to say there was a lot she didn't know about her family. Loudon must have understood because he chuckled.

"In our society, the position of Overlord is one of strength and power. Certain criteria must be met before you assume the mantle."

"Like a primus form," Kira supplied slowly.

He nodded, a flash of appreciation at the example crossing his face. "Very good. That is one. Every House has their own criteria, certain checkboxes that must be ticked off."

"And someone who doesn't meet the qualifications is passed over," Kira guessed.

"In rare instances, a House might decide to follow another, but such occurrences usually only happen in times of turmoil when a different type of leadership might prove more advantageous."

Kira thought she saw where he was going with this.

"In every way but two, Harlow was the better choice for Overlord. His military acumen was unrivaled. The lack of primus wasn't much of a concern since he had no trouble fighting against them," Loudon said.

"But my father became Overlord."

Loudon inclined his head. "I knew them both when we were young. They were like night and day. Your father had this way about him. He was charming, charismatic. People followed him. Drawn to him in the same way they were captivated by your mother."

"And my uncle?"

Loudon's gaze was far away, with his mind mired deep in memories of long ago. "He served from the shadows. He was Harding's strong right arm, doing what the Overlord couldn't or wouldn't do for himself."

Kira cast a sideways look at him. "It seems like you think my uncle should have been the one to be Overlord."

Loudon paused, his laugh surprised. "Oh, no. I don't care about such things. Your father was a good leader. He did the best he could to protect our people."

The sound Kira made was unconvinced. From the way Loudon spoke, that was hard to believe—especially when standing in the presence of memories of the dead.

A soft splash behind them drew their attention.

Harlow stopped several feet away, two flowers the size of Kira's head cradled in gentle hands. One was a soft baby blue, a white stamen jutting from its middle. The other was the color of a yellow daisy, bright and cheery.

"Loudon. Niece." Harlow's greeting rumbled through the room.

"Overlord," Loudon said, stepping away from the cluster. "I see you've brought your weekly offering. You're a few days early, aren't you?"

Harlow's gaze lingered on Kira a few seconds before shifting to Loudon. "Liliana and Harding have been on my mind often of late."

Understanding and sympathy filled Loudon's face. "I was explaining to your niece about the *etheiri* and her father."

Harlow was quiet, his expression hard to read. Finally, he bent, placing the flowers to float along the water. Their petals touched as if holding hands as they bobbed in the waves his disturbance had caused.

"Would you like to see a memory of Harding now that you know more?" Loudon asked.

Kira's smile was stiff. "Not right now. Perhaps another time."

"Yes, you should be resting for tomorrow," Harlow said, finally standing.

Uncertainty filled Loudon's expression as he glanced between the two of them. "What is tomorrow?"

"The *uhva na* is ready." Harlow's voice was deep and calm as it flowed through the space. "Wren has a plan to test the initiates before making his final decision regarding those who will attempt the Trial of the Broken."

Loudon had concern etched on his face. "So soon? I thought we were going to wait until a more appropriate time." His glance at Kira had her stiffening, leaving her with no doubt as to the real reason he wanted to wait. "If we are too hasty ushering them along this path, it can cause unnecessary damage and leave them ill-prepared for what they face after the *adva ka*."

"The *uhva na* has opened. The Mea'Ave has decided," Harlow said, his words final.

Loudon's mouth snapped shut on what he'd been about to say, his shoulders slumping as he conceded the battle.

Harlow's gaze softened, and he clasped the other man on the shoulder. "There is precedence. It's rare for our young to advance so quickly, but not unheard of. You know that as well as anyone since you advanced years earlier than most. Graydon is another example. This is sooner than we intended, but that isn't necessarily a bad thing."

Loudon's expression was still reluctant. "I suppose if it's the Mea'Ave's will, I have no grounds to stand against it."

Harlow's hand dropped as he inclined his head. "Commune with Marielle. I know you look forward to these times. I'll see my niece back to the fortress."

Loudon bowed. "As you wish."

Harlow jerked his head at Kira. She walked toward him, sliding one last glance at Loudon as she passed.

Their conversation had been unexpectedly insightful, revealing new depths to Roake's tapestry. Everyone else she'd met had nothing but nice things to say about her father, yet Loudon seemed to think the wrong twin got the accolades. Because he'd once been in Harlow's pod and as a result was unwaveringly loyal? Or was it because he saw something the rest didn't or weren't willing to share?

They were interesting questions to ponder.

Finn shadowed them as they disappeared through one of the tunnel offshoots to the main cavern.

Kira felt the path tilt upward, the climb a gradual one as they ascended. Eventually, oshota clad in House Roake colors came into view, guarding a staircase leading up. Above their heads fluttered the deep blue of House Roake's banner.

The oshota murmured greetings to their Overlord as they passed, their curious gazes flitting to Kira and then away.

Seeing the question on Kira's face, Harlow explained, "The *etheiri* welcomes all, but the individual pathways belong to the Houses. Roake defends what's ours."

"Are you expecting an attack?" Kira asked.

"Such an occurrence is always possible. I find it wise to be prepared."

Paranoid. Always ready for the worst outcome. Who knew such traits were inheritable?

"How did you find the *etheiri*?" Harlow asked.

Kira cast a significant glance behind her.

"I would have been informed if you'd passed through here."

She lifted her eyebrows in surprise. "Keeping tabs on me?"

His answering smile was slight, a micro expression similar to one she'd seen on Graydon. "Did you expect any different?"

Kira thought about it and then shrugged. "Not really."

In his shoes, she'd likely do the same.

Finally, she answered. "Graydon showed me your ocean and the *feilli*. I found the cavern from there."

Harlow made a show of looking around as if to say he didn't see Graydon anywhere.

This time Kira's grin was crooked. "He was called away on

important business."

Harlow shook his head. "That boy hasn't changed."

Unprepared to have a man such as Graydon referred to as "boy", Kira bit back a laugh. It somehow seemed wrong using a word such as that to describe someone as dangerous and deadly as Graydon. She supposed it pointed to the type of relationship the two shared that Harlow could get away with such things.

Harlow's gaze was oddly fascinated as he took in her amusement. "He is the emperor's man. It's unlikely that will ever change."

One corner of Kira's lips quirked up. "Romantic advice, uncle? I didn't think we had that sort of relationship."

Harlow tipped his chin. "You're right. We're not typical uncle and niece. The formation of our bonds was delayed, but that doesn't mean they cannot be built."

Harlow didn't strike her as being overly sentimental. He was too focused on his mission, that of protecting and securing his House. It was one of the reasons she couldn't help questioning his insistence on her presence there. She was a stick thrown into the highly efficient cogs of his world. Why go to such lengths to ensure she remained when it would be easy to let her *ki* poisoning run its course?

Was it really because of duty? Or was there something more?

"I was surprised to see you in the *etheiri*," Kira finally said.

Harlow's passage was silent as he padded beside her, unable to hide the deadly grace with which he moved. Like Graydon, he was a predator. A killer. The way he passed through the world made that easy to see.

Their similarities weren't surprising. After all, her uncle had trained Graydon into the force he was.

"Why would that surprise you?" he asked. "The *etheiri* is where we go to grieve."

"But the Sorrowing happened ninety-two years ago," Kira said, watching him carefully. "That's a long time to cling to the past."

Harlow looked at her. "Is there a length I should shoot for? Perhaps twelve years is enough?"

Touché. *Well played, uncle,* Kira thought as she tipped her chin at him.

"We're not humans. We don't grieve in the same way. Our lives are long; our memories longer."

They reached the top of the stairs, stepping out under a starry sky, the fortress lurking above them, its smooth walls waiting for a signal before revealing the door Kira knew waited.

She hesitated, looking up at the sky. "A place like that only serves to keep your pain fresh."

She couldn't see the purpose behind such a thing.

"I agree. The *etheiri* is a double-edged sword." He took in the stars. "Loudon is one of the most disciplined people I know, yet he spends more time in that place than is wise. For the unwary, the *etheiri* can become a crutch, an endless reminder of what they've lost."

Kira studied her uncle. "Yet, you still visit regularly."

He looked at her, his face difficult to read in the dark. "Sometimes, I find myself in need of remembering what failure looks like."

In light of Loudon's revelations, his words were oddly revealing. And concerning.

"How does that help?" Kira asked.

"My twin was taken from me during the Sorrowing, his wife slain steps away from your crib. My niece was stolen." There was a suppressed rage in his voice. It was all the more terrifying for how controlled he sounded, as if he embraced the fury, allowing it to coldly burn until he could unleash it. "My failure was in not protecting my family. It won't happen again."

He blamed himself for her parent's deaths, Kira realized.

That was the piece she'd been missing.

From the sound of it, he didn't seem like he'd done any healing in the years following. His visits to the *etheiri* had kept the wound open, and Harlow had allowed it to fester, bleeding into everything that he was.

"You never found those responsible?" she asked carefully, sensing she was in dangerous territory.

"Not all of them." His answer was soft and succinct.

She'd suspected as much. If he had, the pain wouldn't still be so bright and immediate. Maybe he would have allowed himself to heal if he'd found and punished his brother's killers.

That was the real reason Harlow still visited the *etheiri*. He wanted revenge—and he was using Kira to get it.

That was the only thing she could think of. There had to be a traitor within Roake. Too much damage had been done too quickly. The assailants had known right where to hit them.

He'd said it himself—she was his niece, but they never got the chance to discover what that meant. The bonds of blood and family never developed.

Fishing expeditions were always easier when you used bait you weren't emotionally attached to.

"I see," she said after a long pause.

It wasn't that she blamed him. In his position, she'd likely have done the same. Hell, wasn't that why she'd embarked on her mission? Revenge and a chance to right the wrongs done to her.

"I'm not sure you do," Harlow said. "Either way, it's best you head to bed. Tomorrow will be eventful."

"So, people keep telling me." Kira readied for the door to appear.

Harlow remained where he was. "One last thing, niece."

She paused, looking at him in the dark.

"Three unidentified objects left orbit around Ta Da'an while the barrier was down."

Kira fought to cover her surprise. "Is that so?"

"You wouldn't happen to know anything about that, would you?"

For once, she didn't have to lie. "No."

He nodded, raising his hand and setting it against the wall. A door shimmered into existence.

Kira paused on the threshold. She might eventually leave this place, but these people were hers in a mixed-up fashion. She couldn't leave them defenseless.

"If I were you, I'd increase your security and add redundancies designed to ferret out traitors. If the Tsavitee were on those ships, they won't come at the Tuann directly like they did in Ta Da'an. They'll use manipulation to de-stabilize your military and government. Expect betrayal. They have a nasty habit of exploiting people's weak spots."

Kira didn't wait for his response, walking through the door with a final wave over her shoulder.

"Sleep well, niece." Harlow's words followed her into the darkness.

*

When Kira finally dragged herself to her room, it was to find a surprise waiting for her as soon as she opened the door. Only reflexes honed in the worst life and death situations saved her from a shot to the chest.

She jerked sideways, letting the energy blast skate by her. Adrenaline abruptly flooded her limbs as she prepared to attack.

A blanket floated up from the bed. "Password."

"Jin?"

"Password," the blanket demanded again.

"You know who it is," Kira snapped as Finn moved silently into position behind her, his en-blade already out. At the sound of Jin's voice, he relaxed slightly, shifting to resume his position against the opposite wall.

"I don't plan on leaving the room until morning. You can get some rest in a real bed," she informed Finn.

Truthfully, she was too tired to go anywhere.

Finn eyed the sheet. "I'll wait until you're inside, and the door is closed.

"Not until she gives me the password," Jin insisted.

Kira glared, her lips flattening into an angry expression. "You know who I am."

"Do I, though? You've been in contact with Odin, who is a sneaky, devious toadstool. Who knows what deceptions she's enacted?"

Finn seemed entirely too interested in their conversation for Kira's comfort. In the rooms around them, she could hear people stirring. It wouldn't be long before someone got up the courage to open their door. If they caught Kira talking to a floating blanket, it wasn't going to be good.

"If you don't let me in right now, I'm going to fry your circuits and reassemble them as a toaster oven," she threatened through gritted teeth.

There was a pause.

"Yup, that's definitely you."

Finally.

There was a slight buzz and the field covering the door disappeared. Kira waved at Finn. "I'll see you tomorrow."

He didn't look exactly reassured, but at least he didn't try to follow her into the room either.

Kira closed the door as she heard two others open.

She leveled a glare at her friend. "What the hell was that?"

Jin didn't answer as sharp jolts of electricity darted through her limbs.

Kira held in her yelp, knowing the sound would draw Finn, no doubt provoking an extreme reaction.

When the electricity died, Kira said through clenched teeth, "Jin, you're seriously making me mad."

"With Odin in the mix, I thought it best we up our security precautions."

"By electrocuting me?" Kira knew her voice was edging toward hysterical but found she didn't care. This was extreme, even for Jin.

"I needed to destroy any bugs she might have left on you. I'm not risking a single piece of her coding reaching my hardware," he told her.

She stared at him in disbelief.

"You're paranoid," she told him.

"No, I'm not. I found two suspicious lines in my coding," he argued. "I don't know what they do yet, but I will."

Unfortunately, Jin had good reason for his paranoia. This wasn't the first time Odin had pulled a stunt like this. The two had been locked into this odd war for as long as they'd known each other.

Odin thought it was a game. Jin didn't help matters, retaliating every time she snuck something by him.

"From now on, we're going to have a four-point authentication system and two sterilization sessions any time you return," Jin informed her as he swept around her to cut off her path to the shower.

"Not happening." She sidestepped him and entered the shower.

He stayed outside, raising his voice so she could still hear him over the sound of running water. "I thought you might say that."

Kira eyed the open door with suspicion. He sounded way calmer than he should have.

She finished up, grabbing a clean towel and wiping off before donning a shirt and panties for bed.

Dry and moderately warm again, she headed for the bed, collapsing into it, almost groaning in bliss at finally being horizontal again. She was so tired.

Her eyes had barely closed when the bed moved under her. She popped upright, staring at the covers in horror as they bulged.

"That's why I took the liberty of coming up with an alternate plan," Jin said proudly.

Kira drew aside the sheet to find a small metallic lizard. He cocked his head at her, his movements incredibly lifelike as his tongue flicked out, tasting the air.

"Ta da," Jin sang. "I've spawned. Meet the new mini Jin."

Kira choked, dismay and disbelief written on her features as her gaze lifted. She shook her head.

"What?" Jin asked. "He's cute."

"No," Kira finally managed to say. She shook her head again as if by doing so Jin might listen. "Absolutely not."

Jin happily talked over her. "I've decided due to certain events, you can no longer be trusted on your own."

"What events?" Kira asked through gritted teeth.

Jin ticked them off one by one. "The primus. The confrontation in the classroom. Meeting Odin unsupervised. Jumping off a cliff to have sexy time with Graydon."

Kira's glare burned hotter.

"I've decided I need eyes on the ground, so to speak. This is the best solution." Jin flew a figure eight over the lizard as it rose onto its hindquarters and tried to bat at the drone. He missed, plopping onto all fours. With a dissatisfied flick of his tail, the lizard waddled toward Kira's pillow.

She slowly shook her head again. "What part of *you have to stay hidden and not draw attention* did you not understand?"

"All of it."

Kira rubbed her temples. All she wanted was sleep.

"Mini Jin can be with you while I'm stuck in here," Jin promised. "And bonus, he'll make sure Odin can't get her greedy little claws into my hardware by ensuring you, the weak link, is protected."

This time, Kira snatched the pillow from under the lizard and lobbed it at her friend. It hit him before bouncing to the ground. The lizard righted itself, its mouth opening in a silent mew.

Kira fought the urge to feel guilty, knowing the lizard wasn't a living creature. It was harder than it should have been, mainly because of the pain in her ass hovering in midair.

"Rude," Jin complained.

"What's if he's seen?" Kira asked.

"Min, play dead."

The lizard froze, his surface hardening until he looked like he was carved of stone with faceted jewels as his eyes.

"Min?" Kira asked.

"Short for mini Jin," he explained.

Kira sent him an unamused look. Cute—not.

"The Tuann will never see anything but a very interesting bracelet," Jin promised.

"A very weird bracelet," Kira muttered.

"His presence means I won't feel the need to explore," Jin cajoled.

Kira frowned at him. "You're starting to make a habit of ultimatums, and I don't like it."

Jin's snort was unimpressed. "Too bad."

Kira picked the lizard up. He had a surprising heft to him, his body warm and lifelike despite the metallic sheen to his skin. Had he been green, she might have thought he was real.

She set him on the edge of the bed. "Do I want to know what you used to make him?"

"Probably not."

That meant he'd appropriated Tuann technology for the lizard's construction.

"Did you hear my conversation with Harlow?" Kira asked, changing the subject.

She'd lost. Resisting further would only result in a loss of dignity.

"I did."

"Your analysis?"

Jin was quiet for several moments. "I found it interesting he chose to share this information with you."

"You think it's a trap? Meant to lure us into doing something that tips our hand?"

Jin made a thoughtful sound. "That's unclear, but I suspect your uncle is skilled at political games and intrigue. He will be one to watch."

That had been Kira's assessment as well. "At least we now have an idea of how Odin got on the planet."

She probably used the distraction by the Tsavitee on Luatha to slip through the Tuann's security net along with the other ships Graydon had told her about.

"But we can't assume," Jin was quick to add.

"No, we can't," Kira agreed.

Assumptions had a habit of leading you to mistaken conclusions that inevitably got you knocked on your ass or staring into a Tsavitee infantry squad.

The two of them shared a look. They'd been down this road before.

Kira stretched out on the bed. "I'm getting sick of this."

"Watch for the betrayal from behind. That's how they always come for us."

Kira grumbled an agreement, resting her hands on her belly. "Just when I was getting comfortable."

"Yes, I heard how comfortable you were getting with the commander," Jin teased.

Kira sent him a flat stare. "Stuff it, Tin Man, or I'll have to comment on this weird flirting thing you and Odin are doing."

Jin made a choked sound of denial. Kira hid her grin. She'd thought that might work.

TWENTY

KIRA TRUDGED INTO the Warrior's Hall, feeling out of sorts and tired. The night had been long, but her sleep short. A headache lingered behind her eyes, likely a result of the lack of sleep and the *keeva* she'd consumed.

Most of her fellow initiates were already present, many of them practicing diligently with their wooden swords. The announcement by Wren seemed to have lit a fire in them. No one knew for sure when the trial would take place, but they all wanted their shot at advancing.

Kira didn't blame them. She did too. Hence the reason for her presence despite her need for more sleep.

Blue sat against a wall, tinkering with a device between her legs. She looked up, her expression unwelcoming as she caught sight of Kira.

Guess Blue was still upset about last night.

Kira ignored the small pang the thought brought, telling herself it was better this way. Blue and Raider were part of the past. There was no going back, no matter how nostalgic she'd found last night.

"This is what you've been doing all this time?" Jin asked from her collar.

"There's usually a lot more running involved," Kira told him. "Also, I thought we agreed you would be motionless and silent."

The lizard's face was stubborn as he looked up at her.

"Why don't we get to doing that?" she suggested.

A small huff came from the lizard before it curled around her neck, clasping its tail in its paws to create a torc. "Sheesh, you're so grumpy when you're upset with yourself."

"I'm not upset with myself," Kira said quietly.

"You know people will think you're crazy if they catch you talking to yourself like this," Raider suggested.

Kira jumped, spinning to find him standing behind her.

He was quiet for a long time, his expression unreadable.

Kira wiped her hands on her legs and grasped for something to say. Regret from last night lingered, making it difficult.

"Is that Raider?" The lizard's head lifted, his tail flicking. "How's your hangover, meat sack?"

Raider shuffled closer, bending for a better look at Kira's necklace. "Why is Jin's voice coming out of a lizard?"

Kira was too tempted with the prospect of chucking the lizard down the nearest dark hole to answer.

The lizard preened. "I've spawned a mini me. Do you like?"

A look of horror descended on Raider's face. "The universe doesn't need any more of you."

The lizard blew a raspberry. "How rude."

In this, Kira was inclined to agree. More versions of Jin scuttling around weren't pleasant to contemplate.

"How did he convince you to go along with this?" Raider asked.

Kira was slow to answer, the question taking her off guard. She'd expected antagonism. Anger. Some of the fury the old Raider had been so good at generating to blast her, leaving her feeling about two inches high.

This Raider acted like last night had never happened.

"He has his moments," Kira said, distracted.

Raider's behavior didn't make sense. She knew him as well as she might a sibling. She might not always like him, or he, her, but she knew him backward and forward.

This behavior was atypical. It left her suspicious and on guard.

"If you say so," Raider said before continuing toward Blue.

Kira watched him go, wondering what game he was playing.

"That was weird," Jin said, echoing her thoughts.

Kira made a sound of agreement.

They didn't have time to ponder his shift in behavior as Graydon, Wren, and Maida appeared on the balcony above.

The initiates fell silent, turning their attention to the three.

Wren stepped forward. "As warriors, we must be ever vigilant. It is why every warrior of Roake takes a turn on patrol. Today, you will join the ranks of those who've risked their lives on behalf of this House."

A murmur broke out among the initiates.

Wren held up a hand, and they died down. "One of the most

difficult things a warrior learns is when to use *ki* and when to conserve. On patrol, you can be out for hours, often over the ocean, or in other environments where walking isn't an option. That's why we have flyers and other methods of transportation. Each requires skill and discipline to use."

Graydon's gaze found Kira's, his lips curving in anticipation.

Her eyes narrowed. "I have a feeling I know where this is going."

"In addition to the traditional options, our human guests have consented to teach those willing to learn the art of their waveboards. I caution you to choose your transportation wisely. Each has its own merits along with negatives. You will have to decide what is most important to you."

Wren stepped back as a deep cry of approval ripped from the throats of those around them.

"This is unexpected," Jin muttered. "How much do you want to bet Graydon had a hand in it?"

"Why would I take a bet I know I'll lose?" Of course, Graydon had a hand in this. That was who he was. His warning to be here last night as good as said so.

Jin harrumphed as Graydon's oshota, flanked by Roake's, moved into the hall carrying several contraptions, some familiar, many not.

There were devices where Kira was hard-pressed to figure out how they would allow the user to fly. Others resembled stripped hoverbikes, their frame made of wood, fragile-looking sails poking out the back.

Another contraption reminded Kira of butterfly wings, beautiful, but she suspected impractical.

Kira found what she was looking for cradled in Amila's arms. A waveboard, one of the nicer civilian models.

A tingle of anticipation filled Kira, her hands itching to relieve Amila of her burden. It had been ages, and she missed her old friend.

A broad smile crossed Amila's face as she handed Kira the board.

Kira took it, clutching it to her as if it might try to fly off. "Hello, my pretty."

"He thought you might like that one," Amila said, tilting her head up at where Graydon waited, not having taken his gaze off Kira. When he caught her looking, his lips broadened, reminding her of the things they'd done beneath the moonlight.

Jin whistled softly. "That man is playing for keeps."

Alarm filled Kira as her attention shot to Amila. Luckily, the other woman had already moved on and didn't hear.

"What did I say about making sure you weren't noticed?" Kira ducked her head and examined the board in her hands. It was different than the one she'd had during the war. Likely it would be less powerful since that version wasn't available to civilians. Once, she would have known the specs of every single model, civilian or military. No longer.

It was another aspect of her former life she'd allowed to slip away.

Technology had a habit of never standing still. It always progressed. Learning the ins and outs of this board would be like familiarizing herself with an old friend who had grown in the years since their last meeting.

She looked forward to the challenge.

The board was simple, she found, sharing only a passing resemblance to the monster she'd ridden into battle. For one thing, it was much lighter than her old board, its lines sleek and streamlined, designed for form as well as function. She had no doubt it would cut through air resistance like butter.

Kira flipped the board over, pressing the pedals with her hands and watching as the engine kicked on with a light rumble. The board rocked in her hands as the thrusters idled.

Yes, this thing was a beauty. Attractive. Fast. Agile.

Its only flaw was its delicacy. Judging by its light weight, Kira knew it wasn't a workhorse. There would be no battering the enemies' front line with this. A single piece of shrapnel would likely shred it.

But then, this board wasn't designed for battle. Her purpose lay in other areas.

Kira couldn't wait to see what she was capable of.

"I think I'm in love," Kira said.

The lizard bit her. Kira jumped and glared at him.

"We've discussed this. I'm the only machine you're allowed to love. Everything else is a tool," he informed her.

Kira hummed, her gaze returning to the beauty in her hands. Jin could object all he wanted, but that didn't change things. She couldn't wait to make a few modifications. By the time Kira got through with it, the board's abilities would surpass its designer's wildest dreams.

Kira finally looked up, finding most of the initiates had made their decisions. To her surprise, Blue had gravitated toward the Tuann technology, waffling between the hoverbike and the butterfly wings.

Like Kira, Raider had ended up with a waveboard, one that she could tell from the wear and tear was his own personal board. It had no doubt been sent ahead by Jace.

The rest of the initiates were an even mix between the options, with Devon, Rheya, Blake, and Joule ending up with boards similar to hers. The four of them shuffled toward Kira and Raider as their fellow initiates gravitated toward oshota holding the contraptions they'd chosen.

Raider held his hands up as the four approached. He slid a glance toward Kira, a sly grin forming. She stiffened.

"You four are in luck. You get to learn from one of the best," he stated. "Nixxy, here, was a pioneer of the waveboard."

"Don't you dare," Kira warned.

"Too late." His smile held a nasty edge that suggested he might not be as over last night as he'd appeared. "Have fun learning from her. I have a few questions for the *seon'yer*."

With that, he clasped her on the shoulder and retreated, a bounce in his step.

Kira blanched as she became the sole focus of the initiates. That ass. He knew how she felt about being the center of attention.

Rheya avoided meeting Kira's eyes, looking away, uncertainty in her stance. Kira didn't know what had happened after she'd left the Rothchild demonstration, but the other woman had been different since.

She wasn't the only one, Kira concluded as Devon glanced at where Joule was studying his board.

Kira wouldn't have expected either Devon or Rheya to pick a human piece of technology for this exercise. That they had was interesting—and unexpected.

"Have any of you used one of these before?" Kira forced herself to ask.

There was an outside chance some of them had experience. The waveboards had gained in popularity after the war.

All but Joule raised their hands. This might be easier than she'd thought.

Graydon quirked one side of his mouth at her from where he lingered on the edge of her small group. She frowned at him, taking in the board he held in his hands, a twin to the one Amila had given her.

"Joule, you're with me. The rest of you, I'll check your stances once

I've worked with him," Kira told them. "For now, practice hovering."

Joule's gaze was avid.

"You'd probably have a better chance of impressing Wren if you stuck to technology you were familiar with," Kira told him.

His mouth screwed up in a stubborn line. "I want to learn from you. Besides, the *tilu* is slow and reliant on wind to change direction," he said, pointing at the group using the butterfly wings. He shifted and pointed at the bikes. "The *loaw* is more versatile, but it can't get very high. I've studied most of these, and the waveboard offers the widest range in terms of speed and maneuverability."

Kira propped her hands on her waist as she listened. Who was she to argue with his assessment? He was far more familiar with the flaws in his people's technology than her.

Besides, waveboards really were the best choice—but she might have been biased in that.

"Fair enough. Let's get started."

It didn't take long to demonstrate the basic riding stance. Feet shoulder width apart, the dominant side facing front. It wasn't too far off from a stance you'd use on a surfboard or snowboard.

Joule's face was intent and serious as he copied everything she did. Kira was conscious of Graydon listening from the sidelines as she gently shifted his legs to a better position.

"Balance is the most important aspect of riding." The board was designed to help with that, its controls intuitive.

Kira picked up her board and showed it to him. "Weight distribution is key." She indicated the different spots on the board. "A single shift in balance will cause a reaction."

The others had stopped what they were doing to listen, drifting over to stand by Joule.

Kira set the board down and climbed on, adopting the rest stance. She settled her weight more firmly. The board snapped to life, its engines purring as the antigravs kicked online, allowing her to rise until she hovered a foot above the ground.

"Where you choose to distribute your weight determines where the board goes."

She shifted, demonstrating the different positions and what they did. Back, forward, up, down. Even flipping the tail end out, so she curved around them.

Joule looked fascinated, eager to get started.

At her gesture, the rest broke away to try their hand at what Kira had demonstrated.

Watching Joule make his first attempt was like watching a baby bird try to leave the nest—tentative, slightly awkward, even as he caught on quick.

The other three were already showing off, putting the boards through their paces as they sought to impress each other.

Graydon joined her as she observed them. "Enjoying yourself?"

"Teaching novices to fly is the highlight of my day," she said in a snarky voice.

His smile deepened. "I thought you might enjoy it."

He was right. She had. It had felt good and clean. Simple in a way she'd forgotten. Two things that were in short supply with her current mission.

Graydon left her side as Wren stepped onto the balcony.

"You'll be separated into groups based on the tools you've chosen. I expect you to acquit yourself well during this exercise."

Names were called, and the initiates shuffled as they joined their patrols.

Kira wasn't surprised to find herself in the same group as Graydon. The man was a bad penny who kept finding his way into her orbit.

The four she'd taught and Raider rounded out the group with Aeron joining them at the last second. Kira was interested to note Devon's face shut down as soon as the other boy got near. Whatever had happened between them, the two were no longer friends.

Blue ended up on a different patrol led by Maida, who seemed amused as the other woman chattered excitedly at her.

"I forgot that about you," Raider said, settling beside Kira as she fiddled with the settings of her board. "You always were a good teacher."

Kira paused. "Praise? From you?" She cocked her head. "How hungover are you?"

Raider folded his hands behind his head. "I'll admit it took me a while to see beyond my anger, but now that I do, a few things have started to become clear."

Kira changed another setting, not liking the sound of this.

Raider was a good soldier. Smart and intuitive. His biggest weakness had always been that he let his emotions cloud the clarity of his judgment.

If he was being truthful, he'd picked a hell of a time to fix his issue.

"Sometimes, with people we've known a long time, there is all this baggage. It makes it so we can't see them clearly." Raider's gaze was direct, no hint of the fatigue she'd expect in someone who'd spent half the night drinking. "I'd forgotten how focused you are when on a mission. How much you're willing to sacrifice for its success."

"Raider—"

He sat up, his hand landing on her shoulder. He squeezed, the pressure this side of painful. "You forget they weren't only yours to protect."

Kira stood frozen as he leaned closer. It wasn't anger she saw in his eyes. It was determination. All the things she'd worked to prevent unraveling all at once.

"I don't know what you're trying to protect me from, but it must scare the crap out of you if you're willing to burn not only me but also Blue." He glanced at the other woman who looked positively gleeful as she studied the device the Tuann would soon regret giving her.

He patted her shoulder before leveraging himself to his feet. He paused to stare at her thoughtfully. "It's good to see you've gotten better at lying. I think your performance yesterday might have worked on anyone else."

Kira blinked dumbly up at him, her mind racing. She needed a lie to steer him away from this road he'd gone down. Something that would disabuse him of his observations.

He couldn't know the truth. He couldn't.

It would ruin everything.

If he knew, there would be no stopping him. Patience wasn't in his makeup. He'd charge head first at the Tsavitee, undoing years of work in the process, likely getting himself killed along the way.

For Elise to have a chance, she needed something to come back to. A big part of that something was Raider.

Too much time had passed for her to deny it, Kira realized. Nothing she said would make him believe her.

"Consider this a warning from an old friend—your secrets won't be yours much longer. I'll be right behind you from here on out. Everything you've done finally makes sense."

Kira was mute as she gazed up at him. There would be no swaying him. Not with subterfuge or deception. She doubted he'd let himself be blinded by any of it.

His smile, when it came, wasn't particularly nice. "Brace yourself, Phoenix. I'm your new battle buddy. Through thick and thin. You won't be able to drive me away a second time."

The words read like a threat and a promise.

She couldn't argue, not with Graydon watching them with interest.

Kira gathered her board and stood, giving herself time to think. To plan.

It wasn't enough.

Her composure was shaky as she rose. By the time she straightened, her expression was a mask of calm again, no hint of the turmoil within marring its surface.

The oshota's take off saved Kira from having to form a response. She stepped on her board and hit the turbos, shooting straight up after them.

"You're going to have to do something about that," Jin murmured. "I know."

For now, though, she needed to focus on the task at hand. Raider's threat wasn't going anywhere. She could deal with it and its ramifications later.

She'd been a little enthusiastic in her takeoff, piling too much momentum in it so she soared higher than the others.

Cannons came online, tracking her.

She tensed, bracing to dodge if it became necessary. When they did nothing, she bent her knees and piled on the speed.

Wind snapped the hair around her face as she arrowed toward the rest.

Himoto had always said he could read Kira's mood in the way she flew—happy, sad, angry, or a combination of the three.

If he'd been there today, he would have read her desire to run. It seemed the closer she got to her goal; the more things fell apart.

She took a deep breath, letting the board and the wind work some of the anxiety out of her soul. She performed loops and jumps in midair, taking her time as she got the knack of riding in gravity again.

She'd missed this.

No matter how many times she flew, it was like the first time all over again, when she was an angry, scared girl, outraged at the wrongs done her and painfully aware of the differences between her and her saviors.

The moment she stepped on a board, all those feelings vanished, leaving only Kira behind.

It was the same now. Freedom and control, even as she pushed the boundaries of what was possible.

Up here, power beneath her feet and wide-open space all around, nothing and no one could touch her.

Only when the last of the initiates had made it into the air did she join the rest.

She settled into a relaxed stance, weight balanced, legs slightly bent, her arms and torso relaxed. She hovered in midair, watching as those she'd taught that morning became comfortable with the greater heights.

Waveboards were most effective close to ground. Something about the technology meant they had the greatest thrust near a surface, whether vertical or horizontal. Almost like they needed a physical object to grab onto and propel them forward.

The further up you went, the less forward propulsion you had. Oh, you could make it work, but it burned fuel. The last thing anybody wanted was to be a few thousand feet up while flying on fumes. That was a recipe for a very rough landing.

When used as atmosphere insertion units, it was mainly about the fall, with the engines providing stability until you were close enough to the surface to get adequate thrust.

A roar of sound warned Kira. She glanced up as two boards flew past, with only feet to spare.

Amila waved a greeting before concentrating on chasing Isla down. Her legs bent, her body crouching slightly as the two women zipped through the sky.

Beneath them, a dark ocean stretched as far as the eye could see. A rocky coastline curved to her right, the city a shining gem overlooking it.

"Beautiful," Kira breathed.

In that unguarded moment, the planet's soul bathed her in warmth, its presence a comfortable heated blanket against her senses, an unmistakable welcome in its embrace.

It felt uncomfortably like a homecoming.

She instinctively resisted, gently pushing the Mea'Ave away.

It'd been so long since she'd considered anywhere home. She didn't know if she was ready to open that door again.

However, if there was ever a place to tempt her mind and soul, this was unmistakably it.

A wild and untamed world, incredibly dangerous to the unwary. Populated by people who were loyal to their bones. Yes, their customs were odd, and they clung to tradition with a tenacity Kira didn't understand, but they were also fierce and kind in their own way.

This place would have been an irresistible dream for someone much less damaged than Kira.

"Incoming," Jin murmured.

Kira took in the dark streak headed for her. Graydon looked like something out of a holovid, noble and fierce as he rode into battle on a variation of Kira's board rather than the steed of old.

Graydon's board was a more deranged and bulkier cousin to the one she used. It looked carved from wood; a surprising decision given the extreme forces it endured on a regular basis.

"I'm surprised how familiar the Tuann are with this technology," Kira said as he joined her.

They were too confident and at ease for this to be a new concept.

"You'll find many Tuann are appreciative of human ingenuity. It's not unusual to find human inventions that have been modified for our use." Graydon allowed himself a small smile. "Your chosen people have proven themselves quite creative; something mine find endlessly fascinating."

Kira would have liked to ask more but was forced to wait as Wren and several others shot across the water in a wedge pattern.

"We should follow," Graydon informed her.

Kira didn't argue, racing across the sky after the patrol. She settled into a position at the back of the wedge, Raider slightly in front of her. Devon and the rest on the opposite flank.

Finn and Graydon took their spots a few lengths behind her, bringing up the rear. His oshota filled in the gaps as they set out.

It'd be easy to grow bored while flying over the ocean. The terrain had a certain monotony that lulled you into lowering your guard. A costly mistake Kira had no intention of making.

The oshota around her spent the time jockeying for position and playing small games, even as Kira noticed the alertness with which they watched their surroundings.

They were miles from shore when Wren raised his fist, signaling a stop. Kira's board bobbled as Wren's voice echoed in her ear, making it sound like he was standing right next to her.

"You may break formation if you like. Solal and Amila, keep watch on the perimeter. For the rest, you're free to explore."

How was he projecting his voice? None of them wore comms, a fact she'd been surprised about but now understood.

"Jin?"

"I don't know," her friend told her. "Best guess, he's manipulating sound waves in some way."

The implications of that were astounding. If you could manipulate the sound waves to carry your voice, you could do the same to others. As a tool for spying, it would be virtually undetectable.

Graydon's board dropped to match her trajectory as Finn broke away to monitor them from above. "How about a small wager?"

Raider glanced over, maneuvering to parallel their flight path.

"What did you have in mind?" Raider shouted.

"A race. Loser owes the winner a boon."

Kira scoffed. Like she was foolish enough to fall for that. Knowing Graydon, he'd have already skewed the odds in his favor.

"I'm game," Raider's smile was wicked as he shot a challenging glance at Kira. "Unless you're scared?"

She aimed a flat stare at him.

Raider shrugged. "I didn't want to assume since you've been living the soft civilian life."

A small smirk teased Graydon's lips as he waited. Why exert himself when Raider was doing the work for him?

Kira's eyes narrowed. Were the two of them working together to taunt her into this?

After a moment of consideration, she shook her head. Naw. Raider didn't like the Tuann enough to team up with them.

She rethought that conclusion seconds later when Graydon said, "Yes, we wouldn't want to force you to do anything you're not comfortable with. You are, after all, only barely out of your infancy."

The lizard snorted against her neck, knowing that word was guaranteed a reaction.

She didn't disappoint. Rising to the challenge was almost a compulsion. Letting Graydon have the last word wasn't an option.

"There has never been a day when you could out fly me, Raider," Kira declared, before fixing Graydon with a look. "You sure you can keep up?"

His chin bent down. "Only one way to see."

Trash talk, how she'd missed it.

Graydon was about to lose. Even better, both he and Raider would owe Kira a boon.

Her lips curved in anticipation.

Graydon was about to learn the true terror of facing a Cur in battle.

Graydon's expression darkened with expectancy at the challenge he saw on her face, saying without words he was eager to pit himself against her skill.

They'd see about that.

Graydon spread his arms, closing his eyes and tilting back as gravity pulled him down until he fell into a smooth backward dive.

Twenty feet above the waves, his board woke with a roar, bringing his descent to a quick stop as he shot forward, the force of the board's thrust kissing the surface, water flying up around him.

Raider flashed a maniacal grin at her. "Like old times."

"I beat you in those times," Kira returned.

"Things change," Raider promised. "It's not going to be as easy this time."

He followed Graydon, his board cutting through the air with ease.

She stared at the two and shook her head. How did she let herself be talked into these things?

"This should be interesting," the lizard observed from her collar. "What are you going to do?"

"What do I always do when issued a challenge?" Kira crouched, her blood pounding and excitement bubbling in her veins as that piece she'd been missing all those years slid into place.

"Yes!" Jin hissed. "Show them what they've woken."

Kira cut the engines, dropping into a smooth dive, the ocean below rushing up to meet her. She waited until the last second to switch the engine on, the abrupt change from falling to flying threatening to topple her.

She hung on, keeping her balance as a joyous whoop escaped Jin.

She streaked after Graydon and Raider, closing the distance quickly. Neither man was serious yet, letting her catch them easily.

They traded looks, agreeing without words.

"Here we go," Kira whispered.

As if of one mind, they kicked the engines to maximum, rocketing over the water.

The board bounced under her, the vibration settling in her bones and jarring the teeth in her skull. Kira loved every moment of it as she fought for more speed.

Graydon was the first to take the lead, the other two sliding into his wake and letting him take the brunt of the wind.

They were still testing each other, looking for strengths and weaknesses.

Soon, though, it would be time.

Raider gestured at Kira behind his back, sliding her a signal from a time when they'd both been Curs, telling her to flank Graydon.

Sounded good to her.

He slid right, and she went left, the two moving as one to overtake Graydon. Kira put on a burst of speed, shooting past him easily, Raider doing the same on the other side.

They traded victorious looks as they kept Graydon trapped behind them, drifting to block him anytime he tried to pass.

Between one second and the next, their mood turned serious as each concentrated on winning. First, Kira edged out Raider, minutes later he nudged past her board, Graydon bringing up the rear.

They tucked in close, flying only feet off each other's flank. A single mistake could kill them all.

Kira didn't care, crouching and coaxing more speed out of her board. An exultant feeling of victory shot through her as she bypassed Raider, leaving both men behind.

Jin shouted wind speed and directions in her ear, allowing her to concentrate only on flying.

The sharp sense of danger sent her instincts clamoring as a roar split the air behind her.

Kira dodged left as a force rose from the deep below, the soundless toll of a bell ringing as a massive form breached the waves. Up and up it rose, the whiskers and mane trailing behind it as water cascaded off its form. The shadow of the rest of its body still darkened the water beneath as Kira gaped.

The close call she'd just had was insignificant when compared to the massive creature still rising toward the sky.

Lu-ong.

And this one was no baby.

"Evade," she screamed in the next moment as another *lu-ong* breached the surface directly beneath her board, its open mouth and very sharp teeth aimed straight at her.

TWENTY-ONE

RAIDER BROKE LEFT, Graydon doing the same as Kira hit the thrust, shooting out of the way of the *lu-ong's* giant teeth as it shot up into the air where she'd been seconds before.

Kira wove over the water, her path looking like something a hummingbird hopped up on nectar might take. All around her, *lu-ong* breached the surface, their bodies arching impossibly high as they reached for the sky above, doomed to inevitably fail as they hit the apex of their leap and made their journey to the water waiting below.

Their bodies were long and serpentine, their tails not even clearing the waves before their heads dove deep again, only to breach seconds later.

Kira couldn't spare more than a moment of admiration for the sight before she had to focus on the task of simply surviving the minefield she suddenly found herself in.

Kira banked right, avoiding another scaled form. Raider had already disappeared behind the massive obstacles.

Jin let out a low whistle. "Now that's an impressive sight."

Kira couldn't have agreed more. Despite the danger setting every one of her senses on high alert, she hadn't felt this alive in years. She skated a hair's breadth from death's embrace, but she couldn't bring herself to escape just yet.

She didn't get the sense that the *lu-ong* meant her harm. She was an ant next to a mammoth who was trying to walk—or swim in this case.

They almost felt playful, joy trembling through the air.

Jin seemed to agree as he snorted. "Let's see what they've got, Nixxy."

Kira crouched. "I thought you'd never ask."

In the confusion, Graydon had managed to get ahead. At her words, he glanced back, catching her eye as he tipped his head in invitation.

Her smile was almost feline in satisfaction. Challenge accepted. The race wasn't over yet. Only the terms had changed.

Graydon dove for the water, Kira fast on his six.

Here, reflexes reigned superior. An instant of doubt, a single millisecond of inattention and she'd be dead. Either dashed on the waves below or crashing headfirst into the bodies of the *lu-ong*. Somehow, she didn't think she'd be the winner in that scenario.

Graydon veered right, slipping through the small arch that had formed under the *lu-ong's* body as it completed its return to the sea. The space narrowed, the gap fast disappearing as Graydon raced through.

Kira's stomach was tight as Graydon courted death. The *lu-ong* had to be thousands of pounds of hard muscle. If its weight crushed him, Graydon wouldn't survive

He shot out the other side seconds before the gap vanished, a massive sheet of water from the *lu-ong's* body crashing into the waves, water rising to obscure her vision. When the water settled, Kira caught sight of Graydon waiting on the other side, a challenging smile aimed her way. Beat that, he seemed to say.

Kira rolled her eyes. Show off.

Jin clung to her neck. "There's a pocket opening up twenty degrees off the port side. Burn, baby, burn."

Kira didn't question his observation, too used to him as her co-pilot, picking up details that freed her to focus on other things. It was why she could be so confident, even when shit was hitting the fan, and victory wasn't assured. She knew she was never alone. Jin was always at her side.

Her legs tensed, and her altitude abruptly dropped, sending her stomach rocketing into her throat.

Her senses opened, adrenaline pumping through her body. The board hummed a siren's song under her feet. Every second she spent on it, her movements got crisper, more confident, until the board was an extension of herself. A weapon and tool, the same way the en-blade was for the best of the oshota.

On a board, Kira was nearly untouchable. Perhaps it was time House Roake learned that.

A *lu-ong* the color of sapphire, silver edging his crest, surged up from the deep, leaving Kira with little time to dodge or evade. Stopping was out of the question.

Jin screamed in her ear.

"Hold on," she yelled at him.

Kira reached for more speed, bending her knees and using her heel to hit the thrust as she straightened abruptly almost like she was jumping. She pulled her feet up, so the flat of the board was aimed at the *lu-ong*. The technology that allowed her to hover caught on the scales, almost like it was a vertical road. Instead of flying along the waves, she was using the *lu-ong's* body as her path.

Up and up she went, weaving between the ridges along its back, the end approaching, nothing but clear sky before her. Kira hit the end of the *lu-ong's* body, shooting into the air.

She crouched, the sky tumbling around her, as she cut engines and grabbed the board's edge, flipping, once, twice, three times before falling toward the waves. At the last possible second, she righted herself, hitting the upward thrust. The water bowed under her. For one second, she wasn't sure if she'd acted in time. The board bobbed, catching itself as it protested gravity's hold.

Her laugh rang out as she shot away again in time to catch sight of Graydon playing tag as a *lu-ong* chased after him, cutting through the water only to spring toward Graydon at the last second.

He flipped, narrowly evading the *lu-ong's* teeth, before veering to avoid its mate as it shot out of the water.

Deep chuckles rumbled through her mind, the sense that the *lu-ong* considered this a type of dangerous game strengthening.

To her left, Raider had found his own *lu-ong*, racing up its side with the same crazy grin she knew had been on her face. During the war, they'd rarely rode the boards for the simple joy of it. Riding had become a means to an end. It had made them forget why each of them started riding in the first place.

Kira, because it tamed some of the turmoil that always seemed to dance beneath her skin. Raider, as a means of escape from the shitty adults in his life and as a way to channel his fury at the world.

For her, it had always been the feeling of pushing her body to the limits, defying the laws of physics simply because she could. One-upping her friends with tricks that took months of practice to pull off, only to watch them do the same to her.

Loss threatened to steal some of the joy from the afternoon.

Here, IN this moment, she could admit how tired she was of carrying the weight she'd freely accepted. She knew it would be so easy to take what Graydon and House Roake were offering. A home. A place to belong. People to share it with.

But what happened when her past came knocking? Would they accept the flaws and the scars? The nightmares?

Right now, Roake had a pretty dream of who they thought she was. The babe stolen from them, now returned. A victory they could reclaim against loss and tragedy.

They didn't see the person she was. Someone who had survived despite herself. It hadn't always been pretty. She'd done things that kept her up at night. She didn't know if they could accept that.

Part of that was her fault. She hadn't given them a chance to know her.

Kira's gaze lingered on Graydon's powerful form as he streaked across the waves, yearning a knot in her chest.

Wishes and hopes were for children, something she'd never had a chance at being. She did what was necessary. Even when it was difficult.

For a split second, her resolve wavered, wanting wrapped up in desire.

But in the end, one thing had always been clear. What the Tsavitee wanted was something she would never allow them to have.

They were locusts. Consuming and destroying everything in their path. Her goal wasn't the lower forms; it was the ones pulling strings behind the scenes. The ones Himoto hadn't believed existed until too late.

But the Tuann might believe. The statue of their enemies of old proved as much.

Her conversation with her uncle made her think they knew more than they were telling. Roake might prove a valuable ally—if she could take the risk of trusting them.

That was the sticking point.

Graydon was an honorable man. She knew this to her bones. She might not like his method of getting what he wanted, but she never doubted he always had the best interests of his people at heart.

But did those interests align with hers? Could she trust the people around him as much as she did him? Those were the real questions.

She didn't have an answer, and until she did, she was stuck in the middle. Too afraid to move forward, knowing there was no easy way back.

The higher forms had an agenda. A plan. One that shifted and warped every time she thought she caught hold of it. The Tuann were part of that plan. Something told her they were the linchpin upon which everything else turned.

She needed to learn how.

"We have to protect this," Kira whispered.

"We will, Kira," Jin told her in a soft voice. "And I'll be right there with you. To the end if necessary."

The lizard nuzzled her cheek before biting her gently in rebuke.

"There is no me without you," he said. "Remember that when you think about leaving."

"I never intended to let myself fade into the night," she said.

"Why didn't you tell me? I thought I knew everything."

He did. The important stuff anyway.

"At first, it was because I didn't want it to be true. If I ignored it, it meant it wasn't happening. Then when I couldn't hide it, things had changed, and I had to focus on what I could control."

"In other words, you buried your head in the sand and hoped this would pass you by," Jin drawled.

Kira's grin was quick and repentant. That was as good an explanation as any.

"Ah, well, you wouldn't be the first." The lizard uncoiled from her neck, reclaiming her shoulder.

Kira was first out of the field of *lu-ong*, Raider and Graydon following shortly afterward as she began to head to where the patrol was forming up.

"We don't have to do this alone anymore. There are options," Jin said.

Kira glanced down, aware of how the lizard was staring at Graydon as he approached, his face relaxed, like the rough edges had been chiseled down and worn smooth. He'd enjoyed their time with the *lu-ong*.

"You trust him?"

"Don't you?" Jin asked in a pointed voice.

Kira barely hid her flinch. Jin had a point. She didn't let herself get close to people for a reason. That the commander had already breached her defenses several times, meant she trusted him at a subconscious level.

She knew in her bones he wasn't working with the Tsavitee. She'd seen too much of him to think him anything but honorable. Battle had a way of bonding you, of showing you the darkest and best parts of a person. It could lead to feeling incredibly close to the person who fought at your side in a very short amount of time. It stripped the walls that most people kept between them and others, reducing them to their most basic selves.

Graydon had a soul filled with light and dark. He was a terror to his enemy but never those he was loyal to. If she had him in her corner, she knew he wouldn't step out of it even under the most insidious of pressure. He held a strength that most only aspired to.

There was confidence in everything he did. He was the steady rock when everything else had gone to shit.

And if he decided she was a threat to the ones he loved, he would seek to destroy her. She didn't think there'd be any coming back from that.

Not only because she wasn't certain who would win in a real fight.

Graydon rode his board, his posture easy as he glanced at her in curiosity, as if sensing the dark place her thoughts had turned to.

"I won," she told the two of them.

Graydon's grin was seductive. "Debatable."

"First out. I count that as a win," Kira shot back.

The tension in Wren and the rest of the oshota distracted them from their friendly argument.

Graydon straightened, the relaxation of before falling away. Everything about him changed. Gone was the mischievous playmate who'd dodged the *lu-ong* with her. Now, he was the Emperor's Face. Someone who wore his power like a mantle, not like it was a burden but rather a duty he cherished and respected.

"What is it?" Graydon asked in a normal voice despite the fifteen feet between them.

"A distress call came in," Wren said.

"Where?" Graydon demanded.

"Lenay quadrant. Fishing boat. It sounded like a *lu-ong* had attacked their vessel," Wren answered.

More than one person slid an uneasy glance at the *lu-ong* below. Interestingly, the creatures had cleared out in the past few minutes, not breaking the surface as often—almost like they sensed what was happening.

"It's been a long time since the *lu-ong* have been in these waters,"

Graydon said. "Perhaps the time away has opened the door for misunderstandings between them and us."

Wren shook his head. "Harlow never lifted the restrictions on the *lu-ong's* nesting grounds in the hope they would return. No one should be out there."

"And yet they are," Graydon said, his expression distant as he considered.

His eyes met Kira's, the same thought in her mind as well. It was very hard not to see Tsavitee influence behind everything. They'd been the rot that had destroyed so much of her life already. However, jumping to conclusions and chasing ghosts that weren't there was just as dangerous.

Could be this was someone breaking the rules. Maybe they didn't realize the *lu-ong* were back. That made this Tuann business.

On the other hand, it could be this was the first move in the war the Tsavitee started on Ta Da'an. Only one way to find out, and that was to investigate.

Graydon made an abrupt gesture. Amila and Isla nodded, dropping out of the formation before hitting their thrusters and racing toward the distress call.

Graydon glanced at Kira. "I want you with me."

Kira nodded.

"You're to follow orders," Graydon told the initiates in a hard voice. "If I get word that you're creating a problem, forget the trial—you'll be kicked out of Roake."

Wren didn't argue. If anything, his expression hardened, becoming even more unrelenting than usual. Kira had a feeling his preference would have been to send the initiates to the fortress.

"On me," Graydon told Kira.

The lizard clasped his tail with his paws, tightening his grip around her neck. Good thing too, because Graydon and Kira didn't wait for the rest to sort themselves out, arrowing after Amila and Isla without delay.

Raider fell into position off Kira's starboard side, keeping pace easily. The rest of Graydon's oshota, and a few of Roake's, did the same around them. They moved with the ease and purpose of people who'd performed this task on countless missions with each other. They didn't wait to be told what to do; they simply did it. They were a well-oiled machine that communicated without a word spoken.

"Kira, try not to do anything foolish," Graydon warned.

"It's like he doesn't even know you," Jin quipped.

Irritation chased across Graydon's face. It looked like Jin's remark hadn't gone unnoticed. "And keep him out of the way."

Kira snorted. Fat chance of that. Jin thrived on throwing himself headlong into danger. He gave her shit, but he was nearly as reckless. At least she employed foresight, thought through some of the consequences before discarding them as unimportant.

His thinking was more along the lines of "I saw, I wanted, I took." Consequences only came into play after the chips were down, and the smoke had cleared.

The small fishing boat came into view. Made of wood with a tall mast in its center, its sail was built from a shimmery, silver fabric. The boat looked fast and sleek if not for the massive *lu-ong* coil wrapped around its bow, threatening to drag it into the water.

Instead of a propeller, it looked like it had some type of technology that would allow it to hover a few feet above the water under normal circumstances. These were not those.

The crew huddled on the far end of the boat away from the *lu-ong*. No matter how strong Tuann craftsmanship was, it wouldn't be long before the boat went under or cracked under the strain.

Raider made a small exclamation, the curse carrying. "Looks like you're not the only one those creatures think is a tasty snack."

They traded grim looks as they circled the boat.

Kira saw her first impression had been wrong. The *lu-ong* hadn't just gripped the boat with a serpentine coil. The rest of its body surrounded the boat as well, creating a small well in the middle where the ocean frothed from its movements.

"Anybody ever seen a mad *lu-ong* before?" Aeron asked.

Graydon's oshota all shot glances at Kira, the memory of a baby *lu-ong* attacking her vivid in their eyes. There was one difference, that *lu-ong* had a Tsavitee control collar on it. It hadn't attacked of its own will.

This *lu-ong* had no such device forcing its actions.

It made their jobs both easier and more difficult.

"Amila, Solal, get the *lu-ong's* attention," Graydon ordered.

Their agreement came in a wordless cry. The two broke off from the formation to dive bomb the *lu-ong's* head. Kira held her breath as the *lu-ong* snapped at Solal, nearly catching him. He swerved at the last minute as Amila came from the other side, a blast leaving her hand and striking the *lu-ong's* temple.

They broke off, getting distance before making another run.

The rest of the group circled high overhead out of immediate danger. Watching, observing, analyzing.

The *lu-ong* was massive with pink whiskers and a neon yellow fringe. Its body was dark. In the ocean, it would be nearly indistinguishable from the waves.

As she watched, it hissed at Amila, baring fangs easily as long as Kira's body. Its fringe flared, like a king cobra's hood right before it struck.

The *lu-ong* curled closer to the boat, its coils tightening, forcing the boat's bow deeper into the water.

"That boat isn't going to last much longer," Jin warned. "My analysis puts a threat of hull breach due to stress at seventy-eight percent. Your time is limited."

Urgency and desperation beat at Kira as Solal and Amila dipped and wove around the *lu-ong's* head, narrowly avoiding being turned into a Tuann-sized snack. They moved almost too quick to follow, but not quick enough.

The *lu-ong's* fringe flared again, its mouth opening as a ball of pink light shot out like a laser. Graydon flung a hand out, energy forming around Amila.

The light bounced off the shield with a sound loud enough to break eardrums. A fist punched Kira in the chest, the board bucking under her from the reverberations of power.

Raider cursed as his did the same.

"Get distance," Wren cried. "Indya, Veer, support those two."

The oshota from Roake obeyed, the rest of them climbing.

The *lu-ong* hissed again, her head snapping forward when one of the oshota got too close.

Amila's hands glowed white-hot, creating a streak of light as she aimed at the *lu-ong's* neck. Kira saw the danger before she did as the *lu-ong's* tail rose out of the water behind Amila. Kira screamed a warning, already knowing it was useless.

Her body acted without thought, closing the distance between her and Amila as the tail loomed larger with every second. Twenty feet. Ten. Almost there.

Kira braced seconds before impact. She hit the other woman, sending them tumbling through the air, the tail crashing into the space they'd just been.

Kira let go, letting Amila spin away from her.

The oshota glanced at the disaster that could have been before giving Kira a sharp nod of thanks.

It was all they had time for, the *lu-ong* already gearing up for another attack, vicious in its defense. Kira and Amila immediately split, racing away from each other and forcing the *lu-ong* to choose its target.

Light and energy that Kira was beginning to associate with *ki* rent the air, shields snapping into shape as the *lu-ong* attacked. Whatever ability existed in the Tuann to shape the energy of the world around them, also existed in the *lu-ong*—only magnified.

They were going to lose unless something changed.

That was unacceptable.

Come on, Kira. See what isn't obvious. There was always a way. She just had to find it.

Kira studied the *lu-ong* and frowned. There was something about the way it was arranged around the boat. Almost protective. She swung wide for a better look, forcing herself to ignore the battle.

Sometimes you served on the front lines. Other times you had to take a step back and see what others couldn't.

Raider broke off, dropping into place beside her. Their formation tight. "What do you see?"

"It's almost as if she is protecting something."

The rightness of those words settled into place. There was something down there. Something desperate and afraid and needing help.

"Jin, can you tell me anything about what's below the surface?" Kira asked.

The lizard unwound, perching on her shoulder and staring at the spot the *lu-ong* guarded with zealous intensity. After a long moment, the lizard shook its head. "No, I think she's doing something to disrupt my sensors."

"Shouldn't that be impossible?" Raider asked, voicing Kira's thoughts.

"I'm beginning to think there is a lot more to these creatures than the Tuann want us to know," Jin responded.

Kira agreed, but their questions would have to wait until the danger had passed.

Kira studied the fishing boat, her mind sifting through the

information. The *lu-ong* rearranged its coils to cover that pool. Her gaze caught on something she hadn't noticed before, a line stretching from the boat into the water.

Suspicion dawned.

Kira broke off, looping up and around before darting toward the *lu-ong*, her path not straying even as the *lu-ong's* eyes locked on her.

"Kira, what are you doing?" Raider asked in her comms, sounding tense as she headed straight for that small dot of water the *lu-ong* guarded.

"Not to side with the meat sack—because bleh—but I'd kind of like to know that myself," Jin said from his spot on her shoulder.

Kira was silent. He wasn't going to like this plan and she didn't have time to argue.

"Why are you flying directly over that energy field the *lu-ong* is creating?" Jin asked, sounding more alert

"What better way to see what it's hiding?"

The lizard spun, its mouth dropping so it stared at her in consternation. "Are you crazy?"

Her grimace told the answer.

"You are," he wailed.

"Sometimes I wonder that myself," she confided.

She'd learned a long time ago to listen when her instincts whispered. Right now, they were telling her that what the *lu-ong* protected was of vital importance. There was a pounding in her head, a rock-solid belief that something needed her help.

It whispered and gasped, its cries echoing in her ears.

It was possible she was imagining things. If so, what a time for her mind to break.

Graydon and his oshota diverted the *lu-ong's* attention just then, allowing Kira to close the distance, Raider right behind her.

"I hope you know what you're doing because there won't be any way we can help you once you're down there," Raider said.

"Have I ever let you down?"

There was a brief pause and then an answer from both Jin and Raider. "Yes. Frequently."

Kira ignored the two sourpusses. It was go time.

Ten feet.

The postage stamp area she needed to investigate beckoned. Its dark depths whispering of safety.

She hoped she didn't break her neck doing this. Maybe they were right—this wasn't the best idea.

Five feet.

"Jin, you think you can fly this thing?" Kira asked.

There was a pause. "Of course, I can. I'm a better pilot than you."

"I would argue with the truth of that statement," Raider grumbled.

Jin ignored him, asking suspiciously "Why?"

Kira didn't answer. There wasn't time. Two feet. Her timing needed to be perfect.

Graydon's horrified expression caught her attention. He looked incredulous, then furious. "Don't you dare."

"Wish me luck," Kira said with a crooked smile.

She stepped off the board, Graydon's roar surrounding her.

She plummeted. Gravity and the speed she had been flying at pulling her down in a soft arc.

Water rushed up to meet her. Closer. Closer.

Kira pressed her legs together, pointing her feet and crossing her arms over her chest. She braced. This might hurt a bit. She'd intentionally slowed before the jump, so she didn't crush her bones on impact. Hopefully, it would be enough.

The roar of a board approached. Graydon's face was intent and set as he arrowed to intercept her. The *lu-ong's* head rose on Kira's other side. She spat a thin stream of fire that crackled, splitting into two serpentine bodies only feet away from Kira, bypassing her before crashing together on her other side.

Graydon broke off, evading an unfortunate barbecuing.

Part of the serpentine body of the *lu-ong* rose. Only an impossible flip and a hard shove of Graydon's own *ki* saved him from death.

An enraged cry escaped Graydon at his failure to reach her.

Kira took one last deep breath, filling her lungs seconds before she hit.

The water closed around her like a fist. The satisfaction she felt at landing nearly dead center in the circle was fleeting.

Nothing had prepared her for this.

Panic and fear wrapped around her. She fought against gasping as everything she hadn't picked up on above came crashing down all at once.

For a moment, her focus wobbled, overwhelmed by what the creature below was projecting. Her vision darkened as she struggled.

306

Faltering now would mean death.

From somewhere, she rallied reserves she didn't know she had, pushing out with her mind as Joule had taught her. The manipulation of *ki* was only constrained by the imagination. Form a picture, exert your will. The *ki* would answer, he had promised.

She pushed out with her mind, imagining a thin, permeable barrier between her and the owner of those feelings. Not enough to block them, but enough so she could create space to breathe.

There was the smallest lessening of pressure on her mind. Enough to realize the mind encroaching on hers was young. A babe compared to the ancient creature attacking the boat above.

A child. In danger. Scared and alone.

Even as Kira struggled to adapt to the sudden onslaught, she sensed the child weakening. The mother raged, and Kira got the briefest of glimpses of the battle above, a sheet of fire surrounding the mother and boat even as the Tuann and Graydon fought to follow Kira.

Raider let out a battle cry, swooping dangerously close to the mother's head as she rearranged her long body, covering the opening Kira had used. There would be no getting out that way. Not until Kira did what the mother had called her here to do.

That was okay. Kira hadn't expected anything else.

Kira kicked out, flipping herself so her head was pointed down. She swam deeper.

There, below her in the murky depths, a smaller version of the *lu-ong* wreaking havoc above drifted.

The baby's thrashing was weak. A dim welcome wrapped around her. She struggled to echo it, trying to push encouragement to him as she studied his predicament.

It was hard at first to understand what she was seeing.

He was in a cage of some sort. One that was much too small for his body. His upper half was outside the cage, his lower half and tail wedged inside. He looked like a broken jack-in-the-box, trying to escape.

She winced at the sight of blood seeping out of a deep gash. She had a feeling the tail might be broken. Not a good thing for a wild creature in the ocean where much bigger predators might come after him.

What she didn't understand was why the mother or the baby hadn't ripped the cage apart. Both should have been able to accomplish the deed with ease.

His body quivered as he held very still, allowing her to examine him.

He snaked his head around, and Kira went stock still, conscious of the very large teeth close to her body. He might be a baby still, but he dwarfed her. The last close call she'd had with these creatures flashed through her head.

It wouldn't take much for him to chomp her in half.

He looked at the cage and then at her, a question forming in her mind.

He was sapient, she realized with a start.

All the more reason to figure out a way to free him.

She reached out, bubbles escaping as she hissed when the cage burned her hands. There was an unpleasant sucking sensation that made her light-headed.

She imagined it was ten times worse for him. No wonder he was weakening.

The cage was sucking the life right out of him.

Urgency whipped at Kira. She didn't have time to figure this out or go slowly. The baby was fading, the brilliance of his mind dimming against Kira's.

A brief flash of fire flickered in her mind.

She hesitated, guessing what the *lu-ong* wanted.

Another image flashed; this time of a tiny candle next to an erupting volcano. Ah, Kira understood now. Different types of fires with different strengths.

The cage was made by the Tuann. They wouldn't have created something that might kill them every time they handled it. Because Kira was Tuann, she had a better chance of destroying it.

She touched her cuff and grimaced. Perhaps not. Access to her *ki* was nearly impossible with this.

That left trying to do things the old-fashioned way. Muscle through and hope for the best.

Kira grasped the bars of the door, setting her feet against the bottom bar of the cage, careful not to step on the *lu-ong*. Lightning bit through her as the power of the cage tried to suck her down.

She gritted her teeth and strained, resisting.

At her core, her energy flickered, trying to answer her need before guttering like a candle faced with a strong breeze.

Kira persisted. The cage's door creaked up an inch. Almost, but not enough.

She shoved again, reaching for the *ki* at her core by instinct and sliding off that same glass wall. This time, the mother shoved against her mind at that exact moment. Abruptly, her vision shifted, the watery scene fading as the cosmos danced behind her eyes.

It took several seconds to realize what she was seeing weren't stars but rather the tapestry of energy that made up every living thing. Like the *feilli* from yesterday, it sparkled and danced.

Curiosity compelled Kira to reach out, touching the aura that curled off one of those lights. The faint glow touched her skin, shifting colors until it turned a brilliant purple. She glanced out over the glittering lights that reminded her of the sun. Many were darkened and damaged, almost eclipsing the brilliance of those that remained.

Somehow, she knew those darkened parts were the pieces of herself she'd destroyed over the years. The parts she'd willingly sacrificed to protect those she loved.

Regret at the desolation moved through her, even as she knew she wouldn't have changed anything.

Those darkened bits were a reminder of what she'd done to protect her friends. They were something to be cherished. They meant she'd fought, even when it had been hard.

The small serpentine body of the baby *lu-ong* wound through the shimmering lights resting at the heart of her. He nudged a few in curiosity, making a pleased sound as they lit up—almost as if they were welcoming his presence.

He didn't only pay attention to those that shone with a brilliant light, but paid equal respect to the parts she would have said were dead and ruined. They gleamed, captured star fire glittering in their deepest hearts. It was as if the *lu-ong's* presence had woken them from a deep sleep.

Finally, the *lu-ong* drifted to a stop in front of her. He hovered in the vast space, his frills fanning out, the whiskers around his mouth and his beard reminding Kira of a wizened old man.

We accept, daughter of Harding, he told her.

She didn't get a chance to ask what he accepted. Fire lanced through her as her consciousness slammed into her body. She floated, the baby *lu-ong's* surprisingly wise eyes resting on her. Power crackled along her skin. Not since the first time she'd used the burst, had she felt like this.

It's time you fulfill the promise of your ancestors and reclaim your birthright, child. The *lu-ong's* voice held the weight of ages as it echoed in her head.

Kira reached for the cage again, almost as if in a dream, visualizing what she wanted to have happen. A picture and clarity of intent was needed. Discipline of the mind was as important when using the *ki* as discipline of the body was for a warrior.

The cage glowed white-hot, pieces of it melting as the water bubbled from the output of energy she was releasing.

Its bars snapped. The *lu-ong* streaked free, the water echoing with his exultant cry.

His body undulated, scales brushing Kira as he surged forth.

His tail caught on the cage, jerking it forward. It crashed into Kira, its edge hitting her head.

Light glimmered above, darkness encroaching as she sank into unconsciousness.

Jin was going to have nothing but I told you so's for this.

TWENTY-TWO

KIRA DISAPPEARED BENEATH the surface of the waves; the *lu-ong's* body slamming over the space where she'd fallen.

A roar of denial escaped Graydon. His entire world froze, as if she'd taken the warmth and light with her. Endless years yawned before him, the knowledge that he'd never find anyone like her again ingrained deep in his bones.

Terror and fury trembled through him as the Roake around them shouted in dismay as the world started moving again. Fury lit Wren's eyes, the battle-hardened monster within making a rare appearance. One echoed by Graydon's own monster.

Graydon's *ki* magnified Raider's voice. "Damn it, Phoenix."

The human swooped dangerously close to the *lu-ong*, expertly avoiding her as pinpoint pricks of light flared from her mane. Raider spun, closing the distance between him and the *lu-ong*, his skill rivaling that of Graydon's oshota.

Kira's human was a talented warrior when in possession of a waveboard. A fact Graydon knew his first and Wren were taking note of.

Many Tuann viewed humans as little better than untutored children, brash with youth and arrogance.

Raider's actions were proving them wrong today.

"What is she thinking?" Wren gritted out.

"She's being Kira," Raider shouted, making Graydon aware Wren's voice had carried to him as well. "She sees the problem and acts to fix it, leaving everyone else to follow or watch her die."

The human flipped in midair, abandoning the board and landing on the *lu-ong* in an impressive feat.

The human cut against the *lu-ong's* scales with a small knife he must have had hidden on him. He cursed when sparks flew.

"You're risking your life needlessly," Wren informed him. "A *lu-ong's* scales will be impenetrable to that blade."

It was one of the reasons they used *lu-ong* scales as the seeds for their synth armor.

Raider's pace never slowed as he leapt off the *lu-ong* and onto the board as it flew by.

"Then what do we do? I'm not leaving her." Raider muttered to himself in a voice Graydon didn't think they were meant to overhear. "Even if she thinks she's invincible."

"Get clear and form up on me," Graydon ordered

Power amassed in and around Graydon as he channeled it from within and without, feeling as it coiled around him, dripping from his fingers. He molded it with intent. The time for mercy had passed with Kira's action. All he could do now was focus on the kill.

He gestured, hurtling the strike at the *lu-ong*, changing direction at the last minute, so it slammed against the *lu-ong's* neck instead of splashing off its shield.

Graydon had been created for war. It was in his blood, imprinted on his bones and woven through his flesh.

His people had never been peaceful. They were beings of destruction; their darker urges guided by the rules they'd imposed on themselves for reasons he'd never shared with Kira.

Graydon was their crowning achievement. A warrior. A protector. The epitome of everything their race strove to be.

And right now, his blood yearned for vengeance.

"Solal, *ezie* formation," he snapped.

There was a chance she was still alive. A small link stretched from him to her, razor-thin but there nonetheless. He clung to that chance with all he had.

"Keep the *lu-ong* distracted. I'm going in," Graydon said.

"Not without me," the human retorted.

Graydon fought a sense of irritation before relenting. Graydon could use him. And Graydon was nothing if not practical.

The *lu-ong* was a difficult adversary, its skin nearly impenetrable to all but the most destructive of weapons. It had few weaknesses, and of those, it would take both skill and luck to take advantage of.

"Very well," Graydon agreed.

"Don't slow us down, human," Wren said.

"Please. One giant serpent has nothing on the Tsavitee warbirds we used to tangle with," the human said derisively.

Graydon bared his teeth in a bloodthirsty smile. "I guess we'll see soon enough. The rest of you, create an opening. I'm punching through. Stay on me—if you can."

Raider let out a whoop that Graydon took as agreement.

Graydon angled toward the *lu-ong*, picking up speed, his world narrowing as he sized up his opponent. This was going to be close. Power built in his hands and arms, Graydon forming his intent, honing it to a razor-sharp edge.

Under his armor, he knew lines and runes had formed under the skin of his arms, the delicate swirls and swoops glowing in preparation as he fed more power into them.

Every Tuann was born with certain attributes. The Mea'Ave upon birth read their souls and determined what they would need for the life to come.

Through relentless study and training you could add to the marks you were born with, achieve power through stubborn will.

The Mea'Ave only opened the door. You had to demonstrate the will and capacity to walk through it.

Only a quarter of those born with marks ever unlocked them and were blessed with their power. Of those, only a small percentage ever added to them.

Graydon was in those elite ranks. He was more than what he'd been born, possessing a rare will and determination. He'd only ever glimpsed his match in a woman who was too stubborn for her own good and so noble he feared what the universe might do to her if she wasn't protected.

He would not see that light extinguished. The Mea'Ave give him strength for what was to come. He'd need every ounce of its blessing today.

He built the feedback within, gritting his teeth against the onslaught of pain, his skin feeling at once too tight and too thin for the pure power housed in it.

"Time to dance, beautiful," he whispered to the *lu-ong*.

Light and power trailed from Graydon. To those on the ground, it would look like he grew wings of the purest black.

"Something has changed," Solal shouted.

Graydon swallowed the power as a smaller version of the *lu-ong* shot up from the depths, a small screech escaping it as it leaped into the air.

"She was protecting her baby," Amila whispered.

Graydon held the energy in, fighting the urge to expel it. Had he been any other, the action would have been impossible. He'd lived his life by control in all things. His *ki* was no different.

He stared at the water as the mother hovered over her child, trilling a greeting. No bright red hair the color of blood surfaced. Not even bubbles to mark the spot where Kira had gone under.

"Come on, Phoenix." The depth of emotion in Raider's voice betrayed him. He might pretend to hate Kira, but he cared for her in the same way Graydon had seen in siblings. Half antagonist, half fierce protector.

Come on, woman, Graydon mentally urged.

The *lu-ong* whipped around when Solal strayed too close, the deep cry they were known for echoing through the air.

"She's been under too long," Wren said grimly.

Surface, Kira. You can do it.

Long seconds ticked by with no sight of her. That small link they shared thinned.

Graydon bared his teeth. He didn't think so. If she thought to surrender so easily, he would teach her the true meaning of being Tuann. She didn't get to quit. She didn't get to go out like this.

Not ever if he had his way.

He would do anything to protect that woman, even if it meant killing a being many among the Tuann considered sacred. Harming one carried a steep price. There was a chance he would face consequences.

He found he didn't care. He'd already betrayed her trust once; he wouldn't do it again.

Power spooled as he prepared a strike. If this meant his position as the Emperor's Face, so be it. Some things were worth sacrificing for, and he knew to his bones Kira was one of them.

The wings he cloaked himself in sparked, looking like they were made of black lightning as he careened toward the *lu-ong* building a spear with the same light as he flew. The *lu-ong* twisted to face him, power building at the base of her throat, aimed right at Graydon.

He braced. Only one of them would survive this.

The baby disappeared beneath the surface.

One hundred feet. Fifty. Twenty-five. Point of no return.

The baby surfaced, a small, limp form carried in its mouth. The baby wiggled over its mother's body, depositing an unconscious Kira on the deck of the boat.

Graydon veered, releasing his power into the sea beyond the *lu-ong*. Power crackled in the space where he'd just been. He felt the heat of it pass. His armor, that indestructible material made from the discarded scales of a *lu-ong*, buckled.

*

Kira coughed up water, jerking back to the land of the living with no small amount of surprise.

She gasped, sucking in the air she thought she'd never taste again.

What the hell had happened?

"Kira," Jin shouted through the comms. "You're alive. Thank God."

Kira squinted, trying to get her bearings.

Her head pounded. She reached up and touched it, wincing as pain lanced through her. Her fingers came away wet with both water and blood.

That answered the question of why her head hurt.

Around her, the sound of battle raged. The *lu-ong* screaming its challenge as the Tuann dove at her.

Kira sat up with a groan, her head swimming as nausea curdled in her belly. Her headache increased. She knew this feeling. Concussion. Or at least really close to one.

Soothing cool, like an ice pack on sore muscles, washed over her, relieving the worst of her symptoms.

She glanced over to see the dragon-like head of the *lu-ong* baby she'd freed peeking over the boat's railing, his large, gem-like eyes focused on her. Waves of gratitude lapped at her. Adoration following.

"Glad you're safe, too," she told him.

She took in the rest of the boat as she staggered to her feet, swaying slightly. The baby might have helped with her concussion, but he hadn't healed it. At least not entirely.

She looked over at the huddled group of fishermen. They wore simple clothes, warm looking jackets layered over pants and sweaters.

Kira shivered at the reminder of just how cold she was. Every hint of breeze cut right through her, setting off another round of shivering.

If she didn't get warm and soon, she risked hypothermia.

Right now, though, she had to make nice with these people. Not an easy task with the way they watched her with a deep suspicion edging toward hostility.

She tried a small wave and non-threatening smile. They clumped tighter together. One reached for a club lying against a barrel.

Maybe her smile wasn't as reassuring as she'd hoped.

Graydon landed with a thud between them and her, his back to the strangers, his knees bent, his face a mask of rage.

He looked like a man who'd prepared for war and had already resigned himself to the necessary losses. If he'd been any other, she might have named the look on his face one of terror.

Kira braced. That stunt she'd pulled was bound to draw criticism. As well it should. She'd acted rashly, off-balance by the call for help. She'd been arrogant. This wasn't the before of the burst, where she could muscle her way through anything and come out the other side a little dinged up but otherwise unharmed.

She should have waited. Discussed her suspicions with him.

She understood the chain of command, and her actions, purely motivated as they were, broke that in a big way. She'd take any rebuke he chose to give her.

"I suppose I should explain," Kira started.

Her words seemed to break Graydon out of the thoughts he'd been locked in. He crossed the deck with a few powerful strides. His hands closed around her arms, and he jerked her close, warm lips landing on hers. They were filled with the desperate need of someone who'd lost the most important thing to them. His kiss was scalding hot, a perfect counterpoint to the chill trying to steal her thinking.

Instinct took over.

Kira met his fury with her own, pressing herself against him. Death had come too close today, and she needed a reminder that life wasn't just risk and danger. It was about this too.

Graydon didn't pity her for her upbringing. He'd tasted loss. He understood duty and sacrifice. If she let him, he could meet her on an equal playing field.

The undulating sound of the baby *lu-ong* intruded. They broke apart but didn't go far.

Graydon's gaze was searing as they breathed, millimeters apart.

"That was some greeting," Kira finally said in a voice far breathier than it should be.

His expression hardened, his eyes turning to ice. "You will never do that again."

Kira's mouth quirked. And there was the asshole she knew and was unwillingly drawn to. "We'll see."

"We will not," was his response as she forced herself to step back.

Without his warmth and the hard line of his body against hers, she could feel the full impact of the chill. She was conscious of the way her clothes clung to her, and her hair streamed around her face sopping wet.

"I see you, Kira. I'm not going anywhere," Graydon said.

"We'll see about that," she said as she faced the baby.

"Yes, we will. I'll prove it over and over if I have to—until you trust me with all that you are," Graydon murmured.

Chills skated along Kira's spine. Those words were filled with a promise, the universe recognizing the vow being made and cementing it into place.

As if reading her mind, Graydon smiled, the easy expression doing nothing to alleviate the darkness in his eyes. "The Tuann do not make vows lightly. The Mea'Ave has a habit of making them binding—and this is one I will submit myself to wholeheartedly."

Kira didn't respond. She couldn't.

There was a heat in Graydon's eyes that dared her to deny it so he could prove it. It was both thrilling and terrifying.

She'd gotten used to being alone. It was heady stuff knowing there was someone willing to attack a *lu-ong* mother protecting her young to try to save Kira.

Speaking of, Kira glanced around, noting the rest of the patrol had broken off their attack and was in a holding pattern high above.

Colored globes of light spun dizzyingly around the *lu-ong*. The threat was clear—approach and be incinerated

She slid Graydon a considering glance. He would have had to do some fancy flying to have gotten past that.

"We need to get out of here. It's not safe," Graydon said, one hand resting on her shoulder.

"Not necessarily true." Kira's gaze swung toward the crew. "At least for us. They, on the other hand, aren't so lucky."

An older man met her eyes, his expression surly and uncooperative. The captain, she was assuming.

As if in answer, he lifted his chin, his jaw tight as he tried to stare her down.

The side of her mouth tilted up. Yeah, she had a feeling that was the case.

"Unfortunately for them, they were a little too successful in their day's catch. Their cage caught him." Kira focused on the baby, who still clung to the side of the boat, watching the proceedings with a fascinated gaze.

"Ridiculous," the captain argued. "A cage would never be able to hold him."

Kira's head bent. "Not usually, I imagine." She glanced up at Graydon. "I don't know what it was made of, but it tried to drain me of *ki*."

Graydon's face hardened, his expression smoothing out as it turned calculating.

A couple of the younger members flinched and shifted away.

"What proof do you have?" the captain challenged.

Kira shrugged. "I think the *lu-ong* I freed does a pretty good job of supporting my claim."

Graydon's gaze lifted to the mother *lu-ong* and the spinning balls of fire around her. "As does the fact she stopped trying to sink the boat as soon as you went under."

"Who is she to make these accusations?" the man said, unable to see when the battle was lost.

Graydon's smile was a thing of beauty and death as he aimed it at the captain. "The missing heir to House Roake."

Kira shrugged, and half shook her head before nodding. "The title of unwilling guest works too."

There was a hint of fear in the captain's gaze as he glanced at Kira before his expression firmed.

"I don't care who the *iffli* she is," he spat.

Kira stiffened, the name tugging at memories she'd long since buried. The instructors in the camp used to call them that.

Her hands curled into fists as her emotions shut off, leaving her studying the captain the way she would a poisonous insect.

"House Dethos will not stand for this. I'll be speaking to our Overlord," the man was saying.

Hm. She'd heard that name before. It took only a second for it to come to her. The initiates who'd started the bar fight last night had belonged to House Dethos. Interesting to hear that name again here.

"You do that," Graydon rumbled, his voice deepening until it contained a dangerous bite to it. "I would be most interested to hear why a boat belonging to their House is fishing in sacred waters. These waters were declared off-limits."

"Except for Roake," the captain muttered defiantly.

Graydon's face was expressionless. "Yes, because they were appointed the custodians and protectors of everything that lies within. Your House is welcome to challenge them for their position at any time."

The captain's mouth snapped shut, his eyes flashing mutinously. "We're not currently in a position to win a challenge against Roake."

"Then perhaps you should not trespass in their waters or bemoan what you are too weak to secure," Graydon said with infinite patience.

Kira barely heard the words, her focus entirely on the captain. His gaze darted to her and away.

This wasn't her imagination. He was afraid of her. That, coupled with the use of that word, was enough to send her senses to high alert.

There was a whistling sound from behind them. The baby *lu-ong* wiggled further onto the ship, making those behind them stir uneasily.

Kira ignored them, giving herself space to think as she left Graydon's side and moved toward the *lu-ong*. She stopped in front of him. Taking a chance, she reached out, a small smile escaping her as he knocked his head against her fingers before rubbing his cheek along them while making a sound very like a purr.

Kira's heart stuttered, wonder unfurling in her chest as she set aside the captain momentarily. Seeing the baby under the water hadn't done him justice. He was beautiful and delicate, the suggestion of the mammoth creature he'd be one day there in his face. For now, he was adorable, his eyes multifaceted, his coloring not as pronounced as his mother's.

Impressions raced through her mind. A joyous warbling rising as he whistled and trilled a greeting at her.

He broke off abruptly as the world around them seemed to burn, the very air boiling and frothing.

A form dropped out of the sky, wrapped in darkness as stars trailed behind it. The Overlord of Roake landed heavily on the ship. Hellish fury and the promise of retribution raging from his eyes.

Kira caught sight of the survivor he was, the one who feared loss as much as she did. The one who would destroy his soul if it meant safeguarding those who he'd taken under his protection.

The emotions folded away as if they'd never been as he straightened, his expression containing a calm that almost made Kira think she had imagined what came before.

There was a minute tightening in his expression when he caught sight of Kira's state, the blood oozing from the cut on her head. The half-drowned look and the protective way Graydon hovered over her.

Harlow inhaled deeply, whatever emotions he felt disappearing as if they had never been.

"What is going on here?" he asked, his cool gaze traveling over them.

The captain opened his mouth on a lie Kira sensed even before it left his mouth.

"*Iffli*," she said, using the term the captain had called her. "Is this a common word among the Tuann?"

Her uncle regarded her carefully. "Not one I've heard used before."

"Graydon?" she asked.

Panic deepened in the captain's eyes.

"It is an old one, not often used in common speech because of its origins with our former masters," Graydon said slowly. He saw the captain's unease too.

Graydon snagged a sheet that had been sitting over some bulky cargo. Cages, identical to the one she'd freed the baby from, were stacked all along the wall of the boat.

Graydon sent a chiding smile at the captain. "And you said she was lying." To Harlow, he said, "This is *seiki* stone. The emperor decreed its use as forbidden."

The captain's eyes darted, the noose around his neck tightening. His crew tensed at the implications.

"This is alarming, indeed." Harlow's voice a silky rumble. "The hunting of *lu-ong* carries a death sentence."

"That's not what we were doing," the captain defended. "You're mistaking our intentions."

"Are we?" Kira asked.

Somehow, she didn't think so.

More importantly, the mother and child behind them didn't either. If the Overlord didn't do something about this, they would. Kira got the sense their form of justice would be much bloodier and involve teeth.

"What does it mean?" Kira heard herself ask. "That word?"

People lied about words not hurting. Sometimes words left painful wounds that were more difficult to heal than physical ones.

For Kira, that word was deeply rooted in the identity of those who'd once called themselves her master.

Graydon shifted as if reading her hunger for blood. The change was slight as he readied himself for battle. "Halfbreed."

Kira's smile was humorless. "I thought so. I've heard it before—in the camp where I spent my childhood."

Graydon's and Harlow's attention snapped to the captain.

He snarled a curse.

Kira took a chance, dropping into the Tsavitee language. "Your skin is wearing thin, and your deceptions no longer fool the eyes, skinwalker."

She saw the moment when the captain's resolve faded. He shot a glance at one of his crew members, one who stood slightly apart from the rest. He looked as Tuann as any, if one ignored the eerily smooth skin or the placid detachment with which he observed the situation. Unlike the rest, there was no unease or fear at being faced with two powerful Tuann.

That utter lack was warning enough.

At the captain's mistake, the man's eyes finally filled with emotion. Greed and hunger fought for control. He sprang forward, the skin he hid behind tearing to reveal a Tsavitee skinwalker. Sexless and bald, claws outstretched as his mouth opened wide, he streaked across the deck toward Kira.

She barely had time to prepare, tensing to dodge.

She needn't have bothered.

An en-blade appeared, separating the skin walker's head from its shoulders as the marshal Kira had met her first day on the planet stepped into view, seemingly out of thin air. His gaze was serene as he slashed his blade through the air, slinging the blood from it in one smooth movement.

Nearly identical to the Overlord's, the marshal's armor gleamed in the sunlight. These weren't the ornate ceremonial pieces Liara had worn to greet her. These were meant for war. Plain. Simple. Utterly efficient. Without a hint to announce either man's rank or status.

"I suppose this merits a thank you," Kira told Makon.

The faintest hint of warmth touched his expression. "No need. I suspect you would have had it in hand soon enough. Baiting the creature was a wise move."

Kira was glad someone thought so. The shaking in her hands disagreed. Skinwalkers were nasty creatures, reliant on poison as much as their claws. If he'd managed to nick her or pierce her skin in any way, she might not have survived long enough to make it to a medic.

Kira glanced beyond him to find shock had settled on the crew's faces.

"We didn't know anything about this," the captain tried.

Lie.

Kira wasn't the only one to think so either, judging by the way Harlow and Graydon watched him like lions studying a juicy gazelle.

The marshal transferred his attention to Harlow. "I pulled the record, as you asked. This ship has had two warnings before about straying into protected waters. Whether they knew or not, they're still responsible."

The captain started to bluster a denial.

Harlow raised a hand, cutting him off.

The captain fell silent. The appearance of the skinwalker had knocked some of his confidence out of him.

Before, he had postured, convinced he could talk his way out of this. Now, he realized the waters he'd sailed into were much more treacherous and deeper than he'd previously assumed.

Makon paused, waiting. When the captain said nothing else, he continued. "This ship is registered to House Dethos. They are a small House. It is my opinion this is a deliberate trespass on our authority and should be treated accordingly."

Harlow studied Graydon. "And you?"

Graydon's smile was the stuff of nightmares. "They've directly broken several of the emperor's laws."

"We haven't," one of the crew pleaded.

He flinched when Graydon's attention settled on him, white-hot and edged with violence. "You were caught with a *lu-ong* in your cage. Found to be hosting an abomination created by an enemy that has already attacked us once. Had the Tsavitee gotten a hold of a *lu-ong* for their experiments, the damage done to us would have been catastrophic. There is no other way to interpret those actions."

The faces of the crew paled further, fear permeating off them in the face of Graydon and Harlow's regard.

Kira had to hand it to the two. They did intimidation well.

Graydon looked over, a smile tangling his lips as if he'd heard her thoughts.

She rolled her eyes. Yes, yes, he was very scary. That was never in doubt.

That smile died as soon as his attention returned to the captain and crew. "On behalf of the Emperor of the Tuann and standing in for your Overlord, I excommunicate all of you from your former House for grave crimes."

There was an immediate outcry from the Tuann in front of them.

"You can't do that," the captain shouted.

Graydon's jaw was set and hard, mercy nonexistent in his gaze. "I can, and I did. My status as the Emperor's Face gives me that power. I'd tread carefully. I hold your fate in my hand. Be careful not to tempt me to a harsher sentence."

Kira wasn't sure, but excommunication from one's House sounded pretty harsh to her. She'd seen how seriously the Tuann treated the bonds to their House, was living proof to how far they'd go in pursuit of them. She knew how lonely and difficult it was to be an outsider, and she suspected for the Tuann it was much worse.

Humans understood the need to walk alone at times. Not all of them fit in pretty little boxes. Sometimes you became a loner by choice, as she did; sometimes, it was the only path left to you.

Kira didn't regret the captain's fate so much as his crew. For most of them, they were probably only following orders. Now they were going to lose everything.

Still, she didn't speak on their behalf. Graydon was in the right. Sometimes you had to be harsh to protect the many. That they had had a Tsavitee skinwalker in their midst pointed to a rot far greater than she could ever forgive.

"Our House won't stand for it," the captain argued, the veins in his forehead popping. He looked beside himself with rage, his face red and his hands clenched.

"They will," Graydon assured him with a rumble. It was like listening to the crash of mountain ranges. Slow, slumberous, inevitable. "Especially when I open up an investigation into your former House."

The captain sucked in a harsh breath. "You wouldn't."

Graydon's head tilted. "You keep telling me what I will and won't do. That is a mistake. Your Overlord is ultimately answerable for the actions of those in their House. Your casual disregard for our laws points to a dangerous mentality being fostered in your leadership. That is something neither I nor the emperor will stand for."

Shock rendered the captain mute. If he'd been furious at being excommunicated, this proclamation terrified him. Kira couldn't help but wonder if the captain had reason to fear his Overlord, or if there was something she was missing.

The captain's gaze moved to Kira, his expression frozen. When his eyes landed on her, all that emotion he couldn't take out on Graydon found an outlet. Rage spilled into his face.

"You," he breathed. "This is your fault."

Kira braced, knowing what was coming. He needed someone to blame. She was his chosen victim.

Ki gathered around the captain, building as Kira prepared to spring. She needed to disarm him before he could release his *ki*.

She didn't make it more than a step before Makon appeared next to him like a ghost, his sword sweeping up and separating the man's head from his shoulders.

Kira stopped abruptly, blinking at the sudden carnage as the rest of the crew lost their collective minds. Graydon and Harlow snapped into motion, subduing them in seconds.

Blood pooled under the captain's body, spreading until it nudged the tips of Kira's boots.

"I wish you hadn't done that," she told Makon.

He cleaned his blade with a quick flick of his wrist. "Mercy is not always wise, child."

"Maybe not, but I have a feeling he could have told us more about where that one came from." She nodded to the other headless body on the deck.

The marshal's gaze was contemplative as he took in the body of the skinwalker. "You have a point. Pardon my overzealousness."

He inclined his upper body in a small bow.

Harlow hauled one of the crew up, holding him in an implacable grip. "You will return to your House and tell them they are banished from these waters and every ocean on a Tuann planet."

The crew member thrashed, his eyes wild. "You'll destroy our House. We're reliant on the treasures we take from the water. It won't matter what decision the Face makes if we're cut off from our only source of profit."

"Someone should have thought about that before sending you out here to steal a *lu-ong* child," Harlow said, his expression coldly amused.

The *lu-ong* mother's thirst for these men's death beat at Kira. The blood of two of those responsible had assuaged some of her desire for vengeance, but not all. Kira had a feeling if the mother ever found them on these waters again, they, along with any boat they were on, would disappear, not even a piece of driftwood to point to their fate.

Kira wanted to make this point very clear. The last thing she wanted was more deaths. "In case you don't understand the seriousness of this, I'll make it clear. The mother has caught your scent. If she finds you or anyone related to you on open water, you won't have to worry about what Roake will do to you when they find you. She'll solve the problem for them."

Harlow's expression was cruel as he held the crew member motionless. "That goes for the rest of your House as well. She'll know if any of them step into a body of water she occupies. She'll come for them."

The crew member gulped, looking properly chastised.

"We won't answer a distress call from Dethos a second time," Harlow said, releasing him. The crew member stumbled as Harlow faced his marshal. "See that the crew is escorted to their House. Leave the ship for the *lu-ong* to sink. The cages will go to the bottom with the boat."

The marshal dipped his head. "As you command."

Harlow grunted as he moved toward Kira. He stopped beside her to stare up at the *lu-ong* mother. His gaze softened, admiration entering it. This was more than duty. Her uncle held these creatures in high esteem. No wonder he'd come.

As the marshal and Graydon arranged for the oshota above to land carefully so the crew could be evacuated, her uncle studied the baby where he still clung to the ship's side.

"Hello, little one. I am glad you are safe," her uncle crooned.

Kira blinked, not expecting to hear such a soft tone from a man whose defenses had seemed impenetrable.

"Our family has always shared a close bond with the *lu-ong*," her uncle told her as the baby regarded him with wise eyes before touching his nose to her uncle's chest. The baby nuzzled the synth armor before letting out a warble. The boat rocked as he used it as a springboard, diving into the water with barely a ripple.

Harlow smiled, the expression changing everything about him. Where before he'd been serious—austere and harsh—that smile made him handsome.

"Your father could speak with them. He was loved and cherished for it," Harlow said.

Kira moved closer to the railing, looking up at the mother *lu-ong* with curiosity. She waited, hoping Harlow would continue, aching for more information on this man she had never met.

"As boys, we used to swim out as far as we could, and he'd call them to us. We'd spend hours riding and playing with them. Used to drive our parents mad." Nostalgia crept into his smile. A long-tolerated pain lingered around the corners of his eyes. "You hear them too."

His declaration distracted Kira from her study of the mother.

He nodded as he took in her startled expression as if she'd confirmed something. "You are so very like him. Your recklessness will be your downfall."

Kira leaned against the railing before glancing up at the *lu-ong*, relieved to see her fringe had finally settled, some of her rage and anger bleeding away. The balls of fire still hovered as a warning, but they no longer spun.

"How did he die?" Kira asked.

Harlow's expression iced over as he withdrew, his gaze turning distant. "His love of your mother and you compelled him to face his enemy without anyone to watch his back. If he'd waited to go to her aid, he might have lived."

There was an unspoken rebuke in his words.

Kira lifted a shoulder, conceding his point. She'd been reckless. She could own that. "I used to be better at taking others into account."

He blinked slowly, accepting the non-apology.

Kira leaned a forearm against the railing as she struggled to ask the question that had been bothering her. "Do you ever resent me for his loss?"

If he did, it would be understandable.

Harlow couldn't hide his surprise. After a long second, he reached out, his hand cupping the back of her neck. She held herself stiff, ready to defend herself as he drew her in to press a kiss against her cold forehead.

"Sometimes, I forget how infinitely young you are," he told her before stepping back. To Graydon, he said, "Bring her to the fortress. She's cold. I don't want her risking hypothermia."

Harlow didn't wait for agreement, making an impossible leap straight up. He kicked off air, racing across it toward the fortress.

"How the hell does he do that?" Kira didn't realize she'd spoken out loud until the marshal smiled.

"Practice. Perhaps one day you will be able to do the same."

Her expression closed. She doubted she'd be around long enough to learn how.

Makon glanced at Graydon. "I will remain behind. This is House Roake's responsibility."

Graydon's lips twisted. "Just make sure the crew arrives in one piece."

Kira thought it was a good idea to remind the sword-happy marshal of that necessity, given the two bodies he'd already decorated the boat with.

Makon inclined his head, a faint smile gracing his lips. "Of course. It will be as you wish."

Graydon raised his eyebrows at Kira. "Ready?"

He clapped his hands together, his forehead furrowing as power built between them. Sparks flew as he tore his hands apart with visible effort. A board hovered in the air, lowering until he could easily step onto it. He held out his hand and smirked in invitation.

Kira didn't think so.

"I'll find my own way."

He looked between her and the open water, the shore so distant as to be invisible.

"And how do you plan to do that? By swimming?"

Her smile was toothy. Laugh it up, but no way was she getting on that board with him and letting him play knight in shining armor to her helpless damsel.

The low hum of a hoverboard called her attention. Her smile widened as she caught sight of her board skimming across the water.

Suspicion slammed over Graydon's expression.

"I'll figure it out," she said.

Before he could stop her, Kira jumped over the edge of the boat. Her feet splashed into ankle-deep water, the *lu-ong's* coiled body making a surprisingly stable surface as she jogged away.

"Kira, get back here," Graydon warned.

She did a little of her own taunting. "You really should learn to stop underestimating me. It always backfires on you."

As if they planned it, the part of the *lu-ong's* body she stood on rose from the sea. Good thing too, because Graydon looked seconds from coming over the side of the ship after her.

Kira grinned before turning her attention to the task ahead. The *lu-ong* flexed, and Kira shot into the air. Just as she started to fall, the *lu-ong's* head landed under her feet and shoved. She and the *lu-ong* rose, shooting past the rest of the patrol. Kira caught a glimpse of their startled faces, and then she was air born as the *lu-ong* gave her one final push.

For a second she was weightless. All her worries were far below, and she closed her eyes, basking in the stolen moment.

Her eyes snapped open, a fierce grin on her face. This was going to be so much fun.

The hoverboard carrying the lizard streaked along the *lu-ong's* body as Kira started to fall. The board hit the edge of the *lu-ong's* body and grabbed air. Kira stretched, her fingers touching the edge of the board before she grabbed it, slamming it under her feet as gravity pulled her down.

"Unnecessarily flashy, don't you think?" Jin's voice was dry.

"Perhaps," Kira conceded. "But it was fun."

"I can't argue with that," Jin said.

The discomfort of her body was placed aside for now. "What say we give them a little bit more to be angry about?"

The lizard bussed her cheek with several small kisses. "Yasss! I love it when you're devious."

That was all the encouragement she needed as she raced away, the *lu-ong* setting fire to the boat's carcass in a fitting end to the day's events.

TWENTY-THREE

KIRA WAS THE first to reach the outer walls of the fortress, its defenses tracking her as she flew over. Graydon was hot on her heels as she came to a halt inches above the ground. Graydon landed seconds later.

He was off the board and striding toward her moments later, his expression fierce as he moved with a predator's grace.

Tension crackled through the air between them. The close call Kira had had, coupled with what they'd uncovered on that boat, pulled the thread between them tight.

Shivers skated along Kira's spine at the intentness on Graydon's face. His gaze was focused. He looked at her like a conqueror seeing something he wanted.

Except Kira had never been good at making things easy on other people.

He stopped a breath away, looming over her and sending a forbidden thrill through her. His gaze was thoughtful as he smoothed his fingers down her cheek.

"You enjoy games," he murmured. A wicked smile grew on his face. "So do I."

Kira blanched. "Wait."

That hadn't been her intent. She'd simply gotten caught up in the fun of it.

Graydon's expression was merciless. "Too late. You opened the door. I'm simply walking through."

"That's not what I did," Kira denied.

He leaned toward her, his gaze playful and sultry. "The Tuann only play with those they consider theirs."

"I didn't grow up Tuann," she pointed out desperately, sensing her actions had cost her more than she'd anticipated.

Graydon straightened as the rest of the patrol landed.

"You have more of us in you than you want to admit," he told her as Harlow stepped into view. "Don't worry, I'll be more than happy to play with you. Anytime. Anywhere."

Kira's choked sputter had him grinning as he moved toward the Overlord.

"Uh oh, that backfired on you," Jin said as Harlow and Graydon conferred, Wren and Maida joining them.

"Not another word out of you, Jin."

"No problem, but we both know it's the truth." The lizard rearranged himself around Kira's neck so he could have a better view of the proceedings.

Quillon walked toward Kira. "I hear you decided not to take my advice on taking it easy."

Kira's expression was slightly guilty in the face of the healer's displeasure.

The skin around his eyes tightened as he held out his hand. Knowing what he wanted, she placed the wrist with the inhibitor on his upturned palm.

His forehead creased, his eyebrows drawing close as he frowned. Unlike the other times he'd checked the inhibitor, she could almost feel the flow of his soul's breath sifting through her, pausing to linger in certain places.

A feeling of puzzlement floated up toward her from his *ki*.

"Is something wrong?" Kira asked.

Quillon dropped her wrist. "No, you've managed to avoid damaging your channels."

There was something in his expression that made her think there was more to it.

He jerked a nod at her before striding off.

"What's going on?" Raider asked, joining her as he glanced to where Wren, Harlow, and Loudon spoke with Graydon.

Kira shook her head. "No clue."

Whatever it was, was serious and not to Wren's liking if she had to guess. Loudon stood off to the side, making placating gestures. His words seemed to have no effect.

Harlow stepped forward. Silence fell as those in the courtyard shifted their attention to their Overlord. "The Trial of the Broken will take place tomorrow. For those of you whose names are called, I wish you luck. The pride of your Houses rests with each of you. Do your best to meet their expectations."

He stepped back as Maida called out several names. Joule was first, followed by two names she didn't recognize. Raider was next and then Devon. She released the breath she was holding when Maida paused and glanced at her, winking as she said Kira's name. Aeron was the last to be called.

Raider nudged her shoulder with a fist. "We made it."

Somehow.

Kira was more than a little surprised. She'd gotten the sense there were those among Harlow's council who would have preferred she sit this one out.

Her gaze lingered on Graydon and the distinct look of satisfaction on his face. He looked like a cat who'd caught a mouse, smug and arrogant as he started toward Kira.

"Congratulations are in order," he said as he joined her.

"Why do I detect your hand in this?" she asked him.

He regarded her steadily. "If you do, will you refuse the trial?"

She scoffed. "I'm not so prideful as to deny myself an opportunity, no matter how it came to me."

This furthered her goals. Who cared how her name got on the list? This was a step toward the *adva ka* and independence, freedom that limited Roake's ability to influence her fate. She'd be a fool to throw it back at him simply because he'd interfered. Him smoothing the way for her in no way denied her abilities.

He studied her, his gaze enigmatic. "Good, because I did less than you would think. I simply reminded a few people that they were allowing their history to affect their judgment. You've more than earned this chance. Had you been raised Tuann, you'd likely have already taken the trial and the *adva ka* decades ago. I'm simply correcting that error."

Sure he was.

The marshal landed in the courtyard, nodding at them before striding toward the fortress.

Graydon exhaled and touched her elbow. "I have to go. Harlow will want to brief the rest of his council and the emperor should be informed. What we found will have grave repercussions."

He wasn't wrong about that. The skinwalker's presence meant the

Tsavitee were moving. Their goals were unclear, but they could still be thwarted if the Tuann acted quickly and decisively enough.

He paused. "Is there anything I should know before I talk to Harlow."

Kira hesitated, torn. Trust had to start somewhere, and Graydon had more than proven himself.

"In my experience, a skinwalker rarely travels alone. He would have had a ship, and there would be more ready to take his place in the event he failed. He might have been on hand for the capture and transfer of the *lu-ong*, but he would have needed help getting off the planet with his prize. This could mean he had a companion in the wings waiting for him, or—" Kira stopped, uncertain. Not many wanted to believe the worst of their own.

Humans hadn't.

"Or there are already people in place helping him," Graydon finished.

Raider cursed as Kira reluctantly nodded.

Graydon stared into the distance. "If you're right, it would point to a far wider plot. The implications would be dire."

Kira glanced at Raider. She'd need to be careful in how she phrased this next part. The Tuann's secrets were theirs and not something she could reveal without their permission.

"The Tsavitee—are they linked to those you showed me in the Hall of Ancestors?" she finally asked.

Raider's lips parted with interest, his sharp mind already digging into what she wasn't saying.

Graydon cupped her nape, pressing his forehead to hers. "Don't ask me to share secrets that aren't mine to give."

She took that as a yes, or as close to it as she was going to get right now. She didn't blame him. She'd made a statement by keeping herself apart. She didn't want to be considered Tuann. By rights, she couldn't very well expect them to treat her as one now.

She was an outsider, and outsiders couldn't be trusted with some information.

She stared into his eyes. "I can only ask the same of you."

It was as close to an admission of what she was hiding as she could get. If it was just her, she might risk it, but there were others counting on her. Their secrets weren't hers to tell.

Graydon stared at her, his gaze penetrating as he tried to find the things she hid. "I understand."

She thought he might.

His thumb brushed the side of her neck in a caress. He nodded abruptly before striding away.

Blue joined them seconds later.

"How was your patrol?" Blue asked.

"Eventful," Raider said.

Kira studied Blue with narrowed eyes. To her surprise, the other woman didn't seem particularly put out about not being on the list for the trial.

Blue was every bit as competitive as Raider and Kira. Being left out should have had an effect on her, yet she seemed almost chipper.

It only took a minute for Kira to understand why. Blue not being able to compete in the trial meant her time with the Tuann—and their technology—would be extended. If she knew anything about her friend, it was how attractive that possibility would be.

Blue met Kira's gaze, a note of apology gleamed before her attention flitted away as Blake and Rheya approached. Blake looked his normal grumpy, reclusive self while Rheya's steps dragged, her face making it clear she'd rather be anywhere else.

"Do it," Blake rumbled.

Rheya's shoulders bowed before her chin came up, her gaze meeting Kira's.

"I wanted to apologize for my actions the yesterday," Rheya said.

Kira waited. When Rheya offered nothing else, she asked, "Which actions might those be?"

"For my part in bringing up the battle for Rothchild," Rheya said stiffly. "I didn't realize you were in that battle. If I had, I would never have done what I did."

"Why did you?" Kira asked.

Rheya's gaze left hers, wandering over to where Aeron goofed off with a couple of his fellow initiates, causing them to laugh and shove each other. Loudon lingered behind them, monitoring their actions closely as he listened to an oshota.

"I listened to someone I shouldn't have," Rheya said finally. "It was wrong of me. Please forgive me."

Kira studied the younger woman for several seconds.

"Both of our parents lost children during the Sorrowing," Blake informed her. "We've grown up under the shadow of their loss. You could say we let that affect our actions."

Kira thought she understood a little better now. It would be difficult to lose a child under any circumstance. The effects of it would spill into your everyday life for a long time after. These two had likely grown up being compared, on purpose or not, to their siblings. It would likely have made them competitive and out to prove something.

Then came Kira. A reminder of the very people they had probably resented and wished for their entire lives.

Kira rubbed her chin, catching Blue and Raider paying careful attention. She scowled at them. Neither hid their eavesdropping.

Kira shook her head in resignation and looked at Rheya. "There's nothing to forgive. You did what they asked and found a battle you thought illustrated your point. I probably overreacted. I have a reputation for that."

Rheya's expression turned uncertain but hopeful. "Thank you."

"Why weren't your names called?" Kira asked. The two were obviously qualified. Their skills set them apart from the rest.

"We've already passed the trial," Blake supplied.

"Then why are you participating in this training?" Raider asked.

He shrugged. "We're waiting for our apprenticeship to be announced. Until then, the Overlord insists we continue improving our skills."

"Also, this is a rare chance," Rheya said. "Wren and Maida are here to prepare you for the *uhva na,* but they're also here to look everyone over and decide who they want as an apprentice. An apprenticeship with either one would be considered a coup."

Devon strode past them with his head held high; his posture almost brittle. There was a raucous laugh from Aeron and the other initiates. Joule looked unhappy as they made a gesture at Devon's back.

"What's that about?" Kira asked.

"I'm not sure," Rheya supplied. "If I had to guess, it's because Dethos is a small House who is under Danai's umbrella. As a child of Danai, Devon is likely being targeted for his affiliation with them."

Raider whistled as they watched the rest.

Devon's transformation to primus probably didn't help matters. The rest were jealous and afraid and had latched onto this new information as an excuse.

"They're fools," Blake said, heat in his tone. "Devon would already be gone if the Overlord considered him a threat. Their actions only reflect on them at this point."

"What happens if he decides to leave?" Blue asked.

"He won't," Rheya assured them. "Finding another House to join for training would be difficult at this stage."

Aeron, Kira was coming to realize, was much different than she'd first assumed. That smiling face he'd presented in the beginning was a façade—a clever one, meant to lure the unwary into trusting him. Now, she saw his true colors. Kira was beginning to see he shared many qualities of a bully. He bore watching.

For the moment, she put Devon and Aeron out of her mind as she waved at Joule, catching his attention. As concerning as the other two were, they weren't her problem.

Joule's face lit up, and he started toward her.

"Look at the orphan, running to the mad heir's side. I wonder what that says about you?" Aeron said in a voice he no doubt intended to be heard only by Joule.

Unfortunately for him, Jin didn't miss much—and what he knew, Kira knew as well.

A wall slammed over Joule's expression as his pace slowed, his back ramrod straight. His hands clenched at his side. He kept walking toward Kira, his jaw tight, unable to hide the anger shaking him.

His struggle to ignore the other boy was almost painful to watch.

Blake murmured something to Rheya, and she nodded, not looking any happier.

"Remember what we discussed before," Kira called. "I care little for the opinion of blowhards who haven't even earned the blade they wield. Nor should you."

There was an infinitesimal loosening around Joule's shoulders, and his stride smoothed out, so he was walking instead of stomping.

"Real subtle, Kira." Jin's voice echoed in her comms. "Didn't you tell the boy not to pick fights? Then why are you always starting them?"

Because she had a habit of winning her fights.

The cold, calculating look in Aeron's eyes caught Kira's attention. The emotions seemed out of place in the younger boy.

He blinked, the coldness vanishing, but not before Kira's suspicions were aroused. Aeron's gaze dropped to Joule. This time, he didn't bother trying to hide what he said. "I'd be more careful picking your friends, orphan. You never know when you might take a knife in the back that was meant for them."

Kira stepped forward, unable to keep herself from reacting to the not so subtle threat.

"Kira," Raider rumbled. "Not worth it."

Kira wavered. It went against her instincts to leave a dangerous foe standing. The only thing keeping her from acting was the thought that if she intervened now, Joule would be the one to bear the brunt of the consequences. She needed to be smart.

For now, that meant letting the younger man think he'd won.

Aeron walked away without looking back, the initiates he'd surrounded himself with looking confused as to what just happened.

Joule joined Kira, watching him go. "You're better at this than me. I don't know how you can let their remarks pass by when you've proven yourself equal to even the Emperor's Face."

"Don't let her fool you," Blue cautioned. "She got in more than her fair share of fights when she was coming up in the ranks."

Kira thought about protesting but shrugged instead. Blue was right. She had. She'd been younger than everyone else, at least in appearance. Sometimes the only way to establish dominance was by beating it into people.

Joule stared at her in consternation. "What happened to being the person who didn't care what others thought?"

"I don't. Now."

Once, though, she'd very much cared what her fellow soldiers thought. However, she'd never let that control her. You give people the power they wielded over you.

She'd learned very early not to set too much stock in what others thought unless it got in the way of doing her job. When people failed to obey her orders because they thought she was inexperienced, she'd felt obliged to teach them otherwise.

Joule's expression remained unconvinced.

"The one thing you learn if you survive long enough is what to give head space to and what to ignore." Kira looked away. "That boy thinks he's hot shit, but he's only started on his path. There are much more dangerous things out there than him."

"Also, he sounds like a tiny, yappy dog trying to threaten a wolf," Raider said. "It's cute and all, but we know who will come out the winner in that scenario."

*

Graydon made his way toward Roake's Nexus, knowing Harlow would already be there.

The Overlord had called a war council, and there was no better place than the Nexus for a meeting. It was the battle center of the House. All data flowed through it. There, Harlow could tap directly into the Mea'Ave, boosting his capabilities.

Graydon knew that this thing with the *lu-ong* disturbed Harlow as much as it did him. The implications were disastrous. Worse, Kira's question about the link between the Tsavitee and the Tuann's old enemy had gotten him thinking.

Graydon stopped in front of a smooth section of stone, barely taking notice of the four oshota standing guard on either side. The camouflage Roake was known for using in their synth armor, and adding to with *ki* manipulation, made them impossible to see except to those like Graydon who could use *ki* to sense another's presence.

Graydon held his palm to the wall, flexing his *ki* and rearranging the molecules of the door. He stepped through the opening into a room bustling with activity.

Graydon wasn't the first to arrive. The rest of the council, with a few exceptions, were already there.

Caius stood to one side, his hologram folding its arms. "So glad you could finally join us."

Graydon ignored him, moving toward where Harlow studied a display. The settings for the security of the oceans surrounding the *lu-ong's* nesting waters scrolled through thin air.

"How is my niece?" Harlow asked, not taking his eyes off the information.

"Better than she has any right to be," Graydon said. "That stunt would probably have killed most."

"What happened?" Caius asked.

Makon was the one to explain as Graydon took in the settings. Nothing seemed amiss, which made events all the more concerning.

Caius whistled. "Brazen thing."

"It was reckless," Loudon said, having entered sometime in the last few minutes.

"You can't argue with her results," Maida said. "Had that child died, it could have had repercussions for all of us."

She didn't have to expand on what those would be. All those

present, understood how close they'd skated to danger today. The *lu-ong* were powerful. They were the reason the Tuann had survived their old enemy. A massive debt was owed to them.

They would have forgiven Graydon for killing a mad member of their kind, as had nearly happened on Ta Da'an. It was rare a *lu-ong* lost itself in madness—usually only when they were ready to end their very long lives. But if his actions had resulted in an offspring's death? No.

The *lu-ong* would have sought revenge for that.

"That is no reason to allow her favoritism," Loudon argued.

"It's been decided. Kira will take part in the trial," Harlow said, his tone inviting no argument.

Loudon shifted his attention to Wren. "You agree with me that she's not ready."

The rest of them fell silent at Loudon's continued stubbornness. Not many would continue to defy the Overlord when he'd made his position clear. That Loudon could was a privilege stemming from their past.

Graydon suspected Loudon was running out of rope if the struggle for control he could see on Harlow's face was anything to judge by.

Wren stirred, reluctantly. "Physically. Tactically. She is equal to any of my best."

Caius perked up with interest at the high praise.

"But not in *ki*," Loudon argued.

"For now," Wren allowed.

"This is settled," Harlow ground out. "There will be no more discussion."

Loudon jerked back, staring at the Overlord like he didn't recognize him anymore. Realization shifted to horror. "You plan to make her Overlord."

Harlow's unrelenting stare was as good as an admission. Caius dropped his arms, straightening with alarm. He wasn't the only one.

"How could you consider this? There are years of tests and training that are needed before something like this can be decided. You're not the only one who has to approve her ascendance," Loudon said, sounding betrayed.

"She can communicate with the *lu-ong*." Harlow's words had the effect of a bomb, ending all protest before it began.

The ability was nearly essential for any who hoped to inherit the Overlord of Roake's position.

A heaviness filled the air as the rest processed that statement. Graydon was unruffled. He'd been expecting something like this.

Wren, Silas, and Makon looked equally unsurprised.

Contemplation moved over Caius's face as he tapped his chin with a finger. For now, he was holding his opinion in reserve.

Graydon couldn't help but think Loudon had been willfully blind. Anyone who knew Harlow would guess this was the only logical outcome. That Loudon didn't, meant he didn't know the Overlord as well as he thought.

"You would leave our fate to a child's impulsive hands?" Loudon asked.

Harlow's face softened. "You act like I plan to resign tomorrow. It'll likely be centuries before Kira is ready to accept the mantle of leadership. She is still very much invested in the humans and has a lot of growing to do."

Loudon's head bent as he stared at the ground.

Harlow's gaze moved over the rest. "You know I only accepted the position of Overlord to protect the House my brother died for. It was always meant to be temporary until another could rise to replace me."

Quiet filled the room, a range of emotion flitting across their expressions at this admission.

Graydon didn't say anything in defense of Kira. This was her battle to fight. Right now, some of them saw her as a fragile and breakable doll. They'd soon find out otherwise. Roake was nothing if not clear-sighted. Once she'd earned her place among them, they would hold onto the brilliance that was her with both hands.

Harlow waited a beat before returning to the previous topic. "Now, I want to know how a second-rate House like Dethos slipped through our defenses."

Maida tapped several floating icons. "We still don't know. The moment they crossed into our waters, we should have been notified, but there's nothing."

Caius was the one to say it. "There's a traitor among us."

That seemed to break through Loudon's thoughts as he looked up. "We don't know that."

"It gets worse," Graydon said, his arms crossing over his massive chest. "Kira has indicated there's a connection between our enemy of old and the Tsavitee."

"Impossible," Loudon scoffed. "They're extinct."

"My conversations with her and current events have led me to believe otherwise," Graydon said.

Harlow nodded. "I'm inclined to agree. It fits something I've long suspected."

Harlow paused as he met each of their eyes. "Caius is right. There is a traitor among us. This person worked with our enemy to orchestrate the Sorrowing, and they entered our defense codes so Dethos could slip past unremarked."

"None of us would work with them," Loudon said in a subdued voice. "There has to be another explanation."

"They knew too much about how to breach our security," Harlow said. "That knowledge could only have come from one place."

"Us," Caius supplied.

Harlow dipped his chin in agreement. "Us."

It was also likely the traitor was in the highest echelons of their House.

Graydon stirred. "The emperor has been apprised of the situation. His forces are on standby. They will step in if necessary."

Hopefully, it wouldn't come to that.

Harlow shook his head. "We can't count on him. In many ways, his hands are tied, and what he can do is limited. If there is a traitor in my House, it stands to reason there are traitors in other Houses. Ours wasn't the only one affected by the Sorrowing. He will not be able to hunt them down without risking losing support from the Overlords."

"And yet if we do not find a way to stop this, our enemy of old may come out the winner in this millennia-long game," Graydon said.

That wasn't an option.

"Kira seems to be at the crux of this," Silas said. "The generals at Ta Da'an seemed to recognize her. She spoke their language. I find it interesting they almost seemed to fear her. They ran instead of fighting when they lost control. That's not like them."

Graydon agreed. "Of us all, she probably knows this newest evolution of our enemy best."

Caius shifted. "You have such faith in her. Are you sure your judgment isn't clouded, Little Storm?"

Graydon fixed him with a neutral stare. Not many would dare make such an insinuation. But this was family; sometimes you made allowances. "I have never let my personal feelings affect my judgment. Perhaps your considerable age has blinded you to reality."

Of course, making allowances didn't mean being stepped on.

Graydon had earned his place. Caius would remember that or Graydon would remind him with fist or blade.

"My, how the Storm has grown."

Graydon inclined in a half bow. "I was taught by the best."

Since Caius had been one of those teachers, there was no way he could argue.

Harlow watched the Nexus for several seconds before nodding once. "We will watch and wait. If there is a new plot by the enemy of old, we need to see what it is. The sacrifices of those who have gone before will not be forgotten."

The others nodded. "Never forgotten."

"Dismissed," Harlow ordered.

Graydon lingered as the others filed out. Only when they were gone did Harlow release a sigh and shake his head. "What is it you're not telling me?"

"Many things. You'll have to be more specific."

Once, the look Harlow leveled on Graydon would have been intimidating. Graydon would have spilled everything to his pseudo father. Unfortunately for Harlow, that time had gone.

"Don't play games with me, Little Storm." Anger flashed in Harlow's eyes. There and gone in a second. "I'm the one who taught you the rules."

"I remember," Graydon said with a lazy amusement. "You should know by now how committed I am to our people. I don't play favorites, and I don't bow to anyone's demands. Even yours."

"That's what scares me," Harlow said. "Will you sacrifice her too?"

Graydon's nostrils flared as he kept himself from striking out at the man who'd partially raised him. "I won't have to. We both know she'll do it before I can stop her."

Harlow's expression stilled. "It seems we're at an impasse. Perhaps tomorrow while we wait to see if she passes the trial, we can settle this matter with sparring. It'll be like it used to be."

Graydon's chuckle was dark. "I thought you'd never ask."

TWENTY-FOUR

KIRA FIDDLED WITH the high collar of her jacket, still unsatisfied as she frowned at the reflection in the mirror. The outfit she'd found on her bed last night with a message instructing her to wear it for the trial resembled her old cadet's uniform—if her old uniform one had been considerably nicer and tailormade for her.

Like most things of Roake design, the jacket and pants weren't given to frills. Straight lines and simple details made the fit surprisingly flattering.

Even Kira had to admit she looked striking in the colors of Roake—black coupled with accents of deep blue and silver.

The best part of the uniform was the addition of a thermal regulator, allowing the fabric to warm around her body—keeping her at a perfect temperature. The uniform would provide better protection against the elements than her previous clothes.

Too bad she hadn't been wearing it for her dip in the ocean. It would have made for a much less chilly ride home.

Whoever had commissioned it had spent a pretty penny on its construction. These weren't the sort of garments you'd find just anyone wearing. Their quality spoke of wealth and privilege. The sort most couldn't even fathom.

Kira smoothed an admiring hand on the front of the jacket, trying to puzzle out how she'd come to be in possession of something so nice.

Jin, taking advantage of her distraction, launched a rock at her shoulder. Kira barely felt the high-speed projectile as it bounced off the fabric, a slight shimmer marking the area where it had hit.

Seconds later, the shimmer disappeared, leaving the dark black of the uniform behind.

"It has anti-ballistic properties," Jin observed, drifting closer for a better look. "I've never seen a bulletproof fabric that was this thin or flexible. You'd better keep this out of Blue's hands."

"Do you think it would take a bullet?" Kira asked, twisting and turning as she tested the way the fabric moved with her. It was surprisingly comfortable if you discounted the choke collar.

"We could always test it out," Jin said, brightening.

"Maybe later." The last thing she needed was him poking holes in her right before the trial.

Especially when she was already running behind.

Kira tapped the mirror, turning it invisible before heading to the door.

Jin zipped in front of her. "What do you say I tag along?"

"Isn't that what the lizard is for?"

Jin bobbed in front of her. "My spawn is amazing, but he isn't me. With the Tsavitee presence on this world confirmed, I think it would be best if you had backup."

"I really wish you'd stop calling him that." It sent chills down her spine every time he referred to the lizard as spawn.

"What else would I call him?" Jin asked, sounding baffled. Before Kira could answer, he pressed his argument, "I know he's great, but he lacks my sleek, debonair air. Most important, he doesn't have my offensive weapons. Face it, you need me."

Kira couldn't help poking at his pride. "That sounds like a design flaw to me."

Jin growled. "I was on a time limit. Don't worry, the next spawn will be even better."

What a dreadful thought.

Kira sidestepped Jin, scooping up the lizard and draping him around her neck. The lizard responded automatically, clasping his tail with his paws to create a necklace.

"Don't let him hear you say that. You might hurt his feelings," Kira said, cupping her hand over the lizard's ears as she stepped past her friend.

Jin whirled. "You know he doesn't have feelings, right? He's a machine."

Kira shook her head. The irony in that statement.

She opened the door, waving over her shoulder. "I'll be back soon."

Finn was already there waiting, as he'd been every single time she opened the door. Kira started toward him.

"I would like to go on record and say this is a mistake," the lizard said in Jin's voice.

Kira pursed her lips to hide her smile. "Noted. I'll file it with the advisory board next time we meet."

"Also, you'd better not grow to like him better than me," Jin snapped. "I'll see that you never have a warm shower again if you do."

Kira cupped the lizard, warming his strange metallic skin with her hand. "Don't worry, Jin. You'll always be first in my heart."

The lizard bussed her hand before settling with an irritated grumble.

"Ready?" Finn asked.

Kira nodded. "Any advice?"

He started toward the stairs. "Be true to yourself and focus on your task."

That wasn't enigmatic or anything.

Finn led her through the fortress, their path to the Hall of Ancestors a direct one. There were to be no detours this time.

Despite that, they found the halls crowded with Tuann. Some were in the synth armor of warriors and oshota. Each of them lifted their chins in a sign of respect as Kira passed. Interspersed throughout their ranks were those wearing clothing similar to Kira's. The artisans or those among Roake who had chosen a path not lined with violence.

They cradled bundles of flowers similar to the type she'd seen her uncle place in front of the memorial. As she passed, they bowed and set the flowers at their feet, lining the path behind her on either side with a riot of color.

"What are they doing?" Kira asked.

Her pace slowed as she watched the Tuann acknowledge her passage with reverence and a hushed appreciation, more than one of them touching their chest and then their forehead before offering their hands in her direction.

Finn remained facing forward as he padded down the corridor. "The Trial of the Broken is dangerous. Initiates have died in the undertaking. They're paying their respects to your courage, and asking you to come back alive."

Kira waited for several seconds, taking in the faces of those present. They didn't know her. Not really. Why then had they gone through the trouble? They would have had to take time out of their day to do this. The flowers said this had taken preparation and thought.

"Why?" Kira found herself asking, feeling overwhelmed.

Finn paused, glancing at her. "Because you're a daughter of our House. You're family."

Kira had no response to that, instead choosing to keep her own counsel as they continued. This was much more than she had expected. More than she had prepared for.

"It's kind of nice, if you think about it," Jin said quietly.

Kira didn't answer. She couldn't. Her throat felt thick with emotion.

Finally, they reached the familiar doors to the Hall of Ancestors. Finn stopped in front of them as Kira peered inside. The room was empty. Each initiate would take the trial alone, the rest waiting until the previous had passed or failed—whichever fate and their talent decided.

"I await your success," Finn said.

She didn't answer for several seconds, oddly intimidated. There was something about it all. She'd flown countless missions, faced death numerous times, yet standing here on the precipice, she found herself nervous.

"You've done much harder things," Finn assured her.

She nodded. He was right. She had. Just because the stakes felt high, her entire future resting on the outcome, that was no reason to stress.

"Finn," she said, stopping him. She waited until he looked at her. "In case I didn't say it before—thank you. It was nice to have someone watching my back again."

Even if she hadn't always let him do his job to the fullest extent of his abilities. That didn't mean she didn't appreciate his efforts.

"And I will again," he promised.

Her smile was crooked. "No talking you out of it?"

He shook his head, not bothering to answer as he walked away.

Yeah, she hadn't thought so either.

Kira stepped into the Hall of Ancestors, the statues lining either side of the walkway watching as she marched toward the wall Graydon had shown her the last time she stood here.

She stopped in front of it, her gaze tracing the lines and circles that still reminded her of a stylized version of a solar system's orbit.

"Looks like you're the only thing standing in my way," she told the wall.

Kira settled into wait.

Last night, Rheya had explained how the test worked. Each initiate stepped past the wall on their own. Only once they had passed or failed would the doorway appear again.

The soft fall of footsteps alerted Kira to the fact she wasn't alone. Wren joined her at the wall, studying it in the same way she had.

"I thought Loudon would be the one to see me off," Kira said.

"Normally, yes, but I asked him if I could be the one to prepare you for your trial."

Kira waited, knowing he'd likely reveal his reason soon enough.

"You should reconsider this path," Wren finally said.

Kira sighed. There it was.

She'd been half-expecting this.

She cast a glance at Wren, wondering how he had ended up being the one to broach this topic with her. She could see Graydon—even Harlow—undertaking this task. But Wren?

It wasn't like they were close. He had been clear in his interactions with the initiates. He wasn't their friend and probably didn't care one way or another about their success.

His teachings were amazing—astoundingly so given his cold manner—but he wasn't the type to sit you down and offer advice. No, orders were more his speed.

Kira had to wonder why he wasn't resorting to that tactic now.

"This won't lead where you think," he said, not taking his eyes off the carvings.

Kira shook her head. "It continuously astounds me how arrogant some Tuann are. What do you know about anything concerning me?"

"More than you think," he said.

She seriously doubted that.

He flicked the inhibiter around her wrist. "It takes more than a few weeks to recover from *ki* poisoning. You're risking your life on something that you could conquer easily if you wait."

Frustration was an unexpected sight on his face. He was normally so controlled—almost scarily so.

"Quillon," Kira growled. The healer had broken his promise. "He wasn't supposed to reveal my progress."

"He didn't have to."

Kira paused, taking in his stiff expression.

"You're the other patient he treated for *ki* poisoning," she said in realization.

Wren held still for several seconds, before finally unbending enough to nod. "Indeed. That's how I know you're making a mistake. You're talented, probably one of the best I've ever seen. With time and training, you could be a force to be reckoned with—but only if you resist the urge to take shortcuts."

Not an option. Her mission had already been delayed enough.

Kira faced forward, her back and shoulders straight. "No."

Wren's advice held merit. Regardless of that fact, Kira was still going to ignore it.

He opened his mouth to argue, but a steady glow along the carving's lines interrupted him. Identical looks of surprise filled their faces as the blue filled more and more of the lines, the hard surface of the wall beginning to fade.

"That was quick," Kira said. She'd expected to be waiting hours. Everything she'd been able to gather about the test said it took time to complete. Devon had likely only stepped through the wall a few minutes before Kira appeared.

"Too quick," Wren agreed.

The same oppressive feeling from earlier spilled out as the wall disappeared, revealing the darkness beyond. Fingers of dread and self-doubt wrapped around Kira's heart and squeezed.

"Where's Devon?" she asked, not seeing him appear from the darkness.

Wren shook his head, his body tense as he stared into the abyss.

Kira took a step, only to find her way blocked by Wren's arm.

"Something is wrong," he said, not looking at her. His forehead furrowed as he frowned at the spot where the wall had been. "The *uhva na* doesn't open like this."

She paused as she gazed uncertainly into the room beyond. "All the more reason to investigate, isn't it?"

His expression was grave as he shook his head. "Interfering with another's trial might result in the Mea'Ave refusing you entry when it comes time for your own."

Meaning if she did this, she might not get a second chance until the next time the House trial was administered, which could be years.

Choices. Choices.

Kira stepped past the line marking the wall's previous existence. "If I turned back now, wouldn't it mean I didn't deserve to ascend anyway?"

Faint approval lingered on Wren's features as he joined her. "As long as you understand the risks."

"Don't worry. I won't blame you if anything goes wrong," she said dryly.

"No, because the only one who would be to blame is you and your damnable curiosity," Jin whispered in her comms.

Kira grimaced. He had a point.

There was a low hum as the wall coalesced into existence.

Wren touched it, seeming disturbed.

"I guess that settles the question of what we should do. Our only option now is forward," Kira said, somehow unsurprised to be cut off from their path of retreat.

It seemed fitting somehow—though she was hard-pressed to say why.

Kira started moving; Wren slow to follow. Their footsteps echoed in the cavernous space. The chamber was Tuann made, the same stone that formed the rest of the fortress had been used to create this place as well.

That was where the resemblance ended.

This place, like the Hall of the Ancestors, felt ancient. The mammoth corridor they were in was long and seemingly never-ending.

Kira paused next to a tall, narrow window no wider than her torso. It looked out onto stone and more walls. No view of the ocean or land was forthcoming.

Strange.

Kira touched the windowpane, an interested hum escaping her as her hand passed right through, a tingling sensation warning her she'd interrupted an energy field.

Instead of withdrawing, she stuck her body as far as she could through the field, leaning out. She didn't make it far. The window ledge was at least two feet deep, and the opening was so narrow it was impossible to fit through.

She dropped onto her heels, watching as the illusion of the window snapped into place. A window looking into what amounted to a cave. How strange.

Kira stepped away from it, studying the rest of the hallway as she slowly followed Wren.

Banners at even intervals marked their path, evidence the place had a caretaker. Architecturally, the place was as beautiful and serene as the rest of Roake. It was cold and lonely, somehow—as if the people who had made it a home were long dead.

"Is there another way out of here?" Kira asked.

"Only the Overlord or Loudon can open a passage to this place," Wren said.

Convenient.

"Perfect place for an ambush," Jin muttered.

Kira thought so too.

Maybe she should have let the real Jin come with her after all.

"Be careful. The trial preys on your fears and doubts," Wren said. "Remember who you are at all times. Don't be led astray."

Not going to be a problem.

Every sense she had was on high alert. This place felt ominous. The atmosphere heavy, as if it was waiting for something.

Yeah, dropping her guard wasn't happening.

They moved on, past columns and doors that Kira didn't have to open to know she wanted no part of.

Time felt different here, moving too slow and too fast at the same time. Almost as if they existed outside its constraints.

Their path led them to a circular room where the floor was etched with a complicated repeating pattern. It was a rotunda, the roof high above, impossibly complicated, reminding her of some of the holy places of old Europe.

Their footsteps echoed in the room as they ventured further inside.

The pattern laid into the floor ended in fifteen points along the edge, each one leading to a door that opened to incredible scenes. Some led to landscapes. Snowcapped mountains next to sand-swept deserts. Endless forests followed by oceans as far as the eye could see.

That wasn't all, Kira realized catching a glimpse of a gas cloud billowing across thousands of lightyears' worth of stars. Some doors led to places she had no frame of reference for.

"What is this place?" Kira asked, drawn to the doors.

Wren shook his head. "Something I've only heard about in stories."

"Didn't you take this trial?"

"Every trial is different, customized to the individual."

Kira paused in front of one door. "For what purpose?"

He hesitated, his gaze moving over the different scenes. "We're descended from monsters. This place weeds out those who might waver from the path our ancestors set us on."

Kira stopped. "And who decides the criteria needed to pass."

349

His look was significant. "The Mea'Ave."

Kira's frown was troubled as she took in the room and its doors. She didn't like the thought of trusting the fate of an entire people to an entity she understood so little of.

"Come on. We should continue," Wren said.

Kira hesitated, glancing around one last time. She had a feeling these doors were only the beginning. What kind of power would they bestow on a person?

A dozen worlds existed here; a dozen chances to conquer.

Or to escape into.

They drew to an abrupt stop as they sensed another's presence at the same time.

Kira frowned as a figure stepped out of the shadows. "Joule, what are you doing here?"

He didn't answer, stepping further into view, his hands held up, palms facing them.

"Behind him," Jin warned.

Wren crouched, his hand sliding to the pommel of his en-blade as Aeron moved into view, a Tuann *zuipi* aimed at Joule's back.

"Surprised?" Aeron asked.

Kira shrugged. "Not really. Having someone pose as an initiate is the most logical choice if the Tsavitee planned to infiltrate Roake."

The initiates were essentially strangers to Roake. Any idiosyncrasies would be easy to overlook.

"Lothos did say you were clever." Aeron's smile lacked its normal cheeriness.

Kira struggled not to look at Joule. His terror would only slow her reflexes and make her job harder.

"I had a feeling you would find your way here." Aeron nudged Joule. "It's why I brought insurance. The others were clear that you had an overdeveloped need to protect people. Threaten someone you care about, and you're powerless."

This time Kira held quiet as the lizard slowly slipped from around her neck, making his way under her jacket and onto her back as he headed for the ground.

Kira hoped Aeron didn't notice.

It was possible. The room was dim, and he was far away.

"No response?" he asked. "Not even a sarcastic quip or a meaningless attempt at convincing me he doesn't matter to you?"

"Why waste my breath? It's obvious you've got me. Let him go and then finish the job."

Scorn filled his expression as he abruptly pointed the *zuipi* at her. "Do you think I'm here for you?"

Kira blinked. Was that a trick question?

"I take it you're not?" Her tone rose, making the statement a question.

Rather than answer, Aeron fired the *zuipi*, a bolt heading straight for Kira. Wren appeared in front of her like a ghost, his blade deflecting it.

"Joule, run," Kira shouted.

Joule wasted no time, darting behind one of the doorways.

Aeron cursed, letting him go. Joule was the least of his problem right now.

Wren launched toward Aeron, appearing in front of him in the next second. His en-blade whistled as it sliced through the air. Aeron whipped out of the way, his weapon rising.

It was no use. Wren was already gone again, his attack shifting.

"Are you all right?" Kira shouted at Joule.

His head popped out of his hiding place, and he nodded.

Kira breathed a sigh of relief. Good.

She glanced from him to where the other two fought, wanting to join the battle but also needing Joule safe.

"Go, I'm fine," he said, reading the struggle on her face.

Kira hesitated. It went against the grain to leave someone she cared for unprotected.

"I won't make a very good Overlord if I constantly rely on others to protect me." Joule's gaze was steady. A confidence there that was new. He brought his hands together, creating the pattern for a shield. "Besides, I have this."

Kira's smile was slow in coming. He did indeed. Not so defenseless after all.

She nodded at him. His face was serious as he returned the gesture.

"All right then." She raced into the fray.

Aeron saw her coming, one hand sweeping up in a gesture that had become familiar over the last few weeks. Kira sidestepped the strike, barely pausing as she barreled toward them.

Wren took advantage of Aeron's distraction, planting his foot and shifting the direction of his slice.

It was the first time Kira had seen Wren in action. He didn't disappoint. Every movement was efficient. Nothing wasted. He moved with power and decisiveness; his defense nearly impenetrable even as he attacked.

Kira had a brief second to be grateful he wasn't her enemy. That was all she had time for as she launched an attack of her own, hoping to capitalize on Wren's distraction.

Aeron was surprisingly nimble as he evaded the two of them. Quicker than anything he'd shown in training.

Wren and Kira worked together, reading each other's movements as they coordinated their attacks. Kira was at a slight disadvantage since she had no blade to wield, but she didn't let that stop her, hitting Aeron as soon as Wren regrouped.

The tactic kept the Tsavitee mole off-balance, not allowing him to think beyond the next second. Soon he was fielding their assaults more than he was attacking.

Wren and Kira pressed harder, there when the other withdrew. Timing and precision were key. If either one misjudged even a little, it would result in friendly fire or death by Aeron's hands.

Gradually, Aeron was forced back, step-by-step. He was tiring. It wouldn't be long now.

Aeron faltered. Kira was there in the next second, her fist already cocked as she hammered a blow into his side. He grunted, stumbling.

Kira tasted victory.

Power crackled through the air. A primal part of her screamed danger. She broke off her attack. Too late.

She reached for her *ki*, desperate as it flickered and sputtered in her grip.

Out of the corner of her eye, fire and pain raced for her, impossible to evade.

"Kira!" Joule screamed.

Wren barreled into her. Kira stumbled, falling to the ground. Power sizzled at her back, white-hot heat scorching her senses.

A grunt of pain came from Wren as he hit his knees seconds later.

She scrambled upright, his stunned eyes meeting hers as he toppled to his side.

"No," she moaned.

Get on your feet. Grieve later. Survive now. The fight isn't done yet, the logical side of her said.

Loudon stepped into view; his eyes sad as he gazed at his former friend. The air around him was still saturated with the *ki* he'd channeled.

"Why would you do that?" Kira asked.

Aeron moved toward his side. "Because he's a traitor; that's what traitors do."

They strike from behind when you least expect it.

The serenity and sense of purpose Kira normally associated with Loudon was absent today, leaving behind a cruelness she hadn't seen before now.

"This is your fault," he told her. "If you hadn't come here, I wouldn't have had to do this."

Kira laugh was mocking. "This should be good."

"You forced my hand," Loudon said. "Just like your father and mother did."

The world around her faded, the swoosh of her blood drowning out the sound of everything else as Kira fought to stay where she was.

This was the man responsible for everything. Whatever fucked up reason he'd used to convince himself of his righteousness, Kira didn't care.

He was going to die today.

It looked like her uncle was going to have to wait his turn for revenge. This was one wrong Kira looked forward to correcting.

"People like you always make excuses. It's not your fault. They forced you." Kira reached for calm, swallowing it deep and forcing it to spread throughout her body.

Revenge was well and good, but she needed to create a window where it could be obtained. Losing herself to rage would only get her dead.

The faintest movement on the floor next to Loudon and Aeron caught Kira's attention. Jin's spawn crept nearer, one leg at a time, his progress slow so as not to drawn attention.

"What will my uncle say when he finds out about this?" Kira asked, stalling.

"He's not going to know."

Kira smiled. "Are you sure about that?"

Doubt crept into Loudon's expression. He quelled it, his hands rising as he started to sketch a rune. "It doesn't matter. I did this for Harlow—so he could become the type of Overlord Roake deserves. If his hate is my reward, so be it."

The rune glowed white-hot, pinpricks of light forming. The hairs on Kira's neck rose as it got hard to breathe, the pressure in the room rising.

The lizard lurched forward as Kira wrapped her arms around Wren and threw herself to the side.

Two explosions rocked the room, an agonized scream accompanying them. The stone where she'd been seconds before was now a molten crater.

Kira lurched upright to find the spot where Loudon and Aeron had stood empty except for blast marks all around it, the metal body of the lizard lifeless on the ground.

Kira closed her eyes and inhaled, wrestling with the desire to track the two down immediately. There were things to take care of here.

She kneeled at Wren's side and moved him carefully onto his back. The sight to greet her wasn't a pretty one. A fist-sized hole had been punched through his synth armor. Scorch marks dotted the edges of the wound. Whatever had hit him had burned right through the armor, blackening flesh before cauterizing the wound.

Joule landed next to her. "Is he alive?"

"For now."

This was a fatal wound. Wren needed immediate attention if he was going to survive.

Revenge was going to have to wait.

"Come on, Joule. Help me carry him. We need to get him to Quillon."

Joule moved to obey, reaching for Wren's shoulders.

Wren pushed him away. "No, you need to go after him."

His breathing was labored, and his skin waxen. He looked inches from death—which was where he'd be if they didn't act now.

"Later," Kira said. "You'll die otherwise."

"Stubborn, like all of your family," Wren forced out.

"Complain to someone who sees that as an insult."

His laugh was small and pain-filled before his gaze found Joule's. "Find Graydon. Warn him they're after Devon."

Kira pressed hard against Wren's wound, her mind racing as she put together the pieces. Graydon remaining with Roake even after his duty was done. Wren's concern over Devon. There were only a few reasons she could think of for something like that.

Wren's expression was determined as he focused on her. "He's important. You have to protect him. He's privy to things that if they fell into the wrong hands would devastate the Tuann."

If her new suspicions were right, that was an understatement.

Kira closed her eyes. This right here was why she never wanted to lead again. Difficult decisions with no right answer.

"Can you find your way out?" she asked Joule.

Chances were Aeron didn't come by way of the same path Kira and Wren had taken. He wouldn't have needed to with Loudon as his co-conspirator. The Roake herald would have known how to get in and out. Probably even opened the way for him.

Joule might be able to take advantage of that.

He hesitated. "You're going to need my help."

Her chuckle was strained. "Almost certainly, but I need you to get Graydon more. If I fail, he'll pick up the pieces. Last lesson—always hedge your bets."

The struggle to obey warred with his need to help. She hated to ask this of him. She knew how difficult it was to abandon the battlefield when people you'd sworn to serve beside still fought. However, it was sometimes the only way to victory.

Something broke in Joule's expression—the innocent romanticism of being a warrior crumpled and fell by the wayside. What emerged was someone stronger, if a little more bruised.

He rose. "Don't you dare die."

He was gone before she had the chance to make promises she didn't know if she could keep.

"He will make a fine leader one day," Wren said, his face a mask of pain.

"Yeah, he will." It didn't make Kira any happier to be the one to teach him that lesson.

Wren moaned, his eyes slipping shut as unconsciousness beckoned. "Go. Don't worry about me. I will see my daughter soon."

Time was ticking away, but there was one last thing she had to do before she left. It was a long shot at best. Likely it wouldn't work, and if it did, it would bring nothing but trouble.

Kira left his side, crossing to Jin's spawn. She picked up its lifeless body. "Jin, you there?"

No response came. She sent her senses into the inanimate object. The spark that was Jin was absent. Whatever defense he'd built into the lizard had destroyed its connection to him.

Judging by the silence in her comms, his signal couldn't reach her here.

Kira returned to Wren, kneeling at his side. His breathing was labored as he watched her.

"What are you doing?" he asked as she squeezed the lizard.

"Concentrating," she told him.

It'd been a long time since she'd done something like this.

The lizard heated up, ropes of *ki* spiraling out of it to curl around Kira's hand. Sweat popped up on her forehead as pain hammered her temple.

Wren sucked in a breath. "Don't. It's forbidden."

"I figured."

Things as dangerous as stealing the essence from something and giving it to someone else always were.

The lizard melted until Kira held a handful of silver liquid. She slammed it into Wren's wound. An agonized scream left him.

She thrust her face close to his. "You want to meet your daughter again? You stay alive. She's not waiting for you on the other side. She's here. So, keep breathing."

She didn't wait for his screams to abate, standing and racing away in the direction she suspected the traitors had taken.

The others wouldn't thank her for this if they ever caught wind. Her lifestyle choices and her decision to help the humans hadn't made her popular. If she revealed the survival of the other children who were with her in the camps to the Tuann, they wouldn't be happy.

Kira couldn't bring herself to care. She'd never been good at letting honorable people die. Wren didn't deserve for this to be his end.

If she were lucky, the pain from what she'd done would have distracted him and he wouldn't remember her confession. If not, she'd deal with that if she survived the coming encounter.

TWENTY-FIVE

KIRA RACED THROUGH the labyrinth of hallways. Abruptly, she found herself in a large chamber, the sound of water all around. She stopped, gazing at the darkness pressing close.

Gradually, her eyes adjusted. What she'd at first assumed was black was a thin sheet of water reflecting the stone.

Light glimmered in its depths, reflecting off hundreds of standing sheets of mirrors that reminded Kira of liquid water.

She paused, taking in the impossible scene before her gaze snagged on Devon, his expression startled as he glanced over his shoulder from where he kneeled like a supplicant in front of one of the mirrors, water seeping into his pants. His chest was bare, as were his feet.

"Kira? What are you doing here?" he asked.

Kira started toward him. "Devon, I don't have time to explain, but we need to get out of here."

He rose. "I can't leave yet. I'm still in the trial."

Kira struggled with her impatience. "That'll have to wait. There are people who want to kill you in here. That's a little bit more important."

Life first. Passing the trial came second.

Devon took a step away, frowning in suspicion.

Kira jolted forward, before forcing herself to remain where she was. If she scared him and he ran, it would delay them further.

"I know you have no reason to trust me, but I won't hurt you." Kira held out her hand.

Devon stared at her, those familiar eyes that tugged at her memories shadowed and distrusting.

Kira held still, wrestling with impatience. Loudon and Aeron had left before her. It was a miracle she'd made it here first—one she didn't trust.

Devon's lips parted, and he looked on the verge of reclaiming that step he'd taken away from her when a voice intruded.

"You really should have listened to her," Aeron said, stalking into the room.

Kira placed herself between him and Devon. "Where's your little buddy?"

"He'll be along shortly. His arrogance with you cost him. That explosion you made caused damage." The cheerful smile Aeron always seemed to have ready, was vaguely threatening, no hint of friendliness to it.

"You know who I am?" Devon asked in a low voice meant only for her ears.

"Not a clue. I just don't like letting the bad guys have what they want."

Technically, it was true. Right now, she had theories and suppositions. No confirmation.

Regardless of if he was who she suspected or not, she likely would have placed herself in the same position. Devon wasn't an innocent, but that didn't mean she was going to let him die.

"Come on, Devon, don't you want to take primus form again? It was so much fun last time," Aeron taunted.

Devon went still behind her, his limbs stiff and set. "I knew you had something to do with that."

Aeron's lips quirked. "Should have listened to your instincts." He looked around. "I know why you didn't, though. You Tuann think it's impossible to force another's primus to the surface."

His gaze to Kira. "The *iffli* knows intimately how that feels."

Kira saw Devon look at her out of the corner of her eye, his surprise impossible to conceal. "You have a primus form?"

Kira ignored him, keeping her attention on the real enemy.

"Sure, she does. It's why she interfered. She knows what it's like to kill your allies by accident," Aeron said, tilting his head. "Couldn't stand to see someone else face the same fate, could you?"

Kira held her silence.

Loudon limped into the room, blood trailing him from wounds in his leg and side.

"What are you doing here?" Devon asked.

"He's a traitor. Don't you wish you'd left when I asked?" Kira said, inching toward him.

Things had gotten worse if that was possible. It had taken both Wren and Kira to force Aeron onto the defensive. Alone, facing Aeron and Loudon—even with one of them injured—Kira wasn't confident of her ability to win.

She would have much preferred to run. An option that was no longer available.

"I'm beginning to see your point," Devon said.

Her snicker was quick. He was funny. If he hadn't had a propensity to be an ass or let ambition blind him, she might have even found him moderately likable.

"What do we do?" he murmured.

Kira's gaze flicked between Aeron and Loudon.

"Kira?"

"I'm thinking."

An image shifted in the water. The long, sleek form of a *lu-ong* snaked along the surface, rippling over the water underneath and across the mirrors like an echo. Almost ghostly in how he moved.

"What is this place?" Kira asked.

"It's the final test. Designed to offer you your greatest desire, it can be difficult distinguishing between reality and a fantastical dream," he said.

Kira's head cocked.

"What about memories? Can it show you them?"

Devon hesitated. "Yes. That's part of it. Those with pasts are forced to confront them by reliving the most difficult pieces."

Kira bared her teeth. Good enough.

She had plenty of those moments to relive.

"You choose the depth to which you lose yourself," he said. "Most only peer into the surface. That is difficult enough to survive."

Kira straightened and stretched out her hands, tendrils of *ki* reaching out. Droplets of water lifted from the mirrors and puddles around her to stream toward her. Faster and faster until rivulets turned into airborne rivers.

Loudon's eyes widened. "Stop her. She's trying to pull us into her mind."

Kira grinned. That was the hope anyway.

"Devon, I'm sorry about this," she said over her shoulder.

The water surged before he could finish his question, encasing the four of them. Kira looked up, finding the wizened face of the baby *lu-*

ong peering at her.

I really hope you're right, she thought at it.

As a plan, it was a shoddy one at best. Here's hoping Graydon did his part.

Kira floated as a voice greeted her. "Yo, Phoenix, are you done lollygagging, or can we go kick some Tsavitee ass?"

*

Harlow's blade whistled past Graydon's nose, centimeters separating Graydon from death as he leaned back the barest bit. Had Harlow's blade connected, it likely would have split Graydon's skull.

"Feeling a little enthusiastic this morning, are we?" Graydon lunged, his blade flicking up.

Harlow blocked, barely preventing himself from being skewered in the side.

Now that their greeting was over, the real fight could begin.

The older Tuann bared his teeth, whipping his en-blade around. Graydon evaded, parrying as Harlow pressed his attack. Faster and faster until their blades were a blur—fluid and graceful in a beautiful dance as they tried their utmost to kill each other.

Graydon raised his blade, blocking the Overlord's downward strike. The blades screamed as the combatants locked together

"You've gotten old," Graydon said through gritted teeth, his shoulder and biceps screaming as the Overlord bore down.

"Did I train you to talk or fight?" Harlow aimed a vicious kick at Graydon's knee.

A toothy smile spread across Graydon's face, *ki* flooding him as he strengthened his body. The strike stung, but it failed to break the knee as Harlow intended.

Graydon shoved the Overlord's sword away. He didn't give the Overlord time to recover, stepping into his space and hammering a punch into the other man's exposed side before ducking out of range.

"*That's* how you trained me," Graydon said with no small amount of satisfaction.

Appreciation glittered in Harlow's eyes as he touched his injured side. "Now that your focus has returned, perhaps we can get serious, Little Storm."

Graydon chuckled as he settled into an offensive stance, weight evenly distributed, his arms loose and relaxed. "It's you whose focus is lacking, old man."

Harlow didn't respond, the tip of his blade lowering.

Graydon's legs tensed, his front foot sliding the slightest bit in preparation for his attack.

They burst into movement at the same time, charging each other. Graydon's name ripped through the hall in a scream. As one, Graydon and Harlow shifted to meet this new threat, blades coming up.

The oshota placed themselves between the two inside the room and the screamer.

"Graydon!" a familiar voice shouted.

Joule barreled into the Warrior's Hall. His gaze frantic as he searched. Spotting Graydon, he ran toward him, only to find his way blocked by oshota.

He pushed forward anyway, resisting when they tried to force him back.

Graydon straightened, noting the panic and determination on Joule's face even as he tangled with warriors who had centuries of experience on him.

Ice spread through Graydon. There was only one reason he could think of for Joule to behave in such a manner.

Kira.

"Let him through," Graydon barked.

The oshota hesitated until Harlow gestured for them to relax their guard.

They shifted aside, allowing the barest gap for Joule to pass. He stumbled toward Graydon; his clothing disheveled. There was blood on the knee of his pants, and his sleeve was ripped. He'd been in a fight.

Graydon had been right. Something was wrong.

Joule stammered, his words not making sense.

"Enough," Graydon ordered. "Calm yourself."

He waited as Joule took a deep breath. The boy was nearly shaking, his chest heaving from exertion. Now that he was closer, Graydon saw the sweat on his forehead and the terror in his eyes.

Whatever had sent him here, he'd used every bit of his speed to get to Graydon as quickly as possible.

When Joule's breathing had steadied, Graydon set a reassuring hand on the boy's shoulder, knowing it would steady him. "Good, now give us your report."

Some of the terror leached out of Joule, and he straightened, his expression reflecting a determination and strength that would one day make him a fine leader.

"It's Kira. She's in the Trial of the Broken," Joule said.

Harlow frowned. "She should have hours yet before her time comes."

"She's not alone," Joule said. His composure cracked, grief and shame warring as he met Graydon's eyes. "Wren sent me to tell you they're after Devon."

The mood in the room plummeted, growing heavy and tense as Harlow and Graydon traded a look.

"What of Kira?" Graydon asked.

Joule flinched. "She went after them."

Graydon should have expected as much.

"She's not alone," Harlow said at his back. "Wren is at her side."

"He was injured. I don't even know if he's still alive." Joule's face crumpled, reminding Graydon for all that the boy possessed maturity far beyond his years, he was still a boy.

"And you left her there?" Harlow asked, a dangerous rumble in his voice.

"Ease up," Graydon warned as *ki* built, saturating the room.

"You're a long way from being able to tell me what to do in my own House, Little Storm."

Graydon faced his former mentor, not in the mood for threats. Kira was in danger; he didn't have time for this.

Joule surged forward. "It's our fault. She wouldn't have come here if she hadn't saved Ziva and me. She'd be safe. They would never have gotten close if they hadn't threatened me."

His action stemmed the rising tension, reminding them there were several lives at stake. Finger-pointing and blame could wait until afterward.

Harlow inclined his head. It was the best apology Graydon was going to get.

There was respect on the faces of the oshota around them. Joule's actions had cemented his place among them. They would not soon forget his loyalty to a daughter of their House.

"Who was it?" Harlow asked.

"Aeron." Joule seemed almost hesitant as he added. "And Loudon."

There were small sounds of dismay from those around them. It turned to grief and acceptance as Graydon stood.

"It looks like you've finally uncovered the traitor of your House," he told Harlow.

The Overlord's face was frozen as grief and rage battled for supremacy. The emotions flickered and guttered, extinguished as they left nothing but an implacable determination behind.

Graydon rose. "Stay with Veer."

Joule lurched, his expression earnest. "I can go with you. I can fight."

Despite his intentions, the boy looked on the verge of collapse. Escaping the trial before it was finished would have likely sapped all his reserves.

"You can barely stand," Harlow said. "You've done enough. It's our turn."

Dejection settled on Joule's face, a naked vulnerability that Graydon couldn't walk away from. He picked up Joule's arm, turning it so the boy could see.

There, carved in blue and silver lines, was the mark of the broken, proof Joule had passed his trial. The boy probably hadn't even felt the emblem rise to the surface in the fury of everything that had happened.

"Congratulations," Graydon said.

Joule gazed down in shock. "I don't understand."

"There are more ways to fight than with en-blade or *ki*," Graydon said. "You recognized that. The trial has rewarded you."

Joule traced the lines of the emblem with reverence.

"Watch over him," Graydon ordered Veer. Harlow's oshota gave him sharp nods of respect. To Solal, he said, "Find the human male. I have a feeling we're going to need him."

Harlow considered Graydon. "Why?"

"A hunch."

Harlow dipped his chin, well used to Graydon's hunches. He strode toward the courtyard and the cliffside exit, saying over his shoulder, "There is no time for the long way. Let's take the short cut."

*

Painful howls, the type one might make if their soul was being ripped from their body, greeted them as they stepped into the trial.

"Mea'Ave guide us," Indya whispered.

The screams held an agony so deep it broke the person you were before, leaving behind a pale shell.

It'd been a long time since Graydon had heard screams like that. Not since the Sorrowing when so many had lost so much.

Graydon doubled his speed, careful to stay quiet. Alerting the enemy to their arrival would destroy the advantage of surprise.

While dropping down the cliffs and then using the undersea entrance had cut a lot of time off their journey, it wasn't enough. Every second counted.

Graydon and Harlow's oshota moved quietly with them. Their passage nearly silent as they headed for the sounds of agony.

The *uhva na* sped their way, almost as if it sensed their urgency. The trial was known to test even the Overlord on his rare visits. The rooms constantly changed as the place tried to lure Harlow into staying. That's what it was meant for.

Today, those little gut checks were absent, and the trial allowed them to pass with an unheard-of ease.

In a very short time, Graydon and the rest approached the only room in the structure that always remained the same. A place where memories and dreams intertwined.

This room intended to coax you to stay, its lures nearly irresistible. Graydon had always thought this place was the real test. This was where a person's true colors could be seen.

They spilled into the room, the sounds of dripping water and the pain-filled cries of those caught within the depths of a nightmarish realm greeted them.

Graydon took the scene in with a glance. Kira floated in a bubble, liquid spinning in two separate directions around her to create something that was eerily beautiful. Columns of the watery liquid had speared Aeron and Devon through the chests, raising them to float in midair.

"She's pulled them into her mind," Amila breathed in shock.

Hers wasn't the only surprise. It took an exceptionally powerful mind to swamp another's in this fashion. That Kira could, spoke of a discipline and strength even the members of Roake hadn't been prepared to attribute to her.

Loudon coughed, sucking in air as he sat up from where he'd collapsed. He looked up at them, unmistakable shock on his face.

"Harlow, what are you doing here? Even you can't interfere with the *uhva na.*"

No one moved for several seconds, realizing Loudon didn't know they'd been warned of his betrayal. He either thought Joule wouldn't make it out, or he didn't know the boy had survived whatever he'd done to Wren.

Harlow stepped forward, Graydon circling to his right, putting space between them as he tried to flank Loudon without the other man realizing it.

The boys abruptly seized as whatever Kira had shown them caused their minds to buckle. Loudon barely glanced at them, keeping his attention on Harlow.

If Joule hadn't warned them, Graydon wasn't sure he would have been able to spot the other man's deception. His acting was perfect, not even a hint to show the traitor within.

"I would argue circumstances aren't normal, wouldn't you?" Harlow said, taking another step toward Kira and the rest. "The Trial of the Broken isn't meant to be taken with others."

Loudon hesitated. "The trial opens to whoever it pleases. It isn't my place to second guess its will."

"Is that why you're here?" Harlow asked.

Loudon drew himself up. "As a herald, it's my duty to observe."

Graydon nearly cursed as Loudon retreated a step. The Overlord stopped, frustration in the tightness around his eyes and mouth. Both of them knew they were still too far and Loudon too close to Kira.

Devastation filled Loudon's expression.

"You know, don't you?" Loudon asked finally.

Loudon didn't wait for an answer, whirling and bringing his hands together. *Ki* wrapped around him, boiling the air before surging toward Kira.

Graydon's blood turned to ice as he charged, yanking at his *ki.* Denial roared through him. He was going to be too late.

Out of the watery depths, the ghostly form of a small *lu-ong* appeared. His jaw dropped, swallowing Loudon's *ki*, leaving the man staring open-mouthed at the apparition.

The baby faded as quickly as he'd come.

Loudon remained frozen as Graydon powered toward him.

He seemed to come to himself, reaching for the blade at his side. He never got the chance as Finn shot from the darkness, his en-blade a streak of motion as it bit into Loudon's shoulder.

The traitor screamed as his arm fell to the ground. Sobs echoed in the room as he clutched his wound. Loudon staggered before sagging to his knees.

Finn stood over him, his expression merciless.

Graydon nodded at him. "Well done."

A grunt was Finn's only response.

Graydon put Loudon out of his mind as he walked toward Kira, knowing the oshota wouldn't let the other man out of his sight. It allowed Graydon to focus on what was important.

Harlow joined him, staring up at the watery cocoon Kira had wrapped around herself. "Someone find Quillon and tell him we have a second patient for him once he's done with Wren."

Loudon laughed from his spot on the ground, the sound nearly insane. "You won't be able to save her. There's no way to break the link, and if it persists, she'll kill them all."

Finn kicked the other man in the stomach, satisfaction skating across his face at the sight of the other man's pain.

"How did you get here?" Harlow asked.

"He came with us," Raider said, stepping into the room with Solal at his back. "Wasn't expecting him to race ahead without a by your leave, but it appears it's a good thing he did."

The room was quiet as Raider's lips quirked. "I see the Phoenix is rubbing off on you. I'd watch that if I were you, or you'll end up being just like her."

Finn's expression was stony as he remained locked on Loudon.

Seconds later, Raider blanched at the sight of Kira hovering in her sphere of water. "What the hell is that?"

"The trial," Graydon informed him.

Agonized cries ripped from Devon and Aeron as hazy images flickered in the water's depths. Insubstantial and faded but growing more pronounced with every second they lingered.

Kira was silent and still, even as the other two twisted, unable to stifle their pain.

Raider frowned. "I know that place. It's Atlas right before the battle for the planet." His gaze found Graydon, his eyes hard. "Why is my captain trapped in a nightmare?"

"I have a feeling she did it to herself," Graydon said grimly.

"Why would she do that?"

Graydon's attention moved to Devon and Aeron.

Raider caught his hint. "They're living this too?"

Graydon nodded.

Raider grimaced. "Poor bastards. I wouldn't wish that fate on anyone."

Graydon's hands clenched, frustration at his helplessness eating him up inside.

"I didn't realize she'd held onto this battle so tightly," Raider said softly, his gaze moving over the images.

"You wouldn't." Jin drifted out of the shadows.

The oshota went on the defensive, en-blades appearing in hands. The tension in the room ratcheted up as arrows of energy formed in the air around them.

Raider grimaced. "I forgot to tell you. He's the reason I was able to get here so fast. I was already on my way when Solal found me." To Jin, he said, "You were supposed to stay out of sight."

Jin harrumphed. "Like I was going to listen. Really."

"What abomination is this?" Makon asked.

Jin made an aggravated sound. "These guys are a touchy lot, aren't they?"

"Perhaps it's the fact you're not supposed to be here," Raider suggested as the room hovered on the edge of violence.

All it would take was one jumpy oshota, one misconstrued gesture from Jin, and Graydon would lose control of the situation.

He couldn't afford that with a helpless Kira in the mix.

"He's Kira's friend," Raider said in explanation. "I wouldn't try to hurt him. He's far more dangerous than he looks. Not to mention if you're successful, Kira will likely kill you when she wakes."

"Aw, you say the sweetest things, meat sack," Jin crooned.

"I hate you so much, Tin Can," Raider said without heat.

"Enough," Makon said, his voice holding a bite.

Raider and Jin fell silent, neither seeming afraid. Impressive, since Graydon knew how intimidating the marshal could be.

"What is that thing doing in our home?" Makon asked.

"Where Kira goes; I go. The end," Jin said. "Now, can we get back to saving her?"

Graydon stifled his smile, for once in agreement with the machine.

Jin spun toward him, his voice turning serious. "I practically forced her to come here with the understanding you would protect her. I had to endure her feelings of betrayal. If you can't keep her safe, I'll be more than happy to take her back."

Any common ground Graydon had found with Jin vanished at those words, leaving Graydon to bare his teeth at the pest. He'd like to see him try.

Jin chortled, unintimidated.

Harlow shifted, the small gesture calling their attention like a magnet. "No one is taking her anywhere, and his presence can be addressed at a better time. Right now, extricating her from her own mind takes priority."

Graydon agreed whole-heartedly.

"Tell me about this memory," Graydon said, buying himself time to think.

Raider glanced at Jin. "I don't know why she would be lost in it. This was an early battle. One of the few we won."

Jin floated next to Kira's bubble, seemingly ignoring the rest of them. An illusion, Graydon knew. The drone was a threat. Sooner or later he would need to be addressed. But not now.

"And you?" Graydon asked.

The drone was too quiet. There was more to this story.

"Kira's right," Jin grumbled. "You see too much. It makes you dangerous."

"I suspect the same could be said of you."

Jin might play at the fool. His utter ridiculousness was a shield used to keep others underestimating the drone. The façade hid a deceptively dangerous being.

"What happened there?" Harlow asked.

"We were tasked with safeguarding a planet evacuation," Jin started.

"By the time we arrived, the Tsavitee were already on the ground. They had set up an angel class destroyer in orbit and were picking off any ship that made it into the air. Kira led a strike team to take it down. Successfully, I might add," Raider said with a glance at Jin.

"But not before we lost over a dozen ships," Jin said calmly. "She'd spent time on Atlas. It was her home for a short time after the camp. She knew people there, and she had a lot of friends on those ships."

Dismay crossed Raider's expression. "I didn't know that."

"You wouldn't; she never told you. It was our first engagement as a team. She wanted you to focus on the success of the mission rather than what had been lost. It doesn't mean she didn't feel every one of those losses," Jin said.

"Our family has always been protectors," Harlow mused, staring up at his niece. "Our sense of responsibility is overdeveloped. It's why we've long been tasked with the leadership of this House."

"Kira is a chip off the old block then," Jin said.

"How do we get her out? As memories go, this is a gentle one," Raider said.

Jin answered before Graydon could. "You want to use her link to Raider to gain access to her mind."

Raider's face was puzzled. "What are you talking about?"

"Tuann form mental connections to the people they care about," Jin explained. "It's how they preserve their sanity. The more connections they have, the more stable they are. Deprive them of their connections, and they slowly wither and fade."

"How do you know that?" Makon asked.

Jin snorted. "Please. I know that woman better than I know myself. I've always suspected she needs an emotional connection with others. Our self-imposed exile confirmed it." He focused on Graydon. "It's a good idea, but I'm the better option. My connection with her is stronger. More developed."

For once, there was no hint of laughter or teasing in the drone.

"You're a machine," Makon said. "You won't be able to meld with her mind."

Jin's voice was cool. "You shouldn't judge either Kira or me by your definition of what's possible. People in Kira's vicinity have a way of exceeding your expectations."

"You're not a person," Indya pointed out.

Jin sniffed in insult. "I've never allowed myself to be limited by small minds lacking in imagination. I'm not going to start now."

He started toward Kira. "Are you in or are you out?"

Graydon didn't have to think twice. If the drone said he could do it, Graydon would risk everything to ensure she survived. "I'm up for anything you are, machine."

Jin cackled. "I knew there was a reason I liked you."

Graydon stopped inches from the bubble. "The marshal is right. Our technology doesn't always coexist well with the human's. It could destroy you and me in the attempt."

History was littered with stories of those who'd fallen afoul of the memory pools. They were both taking their lives in their hands by doing this.

"I'm willing to take the risk," Jin said. "Better to try and fail than live with the consequences."

"Strange to find myself agreeing with a machine," Graydon returned.

Jin rotated toward him. "Graydon, this has to work. If she destroys Devon's mind, you'll never convince her to stay. Any progress you've made will be over. She'll cut and run so fast you'll never find her."

Graydon had no doubt Jin spoke true. Kira would blame herself, despite her sharing no fault in matters.

"Then we'd better make sure we don't fail," Graydon said.

Graydon lifted his hand, praying to the Mea'Ave and *ki* around them that this would work. His connection with her was fragile. New. Yet it was stronger than it should be for what could be considered a blink of an eye for many Tuann. If allowed to grow, Graydon knew their connection would blossom into something they would write about for ages.

Kira cared. Even when she shouldn't. Even when it would have been easier to walk away. You just had to look at her actions when she'd saved Devon and the *lu-ong*. Neither scenario had promised her any benefit. Any Tuann he knew would have let things play out with no risk to themselves.

Not Kira.

It was the thing he liked best about her. She threw herself into danger because it was the right thing to do. It was noble and stupid. He'd prefer the woman didn't take such risks.

He refused to lose her now.

Graydon closed his eyes, drifting into a trance. The brightness of Kira's soul obliterated everything else in the room. It burned white-hot, full of an incandescent passion. Beautiful and deadly, overshadowing everything else.

This was why people were drawn to her. Why her humans had gone to such lengths to protect her and why the human at his side had followed her to Roake despite strong opposition.

She was an inferno with the power to destroy or protect.

Graydon had seen few souls as pure as Kira's. It made him crave her, tempting him to linger and let its strength settle his own.

With the ease of long practice, he pushed its intensity back, surprised to find the bright shadow of Jin in his mind's map when

Kira's impact faded.

As one, they both stepped into the water's currents.

Pain surged, threatening to break bones. A thread of consciousness waved and he grasped hold, using it to pull himself free.

Kira's past rose around him. Shadowed and insubstantial as if afraid to show itself.

A boy walked out of the gray, tendrils clinging to his form until he stood in front of Graydon. He was young, on the cusp of puberty, his ears pointed, his eyes wide-set and familiar. His eyes were a bright yellow. His hair was black, and his skin was brown.

There was a familiar sarcastic light in his eyes, and his lips were pulled up in an expression Graydon had seen more than once on Kira's face.

"Jin?"

"In the flesh." Jin glanced down. "Well, in the dream flesh."

Jin held up a hand, flexing the fingers before opening and closing them to make a fist with a look of fascination. His hand dropped, and he looked up at Graydon. "Shall we continue? Kira is waiting."

Graydon was slow to respond, Jin's appearance causing him to reconsider everything he thought he knew. Why was Jin in the form of a boy?

More importantly, why did he resemble so closely a boy Graydon already knew?

"Why did you take that form?" Graydon heard himself ask.

Jin's shrug was dismissive as he stuck his hands into the pockets of a pair of jeans, a decidedly human invention. "It felt right."

The dreamscape shimmered, the half-formed figures wobbling before dissipating.

Jin looked up, his expression wiser than any child's had a right to be. "Damn, I'd hoped she'd stay out of those memories. Nothing good ever comes of revisiting them."

Graydon was still stuck on Jin's appearance and didn't speak.

Jin shook his head in regret. "She's going to hate me for this later, but some things are worth the risk. I hope you don't betray the trust I'm about to put in you."

He didn't give Graydon time to respond. The scene spun.

Graydon ran through a field, trees all around, the dark pressing in, cloying in what it concealed. A small hand was clasped in his as his lungs burned with the need for air.

Kira/Graydon looked back, looking over the boy's head at the tree line behind them. The terrible bay of an animal hunting them floated out of the forest. The creature wasn't far. They'd never make it to the other side of the field in time.

The boy tripped, holding in his cry as he hit the ground. Kira/Graydon crouched beside him and eyes the color of sunny daisies looked up at them.

"Go," the boy whispered. "You'll never make it with me slowing you down."

He was right. They were going to be caught.

Desperation and terror threatened to strangle Kira/Graydon at the thought of returning to that cold, damp place.

The scene spun, and they stood in the rain, a rifle held in front of them. Their hands too small to properly grip it, their arms shaking as they struggled to keep it extended. Failure was too terrible a prospect to consider.

A shadowy monster the size of a giant paced in front of them. "Weakness won't be tolerated. Fail, and you will be punished."

A whimper came from beside her.

"Stay strong," she whispered to the young one.

It was a risk to speak. If their masters caught them, the beating would be brutal.

The boy's rifle clattered to the ground, the sound loud despite the pouring rain. Kira's face remained blank and uncaring. Emotion was pain here, and she was intent on surviving.

The giant's smile was cruel. "It seems we have a winner. Bring him."

The rest of those in the formation remained locked at attention, their bodies rigid as they kept the rifles uplifted. No one spoke. No one breathed for fear the masters would turn their focus to them.

The boy's gasping sobs could be heard as he was dragged out of the formation, stripped and then whipped, the flogger creating long streaks of red the rain washed away.

"We have to leave tonight. The distraction is already prepared. If we wait any longer, we'll be the ones they experiment on next," someone whispered as the boy collapsed and was dragged toward the gaping maw of the door.

Flash. The sky all around, ground to air artillery fire lighting up the air under their feet.

Flash. A Tsavitee demon class, its maw opened wide as it hammered at their armor.

Flash. A scream ripping from their chest as they destroyed the thing they feared.

Flash. The bridge of a ship as humans moved around them.

It was a strain, but Graydon managed to separate his consciousness from Kira's, not allowing himself to be dragged fully into the memory this time.

"You're good to launch, Whiskey One. Stay safe out there," a female said.

Kira limped into view, her foot encased in a cast.

"Don't forget to tell Phoenix to take care of that foot of hers. The rest of us will be happy to pick up her slack," a female said through the comms.

"Ha, fucking ha, Elise," Kira said with a carefree smile that startled Graydon. This Kira seemed younger than the one he knew, only a hint of the shadows he'd glimpsed in her eyes.

She was happy, he realized. Totally and completely.

"Try not to damage the deck on your way out," Kira was saying.

"Never, Nixxy. We'll leave that to you."

"Don't take it to heart, Sunshine," a man drawled. "You know the Phoenix can't stand being cooped up. Goes a little stir crazy."

Kira rolled her eyes as the humans around her ducked their heads, hiding their amusement. "Yeah, yeah, laugh it up, chuckle britches. I'll make sure to remember that next time I'm leading PT." Her expression became serious. "Stay focused out there. I don't want anyone damaging my perfect record because they got careless."

"Not to mention, I'd prefer we didn't look like complete idiots in front of our guests," a man said, stepping onto the bridge.

Seconds later, someone cried, "Commander on deck."

Those present snapped to attention. Kira was slower to move, as if going through the motions was almost more effort than they were worth.

"How are we looking, Captain Forrest?" the man asked, crossing the bridge.

Kira straightened from where she'd been leaning over a console. "Talks have begun, Commander. The rest of the Curs are sitting in their chutes, locked and loaded, and awaiting our orders."

"Very impatiently, I might add," someone said through the comms.

"When aren't you impatient?" Jin groused.

"Kids, let's not fight in front of the parents," the one Graydon had heard called Elise said. "The Phoenix doesn't like it."

The Phoenix in question made a sarcastic face at the console as those on the bridge grinned. It was obvious they were used to the byplay.

That was the way of things for those among the warrior class. They weren't always easy with your feelings, more prone to finding the spots you'd like to protect and then poking and prodding until a hard callous formed, but they were there when it counted.

And Graydon had a feeling this moment in time had counted for Kira.

The shadows he sometimes saw in her had their origins in this memory.

"Look alive out there," Kira said. "No games. We can't chance anything with the entire universe watching our every move. Get in, make sure the comet's not hiding any nasty surprises, and then get out."

"You think they'll name it after us?" someone asked.

There was a guffaw from another. "Why would they do that?"

"Well, we'll be the first to explore it. Sounds only fitting it gets our name."

Kira shook her head as the commander said, "I'll make sure to request that in my report to the higher-ups. Get me eyes on it and then get to the ship."

A chorus of yes, sirs answered him.

The commander nodded at Kira. "You have a go for this mission, Captain. Let's see what your Curs can do."

Kira grinned. "Sir, yes, sir. Sunshine, Bayside, you are go for release. Bring me back some space dust."

The scene spun, chaos and pain all around before going dark. A cry of grief and pain split the air.

When Graydon opened his eyes again, he was back where he began, racing through a field, panic and desperation beating at him, a small hand clasped in his.

TWENTY-SIX

"A LOOP," GRAYDON said softly. "How is she doing this?"

Jin's intangible presence brushed against him. "Technique she picked up in the camps. Hard for someone to find the secrets you're hiding when you shred your memories and force them to repeat."

In front of them, they reached the spot where the boy fell, his hand leaving Kira's.

"You need to find the thing she doesn't want you to see," Jin said urgently. "Right now, you're an enemy combatant. She'll dredge up the most painful memory she can find and relive it over and over again."

"Why would she do that?" Graydon asked as the memory spun. Rain poured down, indistinct figures standing at attention holding rifles.

Jin's unease emanated from him. Graydon got the sense this memory was a touchy one.

"Double-edged sword," Jin said, sounding strained. "The Tsavitee don't feel; not like we do. Overwhelm them with emotions they have no reference for, and you have a powerful weapon against them."

"She rattles their cages until they'll do anything to escape," Graydon finished for him.

"If their minds don't burn out first," Jin agreed.

The boy dropped his weapon and was dragged out of formation as the others whispered of their escape plans.

Graydon tried to see the faces of those standing around Kira and failed. Their features were cast in shadow and out of focus.

"That isn't possible." Graydon backed away and moved down the line. None of them had faces.

The *uhva na* should have pulled complete memories from Kira. You couldn't hide from the Trial of the Broken.

"That's not what you should be focusing on." Jin's flinch was barely perceptible as they finished whipping the boy until his back was raw and bloody before dragging him away.

Graydon stopped in front of Kira. To the unobservant, her expression would seem flat. Uncaring. Not the woman he knew, as she watched a boy beaten in front of her. She'd told him about this memory. About watching a boy whipped until there was barely any skin on his back.

Fire flashed in her eyes, there and gone in an instant.

"There you are," he said.

Hatred burned deep inside her, only to be replaced by something else. Determination.

"What about him?" someone asked.

"There's no choice; we have to leave him. Breaking him out of the isolation cells would take too much time."

Rebellion sparked.

Kira's rifle clattered to the ground as she stepped out of formation, locked on the man who'd had the boy dragged forward. He took in her insubordination, not smart enough to be afraid.

He started to speak. Kira lunged with a primal scream, her smaller body flying at his.

The man's hands raised, the familiar scent of *ki* saturating the air.

"Tuann," Graydon whispered, horrified at his discovery.

Kira never paused. She was on the man in the next second, the weapon she'd disguised in her hand slashing across his throat.

She landed. Her gaze flickered as she spotted Graydon.

"You see me," he said, starting. She was aware on some level of what was going on. He could use that to call her from her memories.

The world slid sideways, the memory replaced by the flight deck of a ship. Humans jostled Graydon, whistling and hollering at where Kira stood on a cargo container. She held a spoon up to her mouth, singing to the accompaniment of a few humans playing instruments.

Kira's voice washed over him, teasing and sensuous. Her pleasure in the act was obvious, written across her face and carried in every note she sang.

The humans were enthralled, held spellbound as she wove her web. A few held up flashlights or glow sticks, waving them in time to the beat.

Her mother was said to have been able to do that. Luatha had long been known for their artisans. Music and art were a part of their daily lives. Kira's mother had won Roake's heart with her voice. She'd been nearly as treasured as Harding.

Graydon knew if he let himself, he could get lost in her music. Instead, he opened his eyes and forced himself to pull away. It was a distraction, meant to lull him into lowering his guard.

As if on cue, the scene shifted back to the bridge.

Kira limped into view.

Graydon padded after her, a hunter on the prowl. "It's not going to be that easy, *coli*. What is it that you don't want me to see?"

The barest semblance of defiance flashed across her face.

There she was, Graydon thought with satisfaction. "You can run all you want. I'll still find you."

"Bring me some space dust," Kira said as the scene started to slide sideways.

Graydon held firm, anchoring himself in place with a flex of his will. Not this time.

The dreamscape hiccupped.

"Something is interfering with Whiskey four's signal," someone shouted.

"Abort, Whiskey one," Kira said. "Elise, get out of there."

"There's something here," Elise argued.

"I don't care what it is. Get on your board and get your ass back here," Kira ordered.

The atmosphere on the bridge shifted, tension ratcheting up.

"Four class three bogeys just appeared on scope," a human said, the voice showing the slightest hint of strain.

Kira looked up. Her expression horrified as the commander's face tightened.

"They're here to stop the alliance," he said.

Kira nodded. "Sunshine, forget about what's out there. You have new orders. Rendezvous with the fleet and provide support. They'll go for the ambassador's ships."

"Fuck," Elise cursed. "I'm on it. Bayside and Champ, turn and burn. Don't wait for us."

The bridge was controlled chaos as orders were snapped out, then relayed down the line. The ship jolted and quivered under his feet as torpedoes were launched, and the guns came online.

"Alert the ambassador and tell the Haldeel to bug out," the

commander ordered.

"Roger that," someone shouted, already moving to obey.

Kira stared at the screen. "We're not going to be able to hold them."

There was grim acceptance in the commander's face. "I know, but we'll do the best we can anyway."

Kira nodded.

Again, the scene tried to wrench sideways. Graydon held firm, his mind threatening to buckle as his nose began to bleed.

Kira's mind was powerful, and her desire not to revisit this next memory even more so.

Graydon couldn't let her run.

Her desperation beat at him, shredding his insides. He didn't relent. This was their best opportunity. He had to act now. Every time she looped, she'd grow weaker. Eventually, there would be no pulling her out. This had to happen now.

Their wills tangled as they fought for control.

The balance wavered before tipping back toward Kira. Jin appeared beside Graydon.

"Sorry, dearest. Time for a little tough love. You need to wake up, and this is the fastest way," Jin said with a sad smile.

The bridge disappeared, the black void of space taking its place, glittering stars caught in its depths. Below him, a moon reflected the light of a strange sun.

"Curs, rally on me. I have a plan," Kira shouted.

"There's no time. We're not going to make it," Elise said.

"Yes, you can," Kira shouted. "Trust me. It'll work."

"I'm sorry, Phoenix. It wasn't supposed to happen like this," Elise said in a broken voice. "I've left you something. Find it. Protect it. Trust no one."

Time skipped.

Kira's scream of denial came as the moon splintered, pieces of it shooting into space from the force of the explosion.

"Pull her out now, before she relives this," Jin ordered.

With the last dregs of his will, Graydon shattered the world around them, the sound of Kira's agony echoing in his ears.

Graydon jolted into his body, the waters of memory and dream holding their shape. They wobbled before crashing down.

Kira fell. Graydon surged forward, catching her body and lowering them both to the ground until he was kneeling in the water.

She screamed; one long, drawn-out agonized sound after another. It was painful to listen to and even more difficult to watch as he clutched her to him, making soothing sounds.

She sobbed, the sounds broken as they reached inside Graydon and twisted. He hated what he'd made her relive, even as he knew it had been utterly necessary.

Gradually, he became aware of her speaking into his chest as he rocked her back and forth.

"They're gone. They'reThey'regonethey'regonethey'regone."

Harlow met Graydon's eyes. His expression almost lost as he took in his niece. The Overlord wasn't used to helplessness. It didn't sit well.

He withdrew into himself, a mask slamming down as his attention shifted to the culprits of what happened. There was no mercy in him as he made his way toward Aeron.

"Shh, I've got you," Graydon crooned. He lifted a hand, pushing her hair away from her face. "I know, *cheva nier*, but you're not alone now. I'm here."

Her pain gutted him.

Jin drifted beside her.

"She sacrificed herself for you," Graydon said softly. A word crept along the edges of his mind, one he tried to ignore, knowing the ramifications of it would change everything.

It pushed forward anyway. Soul bound.

"Yes," Jin agreed. "Not all of her secrets are hers to tell."

It was a warning, one Graydon would do well to pay attention to.

As secrets go, this one was dangerous. There hadn't been a soul bound since the Tuann's escape from their merciless masters.

That there was one now would rock the very foundations of their society if it ever got out.

He was starting to understand the full ramifications of Kira's existence and the potential for danger she held.

*

Numbness spread through Kira as she clutched Graydon, nuzzling her face into his neck. Just one more minute, and then she'd pull herself together.

She needed to face the consequences of this—but not yet.

Even knowing she shouldn't, Kira's head lifted, her lips unerringly finding Graydon's.

She needed to forget, if only for a minute. All of the pain. All of the sadness. She needed to know there was more to this life than death and loss.

Graydon had come for her, dragged her scratching and clawing from the darkness. He was still here, even after he'd seen her in some of her worst moments.

Graydon's hand rose, cupping her nape. His passion matching hers. The kiss was gentle, as if he was afraid of breaking her—until he wasn't.

They sank into each other. The rest of the world faded away. The only thing of importance the way their lips clung, heated and warm. A brand that marked and claimed.

Someone cleared their voice loudly next to her.

It took several seconds before Kira could force herself to draw back, her breathing fast as arousal swam through her veins.

The brutal beauty of Graydon's face eclipsed the rest of the room. The visible battle he fought not to pull her to him and continue their interlude was reassuring. She wasn't the only one fighting not to finish what they'd started.

"As touching as this is, I'm not sure your uncle wants to see you getting busy with the commander," Jin drawled. "I second that sentiment, if you were wondering."

Kira felt drained and weak as she propped herself on one hand. "You couldn't have found another way?"

Jin darted into her chest. Her arms closed around him as his voice came, muffled. "Graydon seemed convinced this was our best option."

Kira dropped a kiss on his smooth metal. "Thank you for coming for me. I know that couldn't have been easy for you."

Jin carried his own scars from those memories.

Jin drew back. "It wasn't."

The other two were starting to recover from their immersion in Kira's mind. Devon bolted upright, landing on his hands and knees as he lost the contents of his stomach.

Finished, he scrubbed at his mouth, looking lost. "How do you bear it?"

Kira's smile was halfhearted. "What other choice is there?"

Their conversation was interrupted as the oshota forced Aeron up and onto his knees, not bothering to be gentle as they did so.

To Kira's surprise, Aeron didn't seem defeated, sitting there on his knees, oshota on either side and one behind him, en-blades unsheathed.

She frowned.

He seemed resigned, if anything.

"Why did you do this?" Harlow asked.

Aeron's head lifted, his eyes finding Kira's. "You weren't supposed to be here. He said you were done with the Tuann."

"So sorry to ruin your plans," Jin said when Kira remained silent, watching Aeron carefully.

Aeron's smile was humorless. "Me too, but that's why I'm here. Insurance, right? For when things go wrong."

His gaze fell on Loudon as black crawled across Aeron's eyes, his skin darkening. "We couldn't exactly trust a Tuann to secure such a valuable prize as Devon. He's going to be the new you, Kira. It's why they sent me."

"Primus," an oshota shouted, his en-blade already swinging.

Aeron's hand shot up, catching the blade. He bared incisors that had lengthened into fangs. Horns curled up from his head as he ripped the blade away. He swung, and the oshota flew back.

"Wrong," Aeron said, adjusting his shoulders as if trying to get comfortable in his new form.

"General," Kira whispered.

Kira's world shifted as her preconceptions were realigned. The generals were like the Tuann; they had more than one form.

Around them, the oshota scrambled in the face of the unexpected threat.

Jin moved to hover protectively in front of Devon and Kira.

The general lunged at Harlow. The world slowed, Kira too far and too weak to do anything but watch as Harlow dropped back a step, a glow building in his hands as the general neared.

A lance of red pierced the dark. It hit Aeron in the chest. He gurgled, blood bubbles forming around the corner of his mouth as he dropped to his knees, a look of shock on his face.

For an instant, nobody moved, surprise holding them immobile.

Finally, they looked to see a figure standing in the middle of the water, a cloak covering their face. The person snapped a jaunty wave in greeting before racing into the darkness.

"After them," Harlow roared.

Kira didn't move as she stared after the stranger. She recognized that cloak.

She should. It was hers, though the last time she had seen it had been on her ship, months ago.

"Oh boy, that's not going to be good," Jin muttered.

Kira shot him a glance, ordering him without words to do something.

He sighed, floating after the figure. "Don't get into any more trouble."

No one remarked his passing, too vested in Harlow's security to notice.

Graydon's oshota grouped around Devon, forming a wall of flesh around him.

Kira's lips parted, and Graydon bent a look of warning on her, telling her without words not to ask.

Her mouth snapped shut. His look was confirmation enough of her suspicions.

On the ground, Aeron wheezed as he struggled to breathe. With the rest distracted, Kira crawled over to him, her touch fleeting and tentative as she examined the wound. It was clean. Almost surgical.

If Aeron got medical attention, he would no doubt live.

"Lothos told me you'd kill me if I accepted this position," Aeron gasped. "Looks like he was right."

"You're not dead yet," Kira told him as she pressed her hand to his wound to stem the blood.

His laugh was clogged and pain-filled. "They call you the Savior. Always whispering of your existence—but you never came for us. We weren't good enough for you to save. You saved all of them, but never us."

His gaze moved over the ceiling, fear of death on his face. Right then, he was a boy despite his form being that of a general, with the same fears the rest of them had.

"Did it ever occur to you to save yourself?" Kira asked.

He scoffed. "Someone has to protect our young from our masters. If we don't, they'll do terrible things to them."

"I know," she said sadly.

"We never were the favored children," he ground out. "Seems not much has changed."

Graydon appeared over Kira's shoulder. "Why are you here?"

Aeron shifted, an agonized groan leaving him. "The masters want their toys back."

Graydon looked over Kira's head toward Harlow. "Confirmation."

Harlow nodded, looking grim.

"Get him medical attention and then fit him with a disruptor," Harlow said. "It stands to reason if the disruptor works on our criminals, it'll work on one of them too. The emperor will no doubt want him interrogated."

Harlow's oshota were gentle as they shuffled Kira to the side, reaching down and securing Aeron.

"See you soon, Phoenix," Aeron said over his shoulder as he was carried away.

"You'll never get close to her again," the oshota carrying him snapped.

Harlow crossed to Loudon, grief and betrayal written on his face as he stared at his friend. Makon and several others stood in a semi-circle around the man, making sure the Tuann wouldn't try to run.

Loudon struggled to focus on the approaching Overlord.

His armor had clamped down on the flesh above the arm, creating a tourniquet and preventing him from bleeding out. It didn't stop him from going into shock, however.

"I always thought there was a traitor, but I was hoping it wasn't you," Harlow informed him.

Loudon was quiet.

"Why did you do this?" Harlow asked.

Still, Loudon didn't speak.

"If I had to guess, it's because of the role he played in my parents' deaths. He was the mole, the person who made everything that happened possible," Kira finally said, coming to stand beside Harlow's side.

She crouched so she could stare Loudon in the eye. "I'm betting when the Tsavitee approached him before my arrival, he tried to refuse. Only the Tsavitee don't like being told no. They probably threatened to reveal the role he played in the Sorrowing if he didn't help."

Loudon glared at her.

"Tell me I'm wrong," she told him.

His face turned ugly. If he could have, he probably would have tried to kill her again.

Kira stood and shook her head.

"Why did you betray them?" Harlow asked. "You were Harding's friend too. He trusted you."

Kira was quiet. She could have told him what she'd learned, but she knew the answer would only hurt him.

She found herself reluctant to do anything that would cause him further distress.

"He was weak and a fool," Loudon bit out finally. "He never should have been Overlord. It always should have been you."

Harlow was still as poison continued to spill from Loudon's lips.

"I did it for you. He was never strong enough to do what was necessary. You were the one who was always meant to lead. You—"

Harlow hammered his fist into the reclined man's chest. Raw *ki* exploded through him. Kira's ears popped from the pressure.

Loudon was dead even as his eyes widened, his body convulsing.

Her uncle slowly straightened. "You fool. All this for a position I never even wanted."

Harlow's head bent.

Grief chased through Makon's expression before it was gone. The marshal met her eyes before inclining his head.

Kira lingered, torn between the need to retreat and leave them with their grief and the need to offer some form of sympathy. Her uncle's friend had committed unspeakable wrongs against him. There were no words that would take the sting of that knowledge away.

She had to try anyway. Kira opened her mouth to speak. Pain devoured her. A high whine escaped her as fire encased her wrists.

Harlow whirled as she brought her wrists to her in an instinctive gesture to protect them.

"What's happening?" she gritted out as the fire burrowed deeper.

Graydon was there in the next second, both men hovering protectively over her as Graydon withdrew one arm, bringing it up so they could see.

Shock and awe were on both men's faces as Graydon pulled her to him, his hand rubbing a soothing pattern over her back.

"Make it stop," Kira managed to get out.

"I can't. It'll be over soon," Graydon said, pressing his cheek into the top of her head.

Sure enough, seconds later the pain eased, and Kira stared at her new injuries. Her skin was unblistered, but it wasn't unmarked. Around each wrist were etched lines, the pattern beautiful and familiar.

The only time she'd seen anything like them was when Himoto had shown her photos or video of her primus form.

"Why are the tattoos from my primus form suddenly appearing?" Kira asked, feeling a spurt of fear.

Graydon touched them gently, smoothing a finger along the lines. Electricity and heat trailed behind where he touched, tugging at Kira's core.

"These are Overlord bands," he said. "They're bestowed on very few."

Her gaze lifted to find pride and a fierce satisfaction blazing in his.

"It means the Mea'Ave has judged you worthy," her uncle rumbled. "Congratulations. You've passed the *uhva na*."

TWENTY-SEVEN

IT WAS SEVERAL days later when Wren finally managed to hunt her down. A part of her had been expecting him.

She'd never know if it was what she'd done that day or Quillon reaching him in time was what saved him. Kira didn't think she wanted to know.

Wren joined her where she leaned on the stone balcony of her new room. It seemed when you passed the Trial of the Broken, you got better accommodations.

This room was bigger than the last and came with more amenities. The balcony was one.

Like her first room, it had come fully stocked with a full complement of clothes. Many were the same ballistic-proof quality of the outfit she'd worn to the trial.

In addition, Kira had found two weapons that made her mouth salivate. They begged her to test their capabilities. One was a sword similar in form to an en-blade and fit her hand like it had been made for her. The second was a bracelet that turned into a whip of light, perfect for those times you couldn't go overtly armed.

Her not so mysterious benefactor had been more than kind.

To everyone's surprise, Kira wasn't the only one to pass the trial. Devon had received his marks at some point before she'd arrived. Joule too, she'd been delighted to discover.

Raider's attempt was delayed by a day so the Overlord could deal with the fallout from events, but soon he too bore marks of his own. He was the first human ever accorded the honor. It had sent shock waves through Roake as a result.

Not that Kira was surprised. She always knew Raider was capable of it. Her former ally was nothing if not tenacious.

The question of Aeron's infiltration had been answered as well. Loudon had been a busy boy over the past few weeks, falsifying Aeron's background and making sure to put him into Devon's orbit whenever possible.

Aeron was supposed to get close to Devon, then find a way to alienate him from the rest of the initiates. It was meant to mentally weaken him and drive him into a corner, making him easier to scoop up in the end.

The trial was over, but the path to the *adva ka* was still long and twisting. No one could tell her when the next one would be called. They simply didn't know. Evidently, the *adva ka* existed based on the Mea'Ave's will. It would allow entrants only when it wanted.

It meant Kira was back in a holding pattern. Not that she minded overly. With evidence provided by Odin that Elise was out in the universe again, it meant her need to find the Tsavitee home worlds was no longer as pressing.

She still needed to find them, but she no longer felt like she was going to come out of her skin from the urgency she felt. Besides, it was going to take time for Odin to sift through the data she'd given her. This had always been a long shot.

For now, Jin's presence on Ta Sa'Riel had been overlooked, Loudon's and Aeron's actions overshadowing his trespass. In light of what had almost happened, Roake was more distracted with dealing with the fallout from that rather than assigning punishment and blame for Jin's presence here.

It helped that Kira's uncle seemed content to pretend he'd known about Jin all along. Kira wasn't going to argue.

She traced the patterns of the marks on her wrists as she waited for Wren to speak.

The *seon'yer* looked pretty good for a man who had been inches from death only a few days ago. Tuann medicine at work. It was impressive, to say the least.

In the end, he said nothing, simply setting a medallion on the railing next to her.

Kira picked it up, tracing the raised ridges. "What's this?"

"Proof of your apprenticeship," Wren told her.

"And you've given this to me why?"

He fixed her with a cool look. "You're bright. I'm sure you can figure it out."

She rolled the medallion in her palm, as she considered the Tuann in front of her.

Wren was a hard one to read. It made dealing with him difficult. Manipulation was out of the question. He saw too much. Behind that stiff reserve was a very smart man. There was a reason Rheya had salivated at the thought of an apprenticeship with him.

He didn't wait for her response, moving toward the balcony door.

"Awful arrogant, don't you think?" Kira commented to his retreating figure. "Assuming I'll accept?"

He stopped, regarding her with an enigmatic gaze. "You'll accept."

Kira set the medallion on the stone beside her, before leaning against the railing and lacing her fingers over her stomach. He seemed very sure of himself. This should be good.

"You called the memories because you couldn't fight them both alone," he said. "You got lucky Graydon and Harlow showed up just as Loudon fought his way free of your trap. Next time you might not be so lucky. I promise that by the time I finish with you, you'll never have trouble with enemies of that caliber again."

Her head tilted. There were many responses she could have given him. Defenses. Excuses. Reasons why she'd chosen that route instead of another.

None of them mattered—because he was right. She hadn't been sure she could take both of them on at once. Not without possibly sacrificing Devon.

"I plan to keep an eye on you," he told her in warning. "Never forget that."

Kira stiffened, internally cursing. He remembered.

Wren moved toward the door, saying over his shoulder, "We ship out in a week; I expect to see you there. It seems the Haldeel have called a quorum. You and the others who passed will be part of a delegation handpicked by the emperor."

Jin rose behind her as Wren disappeared into her room. "Care to explain what that was about."

Kira scrubbed a hand over her face before facing the ocean again. "Not particularly."

"But you're gonna anyway," Jin sang.

Kira's head dropped. "I may have implied the daughter he lost in the Sorrowing is still alive."

Jin dipped. Long moments passed before he said, "I see I missed a few things after my spawn was incapacitated."

Kira grunted. That was an understatement.

"What are you going to do?" he asked. "You know what the group will do if they find out you're sharing secrets."

Kira had made certain promises. Promises she'd broken for Wren. The rest wouldn't be happy if they learned about it.

"I'm well aware of all the ways this could go wrong," Kira said, resigned.

She was playing a dangerous game, with stakes she no longer felt certain she wanted to pay.

After several minutes, Jin floated to the railing next to her. "The Haldeel. Their territory was where Odin said Elise was last seen, wasn't it?"

Kira's lips curved. "And Wren just handed us the perfect excuse to go investigate."

Jin chuckled as he swung toward her door. "There's something I found that I think warrants investigating."

Kira stretched and stepped away from the railing. "I was starting to feel a little cooped up now that you mention it."

*

Hours later, Kira crouched in the shadow of the fortress, watching the perimeter wall, Jin a dark shape beside her.

Sneaking out without Finn discovering and following hadn't been easy. Luckily for Kira, her new quarters came with a balcony, handy for escaping undetected from an oshota who had a habit of staking out her front door.

"Wait for it. Wait for it."

Kira tensed.

"Now," Jin said.

She raced forward as Jin lit up the wall with red tracer dots, showing the safest places for her to ascend. She scaled it in seconds, up and over before anyone had a chance to see her.

She landed softly on the other side, wincing as her ankles protested the long fall.

Jin lowered beside her. "Well, that was a little easier than I thought."

Kira glanced at the wall. Maybe a little too easy. "Getting back into the fortress when we're done with this little escapade will be harder."

The defenses were geared to keep people out, not in, after all.

"We'll worry about that later," Jin decided. "For now, let's get moving."

He led the way, racing over the knee-high grasses with ease as he headed for the forest where Kira typically trained.

An hour later, they were under the trees and nearly to their destination when Kira stopped.

"You can come out now," she said.

Raider stepped from the shadows, his hands in his pockets as he sauntered toward them.

Kira slid a hard glance at Jin. He whistled as he floated into the dark, giving them an illusion of privacy. She didn't have to ask if he'd known Raider was following him. Jin would likely have picked up on the other man's presence as soon as he'd started trailing them.

It seemed this was a discovery Jin thought Raider should know about.

"Following me now?" she asked.

He shrugged. "I did warn you I wouldn't make things easy for you."

He did at that.

"I have a right to know. You weren't the only one who loved her," he said.

He was right. In his place, she would have been just as tenacious.

The instincts that had kept her alive all these years warned that trust was a precious commodity. Once a secret was out, it couldn't be put back in its box.

If she did this, there was no going back.

Could she trust Raider like that?

Kira stepped around him.

"Kira," he protested.

She stopped and tilted her head at where Jin had disappeared. "You coming?"

Shock was replaced by determination as he followed at her heels.

They resumed their trek, Raider silent as he trailed them. Jin was a bobbing shadow in front of them as he scanned the area.

He stopped abruptly, before darting through a pair of trees.

"Found it," floated softly to Kira.

She started after him, stepping into a wide clearing, her steps slowing as the hulking form of the *Wanderer* greeted her. Half covered with branches and other vegetation to disguise it from surveillance, it sat in the shadow of several boulders.

Kira circled it as Raider stared.

"How the hell did you land a ship on this planet?" he asked.

Kira didn't answer, too busy ensuring the *Wanderer* wasn't damaged in any way. She was going to kill the person who'd flown it here. Kill them very dead.

The risks they'd taken. The danger they'd put her ship in—not to mention themselves.

It was enough to short circuit Kira's brain.

"Dead. Very, very dead," she muttered, storming toward the landing ramp.

She pressed her palm to the security lock. It beeped before flashing red.

Access denied.

A high-pitched growl escaped Kira. That little—

Kira's motions were jerky as she popped off the panel. "Lock me out of my own ship? We'll see who's laughing soon."

She pulled out a few wires, crossing them and then splicing another set before slamming the panel in place as the circuits rebooted. Kira waited, barely resisting the urge to tap her toe as it came back online.

Kira stabbed the buttons as she inputted her override code.

Raider didn't comment as she worked.

The light flashed green, and the ramp started to lower.

Jin was the first through, slipping into the narrow gap as soon as it was wide enough. Kira and Raider were forced to wait until the ramp was fully extended.

It hadn't even touched the ground before she was striding up it, her footsteps an angry accompaniment to her mood.

Kira headed straight for the room they called the bridge. Consisting of two chairs in front of the ship's controls, it was small and usually unoccupied since Jin mostly ran the ship's functions and didn't need to be on the bridge to do so.

Today, however, one of the chairs was occupied by a slight figure wearing a cloak.

"You have a lot of explaining to do, young lady," Kira snapped.

The figure turned her head, the cloak's hood sliding off. Curly hair the color of gold slipped free as the occupant looked up at Kira with a crooked grin.

"Auntie, took you long enough to find me. I was expecting you an hour after I shot the general."

Kira's eyes narrowed. "I was trying not to draw attention to you—something you should have been careful about yourself."

The waif seemed less than intimidated as her gaze alighted on Raider. Wonder crossed her face as she scrambled upright, her legs hitting the deck. She brushed her hair from her face and adjusted her clothes.

Her gaze darted from Raider to Kira and back again. "Is that him?"

There was yearning and excitement in the girl's eyes, as if Kira had brought the best gift she'd ever received.

Kira exhaled. This was why she hadn't wanted to bring Raider. It was also the reason she couldn't force herself to leave him behind.

It was time—even if it would upset any gains Raider had made toward trusting Kira again.

The girl nearly bounced with excitement. Seeming the same age as Joule, her hair was short, and her eyes were a vivid amber. A bandanna wrapped around her forehead, hiding ears Kira knew were as pointed as her own.

"Yes, it's him," Kira said.

The girl clapped her hands together and raced forward. Kira stepped into her path, leveling a hard stare on the girl. If she thought she was getting out of trouble because of Raider's presence, she was mistaken.

Chastened, the girl backed up, finding her seat again.

"What are you doing here?" Kira asked. "I left you planetside with someone who would look after you for a reason. Does that person know you're here?"

The waif shrugged, pulling her legs up and crossing them under her. "I got worried when you went radio silent. I hitched a ride on a transport and tracked the *Wanderer* to O'Riley."

Kira should have anticipated this. The girl's caretaker should have as well.

"When I broke into the ship, your friend was here," the girl explained. "She needed a ride but couldn't get the ship to work. Since you keyed me into the controls, I decided to tag along."

"Odin," Kira ground out.

When she got her hands on the woman, she was going to strangle her for putting the waif in jeopardy.

"Why are you still here?" Kira asked.

The girl leaned back, studying her fingernails.

Kira closed her eyes. "Because you couldn't get off the planet without alerting the Tuann of your presence."

The guilt in the girl's face was confirmation enough.

"Kira," Raider finally said. He stared at the girl, thoughts moving across his face as he put the pieces together. "Who is this?"

Kira leveled a warning look on the girl. "Don't think you're off the hook. We're going to talk about this later."

The girl flashed her an unrepentant smile. "Whatever you say, Auntie."

Kira didn't have time to do more than frown as she faced Raider. She hesitated, not knowing what to say.

He tore his gaze away from the girl, his eyes landing on Kira. "Why does she look like Elise?"

Kira's lips parted, but no words came out.

"Kira," he said again. "Who is she?"

Graydon's large form stepped into the doorway. "I confess I'm curious about that myself."

Kira made a strangled sound as Graydon was joined by Harlow. Her uncle's frown was the stuff of nightmares as his gaze moved over those present before stopping on the girl, where it lingered.

She groaned internally as recognition and shock descended. Harlow's accusing gaze fell on Kira.

"Jin," she growled.

"Don't blame me. Their camouflage makes them invisible to my sensors," he said.

"Maybe see about fixing that so we don't keep having unexpected visitors," she said through gritted teeth.

He blew a raspberry at her.

Graydon watched the two of them with an unamused expression. "Harlow's oshota caught sight of you slipping out of the fortress. We decided to follow you." His gaze rose to take in the ship. "Imagine my surprise when we found you entering this ship—your ship."

The girl stood on her chair, leaning against Kira as she peered at the two men. "Is he the one Odin says you have your eye on? I like him; he's handsome."

Kira shoved her off, pointing at the seat with a no-nonsense stare. With a grumpy frown, the girl obeyed, dropping into it only to swivel around. "Sure thing, Auntie."

"Aunt," Graydon repeated, his gaze shooting to Kira's.

Raider hadn't moved, staring at the girl with a growing look of betrayal. His gaze slowly rose to Kira.

Kira gestured. "This is Elena." She took a deep breath. "My niece—and your daughter."

Elena shot the rest a gamin grin. "Nice to finally meet you, sperm donor. Auntie and Uncle Jin have told me so much about you."

TUANN TERMS

Adal – Loosely translated it means the reckoning – challenging to dangerous undertakings

Adva Ka – A rite of passage Tuann must pass

Aksa – Fist sized animal who is stubborn and blood thirsty

Azala – Child

Azira aliri – Cat ear shaped flower

Aza – Polite form of address, ex: Sir or Ma'am

Cheva nier – My love

Choko trees – A tree on Ta Sa'Riel

Coli – Affectionate term of endearment similar to sweet heart

Colina – A formal form of coli

Etheiri – Place of remembrance

Etair – Horse-like creature

Feilli – Symbiotic creatures in the ocean

Fendrik – An enemy on Roake's border

Iffli – Insult. Roughly translated – mutt, half-breed, waste

Kattas – Warrior forms

Keeva – Alcoholic drink

Ki – Soul's breath.

Kueper – A snack wrapped in a pastry

Loaw – Hoverbike

Lu-ong – Dragon like creature who is able to manipulate ki.

Mea'Ave – The soul of the planet

Ooros – Beast of burden, pulls carriages, looks like a cross between a bison and woolly mammoth

Ooril – Night animal

Oshota – Elite Tuann warriors – their name means shield

Seiki Stone – Drains ki

Seon'yer – Teacher or guide

Sirav Rytil – Second chances

Tala dog – Cross between boar and wolf and armored tank

Tilu – A Tuann invention that looks like butterfly wings and allows

the user to fly
Tijit – A small angry rodent
Uhva na – Trial of the Broken. A rite of passage those of House Roake must pass before receiving a teacher who will prepare them for the adva ka.
Ural – Similar to synth armor but not as advanced.
Zala – Infant
Zuipi – Tuann energy/projectile weapon that looks kind of like a bow and arrow

TUANN HOUSES

Luatha – Major House - Kira's mother, Liliana, is descended from this House. Its Overlord is Liara.
Maxiim – Minor house who has pledged allegiance to Luatha. Its Overlord is deceased. Joule is attempting to resurrect the House.
Roake – Major House – Kira's father, Harding, is descended from this House. Its Overlord is Harlow.
Danai – Major House – Overlord is still unknown
Dethos – Minor House who has pledged allegiance to Danai. Overlord is still unknown.
Asanth – Major House
Kashori – Major House

DISCOVER MORE BY T.A. WHITE

The Firebird Chronicles
Rules of Redemption – Book One
Age of Deception – Book Two

The Broken Lands Series
Pathfinder's Way – Book One
Mist's Edge – Book Two
Wayfarer's Keep – Book Three
The Wind's Call – Book Four

The Dragon-Ridden Chronicles
Dragon-Ridden – Book One
Of Bone and Ruin – Book Two
Destruction's Ascent – Book Three
Secrets Bound By Sand – Book Four
Shifting Seas - Novella

The Aileen Travers Series
Shadow's Messenger – Book One
Midnight's Emissary – Book Two
Moonlight's Ambassador – Book Three
Dawn's Envoy – Book Four

CONNECT WITH ME

Twitter: @tawhiteauthor
Facebook: https://www.facebook.com/tawhiteauthor/
Website: http://www.tawhiteauthor.com/
Blog: http://dragon-ridden.blogspot.com/

ABOUT THE AUTHOR

Writing is my first love. Even before I could read or put coherent sentences down on paper, I would beg the older kids to team up with me for the purpose of crafting ghost stories to share with our friends. This first writing partnership came to a tragic end when my coauthor decided to quit a day later and I threw my cookies at her head. This led to my conclusion that I worked better alone. Today, I stick with solo writing, telling the stories that would otherwise keep me up at night.

Most days (and nights) are spent feeding my tea addiction while defending the computer keyboard from my feline companions, Loki and Odin.

Made in the USA
Monee, IL
21 December 2024

75041557R10236